P9-CFH-074

Oberheide

ON THE PRECIPICE

They sat together on the ridge of rock overlooking the swirling river. Their talk was of the ranch, but Lily's thoughts kept drifting as Cade moved closer.

"We don't need any more bloodshed," Lily said finally, rising to her feet.

Cade's hand caught her arm. "There will be no bloodshed."

Perhaps she overreacted trying to pull away. Cade's hand closed tighter to keep her from falling off the narrow ledge. Lily felt the heat of his touch, the overpowering mass of him, and then she was in Cade's arms, her hands scaling the precipice of his shoulders while their lips met and clashed. She felt the iron musculature of his chest against the rounded softness of her breasts, the strength of his hands as they mapped her back. She gulped for air as Cade's kiss wandered to her earlobe, and his hand discovered her breast. As his fingers crept beneath her robe, she melted into liquid heat.

It had been years since Lily had felt passion, but never a passion like this. She was no longer a teenager being taught a lesson in love—she was a woman meeting a man's desire with her own. . . .

Texas Lily

Don't go to bed without Romance...

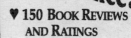

Romantic Times MAGAZINE

Suddenly, romance has a whole new face!

Introducing

TOPAZ
The Gem of Historical Romance

♥ **150 BOOK REVIEWS AND RATINGS**
  ❧ *CONTEMPORARY*
  ❧ *HISTORICAL*
  ❧ *TIME - TRAVEL*

♥ **AUTHOR PROFILES**

♥ **PUBLISHERS PREVIEWS**

♥ **MARKET NEWS**

♥ **TIPS ON WRITING BESTSELLING ROMANCES**

Read *Romantic Times* Magazine
122 page Monthly Magazine • 6 issues $21
Sample Issue $4.00   (718) 237-1097
Send Order To: Romantic Times
55 Bergen St., Brooklyn, NY 11201

I enclose $_____ in ❑ check ❑ money order

Credit Card#_____ Exp. Date_____

Tel_____

Name_____

Address_____

City_____ State_____ Zip_____

Patricia Rice

TEXAS LILY

A TOPAZ BOOK

TOPAZ
Published by the Penguin Group
Penguin Books USA Inc., 375 Hudson Street,
New York, New York 10014, U.S.A.
Penguin Books Ltd, 27 Wrights Lane,
London W8 5TZ, England
Penguin Books Australia Ltd, Ringwood,
Victoria, Australia
Penguin Books Canada Ltd, 10 Alcorn Avenue,
Toronto, Ontario, Canada M4V 3B2
Penguin Books (N.Z.) Ltd, 182–190 Wairau Road,
Auckland 10, New Zealand

Penguin Books Ltd, Registered Offices:
Harmondsworth, Middlesex, England

First published by Topaz,
an imprint of Dutton Signet,
a division of Penguin Books USA Inc.

First Printing, July, 1994
10 9 8 7 6 5 4 3 2 1

Copyright © Patricia Rice, 1994
All rights reserved
Topaz Man photo © Charles William Bush

 Topaz is a trademark of Dutton Signet,
a division of Penguin Books USA Inc.

Printed in the United States of America

Without limiting the rights under copyright reserved above, no part of this publi-
cation may be reproduced, stored in or introduced into a retrieval system, or trans-
mitted, in any form, or by any means (electronic, mechanical, photocopying,
recording, or otherwise), without the prior written permission of both the copyright
owner and the above publisher of this book.

BOOKS ARE AVAILABLE AT QUANTITY DISCOUNTS WHEN USED TO PROMOTE PRODUCTS OR
SERVICES. FOR INFORMATION PLEASE WRITE TO PREMIUM MARKETING DIVISION, PENGUIN
BOOKS USA INC., 375 HUDSON STREET, NEW YORK, NEW YORK 10014.

If you purchased this book without a cover you should be aware that this book is
stolen property. It was reported as "unsold and destroyed" to the publisher and neither the author nor the publisher has received any payment for this "stripped
book."

Author's Note

Despite Mexican laws to the contrary, Texans in the 1830s owned slaves. The American settlers who came to this Mexican state were intent on building the Southern plantations and farms that were suited to the east Texas weather and soil. The ranches that Texas is famed for in Western literature today were not American concepts of this period.

However, not all the settlers owned slaves. For the sake of my story, I have chosen to make my heroine the owner of land, not people. If this creates a setting more modern than the period, I apologize to any historians who might object.

Prologue

Mississippi
Spring 1824

"**D**addy's drinking again!" Alicia's expression was more irritated than scandalized as she swept into the front parlor, her full, ankle-length silk gown billowing out behind with her brisk pace. "What are we going to do?"

"The same thing that we always do, ignore him." Elizabeth consulted the ornate gilt mirror between the front windows, arranging the flowers in her hair more securely and checking her drop earrings for evenness. "Lily will be playing when the guests arrive, and we'll greet everyone and send them in here and they'll not even miss him with all the fun they'll be having. Perhaps we should have some refreshments sitting out so the men will have something to occupy them before the dancing starts. Hannah, see to setting a table out." She directed this last remark toward a black servant making hurried last-minute adjustments to the white organdy gown of the youngest member of the family.

The servant glanced with frustration from the loose waistline to the haughty young woman at the mirror. Lily waved her away. "It's all right, Hannah. I'll be sitting down all evening. No one will notice. This is the night Beth's going to bring Artemis to the asking point. Let us not stand in the way."

The two exchanged conspiratorial glances that said, "The sooner, the better," and the servant hurried off to do as told. Lily took her place at the magnificent new Steinway that had replaced their old harpsichord, satisfied that she was where she wanted to be.

"Lily, it's too early to start playing. Why don't you

have Bessie do something with your hair? It looks like it hasn't been touched in weeks." Elizabeth turned away from the mirror long enough to scrutinize her youngest sister.

Since Bessie had just spent half an hour trying to arrange the slippery golden-brown tresses thus disparaged, Lily merely shrugged and stroked the keys lovingly. The pink flowers Alicia had insisted that she wear in the elaborately curled and braided coiffure were already listing to one side, tugging loose one of the painfully curled locks of baby-fine hair. More strands would come loose before the night was over. Lily really didn't think it would matter, although somewhere deep down inside of her, she wished it would.

"No one's going to notice, Beth. Leave her alone." Alicia's words echoed Lily's thoughts enough to make the younger girl wince as she bent over the piano keys.

"She's sixteen. It's about time she started making someone notice," Beth answered with a sniff. "I've taken my time in making my choice, but Lily will have to start looking right away if she's to find anyone at all. What about young Robert Paul? Surely he must be tall enough."

The young man in question was of the same age as Lily, with a pockmarked face and a way of stuttering that sent spittle all over the person with whom he was speaking. Besides that, he had once tried to put a toad down Lily's back. The idea of setting up a courtship with Robert Paul made her wince even more than the disparagement of her hair. Stoically, Lily crashed into a rousing chord of Beethoven.

Ephraim Porter appeared in the hallway as the first guests began to arrive. A tall man with unruly wavy hair that perpetually fell in his face, he managed to maneuver the rosewood stairs with some degree of grace as he descended amid the apprehensive gazes of his two eldest daughters. The youngest, the one who took after him, was nowhere in sight. Ephraim heard the tinkle of the piano in the parlor and nodded sagely to himself. Elizabeth and Alicia frowned, but he managed the last stair with great aplomb and held out his hand to greet the first arrivals.

"Glad you could come, Harper. Welcome. Have a nip of France's finest with me while the womenfolk talk." To the relief of his daughters, Ephraim steered their first male guest to the study, where others could join them while the women safely entered the parlor, undisturbed by the telltale smell of brandy on their host's breath. Before the evening was over, all the men would smell of the liquors that Porter's Emporium carried with spectacular success.

When Elizabeth drifted by to whisper to Lily that their father had safely installed himself in the study, Lily nodded and continued playing, hiding her disappointment. She would have liked some reassurance from her father, some kind words that would give her confidence for the evening ahead, but she was accustomed to disappointment. She used to be his favorite, but since her mother's death, he had gradually drifted into a world of his own, seldom noticing any of his daughters. Lily felt it the most, but she had more experience in hiding her feelings than her sisters. Already taller than her schoolmates when her mother died, she had learned to hide her hurt at their taunts along with her fear and her anguish, first at the loss of her mother and then at the gradual loss of her beloved father. Her sisters were already grown and mature enough to deal with their losses. Lily was not and probably never would be. Her feelings poured into the music as the guests arrived to fill the parlor with their chatter.

When the room was filled to bursting and the gentlemen sufficiently "under the influence" to begin the dancing, Lily launched into a Virginia reel at a signal from her sister. The music came effortlessly, and she watched as the figures formed, Elizabeth triumphant on the arm of Artemis Cole, Alicia pouting prettily at the handsome Randolph Brewster. The elder Porter sisters were the belles of two states, despite their rather plebeian origins. Every eligible bachelor within sixty miles fell under their spell, just as those of an older generation had bowed to their mother a quarter of a century ago. The only difference was that Alicia and Elizabeth were determined to correct their mother's mistakes. They would marry wealthy men with names from old, established families, not hapless farmers who would have to sell their land before they could make enough to live on—not men like their father.

As the dancers laughed and twirled and worked their way through the reel, Lily turned away. She was accustomed to spending the evening at the piano rather than among the guests. It amused her to listen to the gossip whispered around her when the speakers thought her too engrossed in her music to hear. She had learned a great deal about life that way and knew perfectly well what their neighbors thought of them.

"Well, I can see there will be wedding bells soon for those two," one elderly matron sniffed from somewhere behind Lily.

"Elizabeth and Artemis?"

"Elizabeth and Alicia. It's quite obvious they've both made up their minds. One can't blame them for taking the first chance to get out of this household. Just like their mother, they are, and a more gently bred, refined woman this world has never seen. What she saw in Ephraim Porter is beyond my comprehension. He's turned out just like her mother warned her he would."

Lily scowled and sent the reel into a faster pace, leaving the dancers breathless and in serious disarray.

The whisper lowered, but she could still hear pieces of the conversation. "Pity . . . gawky, like her father. . . . Old maid. . . . Someone has to look after him."

Lily knew without a doubt that they were talking about her. She had heard it all before. She was taller than most men and had a face plainer than the side of a barn. Even her father's well-known charm had escaped her. But she could play any instrument anyone handed her, and play it well. Music was her solace, her consolation, her life.

Lily continued to tell herself that later in the evening when both her sisters announced their engagements. And she continued lying to herself the next day when the house filled with congratulatory visitors and her father hied himself to the store where he could tipple in peace. Music was all she needed. She didn't need handsome men courting her. She didn't need a man's charm to make her happy. She was happy just the way she was.

But she couldn't play in that house full of excited women. Wandering into the garden that had once been her mother's delight, Lily inspected the roses for the first flower and then strolled to the back gate, looking over the picket fence to the dirt road that meandered out of town. To her interest, a peddler's wagon was wending its way down the hillside toward her. Maybe he would have a new book or some sheet music she could purchase.

When the handsome young peddler stopped the wagon at the gate and gave Lily an alarmingly slow smile from beneath a tangled mop of dark curls, her heart nearly stopped beating. When he spoke, she was certain she had fallen asleep and was dreaming.

"I knew fate drew me to this place, and now here's my lucky charm to prove me right. The name's Travis Bolton, my fair lady, and I've come to sell you the things that dreams are made of. Do I dare ask that I make your lovely acquaintance?"

Lily could tell the traveling salesman was not much older than she, but his silver tongue and mellow voice spoke of a world of experience well beyond her own, and his dancing eyes and charming smile were the answer to all her wishes. Here was the chance to make a memory to look back upon when she was old and lonely.

She made a mock curtsy and introduced herself, and the peddler eagerly leapt from the wagon to open the garden gate.

From the perspective of nine years, Lily looked at her tall, dark-haired son and shook her head at her youthful folly. The peddler had certainly given her a memory to last a lifetime.

One

Lily looked away from the eight-year-old studying at the table and glanced out the beautifully glazed window Jim had just installed this spring. She clenched her hands into fists as one of the farmhands outside shook his head in response to something another of them said, scuffed his moccasins in the dust, then turned determinedly toward the house. Hastily donning the apron she seldom wore, Lily opened the back door as if she were on the way to the kitchen.

She had known this confrontation was coming, but she had hoped to postpone it a little longer. Just a little longer. Anything could happen in a few hours' time, a few days. Jim would be coming back. He had to. But a shiver running down Lily's spine reminded her that it had been a month already. It didn't take a month to look for a lost calf.

She stepped down to the ground quickly so the man standing on the wide step didn't have to look up at her any more than necessary. He twisted his hat in his hands and didn't quite meet her eyes.

"Beggin' your pardon, ma'am, Miz Brown, but I thought I orter let you know I'll be packin' my bags and movin' on this evenin'. I got a offer from that Reynolds fella, and I reckon I can't turn it down."

"I'll match the offer, Jack. You know we hate to lose you. You're one of the best men Jim has."

Jack looked as if he would rather eat his hat than answer, but he managed to say what needed to be said. "Ma'am, Miz Brown, we reckon Jim ain't comin' back. We've scoured them prairies high and low. There's been signs of Indians up along the river. A man like Jim don't disappear without word less'n somethin' happened to him. I'm sorry to say this, ma'am, but we reckon Jim's dead, and we can't be workin' for no woman. It don't pay in the long run. Some of the other fellas are lookin' 'round to leave, too."

Had she been at her home in Mississippi, there would have been a dozen chairs scattered along the verandah for Lily to collapse into while sobbing with ladylike grace, but as it was, there was nothing but an acre of trampled grass and dust between the house and the stable and the barn. She wanted to sit on the back step and bury her head in her hands and pretend this would all go away, but she had come a long way in these last years. She held her chin up and straightened her shoulders, even though that made her a head taller than the bowlegged farmhand.

"Tell them to give me a little more time. Jim has been meaning to hire a foreman, someone to take some of the work off him. If I go and talk to the man now, would you work for him?"

Jack knew she was lying through her teeth, but she stood there so proud and tall, her braid glistening gold in the sunlight, her woman's figure hidden behind the shirt and vest and trousers she had adopted for working beside her husband, that he couldn't resist her appeal. Gnashing his teeth at the extent of his foolishness, Jack pounded his hat back on his head.

"All right, ma'am. If you're bringin' a man in here to run things, we'd be willin' to stay a while. Jim was a good man. We don't want no harm to come to his widow."

"Widow." The word ground into Lily's soul as she threw off her apron and walked toward the paddock. She didn't feel like a widow. Would she feel like a widow if she saw Jim's body laid out in his coffin? He was dead. Everyone knew he was dead. His horse had come back with his provisions and his rifle still strapped to the saddle. That had been right after he'd left to look for that calf. The men had searched night and day for a week, but as Jack had implied, there was too much territory out there to find one man, or his body. He was dead, and she was going to have to start facing it.

She should be feeling grief. She should be weeping and donning mourning and asking for some memorial service and feeling sorry for herself. Instead, she saddled the horse and swung up, without the assistance of any man in the vicinity. She had learned a long time ago that men needed her more than she needed them. She didn't make a production of it. She let them think they were being considerate when they told her to do the cooking while they handled the roundup. She let them think that all she did at the ranch was supply their meals and keep Jim's cabin clean and his bed warm. Jim knew better and hadn't minded. Texas was a rough country and he had appreciated all the help she could give. It wasn't as if theirs was a romantic marriage. It had been a partnership. And although she missed her partner, she knew she could carry on without him.

Except in this one thing. The men wouldn't take orders from a woman. This was a man's country. She could ride a horse and lasso a cow with the best of them, but they would never take orders from her. Only if they thought the orders came from Jim would they listen to her at all. Lily would be furious with the stubborn asses if it would do any good, but she had been out here too long to expect anything else. Women were few and far between, and they had to work like dogs to make a living just like the men, but there was still that memory of how things had been "back home," before they'd "gone to Texas." Women were supposed to be too frail and delicate to think for themselves.

Lily had to laugh at applying that description to herself. Kicking the massive gelding into a gallop, she turned the horse toward town. She couldn't remember the last time she had worn a skirt. When she'd first arrived here as a terrified sixteen-year-old, she'd been filled with her sisters' notions of propriety. She had attempted to keep her elegant organdies clean and her petticoats starched as she had been taught. A flight of pigeons over her wash line had been the beginning of the end of that notion. She'd tried the cotton wraps many of the women wore, but that idea had faded by the time Roy was old enough to walk. Without slaves, there were never enough hands to get the cattle to market, to plant corn, to pick cotton, to weed the meager vegetable garden. Lily had learned right along with Jim how to do whatever needed to be done, and skirts just got in the way.

Perhaps if there had been more children, things would have been different. Lily turned that thought away. Jim had accepted Roy as his own and had never shown much interest in having more. The challenge of conquering the land had been sufficient for him—that and the possibility of someday being rich. Lily looked out over the wide-spread acres flowing around her and felt some degree of satisfaction. They weren't rich, but they were on their way to being well-to-do. Jim had always been a hard worker, and the early years of frustration and disappointment had gradually grown into years of plenty.

There was still trouble ahead, possibly even war, but politics was a topic Lily knew little about. If she couldn't handle it with her bare hands, worrying about it wouldn't help. The tangle with the Mexicans a couple of years ago had sent a number of her neighbors back to the states. The epidemics rampaging across Texas had given little time for the hotheads to develop cankers under their saddles after that. But the fever had dissipated this summer, crops were plentiful, and some of the newcomers, with their bellies full, were beginning to swagger disdainfully when Mexico and Santa Anna were mentioned. She and Jim, along with the rest of Austin's settlers, had pledged to be citizens of Mexico when they settled here, but these newcomers had other things on their minds besides the legality of Mexican citizenship.

There ought to be a peaceful solution to the situation, but knowing men, they wouldn't be happy without a fight. Bending her generous mouth with scorn, Lily reined in her horse at the town's pitiful general store. Here was where she would find the land agents and speculators eager to twist money out of the hands of the ignorant and land from the defenseless. The one calling himself *alcalde* looked up from his makeshift desk as

Lily entered and rose with effusive greeting as she turned in his direction.

"Mrs. Brown! What a pleasant surprise to see you here this early in the week. I hope you have come with good news?"

The idlers around the counter in the back turned with interest, but Lily had become quite used to the attention any woman attracted. She could have been a ten-foot bear wearing a skirt and they would have looked at her like that.

"No, I don't, Mr. Dixon. If we had a priest, I'd ask for a service to be said. But that's not why I'm here. I need a man to help run the ranch for me. Can you recommend someone?"

This whole scene was a farce for the sake of propriety, Lily knew, but she maintained a straight face as Bert Dixon looked solemn, took off his hat, and scratched his head. As a lady, she was supposed to acknowledge only gentlemen, and then only those she knew. Since Dixon dressed in frock coats and occasionally wore a tall beaver hat, he was considered a gentleman suitable for her acquaintance. Lily would have preferred to talk directly to the men at the counter, as Jim would have done, but they would have ignored her, most likely.

The store's proprietor wandered over, greeting her with a nod. Lily knew the idlers in the back were listening. All the ever-changing assortment seemed to do was spit tobacco, knock back whisky, and talk of war, but they knew everything that went on in the territory. Any news came here first. She waited hopefully.

"You ought to sell that place, Mrs. Brown." Ollie Clark was tall enough to look down on her, and he did so with a certain proprietary air, as if he were the only man in town who could deal with her.

He was not only tall, he was a good-looking man. Lily had always considered Ollie favorably, since he didn't spit or have rotted teeth and he always spoke to her with the Southern courtesy she had once expected of any man. But his attitude now irritated her already frayed nerves.

"That's Jim's decision to make," she replied maliciously, knowing her feminine refusal to acknowledge her husband's demise would get under Ollie's skin faster than anything else she could say. "Jim has been planning on looking for someone to help him run the cattle while he concentrated on the cotton," she lied boldly again. "I'm just looking a little earlier than he'd planned."

"Now, Mrs. Brown, that place is way too big for a little gal like yourself . . ." Dixon attempted to intervene between the two tall young people, but the look he received for this blatant idiocy sent his words in another direction. "What I mean is, you ought to think about Ollie's suggestion, Mrs. Brown. Settlers are pouring in here by the hundreds. You could sell off part of your acreage and have enough to live on for as long as you liked."

"That's Roy's inheritance you're speaking of, Mr. Dixon." Lily lifted her chin defiantly. "If you won't help me find a good manager, I'll do it myself. I know most of the settlers around here. It may take me a while, but I'll talk to them all, and maybe get better sense out of them than I'm hearing here."

A man in red kerchief and brown-checked shirt, leaning with his elbows against the counter and obviously enjoying this argument, yelled out, "I hear Cade's back in town. Why don't you send her to him? He's got all the experience she needs."

Lily looked up eagerly. "Cade? What is his full name, and where do I find him?"

Dixon looked anxious and shook his head. "You don't want Cade, Mrs. Brown. He's not . . ."

Lily looked at him contemptuously. "Don't say it, Mr. Dixon. If he has the experience I need, I'll hire him." She looked back to the man who had made the suggestion. "Where do I find him?"

She saw the grins going around the room. She knew she was the brunt of some male joke, but she was long accustomed to that position. Holding her spine straight and her chin up, she demanded respect with her silence.

The man in the back pushed his hat back on his head. "Out at the Langton ranch. He's been punchin' for Ralph this past month. People just call him Cade."

Lily gave a regal nod and ignored the hand Ollie held out to halt her. Stepping around him, she sailed toward the door. She would have a foreman before the day was out if it killed her.

July 1835

The prairie grass rippled in a sudden breeze, sending waves of green as far as the eye could see, but one stand remained stationary. Always alert for the unexpected, Cade eyed the unbending grass with disfavor. The circle of buzzards overhead was fair enough warning. He knew better than to go closer, but human nature compelled him to investigate.

A few minutes later, bending over the dead man, Cade jerked out the arrow he had seen from a distance, ripping it from the deteriorating flesh with a sudden viciousness. He had known better.

Swearing, he gazed down at what had once been a man of middle age, his receding hair falling back from the bland features of a farmer, his soft paunch indicating a life of relative comfort. The arrow had protruded from the center of a homespun shirt that had been carefully washed and bleached in the sun until nearly threadbare, and then mended with loving, even stitches. Cade cursed again and then looked at the arrow in his clenched fist. He had meant to arrive in this place without disturbance or notice of his presence. He could well imagine what would happen should he report this body.

Black hair glistening in the sunlight, Cade brushed away the length rubbing against his chambray collar. Eyes dark as midnight gazed in contempt at the arrow's feathering and unmarked shaft. The man's assailant had the devil's own luck to kill his victim with a poor piece of work like this one—a piece meant to resemble an Indian weapon but all too clearly made by a white man's hand.

Cade glanced down at the unlucky bastard at his feet and felt fear clutch at his insides. They weren't going to blame him for this one. Not if he could help it.

Glancing around at the rippling plain dancing in the glorious sunlight, Cade found the spot he remembered. Callously closing his senses to the stench of the dead man, he flung the body over his horse's saddle. This was one murder that wouldn't be solved soon.

Later, after giving the body a decent burial, Cade leaned against the bark of a live oak and sipped at the flask from his saddlebag. Contemplating the snake slithering through the grass in front of him, he felt the ache that the liquor seldom assuaged—the ache of loneliness, a hurt he had carried with him all his life.

Remembering another day and another snake, Cade took a second gulp of the fiery liquid and tried to forget, but the childish voices singsonging through an open window in melodic Spanish still haunted his memory.

The urchin he had once been grubbed in the dirt just outside that window, pushing a stick through the dust in rhythm with the chanting, glancing neither to the left nor to the right as he concentrated on his self-imposed task, even when a large shadow fell across him.

"Ándale, bastardo." The kick was swift and sure, sending the boy Cade sprawling in the dust. "Get back to your whore of a mother." The words were in elegant Spanish, but the viciousness behind them had naught to do with the grace of the people who used that language.

Scowling at the destruction of his dust letters, the boy didn't look up but merely returned to his previous position, a little farther from the man's boot.

The man's curse and the lift of his boot for the next kick was interrupted by a gentle voice. "Leave him be, Ricardo. He harms no one."

"Apaches have to be taught their places when young," Ricardo replied, his belligerence barely hidden beneath the voice of respect he used for the priest in his long black robes.

"He is not just an Apache, my son," the priest rebuked him mildly. "He is the grandson of Antonio de Suela. Who knows, one day de Suela may return. Would you have his anger turned against you?"

"A de Suela would not acknowledge the spawn of an Apache and a whore. Why do you think he left us?"

The priest shook his head and clicked his tongue. "Do not hold your grudges against the innocent, Ricardo. *Vaya con Dios.*"

The man called Ricardo snarled as the priest walked off. The boy a footstep away sat silently drawing his letters in the dirt, not acknowledging the man's presence. The child had the tough, sturdy body of an Indian, not the slender grace of his Spanish mother. The black hair that cropped over his eyes and shirt collar badly needed trimming, but there was a certain dignity in his stoic stance. He knew the kick was coming, but he did nothing to resist it.

Cursing at the priest's interference, Ricardo spit in the dust at the boy's bare foot, then turned on his heel and walked away without administering a final blow. Only when he was completely out of sight did the boy look up, check the entrance to the alley, and reach for the wooden box beside him.

The snake inside coiled and rattled and hissed, and the boy smiled as he refastened the carefully applied leather latches. The snake grew calm as the box was lifted by a handle and swung gently at the boy's side as he slipped down the back street to his mother's hovel, whistling solemnly as he walked. His father had taught him of the Snake's nature. He was quite certain the man named Ricardo would not understand, however. He had almost looked forward to the moment when the man would kick the box. For the snake's sake, he was glad the man had not tried a second kick.

Sitting in the present with the liquor flowing through his veins, Cade wished the child hadn't been so generous. Ricardo had deserved to die.

Two

Lily tried not to think what she was going to say to Ralph Langton when she found him. It was much better to allow these things to come out naturally. A planned speech would just terrify her. As she cantered the gelding down dusty roads, she set her mind to wondering what Roy was doing right now, worrying that she wasn't there to continue their lessons. She was going to have difficulty running a ranch and trying to educate her son at the same time.

For the hundredth time she wondered if she had done the best thing for Roy by coming out here where books were few and far between and teachers were nonexistent. But at the time, the alternative had been too painful to consider. She had come to accept her life out here, and Roy knew no other, but the suggestion to sell the land had set all the old worries loose.

The thought of abandoning Jim's dream prevented Lily from seriously considering the idea of selling. She didn't know for certain that her husband was dead. Perhaps the horse had just thrown him, and it was taking him a while to walk back. He could have hurt himself and some friendly Indians could have taken him in and were nursing him back to health. In Texas anything could happen. She would hope for the best and do as Jim would have done.

That thought held Lily as she found the group of riders making a circuit of the Langton ranch. She hailed Ralph, and the older man halted his horse and turned to greet her. The others ambled onward, expecting him to catch up when he was done.

"Lily! Good to see you. What are you doing out here all alone? Jim would be furious."

He said this with a genial smile that acknowledged his polite phrases had little to do with reality. Lily returned the smile. Ralph Langton was one man who understood that she could hold her own. He had nothing to prove by thinking of her as his inferior. He was old enough to be her grandfather and had been married for more years than she had been alive. He had learned from those years and treated her with the same equality as he did his wife.

"The way things stand, I'll be doing everything on my own shortly," said Lily. "I may as well get used to it. The men are threatening to leave rather than take orders from a woman. I can't fool them much longer into thinking Jim will be back, Ralph." Lily shook her head to keep him from offering sympathies. She didn't want sympathy. She didn't want to cry. She wanted to keep going until she couldn't go anymore. "I heard you have a man named Cade here who has the experience to act as my foreman. What do you think?"

Ralph immediately looked concerned. "Well, I don't know, Lily." At her stubborn expression, he hesitated. "Why don't you ask him yourself?" He yelled over his shoulder, and one of the riders ambling down the road came to a halt and swung his horse around.

Lily had already noted the man. He sat head and shoulders above the others, and his shoulders reminded her of a bull they had in the paddock. Her eyes were always drawn to those few men who stood taller than she, but the size of this one was intimidating to an extreme. Then she realized why the men back at the store had laughed at her. They had told her about the one man in the territory who could make her look small.

Anger welled up in her, as it always did when someone made fun of her height. She should have been born a man, she had been told more than once. Well, she had done her best to turn herself into one. She would behave as one now. She sat straight and tall in her saddle and waited to see the rest of the joke that had been perpetrated on her.

The man's long black hair was straight as a stick but evidently clean. With a shock she realized his bronzed features and angular cheekbones were undoubtedly Indian, although she suspected something of the Spanish in his heritage also, if for no other reason than the proud arrogance of his nose and the jut of his square jaw. The impassiveness of his expression would be intimidating even without his size. This was not a man she could control with a few sharp words.

Lily was almost willing to admit her mistake in seeking him when she noticed the odd way the man, Cade, held his hands on the reins. They were practically sitting in his lap.

In another moment he was close enough for her to see the kitten draped across the saddle in front of him. A kitten! Lily could scarcely keep her eyes from the untidy sprawl of fur until she recognized the unseemliness of the direction of her gaze. Flushing, she looked up to the man's dark eyes. If there was a flicker of something behind that impenetrable obsidian, she could not interpret it.

"Cade?" She had been told he had no last name. Looking at him, she could see he didn't need one. It would be akin to giving a family name to a wolf. She just hoped he didn't have the intelligence of a buffalo. As he continued to stare without speaking, she continued nervously, "I've been told you have the experience to manage a cattle ranch. Is this true?"

"I ran Colonel Martin's operation over near Galveston for a spell," he acknowledged evenly, scratching the kitten behind the ear to keep it still.

Lily wanted to reach out and grab the kitten and tell him that was no way to treat a cat, but aside from the fact that the animal seemed perfectly content where it was, the idea of grabbing anything from such a location kept her face warm. She turned her concentration back to matters at hand.

She had heard of Colonel Martin and the size of his spread and was relieved but still suspicious. "How long is a 'spell'?"

There was a suggestion of a shrug beneath the straining shoulders of his faded blue work shirt. "Couple of years."

"And why did you leave there?"

Throwing the big man a look, Ralph intervened. "He was unjustly accused of killing a man. He spent some time in prison before Martin could get him out. The colonel thought it safer if he went elsewhere to avoid angry suspicions. I'll vouch for Cade's integrity. I'll hate to see him go, but you can offer him a better place than I can, if he wants it."

Lily looked up to see if there was any change of expression on the man's face at these words, but Cade continued looking at her with disinterest. For some reason, his disinterest was as tantalizing as his size and the kitten. She had learned long ago that she was no beauty, but out here men were inclined to pant over anything in skirts. Or trousers, she amended. She was young and had all the necessary female attributes. She expected at least some degree of interest. But he continued to stare at her as if she were part of the landscape.

"I don't suppose you would be interested in working for a woman, would you?" That wasn't the way she had meant for the words to come out, but now they were said, she couldn't take them back.

"As foreman?" At her nod, he questioned, "Would I be required to sleep in the bunkhouse with the rest of the men?"

That jarred her awake. Was he married then? The thought had never occurred to her. Hastily, Lily revised a few estimates and rethought the problem. She was more determined than ever to have this man in her employ. Having another woman on the ranch would be heaven.

"There's a small cabin one of the hands built for his bride, but they moved on a year or so ago. It may not be in good repair, but I'll see that you have what you need to fix it up if that's what you require."

He nodded and exchanged a glance with Langton. Gathering up his reins, he gave Lily a perfunctory nod. "I'll be out Sunday morning to discuss terms."

He rode away, leaving Lily to stare after him with a

certain amount of incredulity. The man was as arrogant as his nose.

Ralph grinned. "He don't talk much, but you hear it when he does. He'll do the job for you, Lily. All you got to do is persuade your men to take orders from a half-breed."

Hell and tarnation. Lily gave Ralph a look of frustration and pulled her mount into readiness. "Why can't anything ever be easy?"

He laughed as she rode away, but it was a laugh of confidence. Lily turned her mind to persuading a bigoted bunch of peacocks that if they wanted a man to give them orders, it was going to be a red man.

"But, Mama, we *always* go into town on Saturday." Tall and stringy, with an unruly lock of dark hair falling across his tanned brow, Roy propped his hands on his hips in imitation of his father and glared at his mother belligerently.

"I'm tired, Roy. I would rather just sit here and admire the sunset. Why don't you go see if there's a ripe watermelon and we'll picnic by the creek?"

"If I had a horse of my own, I could ride into town with the men," he complained, ignoring her suggestion.

Since Jim's disappearance, Roy had become more rebellious than ever. Lily sighed and stared out over the paddock. Her husband had lost a son by a previous marriage to a riding accident, and he had refused to allow Roy to ride. It had been a mistake, but Jim had interfered so little in the raising of the boy that she had allowed this one anomaly, understanding the reason for it. She supposed Jim had made a good father as these things went, but now she was going to have to pay for that one mistake. She wished he were here right now.

"I'll see what we can do about that when the time comes," Lily promised quietly. "Why don't you have Luke harness up the wagon? We'll go to town for a little while."

Instead of whooping for joy, the boy looked suddenly lost and frightened. "Dad isn't coming back, is he?"

"I don't know, Roy. I just don't know." She wanted to take him in her arms and hug him, but he had made it clear some time ago that he wasn't her little boy any longer and he didn't appreciate being fussed over. She would be the first to admit that she didn't know how to deal with this stranger she had carried in her womb for nine months. No one had ever given her lessons in little boys.

Roy blinked back a tear and turned and ran toward the barn. Big boys don't cry. How early they learned. Lily sighed and went to fetch her bonnet.

They hitched the oxen to the stable's corral fence and walked the remaining distance toward the town's main street. Laughter carried from the big barn out behind Ollie Clark's place. Drunken voices drifted out of the town's two saloons. But a few women in calico and bonnet still went in and out of the general store and lingered to exchange gossip along the street. Saturday was the only day of the week when they had the chance to visit, and they drew out the time as long as they could.

For the main part, the women ignored Lily in her trousers and she ignored them. They had little in common. She couldn't discuss babies or recipes and they couldn't talk cattle or cotton. But even though she felt as lonely as she had when her sisters talked fashions and beaux, Lily still felt sorry for women with no more intelligent interests—men didn't have the world's corner on arrogance.

Acknowledging her own faults with a smile, Lily let Roy slip away to the candy counter at the general store while she followed Juanita to the shamble of shacks behind the town. Juanita was a treasure Lily couldn't live without. Juanita was the one primarily responsible for those meals the men thought Lily had cooked. Juanita had practically raised Roy while Lily was working beside Jim in the fields. And if Juanita wished to visit a sick cousin and take her a pie, Lily would gladly tag along to see that she was unmolested. The shy cook and maid was terrified of men—and for good reason.

Lily carried her rifle in her hand as they hurried around

drunken farmers stumbling from the saloon. She seldom stayed in town this late on a Saturday, and Jim had always been nearby when she did. It had been a mistake succumbing to Roy's pleading, but it was too late to change her mind now. She reassured herself with the fact that she knew most of the upstanding citizens of this town and the territory surrounding it. No man in his right mind would harm Lily Brown in plain view of half the town.

But a drunken man was not in his right mind, as she well knew. She nodded a friendly greeting to a man who lifted his hat to her, but she hurried Juanita onward. The street they were entering now was not the most respectable. It housed squatters and ne'er-do-wells who had stumbled into the territory after all the land had been granted and who shifted from one place to another looking for an easy situation rather than going farther westward to find real work. There were women here too, but they tended to be the kind who exchanged their favors for whisky and trinkets. Juanita's cousin wasn't far above that state, but as far as Lily knew, the woman was the only relative Juanita had. She clung to her rifle and slowed her pace to the cook's smaller steps.

"Take your *bastardo* and go to hell, *bestia*! *Yo tengo* better offers than your flea-ridden cabin. I don't need a . . ." The words evolved into a long string of vivid Spanish that even Lily could tell was mostly obscenities. Juanita halted and flushed, glancing toward the shanty where a woman stood outside ranting and raising her fist at some unseen male, and then she hurried off down a side alley. Lily hesitated, her gaze caught by the golden-haired child sitting on the shanty's step.

Gold curls surrounded a placid face that ignored the woman's furious tirade as the child played with a toy in her lap. Lily glanced at the buxom, black-haired woman in the street and back to the child, finding no similarity in their features. And then a shadow moved out of the shanty to fall over the child, and Lily caught her breath.

The child lifted her head and waved pudgy fists, indicating a desire to be picked up. The large man behind her knelt carefully and lifted her into muscular arms that could have crushed but succeeded in holding the toddler tenderly, while catching the kitten that had been lying in the child's lap.

"I offer you a home and respectability, Maria," he offered patiently to the woman who had finally run out of curses.

Lily fully understood the very American reply the woman gave to that offer. Embarrassed at such language as well as the scene she had inadvertently stumbled upon, she hurried after Juanita and out of sight.

It was only later that Lily wondered how Cade was going to keep a child without a woman to care for her—and visions of glowing gold curls began to dance in her head.

Three

Cade didn't arrive Sunday morning as promised. Lily set her jaw and stoically went about her chores, ignoring the grumbles of the men as she set them to their various tasks. She had promised them a foreman, and they were certain she was reneging on her promise. Hung over as they were after a Saturday night on the town, they weren't exactly willing to listen to reason. Nor were they particularly interested in listening to a woman's decisions. She read the rebelliousness in their eyes as she sent some to riding the fields and others to mending fences.

Normally, Lily didn't allow herself the pleasure of anger, but she couldn't stave it off now. She had spent well over a month worrying herself to death over Jim's disappearance, but no one seemed to care about that. Their only concern was for their own male pride. She could lose everything she had worked for these last nine years, and it would all be the fault of every infuriating male she had ever come in contact with. The whole gender was highly overrated in her opinion. She only wished she could tell them all so.

Instead, Lily hitched the wagon, checked her rifle, and headed into town. She had a very good idea where she would find one Cade Whatever-his-name-was.

Lily drove directly to the little shanty on the back street of the now-silent town. She was too angry to know what she intended to do when she got there, but Cade saved her the problem. As she drove through the dust she could see him sprawled along the front step where the child had sat the day before. His long legs appeared to take up half the narrow side street as he leaned with elbows back in the doorway. As she watched, he lifted his arm to drink from a flask in his hand.

He was drunk. Fury flared even higher as Lily swung down near a conveniently placed public pump. Filling the pail with a few hard strokes, she stalked to where the man half-sat, half-lay, blissfully ignoring her. With a single swing of the pail, Lily drenched him from head to toe.

Before Cade had time to do more than splutter and shake his head from the force of the blow, Lily stepped back and launched into the tirade that had been building all morning.

"You're going to cost me my ranch! Do you have any idea how long and hard I've worked and slaved on that blasted piece of land, and you're going to throw it all to the winds while you sit here and feel sorry for yourself? Hell, my husband's gone and I don't even know where he is, but I'm not going to sit around and mope about it. I'm going to keep that ranch if I have to drown you to do it."

He was beginning to rise like some great monolithic beast, stirring massive legs and flexing arms that resembled small tree trunks. If she hadn't been so blamed mad, Lily would have felt fear. Instead, she caught sight of a small golden head peeping out the doorway, and with more courage than sense, she darted forward, grabbed the child, and headed back for the wagon.

That brought the monster to his feet with a roar.

The child laughed and clapped her hands as Lily set her on the wagon seat and her father stormed down the road with murder in his eyes.

Lily picked up her rifle and calmly aimed it at him. "I'm taking her out to the ranch. When you're sober enough to ride out, you can come claim her."

Cade stalked right past her to the oxen's heads. With a swift jerk of his bare hands, he dismantled the yoke, rendering the reins essentially useless. Giving Lily a look of pure rage, he stalked past her again, this time in the direction of the house.

For the first time, Lily felt a trickle of fear run down her spine. She had dealt with the ignorant and the stupid, she had learned how to handle violence, she knew how to demand respect from the best and worst of men, but she had never come in contact with a man quite like this before. He didn't respond in the same manner as other men. She had fully expected this one to follow sheepishly after her when he'd had enough of the drink. For all she knew, he could very well be locating his own weapon right this minute, and she was helpless to do anything but run.

She wasn't running. Lifting her rifle protectively, Lily stepped away from the wagon and the child. She wasn't going to let an innocent get caught in the crossfire, if it came to that. But she sure as hell didn't mean to walk back to the ranch. He broke the yoke. He'd darned well better fix it.

She lowered the rifle again in surprise when Cade staggered out of the house carrying a doll's cradle under one arm and a child's feather mattress under another. The child squealed with delight as he dumped the load into the back of the wagon. Without giving Lily a glance, he stalked back to the house.

When he returned bearing a dresser spilling small cotton garments and glimpses of lace, Lily hurriedly began arranging the articles in the wagon bed and fastening them down so they wouldn't slide too much. The doll's cradle looked handcarved and beautifully done. The doll inside had once had a lovely china face, and her long linen nightdress was now well worn with time. She dodged out of the way as Cade returned and flung in a bedroll and the rails for a child's bed. Without a word, he made one final trip to the house, this time carrying out a splendidly tooled Spanish saddle, a bundle that undoubtedly represented his own meager wardrobe, and saddlebags that appeared too heavy for any normal man to carry.

After dropping the last of his worldly possessions into the wagon, Cade walked past Lily and toward the stable. Unable to do anything else, Lily started to climb into the wagon seat when she noticed a small gray kitten coming around the corner of the house. Deciding that as long as she was adopting the man's family she might as well adopt his cat too, Lily went to collect the stray.

The kitten had other ideas. Scratching and spitting, it leapt from Lily's grasp and darted to the safety of the wagon wheels. Lily was on her hands and knees under the wagon bed trying to remove the animal when Cade returned, leading his horse.

If he had anything to say about his employer's unladylike position, he had the sense to leave it unsaid as he hitched his horse to the back of the wagon and leaned over to scoop up the snarling kitten in one mighty fist. While Lily hastily backed away from his too-close proximity and stood up to dust herself off, Cade dumped the kitten in the child's lap and went around to the front of the wagon to mend the yoke with wire he had brought with him.

Lily climbed to the seat and waited uneasily for Cade to finish. With his horse tied to the back of the wagon, it was quite apparent that he didn't mean to ride. The idea of having the man beside her on this narrow seat didn't sit at all well. If he was drunk, he gave little sign of it as he worked steadily at repairing the damage. She didn't know how she would react when he claimed the remaining portion of the bench. She fully meant to keep the reins to herself, but what chance had she against his obvious strength if he decided otherwise?

Before Lily could thoroughly panic, Cade finished his mending, walked around to the back of the wagon, and throwing himself in, collapsed against the bedroll. He passed out cold before Lily could urge the oxen out of town.

"Esta un monstruo, señora," Juanita whispered fearfully, peeking out the window curtains at the man unloading his possessions into the small cabin in the side yard.

"A monster?" Lily glanced out to see the child dancing happily between the wagon and the cabin. "I don't think so. A giant, maybe, but I think he's gentle." She tried to say the words convincingly to calm Juanita's fears, but the memory of the rage in Cade's eyes and the ease with which he had dismantled the wagon was troubling. If she remembered the fairy tales correctly, sleeping giants should be left undisturbed.

Not wishing to think about that, Lily checked the baking bread. The men would be in for dinner shortly, and she would have to introduce Cade to them, but she had not yet had any kind of talk with him. He had not even formally agreed to take the job. This was no way to manage a business. Somehow she was going to have to regain control of this situation.

Juanita gave her an odd look and went back to her cooking. Petite and slender, her black hair drawn stiffly into a bun that didn't disguise her fragile beauty, she was everything that Lily was not, but they had worked so long together that Lily no longer felt any awkwardness over their differences. Lily's life had been an easy one compared to Juanita's. She could never resent the other woman's more feminine beauty, knowing the high price it had cost her. It was doubtful that Juanita would ever overcome her fears to enjoy the gift of beauty she had been given.

"Men!" Lily thought with disgust. She wouldn't go so far as to say they were all alike, for she knew her husband had been different, but she had seen enough variation on the same theme to doubt that there were many differences. With that thought in mind, she shrugged, set aside her potholder, and went out to confront the beast.

Lily walked out to discover that Roy had confronted the new foreman first. His bronzed face completely devoid of expression beneath an irregular fringe of black hair, Cade stood with arms crossed over his massive chest, waiting for Roy to finish what seemed to be a long and involved tale. As she approached, the half-breed looked up and his features formed into a formidable scowl. She found herself returning a scowl for a scowl, and by the time she had reached the pair, her arms were crossed just as intractably across her chest.

"A man needs to know how to ride," he said, with thorough disapproval in his tone.

"I agree." Lily watched disbelief appear in his eyes before she continued, "And girls need a mother to guide them."

A flicker of understanding crossed Cade's face before he brought it under control. So, he was not unintelligent. Lily waited.

"You have women here who will look after Serena?"

"Juanita and I will look after Serena. In return, when there is time, you will teach Roy to ride."

He frowned briefly, looked down at the rebellious boy with hands on hips, and nodded agreement. "We begin today. I will get Serena."

He found it blamed awful easy to dump his kid in her hands, Lily decided, but he undoubtedly thought she had nothing better to do but sit around the house like other women. It was time she made it understood who was boss.

"The men will be in for dinner shortly. I will introduce you, but you needn't give them any orders until tomorrow, when we've had time to discuss what needs to be done."

Cade turned around to face her again. The fine hair she had woven into thick braids and wrapped around her head escaped in frail tendrils to blow in her face. Tanned slightly by the sun, her features were even and lightly sprinkled with freckles. A generous mouth pulled tightly in an authoritative frown ruined the rather feminine appeal of her gently molded chin.

He replied firmly, "I will introduce myself. You may take Serena to the house."

He walked away before she could argue. Lily opened her mouth, snapped it closed again, and stared after his departing figure with a shiver of rage. Never, in all her born days, *never* had she been talked to like that. Mr. Cade Half-breed was going to have to learn some manners if they were to deal well with each other.

But she had already drowned him with a pail of water and shouted at him like a fishwife this day. She wasn't up to another tantrum. Finding the child toddling toward the flower garden, kitten in tow, Lily sent her feet in Serena's direction.

"Come on, Roy, if I'm to take care of this hooligan so you can ride, you're going to have to learn to help. Grab the cat and I'll get the brat."

It was with satisfaction later that day that Lily brushed the soft, golden, and newly cleaned curls of Cade's child into a halo. She had dressed the toddler in one of the garments she had boldly retrieved from the dresser Cade had carried into his cabin, and the blue muslin and white lace appealed to her nearly buried feminine instincts. Serena was an utter delight, and Lily's heart ached briefly as she remembered the child she had never had with Jim. There had been times when she had hoped . . . but they had never come to anything.

It wasn't as if they'd had a particularly passionate relationship. Not at all like . . . Lily shook her head and set the child down. That was the past and well left behind. She had been no more than a child when Roy was conceived. She knew a great deal more now. Passion was not a force she could live on or rely on. Jim had been just the steadying influence she had needed.

Juanita answered the knock at the front door. It couldn't be said that they lived in a grand house requiring servants for that job, but both Lily and the maid had come from similar situations and had fallen easily into familiar patterns. The first one-room log cabin Jim had built had been added on to over the last few years, until they now had a dogtrot and four rooms up and down as well as the detached kitchen, but it was scarcely a mansion by anyone's account. Lily dusted a spot on her particular pride and joy, the massive walnut dining table, and waited for their guest to be introduced.

"Mrs. Brown, I hurried over as soon as I heard . . ." Ollie Clark ducked through the low front door and removed his hat as he noticed Lily sitting in the old rocker she had brought with her from Mississippi. Had she been wearing something besides trousers, she could have almost been mistaken for any other woman in the territory tending her sewing and children. His gaze stopped at the child at her feet.

"Come in, Mr. Clark, have a seat. You've had word of Jim?" Lily felt her breath constrict in her lungs as she waited for the words she didn't want to hear.

Ollie took the overlarge wing chair that had once decorated a bedroom parlor and wrung his hat between his hands. "No, ma'am, I didn't mean to get your hopes up none. I was talkin' 'bout Cade. The boys were just funnin' about him the other day. He's a drunken half-breed, Mrs. Brown. You don't want the likes of him about the place. Let me explain things to him and send him on his way. It ain't right for a respectable lady like yourself to have to deal with a man like that."

"I can't dismiss a man without giving him a chance, Mr. Clark. Even drunk, he's showed more sense than some sober men I could name. If Colonel Martin could use him, I don't see why I can't."

He took a deep breath. "He ain't even white, Lily. You'll give me permission to call you Lily?" When she didn't reply, Ollie hurried on. "He's half-Indian, half-Mexican. You'd be better off hiring one of your father's slaves. At least they listen when you whip them. Cade's more likely to turn and kill you. He's done it before. You've got to get him out of here."

Ollie was speaking sense from his own point of view. Beneath his placid exterior, Cade undoubtedly had a violent temper. Lily had seen evidence of that already. And Ralph had told her he'd been in prison for killing another man. So Ollie was speaking the truth, but only one side of the truth. Lily knew all about that kind of lie.

"I'll give Cade his chance, Mr. Clark. Jim would want it that way." Lily watched gleefully as she used this two-edged sword to make Clark squirm. How many times had she resentfully heard those words when the men wouldn't listen to her? Now she used them willingly to get her own way without argument.

Clark scowled and rose. "Jim wouldn't have taken on a drunken Indian. I'll set about finding you a decent man to help out. You'll be needing him soon enough." He gave the child on the floor another glance, one of puzzlement, but he didn't ask the question that obviously was on his mind.

And Lily didn't answer it. Sweetly, she held out her hand and offered her best Southern belle smile. "I'm so grateful for your concern, Mr. Clark. Please do come and visit sometime. Perhaps you could bring Miss Bridgewater. I'd be happy for the company."

The name of the young girl whom the town gossip had Clark courting only brought a milder frown to his handsome face. "That's mighty kind of you, Mrs. Brown. I hope you hear from Jim soon."

Lily watched him go with a sigh of relief and a small feeling of triumph. She didn't know why Ollie Clark was suddenly so all-fired concerned with her welfare, but surely she had set him properly in his place.

Now, if she could only say the same for her new foreman . . .

Four

"I ain't workin' for no blamed red Indian! Pardon me, ma'am, but I didn't come all the way to Texas to take orders from the likes of him."

Lily straightened her aching back and sat up, brushing a dirt-encrusted hand across her perspiring forehead as she looked up at the lanky hired hand. "And what did the blamed red Indian tell you to do this time?" she asked a trifle impatiently.

The man scowled. "He said I was to fix the paddock fence instead of riding out like I always do. I ain't no carpenter."

This wasn't the first time Lily had had to field such a complaint, and she could see it wouldn't be the last. Cade had no patience with the hands' inflated opinions of themselves. Tact wasn't precisely his strong point, either. He gave an order and walked away. The men weren't used to that. Jim had been as much their friend as their boss. They were used to giving opinions and arguing and having someone listen. Cade wasn't Jim.

But Cade was all she had, and she couldn't fault his decisions so far, although she could certainly fault his high-handed manner of dealing with people, including herself. Keeping her resentment to herself, Lily replied with as much patience as she could muster, "I told Cade I wanted the paddock mended today. I assume he chose the best man for the job. If there's a better, just let me know and I'll pass that information on to him. We're having peach cobbler for dinner. You can't quit a place that serves the best cobbler in the territory, can you?"

She ought to despise herself for using the feminine

wiles she had once despised her sisters for wielding, but she would use whatever worked to keep this ranch running. If men were fool enough to fall for a pretty expression and a "please," then it was their own danged fault. She hid her grimace behind a beseeching smile as the man grumbled and then nodded respectfully before wandering off to do what he had been told to do in the first place. It was akin to dealing with half a dozen eight-year-olds.

Lily stood and stretched and admired the neat rows of her vegetable garden. She had already harvested a cellar full of cabbage, sweet potatoes, and turnips. The corn was drying and almost ready to grind. There would be plenty enough to eat for the winter. She really ought to assign one of the men the task of hoeing out the garden, but they considered it woman's work and never took the time to get right down into the soil and pull up the weeds that smothered a plant. Besides, she found a certain amount of satisfaction in handling this one chore herself.

She glanced toward the house, where Roy studied his lessons and Juanita kept an eye on Serena. Cade had been with them a month now, and Lily had made no more progress in dealing with the man than she had at the first. The only way she could reach him was through the child. There were days when she wanted to hold a gun to Cade's head and force him to stand and listen to her. Instead, she had learned to make him come inside and wait while she dressed Serena and discussed the topics on her mind. Cade seldom gave any evidence of having heard, but at least she'd had her say. And upon occasion, like today with the paddock, he did give some indication that he had listened.

She looked up to see the object of her musing approaching. Seldom did Cade come back to the ranch before dinner, and if he did, it wasn't to consult Lily. For a moment, resentment welled up in her, but she had learned to deal with that emotion long ago. Quelling any indication of feeling, Lily watched her hired foreman as he crossed the yard in her direction.

His wardrobe apparently consisted of two chambray

shirts—one with a torn pocket and the other with a dark stain on the sleeve—and two pairs of worn denims. As he walked, his muscles strained at the seams of the old clothes, and Lily often caught herself holding her breath, waiting for a thread to surrender to the pressure. She had never before noticed a man the way she did this one, and she hoped her cheeks weren't red as Cade came to a halt at a respectful distance.

"I want to get rid of Williams," he announced as if the decision had been made and Lily was simply the beneficiary of his judgment.

"He's a tad lazy, but he gets the job done eventually. What's he done to deserve dismissal?" Brought back to the mundane, Lily replied with more poise than she felt.

Cade placed his hands on his hips. The woman who paid him was trying to disguise a load of irritation, but he didn't allow that knowledge to deter him. She swatted at a loose strand of yellow hair flying in her face and added another smear of dirt to her brow. He'd had time to get accustomed to her height—he rather appreciated being able to look her in the eye when she started one of her diatribes—but he was having trouble dealing with the idea of all that fragile slenderness doing the work of a man. He didn't have the white man's prejudice about allowing women to work, but a woman who wielded a gun and a horse like a man was another prospect entirely. He had learned to adjust to many things in his life, however. This was just one more.

"He's insolent and disobedient and a troublemaker. I wish to make an example of him." Cade didn't like explaining his decisions, particularly to a woman, but he acknowledged her right to know.

"He's worked for Jim for years. Jim never had any trouble with him." The devil made her say that. True, Jim had never complained about Williams's behavior, but Lily had always found the man annoying. He had a way of sneaking up behind a person and listening when he had no right, and she had never liked the way he looked at her as if she were a piece of beefsteak instead of his boss.

She wouldn't be sorry to see the man gone, but she had to question the reason.

Cade merely looked at her.

Lily refused to be intimidated by his silence. "Look, if we're going to get along, you're going to have to learn to talk to me. I can't just dismiss a man because you don't like him. I don't like him either; but I haven't got a good excuse to send him away. If you have one, say so."

Cade almost smiled. She was growing more frustrated by the minute; he could tell from the way she pulled at her braided hair, tugging the straying strands behind her ear as if they were recalcitrant animals. He liked the way the blue of her eyes matched the color of the soaring skies. He liked the way she treated him as just one more of the stupid men she so blatantly despised. He didn't like having his decisions questioned. But he had already noted that the less he talked, the more she did. If he wasn't going to be jawed to death, he had to answer.

"I'm not Jim." He waited, as if this would explain all.

Lily wiped her hands on her denims and contemplated the broad-shouldered man standing there, blocking the sun. She had to tilt her head slightly to read his expression. It was an odd feeling, looking up to a man. She tucked her hair behind her ear again.

"You're not Jim," she repeated, trying to understand his meaning, or at least drag it out of him. "The men shouldn't expect you to be Jim. If Williams doesn't like you, he has the option to quit. Your not liking him isn't the same thing. I didn't hire him because I like him. I hired him to do a job. Is he doing his job?"

Cade crossed his arms over his chest. "No."

Lily wondered what he would do if she walked up to him, grabbed his finger, and bit it—hard. She had a mad desire to jerk a reaction out of this stoic giant somehow, but obviously logic wasn't going to do it. Sighing, she shoved her hands in her pockets. "All right, have it your way. I don't know where you're going to find someone to replace him; we're shorthanded as it is, but that's your job, isn't it?"

She gave him a challenging look that said more than

her words. Cade shrugged at the added responsibility; he had been prepared to take it anyway. Hearing Serena's cries of recognition coming from the house, he offered the explanation she had sought.

"I sent him back to finish his work last night. He got drunk instead. He's sleeping it off in the bunkhouse right now. I'll take care of him."

He strode off in Serena's direction, leaving Lily to stare after him in astonishment. Why in hell couldn't he have said that in the first place?

Irritation at her ornery foreman dissipated under the demands of the remainder of the day. Later, when it was time to wash for the evening meal, Lily felt as if she were already two days behind. After scrubbing herself thoroughly from the washbowl and donning a clean cotton shirt from her husband's drawers, she went in search of Serena to give her a bath before feeding her. The noise of a wagon pulling up outside distracted her from her purpose.

Having escorted a hungover Williams off the ranch and inspected the repairs in the paddock, Cade was in the yard when the wagon arrived. He didn't recognize the horse or equipage, but he recognized one of the two men on the seat, and he grimaced in distaste. Ollie Clark had visited with Mrs. Brown a few too many times during this past month. The lady wasn't even officially a widow, and already the vultures were beginning to circle.

Rather uncomfortable with the direction of that thought, Cade turned abruptly for the side door of the dogtrot. The lady's excited cries of "Daddy!" filtered through from the front porch even as he reached for the door.

Lily flung herself into the arms of the tall man coming up the dusty walk. He looked older and grayer, but he was still the father she had always adored. Brushing a recalcitrant wavy lock from his eyes, Ephraim gathered Lily into his arms and kissed the top of her head.

"It's been a long time, little mite. After I got your letter, I thought it was time to come and see you. Have you had word of Jim yet?"

Ephraim Porter felt his daughter's head shake against his shoulder, and he stroked her hair as he had when she was a child. He felt the sadness well up in him at the same time as a small sliver of hope took root. Life was always thus, he had discovered long ago; the bitter came with the sweet. He needed a place in her life right now. Jim's disappearance offered the opportunity. Catching Lily's waist, Ephraim led her up the stairs to the house. It was only then that he took in her unladylike attire.

"Lily Porter Brown! What on earth is this getup you're wearing?"

"Don't start, Daddy," Lily warned, pulling away as she reached for the door. Ollie beat her to it, making a small bow as he held it open for her. She gave him an irritated look and stepped inside. She didn't need an audience for this reunion, but Ollie was making it obvious that he meant to stay.

"I knew Jim was going to be too lax with you. I bet you've run roughshod over him all these years. You ought to be ashamed of yourself, Lily Porter. Your mama taught you better."

"Mama died when I was ten. She didn't have time to teach me better." Seeing a sleepy Serena stumble out of bed, Lily bent to pick her up, discovering Cade's presence by the side door at the same time as the men beside her.

She felt both men stiffen as the tall Indian came forward, but ignoring their testiness, she brushed Serena's fair hair out of her face, pressed a kiss against her forehead, and handed her over to Cade. "She just got up. I haven't had time to bathe or feed her yet."

Then remembering her manners, Lily introduced him. "Daddy, this is Cade, my foreman. Cade, my father, Ephraim Porter." She stepped aside so the men might shake hands, but neither made an effort to do so. Frowning, she watched Cade nod his head stiffly, then turn to her.

"You have company. I'll see to Serena." He didn't even bother to take proper leave of her guests before turning and stalking out, carrying the child with him.

"Who in hell is that and where are your servants, Lily?

What kind of place is this that Jim has brought you to? You ought to have some chaperone, someone to deal with the likes of that . . ."

"I've been tellin' Lily that for some time now, sir. Maybe you can make her see sense. Cade's a drunken Indian and a cold-blooded killer. She shouldn't have no truck with the likes of that. It's Jim's fault for not allowin' slaves and hirin' an overseer like everyone else does."

Lily put her hands on her hips and glared at Ollie. "As law-abiding Mexican citizens, we're not supposed to have slaves. That's half the problem we're having with the Mexican government right now: people like you think you can make your own laws. And I happen to agree with Jim. Slaves are a poor form of labor."

"So is a murdering Indian—"

Ollie's tirade was halted by Ephraim's interruption. "Let's not argue. I've had words with Jim over this before, and there's no sense trying to change his mind. It's disrespectful to talk of him when he can't defend himself."

Relieved, Lily turned her back on Ollie to study her father's tired face. "You've had a long journey. Let me make up a room for you so you can wash and rest. Juanita can keep our dinner warm until you're ready to eat." Selfishly, she made it clear that Mr. Clark wasn't being invited. He might be the best-looking man in town and always solicitous of her well-being, but he was also an opinionated ass.

After preparing the loft over the main cabin for her father and sending Ollie away, Lily went in search of Cade. His rudeness was as inexcusable as her father's. She had no intention of living between two warring factions if her father had come to stay, which she very much expected he had.

She found Cade sitting on the front step of the cabin he had taken as his own, feeding Serena pieces of pecans from his hand. At Lily's approach, he put the remainder of the pecans in the child's lap and stood, brushing his hands off against his denims.

"If you won't be needing me, I'd like time to find another place for Serena. I'll pay rent."

Lily stared at the overgrown idiot with astonishment. God had simply given him too much of everything except brains. She was too aware that her eyes only came level with the spectacular breadth of Cade's shoulders. If she allowed herself to look, she could see the smooth copper of his skin beneath the open V of his shirt, but she forced herself to meet those obsidian eyes instead. She could read nothing at all behind them, and the thought made her want to shiver.

"My father has already run one plantation into the ground. I don't intend to give him a chance to destroy another. You're the foreman, I'm the boss, and he's only a guest. I just ask that you be polite to him. I dislike argument."

At last she had drawn a reaction from him: Cade's eyebrows rose a hair as he met her gaze. Lily felt a certain amount of satisfaction at finally getting through to him.

Cade knew better than to think it would work, but he was relieved not to have to leave immediately. Serena needed the security of a home and the attentions of a woman. Those commodities were not easily found in the life he led. Besides, he was beginning to enjoy Juanita's peach cobbler.

"He'll not like it," Cade warned.

"He didn't like Jim, either, but that didn't stop me." With that retort, Lily spun around and returned to the house.

There were a lot worse things in life than what her father didn't like. It had been a hard lesson to learn, but she had learned it well.

Five

"I want you to come home with me, Lily. I think I've seen and heard enough these last days to convince me this isn't any place for a woman alone. The work isn't suitable for a lady, there's still Indians close enough to be dangerous, and from all I hear, there's war in the air. They're saying the Mexicans are holding American prisoners in Coahuila and planning to shoot them. There's going to be repercussions, just you wait and see."

"Daddy, I'm not going to leave. This is Roy's inheritance. This will all belong to him one day. I've got to hang on to it any way I can. And you talk as if Jim isn't ever coming back. He could turn up tomorrow. What would he think if I had already hightailed it back home?"

"He'd think you were a sensible woman." Ephraim set his coffee mug down on the table and glared at his stubborn daughter. They were too much alike in many respects, neither one of them willing to give any quarter. But he was right this time; she would just have to recognize it.

"I'm not going, Daddy, and that's final. I don't belong back there anymore. I never did. This is my home and I'm going to stay." Lily stood up and carried her plate to the sink. Jim had installed the pump in here several years ago, before he built the kitchen, and she was proud to have it. It wasn't the same as having slaves to haul and carry for her, but she preferred it just the same. She liked having something of her own, and this house was hers.

"Not by yourself, you can't. Hell, honey, you're the only woman within twenty miles, far as I can see. These men aren't made of stone. You've gotta have someone here to protect you. It's been over two months since Jim disappeared. You're going to have to start facing facts. If you're too stubborn to leave, you'll have to start looking for a decent man to look after you. That Ollie Clark seems like a fine, upstanding young fellow. He owns that store back in town, don't he?"

Lily sighed and ran her fingers over her temple, where a throb was beginning to build. She loved her father, but he was beginning to get on her nerves. The fact that Ollie owned a store like her father did had impressed him. In her father's eyes, that would make any man fine and upstanding. Maybe he was right, but she had no intention of putting herself in a man's power again. Jim had been a good man, and he was willing to let her work side by side with him, but he had never wanted to hear her opinions. Men never did. Now she had the opportunity to do things her way, and she fully intended to take advantage of it. The labor-intensive cotton would be the first to go.

She looked up as Roy burst into the house, his narrow face lit with inner excitement as he found her and began to extol upon his latest accomplishment. Letting Roy learn to ride was one of those things that Jim would never have allowed. Lily was quite certain she had made the right decision in throwing over that command.

"Mama, Cade says I'm almost ready to ride to town. Can I, Mama? Please?"

Sighing, Lily tousled Roy's hair and wondered if she'd gotten her hopes up too soon. Roy was only eight. Surely that was too young for such a ride. She would have to talk to Cade. That would be easier than listening to her father's arguments.

She stepped outside before Cade could cross the yard to the kitchen where Juanita kept Serena. Roy piled out of the house after her, sensing the confrontation to come.

"Cade!" Lily knew she spoke too sharply, but it had been a long day. She combed her fingers through Roy's unruly curls as she waited for her foreman to turn and find her.

When he did, his gaze went not to Lily but to her affectionate hold on the boy. It was twilight, and the shadows were quickly covering Cade's features, but Lily could almost swear she saw a look of longing in the man's eyes before he raised them to her. When he did, the usual opaque barrier met her gaze. She could easily have been wrong, but she softened her voice when she spoke.

"Roy says he's almost ready to ride to town. That's a long distance. Don't you think it's a tad soon?"

His voice, when it came, was thoughtful and not its usual curt tone. "He learns quick. He ought to be rewarded. It can wait until several of us are ready to go."

Cade was right, of course. Lily had been prepared for a confrontation, but it had only been her own frustration and anger speaking. She couldn't erase that glimpse of longing, of loneliness she thought she had seen in Cade's face. Perhaps he had some human traits, after all. After a few short words, she released him and took Roy back into the house.

Lily pacified her father when she returned by turning the subject to her sisters and how well they were doing, while making certain that Roy scrubbed himself down good before going off to bed. The pressures of all the things that had not been done this day was rapidly giving her a throbbing headache. She finally gave her excuses and retired to the room she and Jim had shared. The possibility that her father was using her absence to search for Jim's store of liquor no longer worried her. He was a quiet drunk, and there was no one out here for him to embarrass but her, and she was beyond embarrassment right now.

Not bothering to light a candle, Lily closed the door between her bedroom and the dogtrot and leaned against it with relief. It was times like these when she missed Jim's company. He had been a buffer between her and the rest of the world, a source of support when she needed it, a calm companion who could make the day's catastrophes look like molehills in the light of his reasoning. These months of independence were beginning to teach her how tediously lonely life could be. If only she could rely on her father just a little bit . . .

Lily drifted to the window and stared out at the tidy assortment of buildings she and Jim had painstakingly created over the years. There were no slipshod lean-tos and ramshackle barns here. All the buildings, from the lowly kitchen to the house itself, were as solid and dependable as Jim. They weren't showy or extravagant. There were no fanciful shutters or useless adornments, nothing remotely stylish beyond the practical lines of timber and clay, but she didn't need fanciful. She needed the security of four walls and a roof over her head, and Jim had provided them.

Just as he had provided her with a name and a father for her child. Lily turned away from the window and stared at the low-slung rope bed she had shared with her husband of nearly nine years. Her childish dreams of love and romance had been permanently killed before she had even met Jim. Except for children, he had given her just precisely what she wanted. Why did it feel as if he had never existed now that he was gone?

And she was quite certain that he was gone. Practical Jim wouldn't even have a ghost to come back and haunt her. If he were alive, he would have found some way to send her word. Lily knew that as well as she knew her own name. Jim was gone and he wasn't coming back.

Staring at the empty bed, Lily felt the loneliness sweep in and curl around her like the notes of the flute in the dry air outside.

Flute?

Grateful for this distraction, Lily turned back to the open window and stared out. Music was a rare commodity in these parts. Her heart hungered for it, grieved for its absence, and longed for it more than she had ever desired or wanted love. Love was an ephemeral thing, but music was real, so real she could almost taste the notes floating over the still night air.

Knowing sleep would elude her anyway, Lily sought the source of the unusual sound. Not wanting to disturb the rest of the household, she slipped through the window to the ground. Men's trousers had many advantages—getting in and out of tight spots was one of them.

Following the notes of the flute through the quiet night

wasn't difficult. She could hear the restless shuffles and low nickers of the horses in the paddock behind her. The music came from the opposite direction, from the low knoll ahead. Loblollies and oaks shaded the grass there. She and Roy used to picnic beneath the trees, before Roy decided he was too big for "baby stuff." She would have to take Serena up there one of these days.

She didn't want to think about Serena either. Cade could take the child away any day, and there wouldn't be a thing Lily could do about it. She was trying to be practical, giving the care of the child to Juanita for much of the day, but Serena was so much like the child Lily had always wanted that it was impossible to ignore her entirely. That was one more piece of the day she didn't have to think about tonight.

Her goal was to find the music, and she wouldn't let all the day's worries and fears confine her. A breeze lifted the loosened strands of her hair and blew them backward as she floated across the yard and toward the hill. The moon was just appearing on the other side of the barn, a silvery spectacle against the black of the sky. It wasn't full yet, but she could feel its pull. Lily shivered and listened to the night creatures harmonize with the notes of the flute as her feet reached the grass beyond the dirt farm yard, and progressed upward.

By the time she reached the top, Lily knew what she would find, but she didn't hesitate. The magic of the music was a rarity for which she would defy the laws of mankind. Already the throbbing in her head had lessened, and her body felt loose, floating, at one with the world around her. This was the way it had once been and never would be again.

Tears formed in her eyes at that thought. She didn't allow them to fall. Without a word, she sat down near the man who was skillfully pouring his talents into the crude reed instrument.

Cade had seen her coming. The overlarge white shirt she wore caught in the silver rays of the moon and carried like a ghostly image from the house up the hill. He had thought the household asleep long before. He hadn't meant for any to hear but himself and the stars, but she didn't disturb the oneness between them. The music accepted her into its tightly drawn circle, and he continued to play until the song wended its way to the end.

Then he put the flute aside and turned his gaze to her.

It was impossible to conceive that this incredibly large man could produce such flawlessly delicate music, but Lily knew better than to speak of miracles. She held out her hand in a pacifying gesture for her intrusion. "I miss music more than anything or anyone else I left behind," she whispered.

Cade's enigmatic gaze revealed nothing. He crossed his arms over his raised knees and nodded. "Music speaks to the soul."

Lily didn't know how he could be so perfectly attuned to what she had thought was her hidden secret, but she nodded gratefully for his understanding. "I wish I had something as easily transportable as a flute. Jim said we couldn't bring a piano."

Guilt wormed its way to Cade's insides. She was being brave, talking of her husband when she had no knowledge of his whereabouts. He heard the pain in her voice; the music had reached out to it. He very possibly had the power to intensify that pain—or to relieve it. Uncertainty kept him from revealing any more. He didn't know her, and she didn't know him. It was better to keep silent.

"They have a piano in town," Cade found himself saying. He'd stood outside Clark's barn any number of times, listening to the intertwining of notes, contemplating the means of making such a joyful noise. The player hadn't been expert, but he'd never heard anything like it before.

Apparently this was news to Lily. She looked up at Cade with something akin to excitement burning in the pale blue of her eyes. "Really? Why didn't anyone tell me?" Then she shut up and her gaze drifted to the pasture beyond the trees.

Her husband had known. He could see that suspicion forming on her face.

"I suppose that's what they do in town on Saturday

nights," she murmured. "Jim told me it was too rowdy to stay after dark."

"The other women stay," Cade said without inflection. He'd watched them, the ladies in their best calicoes with an occasional rustling taffeta here and there, the whores in their brightest colors. So many females in the flesh all in one place had been a tantalizing opportunity of which he couldn't avail himself. He'd stayed out in the night, listening.

Lily had never been close to her sisters, but she had grown up in a household of females and missed the feminine discussions and laughter and shared secrets. Juanita couldn't fill that need entirely; she had been too damaged by her past to speak in more than monosyllables much of the time. Ralph Langton's wife was so much older than Lily that there wasn't much common ground between them. Lily didn't know much about the town ladies, but there was no reason she couldn't meet them somehow, if she put her mind to it.

"I wish I could hear the piano," Lily said more to herself than to anyone in particular. Actually, she wished she had a right to play the piano, but that was beyond her ability to speak.

"I'll take you in if you wish to go." Cade wasn't certain why he had said that. He certainly hadn't planned it. Now that it was out, though, he felt a certain pleasure in the thought, if just to see the fury on the faces of the other men when he entered with the coveted Mrs. Brown on his arm. It would go a long way toward alleviating a myriad of stings.

Cade didn't expect Lily's acquiescence, however, and when she spoke, he almost didn't hear her reply.

"I would like that, thank you. I don't think Juanita would mind watching Serena, and my father can look after Roy. Do they have other instruments besides the piano?"

Cade's fingers idly stroked the flute as he turned his gaze fully on the woman sitting in the grass before him. He had never met anyone quite like her before, and he was having difficulty placing her in any category that he knew how to deal with. She was white and female, which should put her completely out of bounds for any conversation at all. But she was his boss, and as such, there had to be a certain amount of communication. She wore trousers like a man, and to a certain extent she spoke like a man, but he couldn't treat her with the same deference as Ralph Langton or with the scorn he felt for the ignorant farmhands he worked with. If she had been a whore, he could have had certain expectations, but she was a lady. How the hell should he treat a lady who wore pants?

"Fiddles, sometimes," he responded automatically while he struggled with the problem.

"Is there dancing?" she asked anxiously.

It was then that Cade realized that this woman didn't see categories as other people did. She saw people through the eyes of a child, as they related to her and not as other people saw them. It was rather amusing to realize that he had been avoiding her like the plague to keep from offending her ladylike sensibilities when she was more likely offended by his avoidance than his presence. That's what he got for assuming all white women were alike.

"They dance," he agreed.

Cade was enjoying looking at her. Her hair had the sheen of gold in the moonlight. He wished she would let it blow free instead of always wearing it bound in that braid that never quite held all the silky tendrils in place. She was small-bosomed and slender-waisted, but in the revealing denims, he could see that her curves were in all the right places. Her skin glowed golden from exposure to the sun, but he suspected that beneath her billowing shirt she was as pale as the moonlight. It wasn't a thought he should dwell on.

"I don't dance," Lily informed him pointedly.

Even though he had known she would draw a line somewhere, Cade felt a bitter disappointment that it had come so soon. So much for the manners of a child. "Neither do I."

At his sudden gruffness, Lily hastened to explain. "I never really learned. I was always playing the piano for my sisters and their friends. I . . . Well, I married young. Jim doesn't dance."

Cade smiled then, a genuine smile that said he found something immensely pleasant or vastly amusing. He rose to his feet with a grace that belied his size and offered his large hand to help her do the same.

"You had best sleep tonight if you are to stay awake tomorrow."

His hand was brown and callused, but warm and gentle as it enfolded hers. Lily was quite aware that what she had just done was utterly insane, but she didn't care. Her soul longed for music and this man had just offered it to her.

Releasing his hand, she turned back toward the house without a word of parting.

Six

As they drew closer to the barn, Lily could hear the tinkling sounds of the piano over the noise of voices and laughter, and her heart began to pound with excitement. She had never really been to a dance before. She didn't know what would be expected of her and she was half terrified, but the sound of the piano kept her going forward.

The fight with her father faded as she drew nearer. He had been opposed to her staying in town without him, but she wasn't going to have his drinking ruin her very first evening out. Besides, he would no doubt raise the roof if he knew Cade was the one escorting her. It was much better this way, all on her own, without family or memories. Being a stranger, Cade didn't count.

Just the same, Lily was grateful that Cade had cleaned up for her. He'd had his long black hair trimmed to his shirt collar, and from somewhere he had acquired a decent white homespun shirt that he wore covered by a leather vest. If one liked sun-bronzed features and arrogant Spanish noses, he could be considered a handsome man. His looks didn't concern her so much as another subject, however. Just outside the barn she stopped and laid a hand on his arm.

The action halted Cade in his tracks, and he turned to look down at her quizzically. He had been all but holding his breath since she had walked out of the house wearing that blue gingham dress. The top molded to her firm young breasts, and the oval neckline revealed more of her milky skin than those hideous shirts did. He was having difficulty keeping his thoughts from straying to the long legs he knew existed beneath the loose skirt. Somehow, just knowing those legs were bare beneath the folds of material was more arousing than seeing them encased in denim every day.

"Cade, do you drink?"

That was a damfool question, and it jarred Cade out of his daydreams. He looked at her suspiciously. She wasn't given to fool questions. "Does a pig eat?" he asked, with a certain amount of surliness.

Her full lips tightened briefly, then relaxed as she removed her hand. "I meant hard liquor. They'll have refreshments, won't they?"

"Ollie isn't doing this out of the goodness of his heart," he agreed.

Lily took a deep breath and tried for a voice of reason, unaware that her companion had suddenly become distracted by the movement of her bodice. "There will be lemonade and the like, won't there?"

"For the ladies." Watching her breathing, Cade wasn't following her drift with any degree of accuracy, so he agreed without caution.

"Then there will be something to quench your thirst besides liquor." She finished her thought with a degree of satisfaction.

That caught Cade's attention. He stared at her as if she had lost her head. "Men don't drink lemonade."

"You sound just like Roy telling me he's too big to go on picnics. Real men would have the courage to do whatever they damn well liked."

Lily lifted her skirts and strode off before he could react. Cursing, Cade followed two steps behind her. So much for his notion of arriving with a beautiful woman on his arm. He should have known that Lily Brown wouldn't lower herself to being escorted by a mere male. Oddly, he was quite certain that the fact that he was a half-breed hadn't entered her bigoted little mind. Being male was sufficient to lower him as far as he could go.

Cade was too angry to concern himself with the impression he made as he entered the barn where he had never dared trespass before. He consciously avoided making trouble, but his thoughts were on the swaying skirts of Lily Brown and not the people standing around watching him enter. It didn't take two steps into the barn to realize his error.

Ollie Clark stepped into his path, blocking Cade's view of Lily. Instantly on the alert, Cade felt the watchful attention of several of Ollie's cohorts on the sidelines. He hadn't intended to make trouble, but he certainly didn't intend to run from it either. Straightening his shoulders and directing his gaze to the tall man in front of him, Cade waited wordlessly.

"Indians ain't allowed in here. We've got white ladies present."

Ladies, whores, and creatures of indeterminable sex or status, but Cade didn't point that out. He merely waited.

Irritation flared in Clark's eyes. "I'm askin' you to leave, red man."

A hissing intake of breath behind him was all the warning Ollie received. Before he could spin around, a furious virago in blue gingham swirled past him and grabbed the Indian's arm, sending shooting sparks of blue fire from her eyes as she spoke.

"Cade is my escort and I'll be damned if either one of us leaves, *Mister* Clark." Reducing him to the status of "mister" after his hard-won promotion to "Ollie" wasn't sufficient. Lily glared at him. "And for your information, Cade has more of a right to be here than anyone else in this town. Both Mexicans and Indians were here before us. You'll be lucky if they don't run you out of Texas before this is all over."

Realizing Cade had no intention of budging from this encounter, Lily threw him a sharp look, released his arm, and lifted her skirt in imminent departure. "I am in need of a lemonade, gentlemen. I trust you'll find a way to settle your differences amicably."

She stalked off, daring either of the two men to follow her. Cade was swifter on the uptake. With a nod to Clark, he turned and followed in Lily's direction. He had never been escort to a lady before, but he had the vague impression he was supposed to see to her needs. Lemonade had a certain appeal.

When the long arm reached around her and through the crowd at the refreshment table to produce two cups of lemonade, Lily breathed a sigh of relief. Cade wasn't thoroughly thickheaded, then. For the first time, she allowed herself to relax and listen to the music.

The noise of the crowd almost drowned out the tinny sounds coming from one end of the barn. Under Cade's guidance, Lily found herself watching as the young pianist dutifully picked at the notes while following the lone fiddler's directions with anxiety. The dancers seemed oblivious to the lack of inspiration in the piano player. As long as there was noise, they laughed and clapped and swung through the motions of the dance. Perhaps there was something to be said for hard liquor after all.

Cade watched the disappointment in Lily's eyes and was angry at himself for bringing her here. Jim Brown had the right idea after all. A gentle lady accustomed to the finer things in life had no place here. Already she had been rudely insulted and disappointed. The rest of the night would only bring worse.

Perhaps he could correct the situation in some small way. Because of his size, people weren't much inclined to argue with him. He was fully confident that he could do almost anything he wanted within reason. Playing a flute seemed purely reasonable to him. It couldn't be any worse than what they were being subjected to now.

Leaving Lily wistfully watching the piano player, Cade found a bale of hay near the fiddle player and pulled his instrument from his back pocket. He'd heard the tune before; while it wasn't one he was inclined to play in his moments alone, the notes were easily learned. In a minute or two, he added his music to theirs.

The high, lilting notes of the flute caught Lily's ear before she even realized Cade was no longer by her side. Looking up in surprise, she found him sitting on a hay bale, leaning against a post, piping the tune with a vigorousness that would have shamed a concert musician. His own music was much more beautiful than this simple song, but she had to admit that his leadership was already inspiring the other two pitiful musicians.

Cade's action gave Lily the courage she needed. She might never have been to a dance before, but she had played a piano at many. The child on the bench couldn't raise too strenuous an objection to a little help. With a slight lift to her chin, she made her way to the piano and took a seat next to the young girl.

The dance tune came to a natural end, and while the dancers were laughing and gasping for air, Lily smiled at her surprised companion. "I used to play at dances when I was your age. Would you mind if I joined you for a while?"

"No, ma'am. Mama usually does this, but she's down ill. I don't rightly know all the tunes like she does."

"Well, I'll see if I can remember some, and you can pick up when you recognize them. How's that?"

The girl looked more than relieved, and soon Lily found herself in heavenly bliss with her fingers once more striking ivory keys. The instrument was old and slightly out of tune, but with a little work, she could pump a rousing noise from it. It wasn't Beethoven, but it was lively and fun, and the dancers responded to it instantly.

Cade watched as the strained features of Mrs. Jim Brown, farmer's wife, relaxed into the laughing, glowing excitement of Lily Porter Brown, musician. It was a miracle to him to discover that a woman could have more than one face. He had more or less lumped females into certain categories relative to their sexual availability. Lily Brown transcended those categories.

Relegated to the band, where he couldn't offend the sensibilities of the ladies present, Cade found himself ignored if not accepted, and he began to enjoy himself. He had never played for an audience before, but he appreciated the difference in their response now that he and Lily had enlivened the music. Someone else came up trailing a guitar and joined in on "Piney Woods," and the crowd began to hoot and holler with joy.

The girl at the piano was dragged off by a young boy

who led her into the dancing, and Cade was suddenly reminded of something Lily had said the night before.
She'd never experienced the pleasure of dancing because
she had always been the one playing the music. She certainly didn't seem to mind it. Her face was aglow with
pleasure and he had never seen her happier, but the foot-
stomping excitement that the music generated was beginning to affect even him. Cade wanted to know what it
would be like to have a woman in his arms, swinging her
through the steps like the other men were doing with their
wives and girls. Would Lily be feeling the same way?

Lily laughed and looked up at young Anna's father
when he came over at the end of the song to thank her for
helping Anna out. Alan Whitaker's gaze proudly followed
his daughter as she shyly sipped lemonade with her partner, and Lily could see that he was happy because his
daughter was happy.

"She's a charming girl and I'm glad to have been of assistance, Mr. Whitaker. I can remember myself at that
age, dying for a chance to dance and stuck at the piano
instead. Besides, I'm being entirely selfish. I love to
play."

"Anna's terribly shy, and we've been worried that she
doesn't get a chance to talk with young people her age. I
don't know how you did it, Mrs. Brown, but I have to
thank you."

"Anna did it all on her own," Lily assured him. Before
she could say more, a large shadow loomed behind her,
and she looked up to find Cade towering over her.

"Do you think they could do one song without us so I
might have the pleasure of the next dance?" he asked
formally.

Lily looked startled and Whitaker frowned slightly, but
Anna and her new friend had just come up beside them
and the girl offered shyly, "I'll play for you, Mrs. Brown.
What would you like to hear?"

It was settled. Feeling a quiver of excitement, Lily took
Cade's hand and rose from the bench. "Do you know
'Molly Cotton-tail'?" It was an easy song, one every
child learned, but great fun for dancing. Lily smiled at the

child's eager nod. She was finally going to get a chance to try dancing.

Lily's excitement was irresistible. Ignoring the fact that he would most likely get his head blown off for daring to lay a hand to a white woman, Cade led her out to join the dancers. Langton and his wife were there, and they came to join the circle beside them. Cade hid his surprise and scorn as Maria haughtily joined them, towing one of Lily's farmhands behind her. Maria was a whore at heart, but she hadn't denied him her bed as many another had done before. Cade wouldn't begrudge this offer of friendship now.

Unaware that a small cadre of friends and neighbors were forming a protective circle around them, Lily laughed and took Cade's hand as the music began. She had waited for this moment all her life, and she expected to enjoy it to the fullest. She no longer had a man of her dreams to picture in Cade's place. She merely wanted to be herself and to enjoy the music and this small piece of life. It was a wonderful freedom that she had never before experienced.

Cade watched in amazement as Lily spread her wings and flew. She didn't need anyone's protection. The sheer delight on her face as she swung from arm to arm around the circle, her feet scarcely touching the floor, was enough to stop even the hardest heart from treading on her happiness. Cade almost half-believed that life had some meaning beyond mere existence as he watched her. He wouldn't need liquor if he could always feel that kind of joy, even secondhand.

Lily collapsed, laughing, into his arms as the music came to its end. For a moment, Cade was holding her, supporting her slenderness against him while she recovered her breath. He had no right being aroused by innocence incarnate, but his body suddenly erupted into a raging tower of flame. While Lily laughed, Cade burned.

The evening ended simply enough. Lily played a few more tunes until the drunken farmers became too rowdy for gently bred females, then she accepted Cade's escort to the wagon waiting outside.

Cade deliberately kept his distance, but he could feel every movement Lily made as she walked beside him. He drank in the clean scents of her soap and rosewater and burned in every place she had touched him this night. Remembering the priest's preaching of purgatory, Cade knew he had found it right here on earth as he walked beside this completely unobtainable woman.

He should have been feeling relieved that no one had offered to shoot him for daring to invade a territory that had always been off limits. Mostly, Cade wished he'd taken the opportunity to get drunk so he would be feeling numb now instead of burning like a lovesick schoolboy. As Lily called farewell to her newfound friends and neighbors, Cade worked at reining in his lusts. It was lust in the plural, he knew. He didn't want just her body, although that would go a long way toward easing some of the ache. He wanted everything about this woman. He wanted her joy, her home, her family, all the things he'd never known—and would never know.

Scowling, Cade stared at the oxen's rear ends as they pulled the wagon down the road toward the ranch. Lily was humming beside him, totally oblivious to his predicament. She was his boss. She was white. She was an American. She was a lady. He built the barricade of bricks between them with conscientious thoroughness. He should have dragged Maria off to a dark corner and eased his hungers before he left the safety of the lighted barn with this woman.

"You'll never know how much I appreciate this, Cade." Finally sensing her companion's silence, Lily reached out to him in the only way she knew, with words. He had given her an evening to remember for the rest of her life. She wished there were some way to show her gratitude.

Cade gave a surly grunt.

Surprised, Lily turned to study the man beside her. His size was still a little intimidating, but he had touched her with the greatest of gentleness all evening and had not once stepped on her toes. She was beginning to feel almost comfortable in his presence, if only she could break through the reserve he maintained between them.

"I mean that, Cade. I've been dying inside without music. I hadn't realized that until tonight. I feel alive again. It's the most wonderful feeling. I wish I could make you feel it too."

She did. She could. He wanted it too. But he didn't think what she had in mind was the same as what he had in mind. Still, the opportunity availed.

Cade pulled the wagon to the side of the road beneath a stand of oaks. The darkness engulfed them, the leaves blocking out even the stars' light. Lily's soft fragrance wafted around them.

Without a word of warning, Cade slid his arm around her waist and drew her closer.

Lily emitted a smothered gasp as Cade's lips came down across hers, but that was the last protest she made as she found her whole body engulfed in a bonfire of heat that she had not expected and had not asked for but could not fight. Her lips parted beneath his, and the heat of his kiss swept through her insides.

This was insane. She hadn't felt this way since she was a child and didn't know better. She couldn't . . .

But she could. As Cade's hands spread across her back and his mouth took its pleasure and returned it threefold, she very definitely could feel this way.

And with a determined thrust, Lily shoved him away and folded her arms over her aching breasts.

Silently, Cade picked up the reins and set the cattle in motion.

Seven

"Hell, there's land out there for the takin'. Them Mexicans are too lazy to do anything with it, and there's plenty of Americans itchin' to get their hands on it—with our help, of course."

The man sipping his whisky at the table looked at the speaker with contempt. "Santa Anna might have a thing or two to say about that. Do you think it's any accident that Bowie and his lot got thrown out of Coahuila? Or that we got a Mexican army camping on our doorstep? Until we have an army to hold the Mexicans off, we'll not get our hands on any more land. The easy days are over."

A third man shrugged his lacy cuffs from his coat sleeves and disdainfully inspected them for dirt. "There is land to be had if the right people are approached properly. Meanwhile, there's always that swamp down along the river that you can parcel out when this next lot of fools arrives. Unless, of course, you can manage to get the land away from your lady friend. Sold a parcel at a time, it could bring a tidy fortune."

The second man threw back another slug of whisky. "It's not going to be as easy as I thought. And with land prices skyrocketing like they are, she's likely to ask a fortune for any of it. We'll have to find another way."

The first man grinned. "You could marry her. Just think of havin' that tall drink of water in your bed. Right gives a man goose bumps."

"Especially if she learned you've already got a wife back in the states," the elegantly dressed man sniffed. "A lot of men have been getting away with it, but I've got a suspicion your Mrs. Brown isn't the type to take such news lightly."

"How is she going to find out? Her father is easily persuaded. If I could just get rid of that damned drunken Indian . . ."

"Indian?" The third man looked up with sudden interest. "She has an Indian working for her?"

The explanation, when it came, made the stranger smile.

"No, you cannot ride out with the men, and that is final. Get back in the house to your schoolwork."

"But Mama, Cade said . . ."

Lily pointed her finger at the back door, and her rebellious eight-year-old scuffled his feet in that direction. It was almost more than she could take these days, whipping an army of recalcitrant men into line. Thank goodness her father had gone into town so she didn't have to listen to some complaint from him too.

She gave a smile of relief as Juanita came out of the kitchen carrying Serena. At least there were a few women whose support she could rely on. Lily reached to take the child into her arms.

"She is spoiled, that one. *El Monstruo* ruins her." Juanita crossed her arms over her ample chest as she frowned at the laughing child.

Since the night of the dance Lily had avoided Cade by the simple expedient of putting Juanita in her place. Juanita regarded her new status as messenger with suspicion but without questioning. Lily wasn't any more satisfied with the arrangement than the other woman was, but she hadn't come to terms yet with her response to Cade's kiss. She knew it was her own fault for allowing him to take her to the dance. Men had the most ridiculous view of their rights where women were concerned. She should have expected Cade's response, but she hadn't. Nor had she expected her own. That was the part that was giving her trouble.

Lily tickled Serena's belly and sent her into gales of giggles. "What has she been up to now?"

"She decided her dolly should be white and she dusted her in my flour bin. Then she fed my buttermilk to her cat and poured it all over my clean floor and herself and the cat. We will not have biscuits tonight."

Juanita was righteously indignant, but these were still more words than she had spoken in years. Lily smiled and met the maid's flashing eyes. "I don't know of a child alive who isn't a nuisance. What would life be without them?"

Juanita's expression softened momentarily, then grew hard again. "If only they could be had without men." She turned around and marched back to the kitchen.

That was a problem. Lily carried the toddler back to the house for her bath. She was barely twenty-five years old, but she was condemning herself to a life of celibacy just like Juanita was—celibacy and childlessness. They would both grow to be cantankerous old spinsters at the rate things were going.

Jim had at least saved her from that fate, but not by much. Sighing, Lily began stripping off Serena's batter-encrusted gown. Why couldn't men behave with the same civility as women? What made them turn into raging animals at the drop of a hat? Or an eyelid.

She was going to have to come to terms with Cade somehow. Even as she thought it, she saw her foreman crossing the yard toward the barn, another man trailing after him. Perhaps this was the new hand Cade had promised to hire. When the stranger turned slightly, Lily suppressed a gasp of shock, then allowed rage to take over. This had to be the final straw.

Leaving a half-naked Serena in Roy's bemused command, Lily stormed out of the house. She could not believe Cade was doing this to her. It must be his way of getting even.

Cade read the fire in her eyes clearly enough as Lily approached. Even the man beside him could see it, and he shuffled nervously to stand slightly behind Cade and out of range of the first shot. The lady in denims and man's vest looked fully prepared to take them both on single-handed.

Before she could speak, Cade made introductions. "Mrs. Brown, this is Abraham Tulane. He's just come to work for us."

Us. He had his nerve saying "us." Lily glared but kept her tone to a reasonable politeness. "I need to speak with you a moment, Cade." Her expression finished the sentence with "alone." Standing there in half-open work shirt and tight denims, his thick hair brushing his shirt collar, Cade presented a formidable problem all on his own. Lily knew better than to be anywhere alone with him, but anger was the passion ruling her now.

Cade nodded toward the barn. "Go in and choose a mount, Abe. I'll be with you shortly."

He knew what she was going to say, and still he sent the man to pick a horse. Lily could barely suppress the steam she knew must be coming from her ears by the time the man ambled out of sight, and she didn't allow Cade's masculine presence to deter her response.

"What are you trying to do to me?" she hissed. "It's bad enough I have to listen to complaints about you, but what in hell am I going to do when the whole lot walks off because you hired a damned Negro?"

Impassively, Cade crossed his arms over his chest and ignored the glint of sunlight in her hair. "Clark wants you to hire slaves. Tell them he's a slave. Damned if I care what you tell them. I worked with him at Martin's, and he's good. He'll do twice the job of any of those lazy maggots you have now."

It was bad enough that Cade swore in her presence, but his insolence was beyond the bounds of propriety. Lily wanted to smack his enigmatic face, but she had sworn to be reasonable. Holding her breath until her temper returned to a simmer, she tried to approach the subject logically.

"If I tell them he's a slave, they'll treat him like a slave. I can't have that. And I can't have my whole staff walk off the job either. You've got to be reasonable about this, Cade. He might be able to do the job of two men, but he can't do the job of six."

Cade held Lily's defiant gaze. He could still taste the

fervency of her kiss, and the sight of her full lips aroused an unwanted response. He knew he must be losing his mind to even consider this woman in that way, but obviously his body had little to do with his mind. He kept his expression unmoved and his gaze away from her breasts as he answered.

"Let them quit. There are better men out there to be had for the asking. You're the boss, not those griping asses."

When she didn't immediately respond, Cade turned on his heel and walked away. Lily stared after him, wishing for a gun. She couldn't believe he'd said that to her. She couldn't believe that he just might possibly be right. And she couldn't believe she was watching the man's broad shoulders and narrow hips like some love-starved adolescent as he walked away.

As the vision of what would happen as soon as that black man joined the ranks came to mind, Lily groaned and retraced her steps to the house. Maybe Ollie was right. Maybe she should never have hired Cade. But how in hell was she going to find another foreman to do the job as well as he? There wasn't a white man in the country willing to take orders from a woman. She wasn't exactly certain that Cade was taking orders from her. But he was at least doing his job, and out here where men did as they pleased, that was saying a great deal.

Lily didn't want to feel like she was losing control, but she was. That became more evident when her father returned in time for dinner, dragging Ollie Clark with him. Both of them were well on their way to being inebriated.

At least Jim never got drunk. Lily was beginning to appreciate his few virtues more and more these days. Jim might have been boring, passionless, and single-minded, but he was a saint compared to most of the men in her life. Gritting her teeth, Lily saw the men seated in the main cabin, and she headed for the kitchen and Juanita. The evening meal ought to be right entertaining.

Lily did her best to smile politely as the two men

praised the food, complimented her appearance, and even tried to impress Roy with their interest. Roy had grown accustomed to his grandfather's vague addresses, but he didn't take kindly to Ollie's questioning on his riding lessons. He merely gave the handsome guest a look that very much resembled one Cade might have given and asked to be excused.

"You be careful out there tonight," Lily admonished, as she gave Roy a hug and sent him out to join Cade for their lesson.

Embarrassed, Roy pulled away, but he gave an obedient nod. "Cade says I'm good enough to ride out with the others," he reminded her fiercely.

"And maybe you are, but you'll have to save your riding for the evenings now. Your books are more important during the day. Maybe Saturday."

Giving the two men at the table an expressive look, Roy walked out without replying to that. He was going to develop a swagger just like Cade's if she didn't swat his little rear end soon, Lily decided before she returned her attention to her guests.

"Lily, you give that boy too much rope. Your foreman is a bad influence on him," Ephraim admonished his daughter quietly.

"Cade is merely teaching him to ride, Daddy. We've been over this before. Would you rather I went out there and tried to teach him to ride like a man?"

Since that was another topic that had become a sore point between them, Ephraim had the sense to back away before the gauntlet could be tossed. "Now, I know you're doing what you think is right, Lily. You've always been just like me and done things your way. But I think you're old enough to realize you can't always have the things you want. I know I criticized Jim when you wed, and I was wrong, but you ought to know I only want what's best for you."

"I know that, Daddy. You'll just have to remember I'm not a little girl any longer. Would you and Ollie like another piece of cake?" Diverting their attention to food was always the easiest way out.

But not this time. Her father leaned over the table and patted Lily's hand. "You being a grown woman is all the more reason I should look after you. If you're determined to stay out here and not come home with me where you belong, then you're going to have to think about marrying again. Jim would want it, I'm sure."

Lily wanted to close her eyes and scream. It would be such a relief to release the tensions of this day, and perhaps it would end the subject for once and for all. Or it would convince them she needed a keeper even more than ever. Resolutely, she smiled and rose from her chair, picking up her plate to carry it to the sink.

"I'm not in the least bit interested in marrying again, Daddy. Jim hasn't even been gone for three months, and we can't be sure that he's gone at all."

"You know full well what the Indians must have done for him, Lily," said Ollie. "They're hiding out on the other side of the river. A bunch of us are about ready to ride out after them. I can't promise we'll bring back Jim's body, but we'll try. And three months is too long for a woman out here. Your father's right. You need to marry again."

If Ollie Clark thought she was going to be grateful for his reassurances, he was wrong. Lily glared at him. "Those Indians never hurt a soul. You keep your band of drunken renegades away from those people. I don't want them riding down here burning the place to get even with something the lot of you have done."

"Now, wait just one minute, young lady . . ."

Outside, in the warm night air, Cade heard the angry voices coming from the house and hesitated. The open windows allowed the words to float by him in bits and pieces, but he didn't have to hear them all to guess their argument. It had been more or less the same one this past month. The introduction of this new topic of the Indians on the river worried him, but his more immediate concern was the bitter lines of pain that would be etching Lily's face right about now. She had not lied when she told him she disliked argument. The strain was there upon her face every day now. The magical butterfly he had seen that night at the dance had disappeared again.

It wasn't any of his concern. Lily Porter Brown had been given more at birth than Cade had ever possessed in a lifetime. There was no reason in the world to care whether or not she enjoyed what she possessed. But the idea of her marrying Ollie Clark turned his stomach. He turned and walked back to his front stoop.

Lily took the argument for as long as she could, then making her excuses, she left the two men to drink themselves under the table and slammed into her bedroom. She wished Jim had installed a bar with which to lock the door so she could slam that too.

Swiftly, she tore off her clothes and bathed in the tepid water beside the bed. She was too angry to sleep, but if she lit a candle to read, someone would notice it soon enough and she would be made to listen to more drunken entreaties.

Jerking on her long nightgown, Lily cursed the trap of helplessness. She couldn't send her father away. He was her father and she loved him and he was trying desperately to do what was right for her. But he didn't know her anymore, didn't know how much she had changed in these last nine years, and he couldn't understand that he couldn't walk back into his old place in her life again.

Flinging herself against the pillows, Lily crossed her arms over her chest and stared at the room's only window. She wouldn't cry. She would sit here and figure out a way to end this ceaseless argument.

But her head hurt just to think about it. She wished Jim were here. That was the only solution that came readily to mind.

To her surprise, as if her wishes had conjured up a ghost, a masculine apparition appeared in her window. As it stepped through the opening, Lily realized the towering shadow couldn't be Jim, but she couldn't believe it was who it looked to be, either.

Cade held out his hand. "Come. I will show you the music in the night."

She didn't know if it was rebellion or quixotic dreaming, but Lily took Cade's capable hand. At least he would take her away from those two drunken oafs in the other room.

Eight

Adding only a robe over her nightgown and a pair of leather moccasins, Lily followed Cade through the window and into the mysteries of the night. When she was younger, she had seldom been allowed out of the house to explore the darkness. After she had married Jim, she had been tied to his wishes in the evenings. It hadn't occurred to her that she was free at last to do as she pleased.

Only she shouldn't be doing it with Cade. Lily knew that, but she continued to follow him—past the small knoll and the oaks overlooking the house, along the creek that led to the river, and up a narrow path through the trees to a ridge of rock split by a single pine.

Standing there they could look out over the tiny lights of the farm to the faraway lights of the stars. In the distance, Lily could almost imagine that she saw the lights of town. Complete silence engulfed them until gradually, one by one, the bullfrogs began to call.

As she listened, there were other sounds. Crickets wove an intricate serenade punctuated by the staccato beats of an owl's cry. The almost inaudible whine of mosquitoes by the river produced a different music, and the occasional splash of some creature of the water mingled with the contented gurgles of the current. It was music of a different sort than she knew, but it was fascinating just the same.

Wrapping her robe around her legs, Lily sat upon a tuft of grass beneath the pine and scarcely noticed when Cade took the place beside her. They sat in silence until the howl of a distant coyote made her shiver.

"He sings for his mate," Cade reassured her.

"Does he think the sound of his loneliness will attract her?" Lily asked wryly.

"I'm sure it is the beauty of his song." His voice contained almost a hint of a chuckle.

"I'm sure that's what he thinks."

Her scoffing hid an undertone of bitterness, and Cade was silent for a while.

"Men often hide their fears with actions," he finally said.

By this time, the anger of the day had leeched out of her and into the cold stone. Wrapping her arms around her knees and resting her head upon them, Lily reluctantly gave his statement some thought. Cade had a way of saying things that made sense, even when she didn't want to admit it.

"I suppose a man who wasn't afraid would be a fool. I just find it hard to imagine someone like you being afraid."

Cade's low laugh wasn't amused. "Because of my size or because of my birth?"

Lily considered this. "Both, I suppose. To me, Indians are like the wolves, fearless of anything. All I have seen or heard of them is the damage they have done. And your size makes you seem invulnerable, even though that is ridiculous. A bullet knows nothing of size. Perhaps it is your attitude. You look as if you scorn everything, even death."

"I do not mean to give that impression. And Indians aren't fearless. As you say, only fools are without fear. They are just better at disguising their feelings. If Clark takes his band of men against the Indians as he threatens, he will find old men and women and children. Ride with him, and you will see their fear."

Lily didn't ask how he knew of Ollie's plans. Half the ranch could have heard his shouting. Instead, she asked, "How do you know what he will find? Have you seen them?"

"They are related to my father's tribe. Their fathers and sons were massacred by Comanches several years ago, and many others were lost in epidemics. They try to live by raising squash and corn and fishing from the river. They mean no harm. This land has been theirs for centuries. They do not understand the difference since the white man's coming."

"I do not know how to stop Ollie," Lily murmured. Somehow she was disappointed that Cade had brought her out here to tell her this. He could have said as much in the morning in the middle of the yard.

"I know how to stop him. Just tell me if you learn when he is to leave."

"We don't need any more bloodshed." Lily rearranged her legs in preparation for rising.

Cade's hand came out to catch her arm, and he was suddenly very near, hovering over her, his dark face dangerously near. "There will be no bloodshed."

Perhaps she overreacted, trying to pull away. Cade's hand closed tighter to keep her from falling backward off the narrow ledge. Lily felt the heat of his touch, the overpowering mass of him, and then she was in Cade's arms, her hands scaling the precipice of his shoulders while their lips met and clashed.

The sounds of the night were nothing compared to the ringing in her ears as Lily felt the brand of Cade's tongue and instinctively opened to it. She gasped and swallowed and clung tighter as he delved for her soul and almost found it. She knew the iron musculature of his chest against the rounded softness of her breasts, the strength of his hands as they mapped her back, and the welling of desire that existed between the two of them. It had been years since she had known passion, but she remembered it with terrifying clarity.

She knew she had to break away, but there was nothing threatening in the hunger of Cade's kisses. Perhaps that was what called her to him so readily. His need seemed to be as great as hers. His hands and lips gave as much as they took, and they grew strong with her response. It was intoxicating to the point of madness to have this man reduce her world to the heat of his kiss and the press of his body as he lay her back against the grass.

Lily gulped for air as Cade's kiss wandered to her earlobe and his hand discovered her breast. As his fingers crept beneath her robe to touch her through the thin material of her gown, she melted into liquid heat. Desire poured through her with such rapidity that she could sooner catch the moon than stop him. She wanted his large hands against her skin. She wanted to touch him.

When she succeeded in peeling back his shirt and running her fingers along the ridges of his chest, Cade gave a gasp of surprise and surged against her. The hardness of his arousal rubbed into her, but Lily had lost all ability to understand the implications of what they did. She turned her lips up for his kiss, only to find herself abruptly shoved away.

In astonishment, she watched as Cade sat up and struggled with his shirt, turning his back to her. And then with a cry of protest at this callous rejection, Lily leapt to her feet and ran heedlessly down the hill.

Cade was on his feet and after her within seconds, but she was fleet of foot and recklessly unaware of the treacherousness of the ground. He took it more cautiously, wanting to be certain one of them came out of this whole so as to carry the other back. Cursing beneath his breath, he watched her take the lead to greater lengths. He wasn't going to let this happen again.

With a burst of speed when they hit the open prairie, he closed the gap. She was like a terrified bird with injured wings, running and desperately trying to take to the air, without success. He didn't want to harm her with capture, but there seemed no other choice.

Cade grabbed Lily's waist and spun around to take the impact as they fell to the ground. The fall knocked the breath from his lungs, and he could only hold her struggling figure while he gasped for air.

"Don't, Lily," he managed to get out as she flailed wildly with arms and legs, seeking to punish.

His use of her name made no impression. Lily turned in his grasp and tried to sink her teeth into any flesh she could find. Cade turned over and flattened her against the grass, effectively trapping her.

"You don't want what I have to offer," he informed her coldly.

His words finally penetrated some still-functioning part of her brain, and Lily gave up her futile struggles. Even now, she could feel the desire flare up between them, a heat that boiled and simmered every place that they touched. She tried to move her hips away from the encroachment of his, and he shifted slightly to relieve the strain.

"If I had taken what you offered back there, I would have brought you pain and possibly given you a bastard to bring you shame. That isn't what you want."

Of course it wasn't, but logic wasn't the best defense against what she was feeling. Lily turned her head away so Cade couldn't see her eyes. Grass bent and tickled her face, but all she could think of was the solid masculinity of him straddling her hips. She burned with desire, and she hated his rationality.

"Get off me!"

"Not until you tell me you understand. Serena's mother was my woman some years ago. She was desperate and I took her in and she repaid me with her services, but I am big and she was small and she hated every minute of it. She left me for a whore's life and returned only to dump Serena on my doorstep. I doubt that she is even mine. Her mother only meant to get even. Is that what you want of me?"

Lily shuddered and tried to make her mind overrule her body, but even as common sense told her to listen, her body ached for what it couldn't have. "Get off me," she whispered raggedly.

Realizing the sense of this order, Cade reluctantly pulled back, even going so far as to yield her arms while he moved to a crouching position beside her, ready to run after her the instant she tried to get away.

She didn't. She lay sprawled there a minute longer, gazing up at the night sky and not at him while she recovered her equilibrium.

"Why?" she finally asked. "Why did you do that just to stop?"

"Because I'm a man and a fool," giving her the answer she already thought for herself.

"This doesn't make sense. I'm a married woman." As if that explained everything, Lily threw her arm over her eyes and refused to look at him.

"Tell me about your husband. What does he look like?"

Thoughts of Jim settled her churning insides somewhat. Jim had never done this to her, never turned her body and her emotions into roiling waves of tumult. "Jim was safe and sane and didn't ask impossible things of me. He was twenty years older and had been married before. He lost his wife and son and wasn't interested in anything but a partner to help him out here. He was grateful for all the help I gave him. I wanted to give him children, but I couldn't."

Cade had other interests besides where this revelation was leading him. He didn't want to know that she was starved for passion. He knew that already. And he didn't want to translate the remark about children. He preferred thinking of Lily and Roy as the happy family he'd never known. What he wanted to know was whether or not it was Jim's body he had found that day out on the prairie.

"Tell me what he looked like." The age was right. He'd been telling himself all along that the man he'd found had been too old for her. She had burst that bubble.

Lily sat up and stared at him. The shadows of the night hid Cade's eyes, but she knew they were fixed on her with intensity. "He had lightish brown hair that was starting to recede. He complained that it made him look old, and he always wore a hat to hide it. He was about my height but he weighed quite a bit more."

As she hesitated, trying to think of how else to describe him, Cade prompted, "What was he wearing the day he left?"

Lily really did stare at him at that. Recognizing the importance of what she had considered to be an idle question, she considered the answer carefully. "He was wearing that old homespun shirt I made him. He didn't like to get his good ones dirty out on the range. And he wore suspenders because the pants he wore wouldn't fit over his stomach."

Cade groaned and turned away, staring out over the waving grass with a sickness where his heart should be. Much as it convenienced him to let other people think so, he wasn't made of stone. And he knew what he had to tell this woman was going to bring her grief.

"Jim is dead," he told the horizon.

Lily held herself still, willing the pain to slide through her. It was too late for tears, but the hollow inside her emptied a little bit more. Aware of the tension in the broad shoulders of the man beside her, she asked carefully, "How?"

"You don't want to know that." Cade did, though. He wanted to know who had deliberately killed an innocent farmer and tried to disguise it as an Indian attack. One man immediately came to mind, and the reason was sitting right next to him. "I don't think he had time to suffer. I buried him out on the prairie. I can take you to him, if you like."

Lily breathed again, slow, pumping gulps to fill her lungs with air. Her husband was dead. She had known it but hadn't believed it until this minute. Jim was never coming back. He was never going to be there to hold her hand again. He was never going to be there when the corn burned in the summer sun and the calves died in the January blizzard and the cotton drowned in a spring flood. Never again would he tell her that everything was going to be all right, that they would work it out somehow, that things were going to be bigger and better next year. She had always believed him. She had held to his security and believed he was more powerful than God even when she was working beside him in the cotton field and cursing their lack of help. And now he was gone and there was no one to believe in. Except herself.

"I'll have to tell the others. Someone will have to find his grave and verify it's Jim. There needs to be services."

She ought to ask how he died, but she really didn't want to know. There were too many ways a man could die out here, and none of them were pleasant. She was better off not knowing.

Remembering the accusations that had flown the last time he had reported a killing, Cade was reluctant to comply, but he understood the nature of her request. "I'll lead the men out there."

To his surprise, Lily shook her head. "No, you'd better not. They're suspicious enough as it is. They'll never believe you didn't kill him. There . . . there won't be enough to show that you didn't, will there?"

It was Cade's turn to shake his head.

Lily gave a brief nod of acceptance and stared off into space as she tried not to think of what that silent gesture meant. Jim had been dead for nearly three months. She hadn't lived out here this long to remain ignorant of the effects of death. "You'll have to tell me how to find this place," she murmured, just to put something in the silence. "Is there a marker or anything? I'll tell the men that a stranger passing through heard of Jim's death and told me about the body he'd buried some time back. I don't think it's too much of a lie."

Astounded not only that she understood his difficulty without questioning but also that she acted on the knowledge, Cade gave her the directions that would eventually lead to the recovery of her husband's remains. She could do with the information as she wished, but he was beginning to think it might be wisest not to tell anyone for a while, a long while. If she was ready to accept the status of widow, though, he couldn't stop her. It was on his mind too strongly as it was.

Cade knew what he was thinking was impossible. He knew all the odds were against him. But remembering the passion they had shared, he couldn't quench the one thin flame of hope rising within him. Here was the answer to his quest—in this one lonely young widow with a desire as hot as his own and eyes that didn't see the color of his skin. He didn't know if he could do this to her. She deserved a great deal more than he could offer right now, but he couldn't squelch the hope. He had to have something to make life worth the trouble of living.

Unconsciously, he reached for the flask of whisky that wasn't there.

Nine

Lily halted the vociferous complaints of her angry farmhands over Abraham's hiring with the simple expedient of holding up her hand and informing them that she needed volunteers to bring back Jim's body. The startling change of subject silenced them enough for Lily to give her prepared story of having received the information from a stranger passing through.

It would have been an easier tale to tell if she had waited a day or two until she had had the opportunity to go to town and actually to be seen with some stranger, but the information had her nerves frayed and this group complaint was about to push her too far. The fact that Ollie Clark—having drunk himself into a stupor on her parlor floor the night before—now stood behind her with an I-told-you-so grin only made her need for control more urgent. Lily could feel the grin slide off his face as soon as she made the announcement.

They inundated her with questions. Thinking wryly that these men didn't know the meaning of the term "order," Lily merely stood silently and waited for them to grow quiet again. Out of the corner of her eye she saw Cade approaching from the barn, a lariat in his hand, but she didn't acknowledge him with so much as a look.

"I've had the information for several days. I just wasn't ready to believe . . ." She still wasn't. She hesitated, trying to hold back her grief until she could speak clearly again. The moment was effective. The men grew solemn and Jack stepped forward.

"Tell us where to look, ma'am, and we'll do our best."

As Lily described the place Cade had told her about the

night before, Cade and Abraham began saddling horses. Several of the protesters did the same. Unsmiling, Ollie waited until she finished, then he too saddled his mount and joined the others. Lily had expected at least some word of comfort from him, but his mind seemed to be otherwise occupied.

She didn't want to go with them, and nobody suggested that she should. A man dead and buried for three months was not a pretty sight. For once, male gallantry had its use. Lily watched with an aching heart as they rode off, then turned to find her father right behind her.

"Why didn't you tell us sooner?" There was concern in Ephraim's voice, but also a hint of suspicion. He was beginning to learn that there was more to this Lily than the one who had left home at sixteen.

"And give you and Ollie one more ax to hang over my head? I seriously contemplated never telling anyone. At least this way I've kept Ollie from going out and chasing an innocent band of Indians."

Ephraim looked at the dark circles under his daughter's eyes and shook his head. "You can't carry the weight of the whole world on your shoulders, little mite. If your foreman is as good as you say he is, he can run this place through the winter. Come home with me and rest a spell. You'll look at things much clearer after you've been away for a while."

For once, his advice seemed almost sensible. She needed to get away, to rest her weary head, to avoid responsibility for a time. Only her memory of what waited for her back in Mississippi kept her from acquiescing. The snickers behind her back, her sisters' nagging, the empty days would just be another battle. At least here she was battling for something that made sense.

Lily hugged a solemn Roy and pulled him down into the rocking chair with her. For once, he didn't wiggle away but rested his head on her shoulder, desperately trying to hide his sniffling. They had both known this day was coming, but there had been no way to prepare for it.

Juanita brought hot coffee and cake, and Serena and her kitten toddled along beside her. Roy jumped down and crumbled a piece of cake on a plate, but the adults simply sat sipping the coffee, waiting.

It was some hours later before the clatter of hooves outside warned that the riders had returned. The late September day was warm, and Lily continued sitting in the cool darkness of her front room. She hadn't given any specific orders as to what the men should do when they found Jim. She had left that up to them. All she wanted to know for certain was whether it was Jim buried in that shallow grave.

Ollie and Jack knocked on the front door and Ephraim let them in. Jack had been with Lily and Jim the longest of all their hired hands, and it seemed appropriate that he be the one to break the news. Holding his hat in his hands, he swallowed nervously before speaking.

"I'm pretty certain it were him, ma'am. The clothes were right, and the size. And he had that bad tooth on one side. I'd guess it were Jim. Can't rightly say what happened to him, though. We buried him up good and proper and put up a cross and said a few words, if that's all right with you, ma'am."

Lily had never played the part of Southern belle even when she had first arrived in long skirts and petticoats. She looked the part even less now in her men's trousers and long-sleeved shirt. But something in the way she held herself as she sat in the rocking chair, her chin tilted and her eyes full of grief, reminded the men forcefully of the lady that she was.

"Thank you, Jack. I knew I could trust you to do the right thing. Someday . . . You'll have to show me where the grave is so I can put flowers on it."

Ollie wasn't quite so reticent. "You know damn good and well it was those Indians that killed him, Lily. I'm going to get me a bunch of the men together and go after them."

"Shut up, Ollie." Lily rose from the chair, suddenly losing all resemblance to frail Southern womanhood as she looked him directly in the eye. "If those Indians are on my land, I'll have my men shoot you for trespassing.

This is a house of grief. I don't want anymore bloodshed. Now get out of my sight."

Making it easy for him, she walked out in the direction of her bedroom.

Furious, Ollie looked to Lily's father for support, but Ephraim merely looked old and tired. He shrugged his shoulders and said to Ollie, "You'll not bring Jim back by shooting someone else. And you've got no proof it was Indians. Leave it be, Ollie. Lily has a soft heart but a hard head. If she thought it would help to light out after those Indians, she'd be on her horse now. Go home and sleep it off."

Ollie left, and word of Jim's death filtered out rapidly after that. The Langtons were the first to arrive, bringing several of their kitchen slaves and a side of beef for barbecuing. As the meat cooked, others rode up in groups of two or four, and before long, the dusty yard was filled with wagons and horses and people standing in small groups, gossiping.

Lily hadn't realized that she and Jim were so well known. There were people out there that she hadn't seen in years, ones they had arrived here with as new settlers and hadn't seen since. There were people from the town, people she had only met at the dance, and people she could swear she had never seen in her life. It was an incredible turnout, and she would have cried in gratitude had she not realized that death was as good an excuse for a social gathering as anything else.

One of the men carried her rocker out to the front porch, and all she had to do was sit there and accept the condolences of her neighbors. Everything else seemed to be taken care of. Lily caught a glimpse of Juanita's cousin ordering the black servants around in the kitchen yard, and Jack and the men were busily handling the multitude of animals and hauling out some of Jim's barrels of home brew. This was obviously going to be an all-day affair.

Her eyes unconsciously sought Cade. She caught only one glimpse of him as he helped the servants carry out the side of beef for slicing. He evidently meant to make himself as scarce as possible with this crowd. Perhaps that was the best thing. On top of Ollie's loud complaining about the Indians, there were ugly rumors circulating about General Cós and an army of Mexican soldiers landing in Copano Bay. Lily couldn't believe any ship could carry enough soldiers to carry out the number of atrocities being circulated about them, but just the arrival of a Mexican army was sufficient to be worrisome. She didn't like the mood of the crowd as the day wore on. With his mixed blood, it was probably best for Cade to stay out of sight.

As the sun threw its dying light over a crowd stuffed with beef and beer and too drunk to do more than seek their horses in respectful silence, Lily noticed a plume of dust rising on the road from town. Several others saw it at the same time, and they came to a halt in whatever they were doing to watch.

Standing by the well, Lily sensed Cade coming to stand behind her. Whoever was creating that dust was traveling at a high rate of speed. Good news never came fast. As Cade dipped water from the bucket and drank, Lily crossed her hands in front of her and prayed. For some reason, free food and drink had not increased the festivity of this gathering, and she felt the tension as everyone gradually became aware of the approaching rider.

In sweat-soaked shirt and stained leather vest and hat, the rider swung down from his horse and spoke to the first men crowding around him. Lily watched wordlessly as Bert Dixon in his black brocade waistcoat pounded the back of a hatless man in buckskin. The crowd beginning to form around the newcomer had a faintly familiar shade to it. None of them were the settlers and their families, who formed the bulk of the people here today. These were the land speculators, the lawyers, the traders, the men without any permanent job or home who had come here these last few years looking for the promise of wealth that Texas offered. Lily didn't like the sounds of their excitement at all.

Eventually, the reason for it filtered back to her. Giving Cade a nod of acknowledgment, Jack informed them both, "Austin's declared war on them bastards in Mexico. There's fighting in Gonzales. He's calling for an army to drive that damned General Cós back to Mexico. We're all going to have to go. We damned well can't be dictated to by the likes of that bastard Santa Anna."

He didn't say "by any damned Mexican," but the look was on his face as he glanced briefly to Cade. Lily stiffened, but Cade merely took another sip from the dipper.

"You're not a soldier, Jack. Let soldiers do the fighting. If everyone joins the army, who will be left to protect those that are left behind?"

The voice of reason could do little to compete with the drunken excitement of war. Already men were saddling up and making war whoops. It was insane. These men had no professional training. Half of them carried only knives as weapons, and most of the rest barely had anything better than a rusted musket. There wasn't enough money in all of Texas to buy them uniforms or guns. What on earth did they think they were doing?

Lily watched silently as, one by one, her men came up to pay their respects and ride off to war. The harvest wasn't in or sold. She couldn't give them any money. The ranch had no weapons to speak of. She could only wish them well and urge them to take whatever dried beef and corn they could find in the storehouse. She didn't even know why she was doing that.

Turning away from the sight of grown men eagerly going to their deaths, Lily glimpsed Serena's golden head lying peacefully asleep on a hay bale. Without a word to Cade, she walked over to the child and picked her up, carrying her into the house and out of the madness.

Cade watched her go with rising disquietude. This land he had grown up in had frequently known the brief skirmishes of Indian battles, but it had never known a white man's war. Its few Mexican inhabitants had always been content to live off the plenty of the land, to watch the sun rise and set in its own time, and to die peacefully with the church bells ringing overhead. Although his father's tribe had gone to war in the past, the numbers of the white men had driven them into the wilderness and a peaceful existence with the land. But Cade was all too well acquainted with hate and greed and knew the devastation they could wreak.

Cade looked up to find Abraham standing in the barn doorway, watching the excited exodus of the crowd. At least there would be one man left to do the work of half a dozen. Perhaps he knew where to find a few more. Catching Juanita's buxom cousin staring boldly at him, Cade thought it might be a good idea to avail himself of her services. The knowledge of the frightened woman alone inside the house clawed at him otherwise.

But even as he took a step toward the saucy wench and she twitched her hips in anticipation, something held him back. Looking up, Cade found Roy standing lost and bewildered by the paddock gate, watching his father's funeral guests roar off into the sunset. Without a flicker of emotion, Cade turned and walked in his direction.

Juanita hissed at her cousin as the woman uttered an imprecation in Spanish. "You do not want that one, you fool. *Esta un monstruo.* You have heard Maria speak. He is not normal, that one."

"I want to see for myself," was the hungry reply.

Juanita followed the direction of her cousin's gaze and shook her head. She knew what it was like to be raped by a man until she was almost split in two. Never, ever would she get that close to a man again. Her cousin was a fool to look at that one. Perhaps he was gentle with the children, but just the size of him should be enough to warn a woman away. Clicking her tongue at her cousin's foolishness, Juanita drew her back into the safety of the kitchen.

Ephraim Porter ran his hands through his faded curls and watched the visitors depart with sorrow and no small amount of uncertainty. He was beginning to understand why his daughter had chosen this place to live. She was accepted here as she had not been at home. These people were more generous, more open, more everything than the polite, civilized world they had left behind. In a country like this, perhaps they had to be.

That still didn't solve his dilemma. There was going to

be a war, and Lily had no man to protect her against it. Ephraim would be the first to admit that he wasn't the man to do it. He knew about wheelin' and dealin', he knew a great deal about liquor, but he knew nothing about protecting women or running a ranch.

Turning, he saw Lily's Indian foreman lifting Roy into the saddle of an awfully darned big horse. The man was going to get the boy killed. Ephraim started to go down the stairs and protest, but the two of them seemed too much in harmony for interference. They rode away before he could have traversed the yard.

Shaking his head, Ephraim sat down on the front step and pondered the situation. His mind kept traveling back to the sight of Roy riding that horse. The boy sure as hell didn't resemble Jim none. Jim hated horses. There wasn't any physical resemblance either. Heck, Roy didn't look like anyone Ephraim knew of at all. That dark, curly hair of his didn't take after Lily or Jim. His own hair had been light before it went gray. The boy's eyes were gray. He couldn't remember gray running in either of their families.

It didn't matter none. Roy was eight years old and fatherless. Something had to be done.

Watching the large figure of the Mexican-Indian riding off over the horizon, Ephraim shook his head and cursed. He was going to have to straighten Lily out about this situation real soon. The next thing they would know, she'd be marrying the half-breed just to give the boy a father.

Remembering the golden-haired child even now being rocked in the front room, Ephraim groaned. It was going to be a darned sight harder to keep Lily from marrying Cade just to give the girl a mother.

Ten

"You do not get these fevers from my people, my son." His chiseled face wrinkled from exposure to the sun of many summers, the Indian drew on the pipe of tobacco his son had brought for him.

"I do not belong to your people any longer, father, I have not since I was eight winters old. My mother took me to live among her people, and it is among her people that I must survive. This is the only way."

The old man closed his eyes and Cade thought he had fallen asleep, but he was merely ruminating. A few minutes later, he opened his eyes again and regarded the son who had grown to bigger proportions than any of his other children.

"You are fortunate to have two worlds open to you. You must choose the best among them, not the worst."

Cade crossed his legs and stared at the dying remains of the fire. The nights were not yet cool enough for the warmth to be necessary, and the close confines of the grass lodge were stifling. As much as he admired his father, his nature rebelled against the stoic acceptance of the fates or gods he couldn't see. He knew his father would welcome him back to the tribe, and there were times when that alternative seemed the easiest, but in the long run, it wouldn't be. He could feel the narrowness of this world close in around him even now.

"Both worlds are closed against me, father, not open. I must find a path somewhere between them."

"You are Lipan. We have need of warriors. You are welcome here. It is you who are closed, not we."

"I am not a warrior," Cade emphasized firmly. How

could he explain to his father that of all the things the Mexican priests had preached during his youth, one stayed with him stronger than most: we are all God's creatures. His father talked of killing men in the same manner as he would a buffalo. Cade was reluctant even to slay the buffalo. He was definitely not warrior material, but his father would never understand that.

The old man stared at his large son, then changed the subject. "Many soldiers come. Perhaps your mother's people are with them."

"My mother's father must be very old by now. He may have other children. I would know of it if his people return to the hacienda."

"It is a foolish quest, my son. Your mother's people are very proud. Your mother was a proud and foolish woman. I could have told her that her people were gone if I had known she would try to run back to them."

"It is in the past. I must make a future."

The old man shook his head at the vagaries of youth. The only time was now. The future took care of itself. "Dove Woman's daughter looks on you favorably. If you wish a future, take a wife. A man must have children to have a future."

"A man must have some means to keep a wife. I can only do that among the white people. Dove Woman would not wish her daughter to leave her home. It is among my mother's people that I must seek for a wife." Actually, he had a better chance among the Indians than he did among the proud Spanish/Mexicans of San Antonio, but to his father, all whites were the same. He did not differentiate greatly between the Americans and the Mexicans. Cade had no intention of explaining about women like Lily. He couldn't explain her to himself.

He had said all that was needed to be said. Communication among the various wandering Apache bands in this part of Texas could be virtually instantaneous when necessary. Although his father had settled with his new wife and taken up the Waco way of life, he still had means of knowing what was going on. Should anyone come to claim Cade's mother's ranch, El Caballo would know about it within days or weeks, and the source would be much more reliable than any paid informant in San Antonio.

Cade waited until his father finished his pipe and emptied it, the signal that he was dismissed. Rising, he made his way quietly into the night outside the overheated lodge. He could stay here the night, but he wouldn't. Something called him back to the ranch. Perhaps it was that bottle of whisky he had picked up back in town.

Lily watched as Cade rode into the yard well past midnight. He had not asked permission to leave or made any excuses for his disappearance. It wasn't the first time this had happened, and she didn't imagine it would be the last. As long as he got up the next day and did his work, she had no basis for complaint. But she wondered which woman back in town had claimed his attention.

They had been carefully avoiding each other this past month. Although there was no lock, she kept her window closed. The glass in it was rare and very expensive and she didn't think Cade would risk breaking it. And if Cade played the flute, the pane was doing a very good job of hiding the tempting music. Try as she might, she had never heard it again.

They had never returned to the Saturday night dance, either. She wasn't certain it was still going on now that half the men in the territory had lit out to answer Austin's battle cry. The excitement generated by the retreat of the Mexican troops in Gonzales had been followed by a brief flurry of greater excitement when the Americans captured Goliad and the military stores there. Since then, many of the farmers had been drifting back to see to their families, and even some of her own men had come back, complaining of bad food and poor orders. The land speculators had never really left. They were too busy selling swampland and counting their coins every time another contingent of settlers crossed the border. So perhaps there were enough people for a dance, but they might not feel like dancing.

Lily was about to return to bed when she saw the streak of light crossing the horizon. One of the men had told her about it, but she hadn't paid him much heed. Without a second thought, she was lifting the window and climbing out to better observe the phenomenon.

Cade saw her as he came out of the barn after wiping down his horse and settling it for the night. He remembered another night when he had seen her in ghostly white, and he almost turned back to the barn to avoid the apparition, but he, too, saw the light brightening the sky, and he stepped forward to admire it.

It was smaller now than it had been earlier in the month, but it was still a magnificent sight. Cade came to stand behind Lily as they both gazed up into the brilliantly lit heavens.

"Such a sign must signal some great change."

Lily felt the vibration of Cade's voice as much as heard it, just as she felt his physical presence more than saw it. Keeping her eyes on the spectacle in the sky, she tried not to react to the powerful pull this man exerted on her, but she might as well fight gravity. She knew her head came just a little above his shoulder. She knew he had only to reach out his arms and she would be within their circle. She could smell the scent of smoke on him, along with the odor of horse sweat and leather and a man scent all his own. She didn't smell perfume. She relaxed a fraction.

"Changes are not always for the better. Do the stars say whether this will be a good or bad change?" Lily asked.

"I think that depends on which side of the stars you stand. Change is always good for someone or there would not be change."

Sometimes he talked like a preacher. Since there hadn't been a man of the cloth in these parts in a coon's age, Lily was quite willing to accept Cade's interpretation of the heavens.

"Which side are you on, Cade?" she asked quietly.

Unwilling to answer the implications in that question, Cade gave the simple truth. "Mine."

His honesty appealed to her. When she felt him move closer, felt his hands lift to her sides, she didn't move away. With disappointment, she felt his hands drop as he stepped backward.

"They say it is called a comet and it is no more than a flying star. Some things never change." Lily wrapped her arms around herself and refused to look back at him.

"Perhaps. You shouldn't be out here dressed like that. You'll catch cold."

That wasn't all she would catch. Nodding to his wisdom, Lily walked away. Cade watched her go, feeling the knot twist tighter in his gut. She could be the pawn that would bring him what he sought. She could be the woman who would slake his lusts. She could be the woman to mother Serena. She could be many things, but most of them would make her better off without him. Could he steal her future in exchange for his own? His father had done that to his mother, but he had not known her as Cade knew Lily. It was much easier to steal a beautiful stranger than a friend.

"Look, Ma, I'm going to join the Greys!" Roy hoisted a carved gun to his shoulder, and with a gray piece of wool pulled over his head and strapped around his middle like a poncho, he sent his horse into a canter.

The New Orleans militia had marched through here earlier in the month, impressing the boy with their shining uniforms and laughter and air of adventure as they sought to join the Texas army. Even Lily had to admit to being impressed at the sight of such a finely-turned-out group of young men, and their gallantry had brightened her day. But after they were out of sight, she could only see them as cannon fodder, and she had been depressed for days.

She wasn't even certain what they were fighting for. Some idiots in town claimed it was for the Constitution of 1824, but that hadn't been worth the paper it was written on and was just as oppressive as this latest attempt to keep Texas corralled. It was much more likely that they were fighting to grab as much land as they could at the expense of the Mexican government and the poor settlers who tried to work this land in peace. Lily wished she could see it as a glorious cause, but she had met some of the principals over the years, and she wouldn't trust any of them with a catfish and a pole.

"He'll be fine with us. You can't worry about him all the time." Cade rode up behind Lily, catching her expression and partially interpreting it correctly.

"He's so young." Lily turned her head up to meet his gaze. "He's all I've got, Cade. I've got a right to worry."

"I'll take care of him as well as you take care of Serena. No man can say better than that."

"I know that." Sighing, she turned and waved Roy off as he cantered after Abraham. It was almost time to drive the cattle to New Orleans, but there weren't enough men to spare. Driving them in from the plains was going to take all the manpower they possessed.

Seeing that she wasn't going to say anything else, Cade rounded his horse to take out after the others. There was more than concern for her son wrinkling her brow these days, but she wasn't the type to confide her worries.

Once Roy had the opportunity to ride out with the men, it was difficult to keep him inside to learn his books. All he could talk about was his pony and how Cade was teaching him to rope cattle and the best way to make the cattle move in the direction desired. Lily sighed in frustration and brushed her hair out of her face one morning when she found Roy's crudely scribbled note stating he had gone out with Cade. She had definitely not given him permission to do so.

She was going to have to put a stop to this before it got out of hand. Going back to her room, she dressed for riding, coming back in time to find her father and Juanita in earnest discussion while Serena sucked on a bacon strip.

At the sight of Lily, the child dropped the grubby bacon and came running, hands held out. "Mama! Play dolly."

Lily swept the little girl up in her arms and kissed her good morning, but she wouldn't allow herself to be distracted from her purpose. Serena had been calling her "mama" for weeks now. No amount of persuasion could convince her to do otherwise.

Juanita glanced anxiously at Lily's riding clothes. "You are going out?"

"Roy rode out with Cade this morning without my permission. I'm going after him."

Juanita looked distressed, and Ephraim gave a warning cough before speaking.

"Some of those hired mercenaries they're calling volunteers kind of roughed up the town last night. Juanita's cousin was one of those injured. I kinda promised her I'd take her into town to help out."

Serena threw up her chubby hands and gave a gurgle of delight when all eyes turned to her. The child couldn't be taken into town on such a mission. She would have to stay here.

Lily nodded her head in agreement with Juanita's silent plea. Juanita demanded very little and gave everything. And after all, her cousin was injured, possibly seriously, and Roy was quite safe—until he got home and she blistered his little bottom.

"I will look after Serena. Roy can miss a few hours of schoolwork. I'll just tan his hide when he comes in for dinner. You'd better take in supplies, and if there's anything else we can do, send word."

Both women understood each other implicitly without saying the words in front of a man. It didn't take much imagination to know what a bunch of randy men out on a lark would do in a town like this one. The Tejano women would be their first target. There wasn't a medicine invented to cure those kinds of injuries.

Lily wasn't used to feeling angry, but she seemed to feel that way most of the time anymore. She knew people were basically good. She knew she couldn't condemn an entire gender for the actions of a few. But she was having greater and greater difficulty finding excuses for those actions. She had to remind herself that Cade and Abraham and those of her hired hands who had returned were good men and would never join in that kind of rampage. Perhaps it was only those men with a military bent.

That wasn't right either, but it gave her anger a better focus than condemning the entire male population. Bouncing Serena on her hip, Lily waved as her father and

Juanita rode off in the wagon. So, today she would have to stay home and play housewife and cook.

She wasn't totally useless in the kitchen. Carrying Serena out with her, Lily contemplated the beginnings of the meal Juanita had already started. The men expected the noon meal to be hearty, and those new hands Cade had hired were particularly voracious. If nothing else, this war or rebellion or whatever they called it made it necessary for her old hands to accept the odd assortment of new ones. Acceptance was easier than doubling their workload.

Contemplating the combination of Tejanos, Negroes, Indians, and some mixture in between that now represented her employee list, Lily took down a large can of beans, popped the bread dough in the woodstove, and regarded a sink full of freshly plucked chickens with relief. She could manage chickens just fine.

When the men rode into the yard at noon, hooting and hollering over some incident, splashing their faces in the well as they leapt from their horses, the aromas from the kitchen were already permeating the air. Lily set the last batch of bread on the table, wiped her hands off on her apron, and determinedly set off in pursuit of her wayward son, Serena trailing innocently behind her.

She located Cade first, and her anger centered on this man who should have known better than to let an eight-year-old ride out when he had other responsibilities.

Cade took in Lily's apron-covered, flour-coated attire with surprise, but her words elicited a genuine expression of startlement from him.

"Where is my son? I'll not have you carrying him out of here every blamed time he gets tired of doing his schoolwork. I ought to tan both your hides for this."

Cade shoved his hair from his face and contemplated her fury with more puzzlement than anger. "Roy's not with me, Lily. I told him he had to have your permission before he could ride out."

Lily stared at him a moment longer before her face went white and her eyes turned desperately to search the men and horses crowding the paddock and yard. Roy was nowhere to be seen.

"Where is he?"

Cade heard the murmur and grabbed her arm before she could collapse. If Roy had meant to ride out and join them, he hadn't made it. Cade glanced blankly at the miles of open plain beyond the yard and felt something in his insides crack. It would be like searching for an ant on a mountain.

Eleven

"I know a few places where he might be. Let me check them first." Cade tried to sound reassuring, but Lily's pale face had his own insides in an uproar. He knew as well as she that the boy would have come looking for him.

Lily tore off her apron and threw it over the fence. "I know some places to look, too. The men will have to feed themselves." She didn't even take the time to explain where Juanita was or why. She remembered all too plainly the day when she and everyone on the ranch had gone out looking for Jim. It was a hopeless task.

At least Roy's pony hadn't come riding back. That had to be a good sign. As the men around them began to grasp that there was something wrong, Lily went to saddle a fresh horse. She didn't intend to come back until she had found her son.

Giving quiet orders to the men, Cade let her go until he caught sight of her mounting the horse and getting ready to leave without a word to anyone. Catching her reins, he forced her to halt.

"You're to be back here in an hour to report to me just like the others. I'll be damned if I'm going to spend the day looking for both of you."

That made some kind of sense, and Lily was too worried to concern herself about his tone. She was just grateful that Cade understood they could do this much faster if they split up. She nodded, and when he let go of the reins, she urged her horse into a gallop.

Cade shook his head at her heedless pace, then gained his horse and rode out after her. Some of the other men were already saddling fresh horses. He hadn't ordered a full-fledged search yet. The time for that would come when all the obvious places had been checked.

An hour later everyone rode back into the yard with no report of any sign of a little boy and his pony.

Lily refused to cry. She and Cade divided the ranch into sections and sent each man in a different direction, leaving one of the hands at the ranch to care for Serena and to set up a message center. Everyone carried a firearm to give a signal if Roy was found. Times were set for reporting in. One man was sent to town in case Roy had decided to wander there. It was all well planned and carefully thought out, but everyone present knew the vastness of the territory to be searched and the impossibility of covering every inch of it.

Cade circled the ranch, looking for some sign of a single horse and a small rider. It hadn't rained in weeks and tracks were few, but he found some cropped grass and drying dung heading out in a different direction than his men had taken that morning, and he set off that way. It looked as if the boy had chosen the same path the men had taken the day he had ridden with them. His hopes rising, Cade eased his mount down the path, keeping a sharp lookout for any differences in the landscape.

His keen eyesight had found Jim's body in the midst of a vast plain when no one else's had, but it couldn't help him find a small boy and his horse when they weren't there to be seen. By sunset, Cade had lost all sign of Roy's passage. He couldn't bear to return to the ranch and report to Lily, but he had to turn around. There was some chance that the boy had already been found and he just hadn't heard the signal.

It was dark by the time he rode in. He had only to see Juanita weeping in the kitchen doorway to know the news wasn't good. The men were idling around the paddock. Ephraim Porter stood on the back steps with his hands in his pockets, staring blankly at the horizon. Lily was nowhere to be seen.

Dismounting, Cade was about to make inquiries when he saw her riding in. Her shoulders were slumped with fatigue, and he didn't need to see her face to know the anguish that would be written on it. He caught her reins and lifted her down, and she collapsed briefly against him— all the evidence he needed to know that she was beyond exhaustion. Her soft curves molded against him without any recognition of where she was or why.

"Go get something to eat. I'll question the men and get back to you."

It was much simpler to follow Cade's orders than to consider the alternatives. The arms holding her were corded with muscles and exuded a strength she had never possessed. Nodding wearily, Lily drew herself away and turned toward the house.

When Cade entered a while later, he found her sitting stiffly in the rocking chair, a sleepy Serena on her lap cuddling her doll. Lily's eyes were blank and full of pain as they met his, and Cade seemed to feel her anguish spilling into him. He was an outsider, a man who never got close to anyone, but somehow this woman had got inside of him. He didn't like the feeling, but there wasn't anything he could do about it now.

"Jack's inquiring at the neighboring ranches. I'm going back out to take another look. I think I know the direction he took. It might be easier to hear him at night."

"I'll go with you." Lily moved to set the sleepy child down, but Cade crossed the room and caught her shoulder, pinning her to the chair.

"No. The men have to get some rest if they're to go back out tomorrow. You need to be here in case Jack comes back with some word." He didn't state the usual nonsense about her getting some rest. If the child wasn't found, Cade was quite certain she would never rest again. There was that much pain in her eyes. She had already lost her husband. The fates couldn't be so unkind as to take her only child.

Cade squeezed her shoulder and Lily stayed where she was. "I'll put Serena to bed in here tonight so you won't wake her when you come back," was her only reply to his gesture.

Ephraim stepped out of the shadows, for once without

a whisky bottle in his hands. "If you tell me what to do, I'll go with you. You've been out long enough as it is."

Cade looked at the older man and tried not to see himself in the bloodshot eyes and shaking hands. He hungered for a drink right now. He had planned on taking a bottle with him. The caricature of a man standing before him put an end to that intention. The liquor would fortify him through the night chill, expunge the pain that seeped from Lily to him, but it wouldn't find Roy.

He shook his head at Ephraim. "The way is treacherous in day. Lily needs you here."

He turned and walked out, leaving father and daughter to deal with one another.

"He called you Lily." Ephraim regretted the words as soon as they were out, but there was nothing else he could say.

"I call him Cade." Lily rose, carrying the child, and headed for the dogtrot that led to her bedroom.

There wasn't any point in arguing. As Lily walked out, Ephraim went in search of a bottle.

It was late when Cade rode into his father's camp. He'd had longer days, but emotion had a way of draining every ounce of strength until there was nothing left. Somewhere out there was a terrified little boy, lost, possibly injured, and he couldn't find him. Cade wanted to rage at the world. Instead, he sought his father.

The older man looked at him with sadness when Cade stated his request. "Had you stayed with us, you would know our ways for yourself."

"You have taught me much, Father, and I am grateful, but even the greatest warriors would have difficulty tracking a little boy without knowing his direction."

"The buzzards began to gather at sunset. You should have watched for them," he admonished.

Cade closed his eyes and let that information sink in like an arrow to his heart. He had not looked for the buzzards because he refused to consider that possibility. Emotion was blinding him. He was going to have to find some way of putting Lily and her son in the proper perspective.

Forcing his fear and anguish back into the box where he kept his feelings hidden, Cade made himself ask, "Where?"

"The wash. I will send your brothers with you. You may need their help."

The wash was a treacherous gully carved out by the river and the spring floods. It was sheer bluff, and the sides crumbled at the slightest touch. If anyone could climb in and out of such a place, it would be his younger brothers. Cade didn't argue his father's decision.

The seventeen-year-old and fourteen-year-old who responded with alacrity to their father's call eyed Cade with suspicion, but promptly gathered their ropes and horses when the orders were given. Sons of the Waco wife Cade's father had taken after Cade's mother ran away, they were full-blooded Indians and had never known any life but this one. Cade knew who they were, but he knew little more than that.

The search took the rest of the night, and the sun was rising over the horizon before they hauled the unconscious child from the creek bed. Cade had to shoot Roy's suffering mount, but Roy was unaware of even that.

The two youngsters helped Cade rig a travois to carry Roy, strapping his broken leg to prevent further damage and wrapping him carefully in blankets from their horses. When Cade offered to have them accompany him so they could be appropriately thanked for their rescue, they refused. He watched his half brothers ride off toward their camp, realizing that he could have been just like them had his mother not "rescued" him by returning to San Antonio.

Lily was out of the door and running toward Cade even though he was barely in sight of the ranch. Her cries brought men stumbling from the bunkhouse into the dawn, still pulling on their pants and wiping their eyes.

Weeping openly, Lily fell down beside the travois to be certain Roy was alive and to test his head for fever. Then she walked slowly beside him, holding his hand, as Cade dragged the litter toward the house.

There wasn't anything resembling a doctor within fifty miles, and Roy's leg had already waited too long for there to be time to send for one. After placing Roy in a bed in the main cabin and treating his other wounds, Lily clenched her teeth in contemplation of the broken bone.

So exhausted he could barely stand while she performed these tasks, Cade still managed to push Lily aside when he read her intent. He met her gaze without speaking, then placed his hands on the child's leg. Keeping everything he felt firmly in check, Cade clenched his teeth and twisted the broken bone into place.

The boy's anguished screams wrenched something in Cade's soul, and he stared down at his large hands on the boy's small leg with horror. With the child's cries echoing in his ears, Cade lifted his hands and held them out before him with despair at the pain they inflicted so easily.

Roy's screams were the first sound he had uttered since he had been found. Reacting differently to them than Cade did, Lily gulped back her tears and shoved the shattered Cade back to his chair. She began wrapping Roy's leg between two boards. This was something she had learned to do as a sixteen-year-old bride, and she'd used it more than once since then. Life on the frontier taught a person many things.

Ephraim handed Cade a bottle of whisky as he collapsed in the chair after the child's cry died. Cade took a sip, felt it burn all the way to his gullet, then silently returned it to the man. He'd had to do hard things in his life, and he ranked handing that bottle back right up there as one of them, right next to listening to Roy's scream. The pain of that sound twisted around his heart.

Lily didn't even notice. Finishing the bandage and making certain that her son was sleeping, she led the way outside before asking questions.

Cade held up his hand to silence her before she could even get started. "I'm going to get some rest. I'll explain later, but you had better be thinking of some way to thank those Indians that your friend Ollie wants to kill."

He stalked off, leaving Lily choking on her gratitude.

Once inside his cabin and safe from accusing eyes, Cade reached for the bottle of whisky on the shelf. He would drown these emotions scalding his insides and never be battered by them again. Sipping the liquor, he closed his eyes and let the liquid relief pour through him. When he was back to normal he would have to take the matter of one Lily Porter Brown back into consideration. He had been blinded too long by blue eyes and blond hair. She was a woman like any other, a means to an end. That was all that mattered. The whisky sliding down his throat concurred.

Unaware of Cade's turmoil, Lily merely sat at her son's side, offering grateful prayers and waiting for him to wake up. Juanita took Serena, and her father reassured the hands and gave them a day to rest. Lily wiped Roy's brow and nearly cried with joy when he woke later that day and declared he was starving.

He didn't make an easy patient, but when she was sure that he had recovered from the blow to his head and that his stomach was full and he was on the road to recovery, she gave him a small amount of laudanum to ease the pain, and he quietly drifted off to sleep again.

It was dark before Lily took the time to go to her room and rest. Cade hadn't returned to the house, so she assumed he was still sleeping. Remembering the look of raw pain in his eyes after Roy's scream, Lily hugged herself and stared out at the stars. Cade was an odd man. He kept too much to himself. But she had seen how much he cared for her son.

Undressing and climbing into bed, she kept that thought close to her heart. She didn't know why it should matter that Cade cared for Roy, but it gave her comfort. Perhaps being unable to share emotions caused loneliness, and she felt a little less alone knowing Cade cared. It was foolish, perhaps, but she needed whatever comfort she could find this night.

Lily slept soundly, completely drained by the activities of the last two days. When she woke, it was to a gloriously sunny morning and the sound of her father and her son arguing, their voices carrying through the open door to the dogtrot. She couldn't distinguish the words, but they sounded more like banter than anger, so she didn't hurry.

They looked up guiltily at her entrance, but Roy waved a biscuit and gestured at his leg. "Granddad says a broken leg will make me grow taller."

"Why, of course." She stooped to kiss his hair. "Did you think you were going to stay the same size forever?"

"I mean *taller*. Like Cade. He's just fibbing, isn't he?"

"Well, I suggest we wait until you grow up and see. Does it hurt very much? Shall I give you something to make it hurt less?"

Roy made a face. "It tastes nasty."

Ephraim nodded his head toward the door, indicating he needed to speak with her. Lily made a few more cursory comments and left her son finishing off some of Juanita's peach jam on another biscuit.

Outside the cabin she confronted her father quizzically. "Is there something wrong?"

"Jack was at the door earlier. Seems Cade is a bit under the weather. I didn't know what to tell the men to do, so I just sent them out to do whatever they thought best. Will that be enough?"

Under the weather. She knew what that term meant. Giving her father a furious glance, Lily stalked toward the barn. Under the weather. Damn. If she didn't have time to get drunk, he had his damned nerve doing it.

She would deal with Cade later. Grabbing the first horse she came to, she saddled it and set out after the men. Two days of holiday were more than she could afford.

Twelve

With the agenda of the day's work settled, Lily rode back to the ranch to settle a larger problem. She couldn't have a foreman who drank. That was all there was to it. It was a bad influence on the men, and she had a personal abhorrence of it. She had watched her father deteriorate into a helpless old man; she wasn't about to watch Cade.

Perhaps he had good reason for seeking solace in a bottle. He must have been exhausted physically, and perhaps emotionally. She hadn't seen him drunk since the day she hired him, so she couldn't really say they had a problem. Yet.

She wanted to excuse him. He had saved Roy's life. That should be sufficient reason to excuse his behavior just this one time. She was certain Cade thought so. That was the way men thought: "If I'm good today, I'm entitled to indulge myself tonight." She had plenty of experience in that kind of thinking.

But it wouldn't do. It just wouldn't do. Perhaps if she explained it reasonably to him, Cade would understand. She wouldn't get angry. She would be calm and unemotional and perfectly rational. He could get drunk on his own time, but not on hers.

To her surprise, Cade was already up and saddling his mount when she returned to the yard. He looked like hell, but he was functioning. He was moving slowly as if he ached all over, and his eyes were fixed and grim as he lifted them to her, but he had managed to shave and push his wet hair out of his face. Even looking like hell he made a striking picture of masculinity in his tight denims and straining shirt sleeves.

"I've given the men their orders. We need to talk, Cade." Lily rode up beside him keeping her gaze fixed on his impassive face.

"We're going back to thank the people who saved Roy's life," he said. "Take my horse and let me wipe that one down. It should make an appropriate gift." Cade caught her horse's reins but made no attempt to assist Lily in descending.

Lily opened her mouth to protest, thought better of it, and did as told. She wouldn't have any idea how to go about finding and thanking the Indians who had saved Roy. Cade did. Perhaps she could read him a lecture on the way.

Later, sitting up on the great gelding that was Cade's, Lily had to wonder what in hell she was doing. She looked back to find Cade riding out of the barn on one of her wilder mounts. The mustang had a vicious temper and no one ever wanted to ride him. If that was the only horse left in the corral, she supposed Cade was doing her a favor by loaning her his horse, but she was skeptical. Throwing another look to the empty paddock and the barn behind it, she couldn't immediately see another animal available for her to ride. She was obviously reading something into nothing. Losing Roy's horse might be leaving them short. If so, the two he tied behind them as gifts would empty the corral. She would have to count heads tonight.

As they set out in the direction of the low-lying pine ridge where Ollie had indicated that the Indians lived, Lily attempted to strike up a conversation.

"I haven't thanked you yet for saving Roy's life. Will you tell me now how you did it?"

"I had help."

Cade's expression was tight and closed as he kicked his horse into a lead position, making it difficult to talk to his back.

Not to be outdone, Lily caught up with him. There was an entire plain to spread out across. There was no reason she should eat his dust. "Some people have difficulty accepting gratitude. That's understandable, but there's no reason to be rude. If this is what drinking does to you, you ought to give it up."

Cade gave her a look that could have turned water into stone, but growing angry now, Lily ignored it. "I am not some dumb squaw satisfied with riding behind you and chewing your food for you, so quit treating me like one. You're the one behaving like an ass."

She was doing it again. She was crawling down his collar and the back of his shirt and getting under his skin. Nobody else ever got close enough to disturb his carefully preserved equilibrium. Only Lily had the unmitigated gall to assume they were equals.

"I'm not in a mood for talking." Considering what he intended to do with this day, he shouldn't get her dander up too high, but Cade wasn't going to let her work on his, either.

"Well, fine, then don't."

With a haughty sniff, the very proper Widow Brown sent her horse—*Cade's* horse—into a canter, its tail swinging arrogantly, and rode ahead. Both tails swinging arrogantly, Cade mused as he watched her hips sway with the motion of the horse. It gave him a proper respect for this day's outcome.

Lily had missed breakfast and the noon meal, and her stomach was growling as they covered the distance to the woods. If Cade had ridden all this way the other night, it was no wonder he had been exhausted. Just as she was about to protest her hunger, Cade came up beside her and handed her a sandwich from his saddlebag and a gourd of water. Lily gave him a sour look but didn't refuse the offering.

As they drew closer to the woods, she fought her apprehension. Like any other traveler through frontier country, she had heard all the tales of the savages who hid like ghosts in the grass and trees and leapt out with violent war cries as soon as their prey showed any vulnerability. She knew of families who had been burned out of their homes and unsuspecting strangers who had been caught on the road by Indians on the warpath. She had a cautious respect for such violence, but if Cade said these were nonviolent Indians, she would take his word for it. Of course, he hadn't exactly said they were nonviolent, but she had to assume she was safe as long as she was with him. And they had saved Roy's life. That wasn't the sign of a savage. She really wanted to get to meet these people she had heard of all her life and never seen, except in people like Cade.

She sent her foreman a surreptitious look. If he was any example of what an Indian was like, she really ought to be frightened. Give him a little war paint, a quiver, and a knife sticking out of his belt and she might be tempted to turn around and run.

Lily reluctantly fell behind as they traversed a narrow path through the thick belt of forest. The late October sun was already sinking behind the trees, and she glanced at the lengthening shadows uneasily. If she had known the ride was going to take this long, she would have insisted that they wait until morning. She didn't like the idea of being out here after dark.

But Cade seemed unconcerned as they maneuvered their way up the river and through an intricate meandering of paths toward his goal. When they finally came upon the valley where the Indians were camped, the sun was gone, and Lily could smell the smoke of cookfires wafting up from below.

As they rode into camp, people eased out of their huts to see. Wary eyes watched from all directions, and Lily grew self-conscious under their inspection. She stopped when Cade stopped, and she didn't flinch when an older woman came up to touch her mount and say, "Cade's."

Cade swung down and spoke sharply to the woman in her own tongue. She gave him a look that didn't appear in the least intimidated before moving swiftly off in another direction. Without permission, Cade captured Lily's waist and swung her down from his horse.

"My father will see us when he is ready. Follow Dove Woman. She will show you where you may rest and eat."

He pointed at the woman now waiting patiently outside a large thatched hut.

The woman didn't smile or speak as she followed Lily inside, but Lily still got the feeling that Dove Woman was suppressing some kind of excitement or amusement. Inside, Lily found herself the center of attention of a number of young girls, and her gaze went hesitantly to the beds set along the walls, occasionally separated from others by what appeared to be neatly decorated buffalo hides. As the woman went to the fire in the room's center, Lily asked, "Do you speak English?"

"Small," was the reply.

That was a good indication of the difficulty of the language barrier. Still, it was better than saying nothing, and it was obvious that the others only meant to stare.

"Do you know Cade well?"

The woman hesitated as if puzzling out the question first, then the answer. Finally, she replied, "Mucho hombre."

Lily had learned enough of Juanita's Spanish to know what that meant. The difference between English and Spanish apparently hadn't occurred to her hostess. "Mucho hombre," indeed. Only a fool wouldn't see that Cade was definitely very much a man.

The woman left then and came back carrying a bowl of water. With gestures, she indicated that Lily should take the bowl to one of the vacant cubicles and use the water for washing.

Tired and dirty from the long ride, Lily was grateful for that offer, but she couldn't fathom how far she could get without cloth or soap. Well, beggars couldn't be choosers. If the woman continued to stand there expectantly, she wasn't going to do more than wash her face and hands anyway.

Cade appeared in the doorway then. Dove Woman began berating him, but he brushed her aside to throw a package in Lily's direction. "Soap. I'll be back later." With a few unintelligible words, he ordered the other woman and the giggling girls to follow him, leaving Lily alone.

Left to her own devices, Lily quickly shed her clothing and scrubbed as much as she dared. She was grateful for the chemise and the cotton drawers she'd made to go under Jim's rough work clothes. They at least provided a modicum of modesty as she attempted to wash around them, fearful that anyone might walk in at any time.

She wished she had clean clothes to put on when she was done, but she donned the dusty shirt and trousers and expectantly sniffed at the soup cooking over the fire. She would like to look nice for Cade's father, but she would rather have a full meal inside her before then.

Dove Woman returned bearing bowls and a ladle made out of a gourd, but without her daughters. She indicated that Lily was to serve and Lily, all too ready to eat, did as instructed. Then the woman indicated that she set one of the bowls outside the door. That seemed somewhat puzzling until Lily decided the other bowl was for Cade and he wasn't supposed to come into the lodge of an unmarried woman, thus the earlier tongue-lashing. Finding that such an idea appealed to her, Lily set the bowl outside and contemplated her own plate.

She had no utensils with which to eat. Carefully, she observed as the other woman dipped her fingers into the soup and began pulling out choice bits to plop into her mouth. It was crude, but Lily was too hungry to argue.

To her surprise, Cade appeared, carrying the bowl she had set out. He sat down cross-legged beside the fire and began to devour the food to the titters of the Indian woman who watched them.

So much for that theory. Giving up on understanding these people, Lily dipped her fingers in the bowl, selected the choicest piece, and somehow maneuvered it to her mouth without dripping down her front. The occasional flicker of Cade's gaze in her direction made her aware that she had not fastened her overlarge shirt all the way to the neck, but she was damned if she was going to fasten it while he watched.

They ate in silence, and when they were done, they washed their hands in the bowl of water.

"He will be ready." Cade rose and held out his hand.

Lily accepted his assistance and followed him out, suddenly aware that a flute and a drum had begun playing somewhere not too far distant.

There was a large gathering of people in the lodge to which he led her. More people lingered outside after Lily and Cade went in. The room was stifling from the heat of the fire and the proximity of so many bodies. Lily's curiosity warred with her need to escape to fresh air. Curiosity won.

As she sat down where Cade indicated, someone touched her hair. Cade spoke sharply and the hand went away, but now Lily was aware that everyone was staring at her. She wasn't used to being the focus of attention and she felt awkward. How had her sisters survived such moments? By laughing and snapping their fans, she supposed. Lily had a feeling that trick wouldn't work here.

The elderly Indian at the place Lily might have called the head of the table—had there been a table—began to speak. Cade answered him without inflection. There were murmurs of approval around the crowd. Lily found the flute player and focused on him, but his music wasn't nearly as interesting as Cade's.

Growing restless, she glanced around the crowd. She saw the faces of two solemn youngsters studying her intently, and she returned their glances. The younger ducked his head and looked away, but the older grinned slightly before turning his attention to Cade. Lily wondered if it was her imagination or if the two didn't bear some slight resemblance to Cade.

She studied the similarities between the older man she assumed to be Cade's father, Cade, and the two boys. The boys weren't full grown yet and it was difficult to tell with them, but she thought Cade and his father at least seemed taller than anyone else in the room. Cade certainly was, even when sitting.

Although Cade's father had a distinctive nose, it was more bulbous than Cade's aquiline feature, and so were those of the two boys. It was hard to see whether their eyes were similar; they were all dark. Cade's eyes were

more long-lashed, but they seemed to have the same al-
mond shape to them as his father's.

As Lily began an inspection of their mouths, she realized that a sudden silence had fallen, and she looked up
to Cade to see a glimmer of amusement before he spoke.

"My father welcomes you. He wishes you a long life
and many sons."

The sons weren't likely, but Lily didn't resent the sen-
timent. "Could you please offer my sincere gratitude for
his help in saving Roy? And if there is anything I can do,
any way I can help ..." Lily gestured helplessly at her
surroundings. Surely she could show her appreciation in
some material way.

Cade turned and translated her words, and the older
man nodded approvingly, gesturing for the two youngsters to step forward.

"These are my half brothers," Cade told her. "They
helped me find Roy and carry him out. I have told them
they may have the horses we brought with us today."

That seemed the very least she could do. Lily nodded
happily at them. Cade must be feeling better now that he
had his stomach full. He was behaving with much more
politeness than he had earlier.

"What should I say to them?" she whispered aside to
Cade.

"I will convey your gratitude and appreciation." He
turned and spoke curtly, in short clipped syllables, to the
two boys. They nodded respectfully, gave Lily one more
look, then turned and went out.

Since this seemed to be an adult gathering, Lily understood that they had been dismissed. There was another
quick exchange of words between Cade and his father,
and then, to her surprise, the women rose and began to
leave.

"Follow Dove Woman," Cade ordered in a low voice.

Well, that wasn't much different from back home when
the men stayed and smoked their cigars after dinner and
the women went to the parlor and gossiped. Following
her guide outside, Lily breathed deeply of the clean air

and resisted the temptation to stay outside to hear if there would be more music. It would probably be impolite.

She followed Dove Woman back to a small tepee she hadn't noticed when they rode in. It seemed odd to see this one nomadic residence among the more sedentary houses of the village, but she wasn't in a position to question. At the woman's gesture, Lily ducked through the low opening and entered a darkened chamber where only the glowing embers of the fire gave her light.

Buffalo robes and blankets had been spread invitingly on the ground. Lily supposed she should have seen this coming, but she really didn't like spending the night out here, away from Roy. He could be suffering with fever by now.

Lily glanced anxiously at the entrance, but the all-male conference could go on for hours if Indians bore any similarities to the men she knew. She couldn't possibly find her way back through the forest alone in the middle of the night.

Resigned to her fate, Lily arranged the covers for the best layer of padding and rolled up in the blanket. Sleeping in the clothes she had worn all day wasn't particularly pleasant, but she wasn't going to be caught sleeping without them. There were no bars on buffalo hides.

Lily was nearly asleep when a large shadow filled the space between the fire's light and her bedroll. She gasped and sat up before she recognized Cade's silhouette in the darkness.

"What are you doing here? Are we going home?"

"After I sleep with my wife."

And with that extraordinary statement, Cade sat down, put his arms around Lily, and pulled her to the ground as his mouth found and ravished hers.

Thirteen

His heavy body was suffocating. The broad chest she had so secretly admired presented the immovability of a mountain when Lily shoved her hands against it. When Cade eased to one side to maneuver his hand between them, Lily tore her mouth away and gasped, "Are you drunk?"

"Not now," was the only reply before he moved his lips to the vicinity of her ear.

"Then you must be insane." Lily tried to wriggle away, but she was becoming very aware of the heaviness of Cade's lower body across hers and the gentle stroking of his fingers against the side of her breast. It had been a long time since she had been aware of a man in this way, in the tingling awareness that made her blood rush and her senses spin.

Cade didn't answer this inanity. Gently, his large hand closed over her breast and his thumb found the peak through the layers of her clothing. Lily gasped and tried to struggle some more, but his mouth closed on hers again, drugging her more thoroughly than any amount of opium.

His tongue found hers while his hand slid beneath the open collar of her shirt to better encompass her breast. The twin sensations sent liquid fire through Lily's veins, a fire she hadn't felt in years, perhaps never. It had all been so long ago, she couldn't remember. She just knew the frightening loss of control as Cade demanded a response, and she gave it.

It was too quick, too sudden. He gave her no time to think. Before Lily knew what was happening, he was

pulling her shirt over her head and cursing the thin chemise beneath. Then his hands were at the buttons of her
trousers and she was trying to push him away, but all she
succeeded in doing was making it easier for him to pull
off the heavy denim.

Even as Cade cursed the drawers that remained, his
hand was touching her there, finding her through the open
seam, and Lily felt the small explosions of her body as
his long fingers explored her carefully. When she tried to
fight his invasion, he caught her hands and held them
over her head. In that moment Lily knew her helplessness. She gave a cry as Cade's narrow-hipped body
moved over her, but his mouth only clamped against her
breast, moistening the cotton of her chemise. Her hips
rose in a frantic search for an answer to the rioting sensations surging through her.

Briefly, Cade lifted his lips to her ear, and Lily thought
she heard the murmured words, "I'm sorry, *querida,*" before she felt the thickness of him pushing into her.

Lily cried out as much in relief as fury as his body entered hers. Cade hesitated at her cry, but there was no
turning back. He released her hands to caress her cheek.
Then carefully, he pushed deeper. Weeping with frustration at her own inability to control herself, Lily dug her
fingers into the taut flesh of his hips and lifted herself in
eagerness.

It was Cade's turn to cry out in relief as he finally
thrust deeper, plunging with such rapidity that in a few
short strokes they were both convulsed with the contractions of their desire. As Cade's body reached into hers,
touching some hidden spring of need, Lily gave a cry of
surrender. Muscles tightening in waves of pleasure, she
pulled Cade into the whirlpool he had created and felt his
explosion with weary satisfaction.

Tears streaming down her cheeks, Lily clung to Cade's
broad shoulders when he collapsed against her. She knew
it had never been like this before. Even now, even after
what they had just done, she could still feel him deep inside her. He filled her until there was nothing left to fill.

Her starved body throbbed already for a repetition. She had never dreamed it could be like this again.

Why in the name of all that was good and holy could this only happen with the wrong men?

Tasting the tears on her cheeks, Cade rolled over, carrying her with him. "I'm sorry, *querida,* I tried not to hurt you."

Not one to place blame where it didn't belong, Lily shook her head against his shoulder. Cade was still wearing most of his clothing and she was in her underwear. They hadn't even taken the time to undress. They were both insane. "I am not hurt," she whispered.

Cade wasn't certain whether to believe her. Her cheeks were soaked with tears, and he had felt how tight she was around him. Despite her height, Lily was a slender woman. What other meaning could there be? He had feared it would be painful for her, but he had taken his chances. It was too late to go back.

"Perhaps it will be better next time," he offered as consolation.

Better? How could it be any better? She was still shivering with the passion he had aroused so swiftly in her. Next time? Lily didn't want to think about that. She knew where this kind of thing led, and though she hadn't got pregnant again since she married Jim, she didn't doubt that if anyone could do it, it would be Cade.

When she lay silent, Cade thought she slept. Relaxing, he adjusted her more comfortably in his arms and drifted off to sleep.

He had done it. He had taken her. Now all he had to do was keep her.

Somewhere in the dark hours of morning Lily gradually woke to the realization that while her backside was thoroughly warm, her front was freezing. Reaching for a blanket, she encountered a barrier in the shape of a massive arm.

As the realization of where she was and what she had done hit her, Lily uttered a dire imprecation, but before she could find some means of escape, the arm tightened around her.

And then his hand came up to stroke her breast, and she jerked at the sudden sensitivity of her aroused nipple. It couldn't be like this again, Lily reasoned, not so soon. But when Cade laid her back against the buffalo robe and pressed his kisses to her throat, she grabbed his hair and dragged him up to her mouth.

It was sensuous slaughter. Cade's tongue was a soft-edged sword that penetrated and accepted no surrender. His hands caught and captured her curves, torturing her with slow strokes until she writhed for freedom. Instead, he found new places to apply his lethal tongue, and Lily was crying for mercy long before his knees came between hers and pushed them apart.

This time, he thrust deep, nearly terrifying Lily from the state of passion he had aroused in her. But Cade's kisses and hands returned to their electrifying caresses, and soon she was finding his rhythm and matching it. She could feel him filling her, touching the mouth of her womb, and her muscles contracted instinctively to hold him until he was groaning and bucking against her imprisonment and they were both thrust again into wild seas.

As she cried out her release, Lily felt Cade's seed pouring hot and heavy deep inside of her, and the sensation convulsed her even more. It didn't seem possible that after all these years she could find what she had lost in one spring evening, but it was there, the heat and the heaviness and the excitement. And the peace.

Cade stayed inside her, merely rolling over and wrapping her in a blanket so they lay bound in a cocoon, touching everywhere possible there was to touch. Their clothes were an irritation they could afford to ignore while the most intimate parts of their bodies lay joined. Aching with the battering that unused muscles had received, Lily gradually slipped into sleep.

They woke again with the dawn. Lily was too sore to respond when Cade's wandering fingers pushed aside her drawers, but he was already swollen with need, and there was no denying him. How could she deny him after all she had already granted him? And when he finally entered her, Lily discovered she was ready to take him after all.

They lay briefly in the quiet aftermath of exhaustion, until the sounds of the camp arising intruded on their privacy.

Cade glanced down at Lily's rumpled chemise with regret now that light was creeping through the cracks. He would have liked to have seen her nude, but there was time yet for that. He would wait and savor the thought until tonight.

As it was, she was beautiful in his eyes with her hair loosened in a golden tangle against the buffalo robe, her wide blue eyes half-lowered and sultry with their love-making, her generous lips swollen with his kisses. His gaze drifted appreciatively over the full rise of Lily's breasts to the dip of her flat waist and swell of her hips. She was a beautiful woman. He had done well in his choice of wife.

Lily's eyes widened as she realized Cade was staring at her, and he caught the flash of blue before she spoke.

"I must get back to Roy. If he's fevered, no one will know how to treat him."

So much for contemplating a lingering courtship of kisses and lovemaking in the grass under the noonday sun. At least she wasn't screaming rape or some other audacity. She had wanted what they had done as much as he had. Cade had worried about that, but he no longer had any doubts about her passion. Although she felt nearly as tight as a young girl, she had a woman's responses, and he was satisfied.

"You are a married woman now; you will have to fetch your own water. There is a creek in the trees behind the village."

Rising unhurriedly, Cade pulled up and adjusted his denims, and Lily felt her heart pound just at the sight of his nimble hands fastening the buttons over his flat abdomen and narrow hips. It wasn't until he walked out that his words sank in and she wanted to heave something at him.

Damn! Since when had she begun thinking with what was between her legs instead of her head? Cade robbed her of all logical thought when he was in her presence. She was behaving just like a sixteen-year-old schoolgirl again. Would she never learn?

But as she pulled on her clothes and found her way to the creek, Lily felt reality closing in on her. She didn't know by what law they had been married and she was inclined to ignore his assertions, but she couldn't ignore the evidence of her own body. Even as she daringly stripped and immersed herself in the cold water, she could see the bruises of his passion and knew the depth in which he had planted his seed. If she wasn't pregnant now, Cade would see that she soon would be.

That shed a whole new light on matters. At least this time the man had taken the time to offer his name, if a man without a name could do that. Lily didn't doubt for a moment that Cade considered them married. He hadn't taken her when he could have because he didn't want her to bear a bastard. In his eyes, what they had just done was legal.

That posed a whole array of interesting possibilities which Lily wasn't quite ready to confront yet. Not on an empty stomach. The thought of a man like Cade in her bed every night was exciting, but if she ever went beyond that thought . . .

Lily shuddered and got dressed. She could feel the walls tumbling down around her already.

Cade returned to his usual noncommunicative self as they ate their meal and saddled their horses. There was no formal farewell when they took their departure from the camp. Several women came out to watch them and Lily waved at the one she recognized, but the smile she received in return could have meant anything.

As they rode out, they could see the two youngsters trying out their new mounts on the hill. The boys gave them a spirited chase, flying down to cut across their path, but then they were gone and only the trees closed around them, and Lily and Cade were alone.

"I didn't think I would ever see the day when I could appreciate a sidesaddle." Lily adjusted herself uncomfortably on the heavy man's saddle.

A flicker of amusement crossed Cade's impassive features as he took in the area of her discomfort. "You should not expect to be ridden all night and get up and ride the next day. We could have stayed."

Lily's cheeks flamed at his casual terminology for what they had done. "I'll remember that," she replied stiffly.

They rode in silence until Lily's curiosity got the better of her. "Cade?" He twisted in his saddle and looked at her questioningly. That was almost sufficient to make her regret saying anything, but she had to know. "What did you mean when you said we were married?"

"You accepted my horse, didn't you?" He nodded at the huge gray she rode even now. "You invited me into your house and brought me a dowry of two mustangs. My father approved. That is all that is necessary."

His satisfied tone raised her anger. "You know that isn't all that is necessary!"

Cade shrugged and walked his mount through a particularly narrow strip between trees. "We can go to town and sign the *alcalde*'s book, if you like. There are no priests. I would take you to San Antonio and a church, but your rebels are probably already there trying to blow holes in the city with their cannon. What more would you have me do?"

"You could have at least asked me," Lily answered nastily. He was too close to truth for comfort. Marriages were a haphazard thing in this country. She would have preferred San Antonio, but after taking Goliad, the rebels were undoubtedly marching to the next city in their path. She didn't want a church that much. But she would have liked to have been asked and to have had her father and son present. She didn't feel in the least married.

"If I'm married, what is my name? Mrs. Cade?"

He tilted his head as if to consider the notion. "Probably not. It might be easiest if you call yourself Señora de Suela. That's my grandfather's name."

"Do you have an Indian name?"

"Just my birth name. I did not stay with the tribe long enough to give myself an adult name. My father is Lipan and does not have a family name."

"What is your birth name?"

They had reached the grassy plain and Cade could turn and watch her now. Lily supposed the flicker in his eyes could be called amusement. She had never seen him laugh, and rarely did he smile, but she was beginning to understand some of his expressions. Or lack of them.

"My father called me something that translates roughly as 'Mighty Quiver.' I never asked him what he was thinking about at the time. My mother called me Luis Philippe, after her father. Do you prefer either of those?"

A grin quirked the corner of Lily's mouth. Mighty Quiver. She could just imagine a screaming baby boy being called that. She suspected his father had a sense of humor even if Cade did not. He was definitely not a Luis Philippe. She shook her head in reply.

"Where does Cade come from?"

"The Spanish word for music, *cadenza.* They thought they insulted me, but they were unaware of the other poor names I had to choose from."

Lily didn't want to ask who "they" were or why they would wish to insult him for his love of music. She knew absolutely nothing about this man. She wasn't quite certain that she wanted to learn any more.

"Cade suits you," she answered decisively.

"And de Suela?" He lifted his eyebrows questioningly. "Or shall I give myself an adult name now? No one will know the difference."

Lily considered this briefly, then shook her head. "I think that is your decision."

"De Suela is an old and respected name. I will stay with it, then."

Lily de Suela. Considering the state of current affairs, a Mexican name wasn't going to be any better than an Indian one, but she wasn't even certain that either belonged to her. Lily supposed if a child came of their night together, she would be glad of a name for it, but she couldn't reconcile herself to the position of wife just yet. She was just now learning to be herself again.

She didn't think Cade was very likely to understand that. The constant rocking of the horse kept the memory of what they had done in the front of her thoughts, but the closer they drew to home, the more her thoughts turned to Roy. She couldn't concentrate on both of them. Roy had been with her for nearly nine years. Cade had barely been around for nine weeks. Roy won.

She was urging Cade's powerful horse faster as the ranch came into sight. It was easier to put everything else out of her mind and let the one love of her life dominate. She needed to see that Roy was well.

Cade let her go. They were on her territory now. In his father's tribe it was customary for women to own the property. He had given all that he had possessed to Lily without reservation. The theory didn't work quite as well in a white man's world, but he had enough respect for Lily to allow her to take the lead in this case. An Indian male was only supposed to see to the protection of his family and provide for them by hunting. His Spanish heritage was a little more confused but not so very different. He would do his duties outside of the home. Inside the home was her family. He didn't expect acceptance there, but he would have to find some way to demand respect. There was time for that.

As he rode up, Cade noted the strange wagon in the front yard. Painted a bright red and decorated with pictures that apparently had some meaning beyond his comprehension, it bore the bold inscription "Professor Mangolini's Traveling Medicine Show" in gilded letters across the top.

Climbing down from his horse, Cade noted with suspicion Lily's uneasy stance on the front porch. She was speaking in shrill tones unlike her, evincing some welcome while glancing nervously at the recipient of her assurances. As Cade came around the wagon and saw the newcomer, he began to understand why.

Professor Mangolini was tall and dark and handsome and smiled at Lily in a way that went beyond casual acquaintance. And he looked just like Roy.

Fourteen

L ily thought she might be losing her mind. What she had done last night was sufficient to convince her she had lost what remained of her senses, but she couldn't believe she was actually standing here staring at Travis Bolton while her father and the man she had just made love to looked on. She must be hallucinating. Perhaps she could just faint and then wake up and find everything returned to normal.

Lord, but he was even more handsome than she remembered. Nine years had chiseled Travis's features into maturity. There were a few crows-feet around his eyes perhaps, but they still gleamed with the irrepressible humor that had held her so fascinated when she was sixteen. She couldn't believe she was standing here talking to him after all these years. She wasn't hearing a word he was saying.

She was thinking of Roy. How was she going to keep him from Roy? Or had Travis already seen him? Would he have noticed? He'd have to be a fool not to. Of course, Travis hadn't known Jim. Maybe he would think she always fell for tall, dark, curly-haired men with gray eyes. That thought sent Lily's glance back to Cade. She had outdone herself on tall and dark this time, but the thick, straight hair brushing Cade's collar didn't have a lick of curl and his eyes were far from gray. What in hell was she going to do?

"Well, Lily, are you going to introduce me to this gentleman here? Your father and I have already introduced ourselves."

She would have liked to have seen that. Trying to keep

her stomach from leaping up her throat, Lily gestured toward Cade. "This is Cade, my foreman. Cade, this is Travis Bolton, an old friend from Mississippi."

Salesman that he was, Travis instantly held out his hand with a smile. Cade looked at him, looked at Lily, and with a rather pointed glare at the latter, accepted the other man's hand. Travis winced slightly at the pressure exerted but remained smiling.

Taking this opportunity to escape, Lily murmured a quick excuse and ran into the house. She refused to believe any of this was happening. She would think about Roy and worry about the rest later.

She found Roy happily playing with a set of toy soldiers and her heart plunged to her feet. So Travis had already been in here. Perhaps God had sent him to punish her. Or save her. She wasn't exactly certain which it would be.

Nine years was a long time. Lily remembered it almost too clearly: her sisters' excitement over their betrothals, the peddler's wagon coming down the hill, and Travis Bolton, sitting bold as life on the wagon seat. He was the most handsome thing she had ever seen in her life, and the tallest. When he had climbed down from that wagon and smiled at her, she had felt dainty and feminine and just the right size. And he had never done anything to discourage that impression. Except get her pregnant and leave without marrying her.

He couldn't have been much more than nineteen himself at the time. That wasn't much of an excuse for what he had done, but it was all Lily could ever offer. She had never even told her father. When she had determinedly stalked Jim Brown two months later, her father had thought it was because she was upset that her sisters were getting married and she didn't have a beau. She doubted if he had ever realized it was because she had to get married or bear a bastard. Until now.

Damn Travis Bolton to hell. He had nearly destroyed her life once. What did he think he was doing here now? Knocking her legs out from under her again? Well, this time it wasn't going to be so easy.

"Look at these great soldiers Mr. Bolton gave me! Are you going to ask him to stay for a while? He has the funniest stories."

Lily tested her son's head for fever and, reassured, tried to ease the inevitable. "Mr. Bolton is a traveling man, Roy. I'm sure there are places he's supposed to be. I imagine Cade has some interesting stories to tell if you'll ask him."

"Cade told me about how he learned to ride once. Did you know he never had a horse 'til he caught a mustang?"

There were any number of things Lily didn't know about Cade. How did a boy who didn't know how to ride manage to catch a wild mustang? Probably wrestled the animal to the ground. Lily held her fingers to her head and felt another ache coming on. She was going to have to handle this and get it over with.

She heard her father and Travis enter, their voices boldly jovial. The two of them made a good pair. Her father had always been better at selling than farming. Cade would be off checking on the men and making certain that the chores were getting done. She was going to have to ask him to eat with the family. She might not be able to mention their "marriage" yet, but she certainly couldn't delegate him to the bunkhouse anymore.

She didn't have to worry about that. By the time Juanita had the evening meal prepared, Cade had washed and joined the others in the main cabin. Lily felt his speaking glance as she entered, wearing the blue gingham she had worn the night of the dance. It was the newest dress she owned. The others seemed too girlish and frilly. The gentlemen politely rose to their feet when she entered. Cade followed their example.

He was furious. She could tell it. But what was she supposed to do? That was Roy's father sitting there. Lord in heaven above, Roy's father. Lily took her place at the table, and when the men had taken theirs, she bowed her head in prayer, then asked them to pass the salt. It was the only thing she could think of to say.

"Travis was heading for San Antonio when he stopped here. I recommended that he find another destination. You know the place better than I do, Lily. Where would be a good place for a man to sell his supplies?"

"His supplies? Your alcoholic cure-all, Travis?" Lily couldn't keep the hint of scorn from her voice. Nine years and he was still peddling garbage, just a finer class of it.

"Now, Lily, don't disparage my medical training. I don't suppose you remember Dr. Joseph from Natchez? I worked with him for several years before he died, and I spent years after that perfecting the formulas for five of his medicines. I was just telling your father about the book I've written detailing my discoveries."

"Do you have bottles of medicine to cure broken legs? Do you have something we should try on Roy to get him better and make him walk without limping? Did your great training teach you any of that?"

Travis managed to look slightly uncomfortable before his handsome mouth bent into a wheedling smile. "Now, Lily, there you go exerting your overactive imagination again. You've done all that medical science can do for the boy. A sip of my rheumatism medicine wouldn't hurt him any if the pain gets too bad, but young bodies heal themselves quite miraculously."

She had to give Travis credit for not wanting to quack a child. She couldn't tell yet whether he had figured out that Roy was his. She should quit antagonizing him. He hadn't done anything that a million other men hadn't done at some time or place. It was just her unfortunate luck that she got caught.

Lily sent Cade a quick glance. She could tell by the depth of his silence that he had already figured out who Travis was. Cade might not say much, but he never missed a thing. She hoped he understood her predicament. She wasn't certain of the law, but Travis could very possibly take Roy away from her if he chose. She couldn't imagine him wanting to, but she wasn't going to allow any opportunity for him to try.

"Who is Professor Mangolini?"

Lily looked up. She hadn't even been certain that Cade could read. Most men out here couldn't, except for the lawyers in their three-piece suits. To expect an Indian to read . . .

Travis sat back and sipped his water. "People are inclined to believe that foreign physicians know more than homegrown ones, and that professors know more than mere doctors. So I have become Professor Mangolini in order to reach a larger number of people."

"To make more sales," Lily corrected.

Travis scowled at her. "You make it sound as if what I'm doing is a crime. That isn't fair of you, Lily. Should I go back to peddling tin pots and pans that fall apart the instant they hit a flame?"

Ephraim looked up in recognition. "So that's where I remember you! You came by that spring the girls got themselves hitched. Tried to sell me an iron skillet that wouldn't hold water. But you had some half-decent bootleg in that wagon when you came back in the fall."

The undercurrent around the table was about to pull Lily in. She saw the glance that Travis gave her and knew what it meant. He had come back after all. Just a little too late.

"I was just trying to make a living. I'd had a good summer that year, if I remember. I came back thinking to court the prettiest girl I'd ever seen, only to learn she'd already been taken. Near broke my heart at the time. It's odd how the world turns so the same people are thrown together a thousand miles and too many years apart."

Odd wasn't the word for it. Cade would bet his bottom dollar that this scalawag had passed through Lily's hometown on his usual route and heard from Lily's sisters that she was a widow with a wealthy ranch now. He'd bet more than his bottom dollar. Surely Lily could see that.

Cade glanced her way, but she seemed totally entranced by the quack. She had a glazed look in her eye even when she was trying to cut the man to ribbons. The man had hurt her once, hurt her badly, but that wasn't always enough for a woman to turn away a handsome man. Cade uttered a curse to himself that had nothing to do with his Indian or Spanish origins.

Somehow they suffered through the remainder of that

meal. Lily gave an expurgated version of her visit to the Indians, exclaiming over the kindness of their treatment and the intelligence of the boys who had saved Roy's life as if she'd actually had an opportunity to see any of that. It seemed to pacify her father momentarily, although he was still giving Cade pointed looks.

When Lily finally begged leave to retire, Cade couldn't take it any longer. He touched her arm, and she swung around as if he had burned her.

"I need to have a word with you before you go to bed. Shall we step outside?"

She turned on him with wide, terrified eyes, and Cade instantly dropped his hand.

"Not tonight, Cade, please. You know what needs to be done. I'll trust you to it."

Cade watched her walk away as a knife pain slit him from gullet to loins. She was going to deny him. She was going to pretend that nothing had happened. She was going to go to that damned bed alone.

He ought to be accustomed to betrayal and deceit. He'd seen enough of it in his lifetime, that was for certain. But he couldn't believe that after what they had shared, she could up and walk away. It surpassed the bounds of all credulity.

But she did so, and like the others, Cade stood and watched her go. Not wanting to hear what was said after she left, Cade made his excuses and went out the back door. He should take Serena and go back to his cabin and get drunk and forget the hell about her. It had been madness to think that he could marry a lady and make a place for himself. He had no illusions about what he had to offer: a gray gelding and some vague hopes. He couldn't even fool himself into thinking that he could offer the passion she had never known, because the passion that had created her child was right there in the house with her. Damn, but why in hell did the man have to show up now?

But seeing Serena and holding her chubby little body in his arms, renewed Cade's determination. He wasn't going to give up. Not without a fight, at least. If he had to invent another rattlesnake in a box, he was going to find some way of showing Professor Travis Bolton Mangolini out of the territory.

Lily evinced no surprise as her window slid up later, after the house had grown quiet. There wasn't any way she could sleep, and she didn't think Cade would be managing it very well either. There just wasn't any easy solution. How was she to explain that?

She was sitting in her white nightgown against the pillows, a colorful quilt across her knees, and her golden hair in a braid over her shoulder. Cade ached at the sight of her, but he was going to have some explanations first.

"He's Roy's father, isn't he?"

Lily made no attempt to deny the obvious. She nodded.

Although he had known the answer, it was still a blow. Cade leaned his shoulders against the wall and shoved his hands in his pockets as he watched her silhouette in the dim light from the window. "Where does Jim fit into this picture?"

Lily gave him an angry look. "He knew. Don't look at me like that. Jim wanted a wife. A married man gets three times as much land out here as an unmarried one. He'd lost his son. Roy was the son he wouldn't have had otherwise. We were both happy with the arrangement."

Cade scowled. "That's why you were so starved for passion that you'd even take a renegade like me. And now you've got your chance to get Roy's father back and you mean to set me aside."

Lily balled her fists into knots on top of the bedclothes. "Don't talk to me like that, Cade. You have no right. What we did was your choice. You never asked my opinion on the matter. And now Travis is here and could take Roy away if he wanted. I'll be damned if Roy goes anywhere without me."

"And I'll be damned if you go anywhere without me." Cade said it quietly, but the threat was still there as he moved away from the wall and toward the bed.

Flinging back the covers, Lily leapt for the long-barreled Kentucky rifle Jim had always kept beside the bed. Grabbing it, she held it steady to her shoulder. "Not one foot closer, Cade. You had your way last night. It's my turn."

"You're my wife, Lily. Do you expect me to sleep out there," he nodded toward the window, "while you sleep in your lonely bed? Or do you entertain some expectations of sleeping with your friend Travis?"

"Get out, Cade. I don't have to listen to that. For once, you're going to have to listen to me. When Travis is gone, we'll talk about what we've done, but not a moment sooner. I'm not ready to be a wife again, Cade. You should have asked me that the first time."

"You were ready enough to take what I had to offer." The barrel of the rifle was pressed against his chest and Cade grabbed it, twisting it out of her hands. "I'll not let him have you without a fight."

The words "and he'll lose" hung unsaid between them.

Lily took the rifle Cade shoved back into her hands and watched in silence as he climbed out of the window.

She wondered what it would have been like if she had welcomed him into her bed, accepted his right to act for her, allowed his strength to come between Travis and Roy. But she wasn't ready to find out. It was time that she did a few things for herself.

But her body felt hollow when she crawled between the sheets without him.

Fifteen

"Juanita, these have got to be the best cookies I've ever tasted, and I've eaten at the tables of kings."

"Who don't serve cookies," Lily murmured at the red flannel shirt she was sewing.

Juanita's shy smile didn't falter at Lily's cynical words. She set another plate of cookies on the table in front of Travis and backed away.

"Of course kings eat cookies, don't they, Roy?" Travis directed the question at the boy bundled beside the fire with his leg propped on a sawed-off stump Cade had carried in for a footstool.

Roy looked up from the pulp magazine Travis had found in his wagon and gave the foolishness of the adults a look that properly put them in their place.

"Who cares what kings eat? I like cookies." And he went back to reading.

"Your child, not mine, Lily. You've ruined the boy." These words were said low enough so no other could hear but the woman sitting in the chair next to his.

Lily flinched, not at the insult—for she knew Travis was being facetious—but at this first mention of what had hung between them these last weeks.

"Jim was a practical man, not a storyteller. He raised Roy the same," she answered calmly.

Juanita came back to pour Travis a new cup of coffee, and he caught her hand and kissed it. "I think I'm in love, Lily. This woman is all a man could dream of. I've always wanted a woman who could cook circles around me."

Juanita carefully withdrew her hand, but she didn't run

away as she was apt to do when a man became too forward. She merely sniffed and flicked the length of her beautifully handwoven skirt in disdain as she moved away. Lily watched this display with curiosity, but Travis seemed impervious to the honor that had just been bestowed upon him.

"Then it's a good thing you never got me," she replied curtly when it became obvious that Juanita didn't mean to speak for herself.

"Cooking isn't the only attribute I admire," Travis murmured, giving Lily a wicked look.

She was saved by a commotion outside that resulted in the entrance of her father with Ollie Clark behind him. Keeping her irritation to herself, Lily inquired pleasantly, "I don't suppose you brought Miss Bridgewater with you, Ollie? I'm purely starved for the voice of another woman."

She was being spiteful and she shouldn't be. The actual truth was that she was beginning to enjoy the attention she had never received as a young girl being courted. Ollie and Travis had taken to fighting over her every desire and snarling at each other in between times. It would be amusing if it weren't for Cade's absence from the picture. He apparently had the impression that he was above such antics.

Which was probably no more than the truth. Cade had a way of coming in smelling like horse manure and covered in straw and still managing to look the part of noble aristocrat. He entered now as Travis was genially inquiring into the events in San Antonio and Ollie was stonily replying. Cade had at least cleaned up to a certain extent, Lily noted as he accepted the cup of coffee Juanita handed to him. He didn't even look at her, but strode to the fire and dropped something into Roy's lap.

Without a word to the company, Cade went over to the small trundle bed they had fixed in the far corner for Serena to use. Before he could lift the sleeping child from the bed, Lily halted him.

"Stay and have some supper, Cade. You must be hungry. Juanita, there's still a little of that corn pone and stew left, isn't there?"

Roy was studying the object that Cade had given him. He held it up to the fire and watched it wink in the glow. "Is it gold, Cade? Is there gold out there?"

His excitement brought the other two men over to examine the rock with the glittering streak through it. Cade adjusted Serena's covers and came back to the table where Juanita was already uncovering a pot left warming by the fire.

"Fool's gold," Cade replied in answer to Roy's question. "Pretty, but worthless."

Disappointed, the two men wandered back to the table, but Roy polished the rock on his sleeve and continued to admire it. Cade ate, ignoring Travis and Ollie. When Ephraim offered him a flask of whisky, Cade looked up and accepted it, pouring a dollop into his coffee.

Lily frowned and shoved her sewing into her basket. Standing up, she crossed over to Roy, who looked resigned at her approach. "It's time for bed, young man. You need plenty of rest if that leg's going to heal."

"Seems to me it can heal just fine right here," he protested, but he was already reaching for the crutches Cade had carved for him out of old tree limbs.

"No sass, young man, or you'll be going to bed directly after supper for a week." Lily gave his head an affectionate lick as he managed to stand and start for the makeshift partition they had erected at the end of the room. Crutches couldn't get him up and down the narrow stairs to his loft.

Roy made polite good nights to the adults and retired without another word of protest.

"He's a fine boy, Lily. He'll be a big help around this place someday." Ollie helped himself to the plate of cookies in the middle of the table.

"I thought you were the one trying to persuade her to sell and get out." Travis dragged the plate closer to him and took two more cookies for himself.

"That would be the best thing for a woman on her own without a man to protect her," Ollie agreed, unperturbed.

"Will you quit talking about me as if I'm not here? Ollie, is there any word in town about plans for Christmas? With the piano there, couldn't we have some kind of festivity? Without liquor, of course." She gave Cade a scowl, and he deliberately poured another swallow from the flask into his cup.

"There's not many willin' to leave their places unprotected that long. We've got people comin' across the river to fight with Houston that don't seem to know the difference between what's theirs and what's everybody else's."

"From the sounds of it, Houston's going to need those men when Santa Anna gets here."

Travis had taken to Texas politics with all the eagerness of an excited puppy with a new toy. He had visited the camps when they surrounded San Antonio, spoken to Austin before he left to allow trained military commanders to take over, and generally scouted his way around until he was familiar with all the players. To Travis, it was watching a new government in the making. To settlers like Lily, it was watching the grass being burned so neither side could fodder their animals. She had no patience with his enthusiasm.

"There ain't a Mexican goin' to return after bein' driven out of the Alamo with their tails between their legs. They're all cowards." Ollie didn't have to look at the stoic man sitting silently at the table, eating his supper. Everyone knew what Ollie was trying to say.

Cade broke off a piece of cornbread and sprinkled it in his stew.

Cade was many things, but he wasn't a loudmouthed braggart like Ollie Clark. Lily got up to bring Cade another piece of corn pone. She might want to swat Cade upon occasion, but Ollie had no right to take cheap shots at him.

Her action didn't go unnoticed, and Travis casually changed the subject. Ollie left soon after, assuring Lily that he would do all he could to see some kind of Christmas festivity was put together.

"I don't know why you entertain that man, Lily. He's got snake oil behind his ears." Travis reluctantly pushed the plate of cookies away but smiled as Juanita poured him another cup of coffee.

Cade coughed on his dry corn pone, and Ephraim stood up to pound him on the back. Lily gave Cade a suspicious glance, but she was tired of the competition. She left the floor open for her father to explain.

"He wants to buy Lily's spread. He's got a store back in town and a hankering to be a rancher. I've been trying to talk her into selling."

"She'd be a fool to sell, especially to a rascal like that one. He's got a friend in town who tried to sell me a piece of land sight unseen. I may be pretty, but I'm not dumb." Travis stood up and glanced toward Lily. "Why don't you come out with me and get a little fresh air? It seems all you ever do is work."

Lily's first thought was to look at Cade and see how he was taking this, but then she corrected herself. It didn't matter how Cade was taking it. He didn't ask her permission to do whatever he wanted. He didn't even behave like a respectable employee. Just because she had been foolish enough to go to bed with him once didn't make her his wife or require her to act like one.

Without glancing at Cade, Lily stood up and reached for her shawl. This was Sunday, and she had on her best merino dress for the occasion. Cade hadn't mentioned it or even seemed to notice, although it was the same deep blue as the gingham he had admired. But Travis had been properly appreciative. But then, Travis always was.

Outside on the front porch, Lily waited for Travis to lead the way. The sky seemed to be inundated in stars and cloaked in black velvet. She breathed deeply, smelling the wood smoke coming from the chimney and noticing a hint of frost in the air.

"I've been waiting for you to tell me about Roy, Lily. How long are you going to make me wait?"

Well, she had known this conversation was going to have to come sometime. She might as well get it over with. Lily leaned against the porch post and didn't look at him.

"What is there to tell? You can see he's doing fine.

This place will be his when he grows up, and he knows it. What more can you ask?"

"You haven't said the words yet, Lily. You haven't said he's mine." Travis caught the front of her shawl and turned her around to look at him. "If you could have waited just a few months more, I'd have been back. I would have married you. We could have been a family."

Lily looked at him incredulously. "How was I supposed to know that? Every night that week your wagon was there, and then one night it wasn't. You left without a word. I thought I was going to die. A few months later, I was almost certain of it. If it hadn't been for Jim, I'd probably have thrown myself in the river. Roy isn't yours, Travis. He's mine and Jim's."

Travis stroked a straying hair from her forehead. "I was nineteen, Lily, and running scared. I didn't have any money, the sheriff was on my back with half a dozen complaints, and you were the best thing that had ever happened to me. What was I supposed to do? Take you from your comfortable home and family and set you up in my wagon? That's why I went to Doc Joseph, so I could offer something permanent."

Lily jerked her head away. "It doesn't matter now, Travis. It's over and done with. Roy and I are happy. You can go on your way without worrying about us anymore. I don't know why you've lingered. You can see we've got all the help we need."

Travis's hands fell to his sides. "And what about me? Don't I have anything to say about this? I've just discovered I have a son, a family I knew nothing about. Do you expect me to just get in my wagon and move on? Do you have any idea how lonely the nights are out there? How many nights I've seen the lights in the houses as I go by and wondered what it would have been like if I'd settled down?"

"Travis, you always could tell a good tale, but yes, I expect you to get in your wagon and move on. You weren't meant for the life we have here, and I'm not meant for yours. You're always welcome to come by and see us, but that's all, Travis. My son belongs here. You can't take him away."

"Is that what you think I'm planning on doing? I'll admit, I've given it some thought. He's smart as a whip and he'd be good company, but he's only a boy. He needs his mother. I need his mother. Marry me, Lily. I can settle down here, set up a regular practice. I feel it in my bones. Texas is the home I've been looking for."

Lily stared into the starlit sky. Somebody had finally said the words. They should be sweet to her ears. She'd had to propose to Jim herself. And Cade had never bothered to ask. But sweet as the words might be, she wasn't ready for them.

"I'm discovering I like being single Travis. I don't need to rely on anyone for anything. I don't know that I'll ever marry again."

"Don't say that, Lily." Travis caught her waist in his arms and began pressing kisses behind her ear. "You just don't remember how good we were together. Let me bring back the memories, Lily. Then you can decide whether you want to go without that kind of loving for the rest of your life."

Travis started to kiss her, but a hand grabbed his collar and hauled him backward. Infuriated, Travis swung a wicked left punch that would have caught anyone else by surprise and floored them. Cade merely held up his palm to deflect the blow and shoved Travis backward.

"The lady said no. Just take her word for it and go back where you belong."

"Dammit, who do you think you are, you overdeveloped buffalo? This discussion is between the lady and myself, and I'll thank you to stay out of it." Travis raised his fist for another punch, but Lily caught his arm.

"Don't, either of you. If I wasn't so mad, I'd laugh. Where were the lot of you when I was sixteen and looking for a dancing partner? Well, I don't need a partner any longer. So go find someone more amusing to fight over. I'm not worth the effort."

Lily swung around and marched in the door without looking back. Cade watched her go, then turned to see if the other man still wanted to challenge him. He had enough whisky in his blood right now to be ready for the fight.

"Don't look at me like that, cowboy." Travis leaned back against the porch post and folded his arms across his tailored frock coat. "I've no desire to have my face creamed into tomorrow's mush to give you a chance to work off the liquor. You don't really think you have a chance in Hades to win her if I can't, do you?"

"I've a better chance than you do. At least I know what a ranch is all about."

Cade walked into the night, leaving Travis to consider that one certainty. Travis might be everything that Cade was not, but the one thing that mattered to Lily besides her son was the ranch.

In anyone's eyes, that pretty much made it a draw.

Sixteen

The Christmas festivities turned out to be Lily's undoing.

They started joyously enough. The anticipation of having a real Christmas get-together after all the years of hard labor and isolation had all the women in the surrounding area excited. Trunks left closed since they had crossed the Sabine were opened and lovingly rummaged through. Remembered customs from Kentucky, Alabama, Mississippi, and even as far away as England and Germany were pulled out and mulled over and converted to the availability of local resources.

Ollie's barn was trimmed with pine and decorated with acorns and pinecones. Magnolia leaves from somewhere to the east were nailed proudly over the door. A sweet-smelling brew of dried orange rind and cinnamon simmered on the fire the men had built near the door. Whisky punch was the order of the day, but the women made no objections to this male addition to their celebration. War was in the air, but for this one day they would ignore it.

Running her fingers lovingly over the piano keys, Lily laughed at the sounds Roy created from the flute Cade had made for him. For one whole day she was going to forget about the concerns of home, the worry over how she was going to pay Langton for the hire of his slaves to pick the cotton, the need to get her cattle to market. These could be the least of her problems. She glanced surreptitiously at Cade lounging against a barn post drinking from a steaming cup of punch and sighed.

It wouldn't work. It couldn't possibly work. She didn't want to consider that it might have to. She looked up to find Travis determinedly heading in her direction and smiled. He'd been out "scouting the territory" after they'd had word that the Alamo was now in the hands of Austin's rebel army. She was glad he had returned in time for the celebration.

"You look positively glowing, Lily. You ought to wear your hair like that more often. It becomes you." He touched the soft loops of gold she had painstakingly arranged over her ears.

"It will all come down before the evening's end," she replied disparagingly, trying to ignore the appreciative gleam in Travis's eyes. He still had the power to make her feel like an attractive woman. She wished he didn't. It would make life much simpler.

"Let the fiddler play, and come and dance with me, Lily, my sweet. I want to hold you in my arms again. It's been a long cold spell since I saw you last," he whispered near her ear as he ostensibly bent over the music on the rack.

"We dance reels here, Travis. You're not likely to hold me much in a reel, so I'll dance with you. But that's all I'll do." Lily accepted his hand as she rose from the bench.

She didn't complain when Cade joined the dancers with Maria. He had played the flute earlier while she had played the piano. It was time some other musician held the floor. But she suspected that wasn't his only reason for joining the dancers now.

She was almost ready to enjoy the competition. Lily knew perfectly well there were ten men to every woman in this room and every female from the age of ten upward had partners waiting in line, but for just this once she wanted to feel feminine and attractive like her sisters. Travis's laughing smile warmed her heart, and though the look Cade gave her was far from smoldering, it was significant enough to give Lily a small feeling of triumph. He wasn't quite as impervious as he liked to pretend.

She danced with Ollie and her father and even Jack. The men had drunk enough that her height no longer mattered to them. A chance to stamp and shout and work off excess energy and liquor was good enough reason to grab a woman by the waist and swing into the music. Lily glanced up once to see even Juanita timidly following Travis's direction as they tried a respectable quadrille.

Lily gratefully accepted the punch someone handed her between sets and laughed with Anna's mother at the piano before Travis came to carry her off again. She didn't have to look up to know that Cade took the place at her right, making him the first man to sweep her around the circle after Travis lost his place in the reel—she could tell by the heat of Cade's hand against her waist, the strength of his grip as he practically carried her along, and the fresh-scrubbed scent of him in this room full of pomades and sweat.

He was there again at the beginning of the next set, removing the cup of punch from Lily's hand and looking down at her enigmatically through dark eyes as he wordlessly held out his hand and she accepted it. Damn, she was not used to men looking down on her. It was an unnerving experience.

Lily felt giddy and unsteady on her feet as the music pounded louder and faster and the dancers swirled in brilliant profusion around them. Ollie twirled her around. Juanita passed by with a flashing smile on her brown face. Travis whispered sweet words as they passed. And Cade caught up with her again, catching her waist and swinging her off her feet with a flourish as the music ended.

When the music stopped and he set her down, Lily swayed and almost fell before Cade could catch her.

Looking down at her suddenly pale face and glazed look, Cade swore under his breath and discreetly led her toward the door, supporting her with his arm as he practically carried her out. He saw her father bearing down on them, but he gave the old man a look that scared him off before hauling Lily through the barn door and into the brisk breeze of a December night.

"Stand here, out of the wind." Cade leaned her against the barn behind the open door, blocking her from view with his bulk.

"I'm all right. It's just the punch. I'd better go back in," Lily whispered unconvincingly as she pushed herself upright and avoided Cade's eyes. She had never felt like this in her life. Her head was spinning and she wasn't at all certain she could continue standing. She wasn't given to queasiness or the vapors. She wasn't even wearing a corset, for heaven's sake. It had to be the punch.

"I only gave you the kind without whisky," Cade replied, blocking her path with the barrier of his arm. Irrelevantly, he added, "The moon is full tonight."

Lily leaned against the wall to ease her spinning head and met Cade's gaze. She was beginning to understand his mind too well, and it frightened her. A shock of black hair fell over his brow and she let her thoughts wander to how it would look if Cade grew just the one long braid of hair down the right side of his head and shaved the left like his father did. She thought he would look very good with feathers and beads in that braid. She wondered if he had tattoos like most Indians were said to have. She didn't even know what his body looked like beneath his shirt.

"I'm fine, Cade. Really I am. I'd better go inside before my father comes after us." She tried to stand, but he was too close for her to get far.

"It's been two moons, Lily. There's been time to know if there's a child."

She had known that was what he was after. She looked over his shoulder at the blue-black night sky. "I'm not that regular, Cade. I can't count the times I thought Jim and I . . ." She stopped, unwilling to reveal any more of the embarrassing details of her intimate life.

Her face was pale against the dark backdrop of the barn, and Cade lifted his hand to touch her cheek. Noting the difference between dark and light, he dropped it again. "In the eyes of my father, you are my wife. We will go to the *alcalde* to please your father. You have only to say when."

He didn't mean to abandon her as Travis had. That was small consolation. Lily closed her eyes and tried to imagine Cade's hand on her cheek, but imagination failed her.

He wasn't a tender man. She had evidence enough of that. She wasn't certain she wanted a tender man. She wasn't certain she wanted a man at all. But if a child existed . . .

"I'll hold you to that," she murmured.

He would have to settle for that much of an admission right now. Encouraged, Cade didn't let his hand drop this time when he reached to touch the falling gold strands of Lily's hair. He had never had a golden-haired woman before. Even Serena's mother had brown hair, although it might have been lighter when she was young. The color fascinated him, but not as much as the woman whose hair it was.

Cade could sense Lily's terror as an animal senses fear. He didn't know whether it was of himself or of her predicament or both. She was frozen with it, but still she stared at him boldly, defying him with her promises. She was a strong woman, but he was stronger, and they both knew it. He had nothing to prove by forcing her further than she was willing to go. Without touching her more, he brought his hand back to his side.

"You will catch cold." Cade offered his hand this time, and hesitantly, Lily took it. Her fingers were cool and slender against his calluses. He held them firmly, feeling the way his hand engulfed hers, enjoying the smooth touch of her palm until they were inside the barn again and he had to release her.

Lily didn't remember too much of the rest of the evening. Her father drank too much and had to be carried to the wagon. Roy got brave and tottered around without his crutches and told the other admiring children stories of how he'd been rescued by Indians until he was so exhausted that Travis had to carry him out at the end of the evening. Most of all Lily remembered Cade silhouetted against a cloudy night sky, reaching for the reins of a panicked mustang, the horse's flaring nostrils and sharp hooves rearing high above his head as he spoke calm words that worked magic.

The crowd that had gathered breathed a collective sigh of relief as the horse whinnied and shied and came to stand restlessly beneath Cade's touch. The drunken fool who had tried to ride him while celebrating the Lord's birth with a shotgun blast was helped from beneath the horse's hooves, bruised and shaken but otherwise intact.

No one came up to thank Cade. The man's wife wept with relief and was led away by her family. Thoroughly satiated with drink and song, the remainder of the crowd admired the performance as an interesting end to a good evening and then wandered off to their wagons and horses. Cade handed the horse's reins to an older man who came to claim him and went to locate his own mount.

A head taller than anyone else, Cade was easily seen as the crowd eddied around him, leaving a distance that made of him an island in a flowing river. He looked so alone that Lily wanted to go to him, but Juanita was handing her a slumbering Serena and Roy was complaining sleepily and Travis waited for her in the wagon. Lily climbed up to the seat, hugging the warm child instead of the man.

She didn't want a husband. She certainly didn't want a husband who never spoke to her, much less consulted her wishes. She didn't want any man who would come in and take over her life and tell her what she could or could not do and expect more from her than she was prepared to give. She'd had enough of that.

But the possibility that after nine years of praying she might finally be carrying a life within her again kept Lily's mind a careful blank. She wasn't certain whether she would wish the possibility away or not should she stop to think about it. So she didn't.

She went about her days as if nothing had changed. The cotton was delivered to town to be ginned and baled and shipped. Now that the Alamo had been taken, and San Antonio was in American hands, more of the men wandered home to help with the harvest and to do the mending and repairing before spring planting began. Lily heard skeptically the news that Ollie had been sent to represent the district in the constitutional convention. The men seemed to think that the war was over and that they had won. Lily didn't think Santa Anna was quite that generous.

She didn't ask Cade what he thought. He was busy morning, noon, and night rounding up cows that seemed in imminent danger of delivery, rescuing calves born on the prairie that would fall prey to wolves and coyotes. Now that some of the hands were tired of playing soldier and were returning from their brief skirmish he had more help, but he seemed to take each birth personally and each death as his own responsibility. Lily scarcely saw him except when he came to eat, and in his exhaustion, he had little to say then.

Cade had even less to say the night he came in soaking wet to find Travis, Ollie, and Ephraim engrossed in deep discussion beside the fire while Lily ran back and forth to keep them supplied with drinks and hot food while attempting to do her mending in between their calls. When she bent to set another pitcher beside Travis and he absently reached out to hug her hips, Cade's composure cracked.

Lily gasped in surprise as Travis's hand was ripped from her side and then Travis himself was quickly hauled from his chair and shoved toward the door. Ollie leapt up, knocking his own chair over as he attempted to interfere, but Cade merely grabbed his collar with his spare hand and shoved him in the same direction as Travis.

Both men came up swinging, but Cade already had the door open, and with the kick of his boot and a block from his shoulder, he shoved them out into the pouring rain and slammed the door after them.

Roy came to the door of his cubicle to investigate the commotion. Lily stared at Cade's calm features for a second, then in an explosion of rage, slammed out of the room in the direction of her chambers. Cade pointed his finger at Roy, sending him scurrying back to bed.

Tankard in hand, Ephraim looked up from the table at the young giant standing in the room's center, water streaming from his soaked clothing as he visibly forced his fists to unclench in the sudden emptiness of the room.

The older man shook his head and took a sip of his steaming drink.

"You certainly do know how to empty a room," Ephraim commented to the house at large.

Surveying the havoc he had wreaked, the overturned chairs and spilled plates, the tracks of mud across clean planked floors, the condemning silence of closed doors, Cade reached for a plate and the hot stew kept warming by the fire for him. Without a word, he filled his plate, sat down across from the old man, and began to eat.

Ephraim raised his shaggy eyebrows, took a drink, and hid his grin in his cup. It didn't seem like the rest of his company was going to return any too soon. It looked like he'd better learn to get along with this one.

Generously, he poured a tankard for Cade and pushed it across to him.

Cade looked at it, then went back to eating.

Seventeen

Lily pulled up her trousers and began to button them from the bottom while she gazed absently out the window. The rain had let up for a while and the sky was a clear blue. She could see the wind catching at the barn shingles and tossing the trees in the distance, but it looked like a beautiful spring day instead of the end of January.

She could see Cade stepping out of his cabin and carrying a laughing Serena across the mud to the kitchen where Juanita would fill her with warm oatmeal and milk. Cade hadn't apologized for his behavior the other night, but she had noticed Travis had begun to treat her with a certain amount of respect, particularly in Cade's presence. Ollie had apparently returned to the constitutional convention and more important matters. His courtship had cooled considerably since Travis's arrival.

She really didn't miss Ollie's company or Travis's liberties. Idly tugging at the top button of her trousers to fasten them over one of Jim's old work shirts, Lily tried to retrieve her resentment at Cade's high-handed methods, but it was too nice a day to hold a grudge. Travis might be Roy's father, but he wasn't her husband and he had no right to assume the liberties of one. Cade had simply reminded him of his place. Travis did upon occasion need a forceful reminder.

But she wasn't at all certain that it was Cade's place to do the reminding. That was what stuck in her craw. If her father hadn't done it, she should have. And if she hadn't, Cade shouldn't have objected. He had no right to do so.

She really was going to have to pin him down and talk to him sometime.

Impatiently, Lily glanced down at the recalcitrant button that refused to fasten. Pulling the edges of her pants together, she failed to make them overlap. She stared at the gap incredulously. She had always been as skinny as a rail, and she certainly hadn't taken much time to enjoy Juanita's cooking these last months. She hadn't worn these pants in a while because they had needed mending. They always had been a little snug, but this . . .

As the reason for the button's obstinate refusal to close began to sink in and she could no longer deny it, Lily looked out the window again in dismay. Cade was already leaving the kitchen and crossing to the barn.

The inevitability of what she must do caused Lily to reach for a belt to cover the gap as she turned her feet toward the dogtrot and out into the brisk wind. She had known the night they had done it. She had known the night of the dance. She had known and had continued to postpone the inevitable. Now wasn't the time to bewail the fates. The time for action had arrived.

Cade looked up with surprise as Lily walked determinedly in his direction. She hadn't sought his company since he had thrown Travis out of the house. She hadn't avoided him either. She had just pretended he was another piece of the furniture she had to work around. Her ability to ignore what didn't please her seemed limitless, and he had observed it with equal amounts of fascination and annoyance.

He couldn't decipher the expression on her face now. There was something particularly expressive about the rounded hollows of Lily's cheeks and the flash of her sky-blue eyes, but Cade's only reaction was a desire to kiss those grimly set lips. He knew how they could melt into the softness of desire. If he let his mind roam, he could almost feel those long, slender legs around him, and his gaze traveled briefly to admire the proud carriage and height of the woman approaching. It had been three months since he had taken this woman to his bed. He burned with the need for it now. Grueling work could quench the worst ache, but right now he was rested and randy as hell just at the sight of feminine curves in men's clothes.

Cade waited where he was and Lily obliged by marching to stand in front of him. Her voice was as cool and calm as a glorious spring day when she made her announcement.

"I think it is time we went to see the *alcalde.*"

Cade stared at her, letting the words sink in. She wore her magnificent hair in a thick braid the color of corn silk, and the wind ruffled wisps of it about her high forehead. His gaze drifted downward with fascinated curiosity, straying from her eyes to the full swell of her breasts against the old shirt, to the hastily fastened belt that almost hid the open button. She was so slender he might never have noticed the slight thickening of her waist, but the evidence was there in the too-tight trousers, and he felt a sudden grip on his insides at the realization of the cause of that snugness.

Cade jerked his gaze back to hers, read the fear behind Lily's false bravado, and nodded carefully. "Tomorrow is Saturday. Will that be soon enough?"

Briefly, Lily closed her eyes in relief, then opened them again to find Cade's dark gaze still fastened on her. If she could just focus on the breadth of his strong shoulders straining at the seams of the chambray shirt, the capability of his big hands, and the strength behind the high-cheekboned structure of his brown face, she would be all right. She knew there were a thousand barriers to what they were about to do, but only one came immediately to mind. "I want one promise from you, Cade."

Cade waited patiently for the ground rules most women seemed to insist upon. Rules seldom inhibited him, but they were interesting to hear.

"I've watched my father drink away our home and our family. I'll not see Roy's inheritance lost in the same way. I know whisky's cheap and everybody uses it, but I don't want a drunk for a husband."

Cade eyed her expression implacably. "You want me to promise not to drink. And if I don't promise?"

Lily quailed at the alternative, but this was one point she had no intention of compromising on. "Then I'll raise the child alone."

Over his dead body she would, but there was no sense in riling her with that pronouncement. She was being as reasonable as a terrified woman could be. He could return the favor. Nodding in acquiescence, Cade asked, "Shall I tell the others?"

Lily considered it, then shook her head. "We'll just go to town as usual. I'd not make a big deal of it. It's not as if there will be a priest or anything."

So it was to be business as usual. As she walked away, Cade watched the braid swaying against her slender back with a mixture of emotions he didn't mean to identify. It had been so long since he had felt anything that he didn't have the knowledge to recognize them in any event. He concentrated on Lily, who had just dismissed him as if she had told him to round up the cattle on the south forty. He wondered what she would do when he made it clear that it wasn't his name only that came with marriage.

There wasn't much opportunity to inquire. Cade came in early that evening, but Travis hadn't taken the break in the weather to travel out as he had hoped. The other man sat propped before the warm fire teaching Roy the rules of chess while Lily moved about the room, helping Juanita set the table, answering Serena's questions, and buttering a pan of cornbread. Cade noticed she had changed into an old dress he hadn't seen before, and his gaze instantly fell to her waistline. The loose dress succeeded in concealing any evidence of expansion. Still, he couldn't help feeling a slight swelling of pride at the knowledge that his child grew there.

Cade took his seat at the table, and Serena instantly clambered into his lap. Before Ephraim could pour him a whisky, Lily plopped down a mug of coffee beside him. Cade took the hint and drank the coffee, shaking his head at her father's offer. At Lily's call, Roy and Travis came to the table. The splints were off Roy's leg now, but he still walked with a slight limp. He hopped into his chair,

chattering about knights and castles and queens while
Travis indulged him fondly.

Lily looked tired, Cade observed as she took her place
at the end of the table and bent her head to say grace.
That proprietary thought shocked him a little. By tomorrow, he would be in a position to see that she got more
rest—not that Lily would see things that way.

Cade cut Serena's food into small portions and saw that
she picked up as much of the squash as the bread. Juanita
ran out to the kitchen to bring in more bread, and Travis
tilted his chair back and asked for more coffee. Lily
started to rise to get the pot from the fire.

Not looking up from his plate, Cade interrupted. "Get
it yourself, Bolton. You've got two good legs and two
hands."

Lily halted where she was, astonished by Cade's speaking out as much as by what he said.

Travis motioned her back into her chair and rose to get
the pot himself. "I thought Indians believed in making
their squaws do the work. Seems odd for you to be ordering a man to wait on himself."

"Squaws wait on men who have been hard at work protecting and feeding the tribe."

Travis slapped his mug on the table and sent Cade a
black look as he returned to his seat. "You're the hired
help and I don't owe you any explanations, but I'm paying room and board, if that's what you're insinuating. I'm
selling my medical supplies. People around here are glad
to have my experience. Just ask Lily sometime if I'm not
earning my way."

That was a provoking comment, but before Cade had
time to summon a response, Juanita entered, balancing a
pitcher of milk in one hand and hauling an iron skillet of
pan bread in the other. Lily immediately rose to help her,
but Cade was on his feet and shoving her back into the
chair before she could do so. He took both the pitcher and
the skillet from Juanita and set them on the table, sending
the terrified maid back to her corner with just a look.

"Dammit, man, you're scaring her. What in hell is
wrong with you tonight?" Since Cade had already re-

turned to his seat, Travis remained in his, but his clenched fists indicated that situation could change at any moment.

Lily was finally beginning to comprehend what was going on, and while she might have been grateful that Cade meant to take care of her, his high-handed methods didn't work any better in here than outside. Telling him that wouldn't ease the tension that had so rapidly built around the table, however. Even the children could sense it. With a look to Juanita, Lily said quietly, "Take Serena and Roy out to the kitchen to eat, will you? They're likely to have stomachaches, elsewise."

"Dammit, Juanita, you stay right here where you belong. If anyone's going outside, it will be me and that thickheaded mountain over there." Travis was already halfway out of his seat as he spoke.

Switching her skirt, Juanita gave him a look of contempt as she reached to take Serena from Cade and muttered a string of Spanish beneath her breath. Cade replied in a word or two of the same language, causing her to give him a swift look before she hurried the children out of the charged atmosphere.

Roy was resistant to departing. Balking, he demanded, "Why can't I stay? I'm no baby. If there's going to be a fight, I want to see it."

"If there's going to be a fight, it will be outside and you can see all you want. Now get out like you're told." Containing her fury at the two men, Lily rose and shepherded her protesting son out the door. When she turned back to the table, both men were still sitting and her father was drinking his whisky and watching them with amusement.

"What was Juanita saying?" Travis demanded, irked by his inability to know what Cade had said.

"If I understood her correctly, she was comparing all men in general to asses." Lily sat down and picked up her fork, hoping common sense would prevail.

"You are being either polite or very naive," Cade commented as he returned his attention to his own plate.

Lily threw him an irate look. "I know what Juanita thinks of men and why. Which do you think I am?"

"A lady is always polite."

"What in hell would you know of ladies?" Travis asked, disgruntled by the entire exchange and the feeling of being left out of something that could be important. There was an undercurrent here that he didn't like at all.

Cade raised his head, much as a buffalo might when aroused to danger. "My mother was a lady. What about yours?"

Before Lily could do anything unladylike like slinging the plate she had in her hand, Ephraim put a halt to the bickering. "I don't think either of you is impressing anybody." He turned to his daughter with a sly glance. "Lily, I think it's about time you started making some choices before somebody gets killed. If you've got your heart set on staying here instead of coming home with me, you're going to have to settle on one man and get it over with—unless you like watching grown men behave like young bucks and challenging each other."

Lily sent her father a furious look. "I could just tell the lot of them to get the hell out and leave me alone, and that includes you, too. I'm sick to death of men telling me what to do."

Cade raised a cynical eyebrow but returned his concentration to his plate.

Travis leapt into the fray with both feet. "Your father's right, Lily. There must be a dozen men out here to every woman. It's a dangerous situation. We've known each other a long time; that's more than you can say about anyone else out here. And you know what else we have in common," he gave Lily a significant look, "so it only seems sensible that we put an end to this nonsense now. You know how I feel about you, Lily. And Roy needs a father. There's plenty of room in this new country for a man like me. You can run the ranch if you want, and I'll settle down to do doctoring and maybe selling a little land on the side and maybe even go into government once they make up their minds what they want to do. You can be the lady you're supposed to be." Strangely enough, he meant every word that he said, and he waited with his heart in his throat for Lily's reply.

Curiosity caused Cade to look up to see how Lily would take this speech. He had enough confidence in her to know she would reject it, but he couldn't help feeling a little uneasy about its implications. He knew full well what she and Travis had in common, and it wasn't so different from what Cade was counting on to hold Lily to her promise. Pushed to the wall, she might suddenly decide that Cade's uncouth behavior deserved punishment. Or that it might be better to be married to a smooth-tongued bastard who would leave her to run the ranch as she wished. Although Lily might reject Travis's words, she might accept his offer just to spite Cade. He would have to be prepared, if so.

Lily felt the intensity of Cade's gaze as it fell upon her. He said nothing, although he knew their whole future could be riding on her response. Her decision suddenly became more real than the life growing within her. Travis was a nice man and Roy's father, but there was nothing between them anymore. Travis would always be a nice man with a shallow character. On the other hand, Cade's character was deep and dangerous and possessed of unknown currents. Still, she would rather face the unknown with Cade than the known with Travis.

It would be hard to think of Cade as her husband in the same way she had thought of Jim. These past months she had not stopped to consider Cade's feelings, wasn't even certain he had any, and she certainly had never consulted his wishes. Not that he had ever consulted hers, either. But somewhere, they were going to have to start doing just that. Somehow, they were going to have to tell the world that they were man and wife and they meant to stand by each other through thick and thin and all the stages in between. It had been hard with Jim. It would be even harder with Cade. She hadn't wanted to consider it. She had better start now.

With a sigh, knowing the explosion that would follow, Lily lifted her fork and smiled as sweetly as she could manage under the circumstances. "Daddy, I hope you'll be happy to hear that I've already made that decision. As a matter of fact, I made that decision before Travis ever got here. Cade understood when I asked for a little time before telling you, but I guess the time is here. Cade and I were married three months ago. I'm expecting his child in July."

To say all hell broke loose put it mildly, Lily thought as she rose and quietly left Cade to handle the chaos for which he had built the foundations.

Eighteen

As the shouting from the cabin became progressively louder, Roy slipped from Juanita's protection and dashed to his mother's rescue. Entering, he found no sign of his mother, but the sight revealed held enough interest to keep him from wondering over her whereabouts.

Cade had neatly captured Travis's arms and held them tightly behind his back despite Travis's height and strength and vigorous protests. Roy's eyes widened at the ease with which Cade kept his grip while Travis and Ephraim shouted at each other and at Cade.

"No damned Indian marriage is going to stand up in a court of law! The boy is mine and I'll be damned if I'll see the likes of you as his father."

Ephraim turned a furious red at this announcement. "The hell you say! Lily wouldn't be consorting with no itinerant peddler. You've got no call . . ."

But neither Cade nor Travis was paying any attention to this protest.

Cade jerked Travis's arm a little higher to keep him from saying anything more damaging in front of Lily's father. "I'll not take the boy from you, but you can't take him from his mother. That's final."

Cade looked up in time to see Roy staring white-faced at them, and he pulled Travis around to see the same. When Cade was certain the other man had taken note, he released him.

Travis dusted off his coat sleeves and contemplated the stricken gaze of his son. When Lily's father began on his tirade again, he ordered, "Shut up, Ephraim," and took a step toward Roy. "Your mother told you to stay in the kitchen, son."

The word "son" had been applied to him by every male in the district as a euphemism for "boy." Roy had never rejected the word before, but in his confusion, he rejected it now. "You're not my father. Don't call me that."

Travis's shoulders slumped slightly, but he didn't give up. "Jim was a better father to you than I ever could be, I'll grant you that. But he's dead now, Roy, and your mother needs a new husband. I'd like to be the man who acts as your father in Jim's place."

Travis was a big man with dark, wavy hair like Roy's own and a way of speaking to him that made him feel they were equals. He'd given Roy toy soldiers and taught him chess and been a good friend these last months. The idea of Travis taking his father's place had some appeal, but Roy was intelligent enough to know things weren't that easy. He looked questioningly at the man who had taught him to ride and rescued him from the river wash.

On his own most of his life, Cade had little experience in dealing with the intricacies of human relationships, but he knew how to deal with terrified animals. Lowering himself to sit cross-legged on the floor, he invited Roy to do the same. Curious, the boy did as expected.

"I cannot be your father any more than your mother can be Serena's mother," Cade told him. "But you need a father and Serena needs a mother and we would like to act in their places. Your mother has already agreed to give me a child of my own, so there is no question about my staying. I will be with your mother for as long as we both live. And she does not want to be parted from you, so we will all live here together. Do you understand?"

His voice was soft and reassuring and totally unexpected from so large a man, particularly one who seldom said more than three words together. His words now were almost hypnotic in quality, and Roy continued to stare at him even after Cade finished speaking.

Travis looked at the two of them sitting there: the broad-shouldered, black-haired Indian and the wide-eyed eight-year-old staring at him with complete trust, and he cursed. "Cade, he's too young to understand. This is between us. Leave Roy out of it."

Cade looked up from his position on the floor. "You're the one who doesn't understand. Lily has made her decision. You're the one who has been left out. You can work with us or get out."

Roy looked from Travis to Cade, then tugged at Cade's sleeve when he didn't seem to be paying attention to him. When Cade turned his head, Roy said, "I want Travis to stay. Can Travis stay too?"

"If he's been messing around with my daughter, I'll throw him out on his ear, dagnab it." Ephraim glared at the traveling salesman who had dared malign Lily's name.

"I'm staying," Travis informed the room in general, turning a defiant glare on Cade when no one raised an objection. "I'll buy my own land and move out. But you can't take the boy from me."

"Fine, but I'd suggest you find your own woman." With that, Cade rose from the floor and held his hand out to Roy. "It's past your bedtime, boy. We'll still be here in the morning. Go on to bed."

Roy was reluctant to go, afraid he would miss something of this new change in his world, but even Travis joined in to issue him out of the room, and with dragging footsteps, he left.

The three men were left with nothing to say. Cade turned to Lily's father and told him, "We're going in to register the marriage with the *alcalde* in the morning. You are welcome to come with us as witness."

He walked out, leaving the other two men to wrangle the night away as they wished.

"It is time you got back on a horse, Roy. You can get in the wagon later if you are tired."

Cade rode up on the gelding he had given Lily as he gave this order, and Lily smiled. This was the first time Cade had ridden the horse since their "marriage." The horse was obviously now considered communal property.

Roy looked uncertainly at his mother, but Lily didn't

attempt to interfere in this decision. Cade was undoubtedly in the right of it. When Travis brought out a small pinto he had recently acquired in his travels, Roy gave in to the command and took the horse offered. Travis helped him into the saddle, and Roy was soon learning the paces of his new pony, delighted with the mount and not in the least concerned with the tension between the adults.

Ephraim took the seat beside Lily, leaving Juanita to ride in the wagon bed with Serena. Travis had saddled one of his horses and rode determinedly beside them, his grim expression not once turned in Lily's direction.

It made for an interesting wedding party, Lily decided as they traveled more or less silently into town. Serena was cold and cranky and whined most of the way. Juanita was her usual uncommunicative self. And the men didn't seem to be on speaking terms.

On the road to San Antonio they met a small band of Tennessee militia on their way to join the forces at the Alamo. Travis stopped to talk with them, but Ephraim kept the slow oxen wagon moving in the opposite direction. Lily looked over her shoulder at Travis's excited shout and effusive greeting, but not until he rode back to join them did she know what had prompted his excitement.

"That was Senator Davy Crockett! He says there's more coming to join him. There's men pouring across the Sabine to help fight Santa Anna. With men like that, Texas will be a republic yet."

Lily sent him an indecipherable look. "The Mexicans have a thousand troops here already. Santa Anna is likely to bring a few thousand more. All you hotheads are going to accomplish is getting us thrown out of our homes."

"Lily, you're going to have to see that Santa Anna can't run Texas from a thousand miles away. He just hasn't got the resources. And his way of thinking isn't ours. We need slaves to grow cotton and make the land pay. What does he want us to do, live on tortillas like his starving peons? We're not lazy Mexicans like he's used to."

Cade gave him a dirty look and, growling something

irascible, kneed his horse ahead of the wagon. Lily watched him go with a curious mixture of pride and fear. She knew nothing about him, but she understood him to an astonishing degree. Only it wasn't her place to explain his position if Cade wouldn't do it for himself. Sometime, though, people were going to have to recognize that he was as much Mexican as he was Indian. It was a volatile combination under the circumstances.

Their arrival in town went unremarked, since Saturday was the one day of the week when the streets were filled. Cade and Travis took care of the horses and oxen while Ephraim helped Lily out of the wagon. She didn't inquire into the argument that had gone on without her the night before, but she noticed the men were being mighty polite to her today. It would have been a pleasant change if they weren't so irritating about it.

By mutual unspoken consent, the entire party turned in the direction of the general store where Bert Dixon kept his office. The town was supposed to build a hall and a place for public records to be kept, but enough funds hadn't been found for it yet. The idea of making their announcement in front of all the idlers at the store preyed on Lily's nerves, but she kept her chin up and took Cade's arm as they entered.

Cade gave her a surprisingly gentle smile as he covered her hand with his and looked around for Dixon. The man was involved in a bickering dispute over a boundary line with one of the newcomers to the settlement, but he looked up instantly when Lily's party approached. A small frown formed between his eyes as he noted Cade's presence, but he came forward eagerly enough.

"Mrs. Brown, this is a delightful surprise. And you've brought your family, too. I don't think Ollie is in this morning; I'm sure he'll be sorry he missed you."

Preferring to establish his position immediately, Cade intruded before Lily could make some polite response. "We've come to sign the marriage register."

Dixon looked stunned. Stepping back, he took in Lily's determined hold on Cade's arm, the rather grim expressions of the men behind her, and could come to no other conclusion but that "we" meant Lily and Cade.

He shook his head slowly. "I doubt that we can do that. Indians aren't official citizens of Mexico. I can only register citizens."

"I am a Mexican citizen, Dixon. My mother is a de Suela." Cade waited patiently for the next objection. He had expected this; it was the story of his life. Lily, however, was unaccustomed to being questioned. For her sake, he would speed the proceedings if he could.

"Have you proof?" Dixon examined the sheet of paper Cade produced from his pocket and shook his head again. "You're not one of Austin's settlers. You'll have to take this to the priest in San Antonio. He can marry you there, although I must say, Mrs. Brown, I wouldn't advise you to go through with this. You have a valuable amount of land out there. It wouldn't do to let it fall into unscrupulous hands."

Cade removed the paper from Dixon's hands and returned it to his pocket. "The ranch is hers, Dixon. If you know anything of Mexican law at all, you'd know it can't become mine even if she dies unless she legally leaves it to me. We're married. We just want it in the public register."

Lily looked up in surprise at Cade's announcement. She had thought a wife's property instantly became a husband's upon marriage. That's the way it had been in Mississippi. It was a positively feudal law; it was hard to believe the Mexicans had gone beyond it.

Apparently Dixon thought the same. He gave Cade a contemptuous look. "Use that line on a fool woman if you like, but don't use it on me. Go find the priest."

Until now Travis and Ephraim had stayed out of the dispute, but when Cade merely turned away at this command, they both stepped in at once.

"What do you mean, you won't register my little girl? She's got as much right to choose her man as the next person. Who appointed you anyway? I know Austin personally. I'll see to it that he hears about this."

Travis overrode Ephraim's verbal protests with a more

overt action. Grabbing the smaller man's coat collar, he lifted Dixon off the floor. "Now Dixon, I might have a personal prejudice against Cade myself, but I'm not going to let you stand here and insult a lady."

By this time they had gathered quite a crowd. Lily glanced around nervously at the onlookers and wished herself a hundred miles away. Some of the women wore furious expressions, presumably because Lily's word had been questioned or because any man dared interfere in the lawful process of marriage. Some of the men were snickering over Dixon's predicament. His position wasn't an elected one, and he wasn't the choice of everyone present. There were other men, however, who seemed to be solidly behind Dixon, and they were making rude comments to each other and looking at Lily as if she were a piece of trash to be thrown away.

Before a general riot could ensue, Cade shouldered his way back through the crowd again, carrying a heavy tome and flipping through it rapidly. Lily stared at the book with surprise. She had never seen it before, had not known Cade possessed such a thing, and couldn't believe he read it as quickly as he seemed to be doing.

He pinpointed a place on a page as he reached Dixon and Lily and began to read from the book in fluent Spanish. When he was done, he looked up at Dixon with a carefully neutral expression.

"I assume since you are *alcalde* here, you will understand the Spanish. Or shall I translate?"

The fact that the Indian was not only reading Spanish but also speaking the language had the crowd momentarily stunned. Then a man in the back called out, "That certainly sounded like a damned Mexican lawbook to me."

Quiet Juanita gazed at the speaker with contempt. "He is reading the law in the language in which it was written. Shall I translate if you do not understand?"

"But we're not Mexican citizens anymore!" someone else yelled. "We declared our independence!"

"No, you didn't. You only declared yourselves to be against the 1830 constitution. That lawbook is the only one you have or you'd not have any law at all," Travis pointed out as he released Dixon's collar. "What did you read, Cade?"

A stranger to the rear of the room made himself heard despite the quietness of his voice. "He read the passage that says a wife keeps any property she owns upon marriage to dispose of as she wishes. Dixon, I'd recommend you register the marriage as requested."

A silence fell over the room as the stranger came forward. Calling him a stranger was incorrect. Although he didn't live in this portion of the territory, almost everyone in the room knew of him or had come in contact with him at some point since arriving in Texas. Stephen Austin was the reason they were all here.

Dixon sputtered but reached for his register. Cade offered his hand to the man who had lent his credibility to his claim, and Austin took it.

"Would that all my Indian problems could be solved so easily," Austin murmured as he transferred his congratulations to Lily. "Do you have any sisters, ma'am? If we had more women out here and fewer men, we'd settle a passel of problems."

"Her sisters aren't quite the same as Lily, sir," Ephraim explained, coming to stand beside his daughter. "She sets her sights on the man and not his money. Don't know that you want too many of her kind, judging by these rascals I see around me." He sent a scathing look to Dixon and his cronies.

"Let's just get this over with and go home," Lily murmured to Cade as he reached for the pen that Dixon handed him.

Cade sent her a look from under his brows that was easily interpreted, and Lily had the grace to blush. She hadn't meant that to sound as it did, but she could see that Cade had every intention of taking full advantage of it. And with a few strokes of that pen, he would have every right to.

She tried to pull her bonnet forward to hide the telltale stain of red on her cheeks. She didn't know what she was going to do when they got home and Cade made it clear that her bedroom was now his, too. She would worry about that later.

As Roy and Juanita stood beside her, Lily carefully penned her name into the book beside Cade's. He had signed it Cade de Suela, choosing his own name as he had said he would. She was now officially Mrs. Cade de Suela.

Nineteen

S etting the pen down, Lily looked up to find Cade's dark gaze fastened on her from beneath a heavy shock of black hair. He bent to give her a light kiss on the cheek, a token to signify their marriage. Any more in this public place would almost certainly cause a riot. As it was, a cheer rang out somewhere in the back of the room and was taken up as they walked through the crowd and out of the store. Weddings were not an everyday occurrence, and anything out of the ordinary was cause for celebration.

Travis elbowed his way through the crowd to place a hasty peck on Lily's cheek, giving Cade a glare of defiance after he did so. "It's customary to kiss the bride. And I'd suggest you get Lily the hell out of here before they decide a chivaree is in order. Ephraim and I will see that the kids get back home."

Cade might be slow to speak, but he wasn't slow to act. He held out his palm to Travis as a gesture of peace. The other man looked at the offering, glanced at Lily and Roy, and resignedly accepted Cade's hand with a firm shake. For the first time in his life, he was putting someone else before himself.

Without further ado, Cade caught Lily's waist and whisked her around the corner of the building and out of sight of the gathering well-wishers.

Lily wasn't prepared for the swiftness with which all this was happening. She had thought there would be time to adjust to her new status, time with her friends and family around her, time to walk beside Cade through town and pretend he really was her husband like Jim had been.

She had imagined a family dinner at home, a long evening ahead to get used to the idea that Cade would be joining her later, much later.

She wanted to protest as Cade threw her up on his gelding and climbed up to join her, but she was too stunned to say a word. She had worn her blue gingham for the occasion and she had to sit sidesaddle, clinging to Cade's firm waist as he wheeled the horse out of the paddock and onto the open road.

They flew out of town as if all the devils in hell were after them, but once out of sight, Cade slowed the horse and turned to inquire anxiously, "Are you all right? I wasn't thinking. The child . . . ?"

Lily leaned her head against his back and gasped for breath now that the horse had found a steady pace. She shook her head in answer to his question. "I rode an oxen wagon out here from Mississippi when I was four months gone with Roy. I am fine."

This was the kind of woman he needed. Cade swelled with a sudden desire to head for the trees and take possession of her in the long grass, but despite her strengths, his wife was a lady. She deserved something better than a grass bed. He didn't have much better to offer, but he would do what he could.

With that in mind, Cade turned the horse from the open road onto the prairie, heading for the distant woods. He sensed Lily's puzzlement, but it was easier to show than explain.

They rode for an hour over increasingly rough terrain as they drew closer to the river. Then Cade turned his horse northward and Lily knew they were on her property, but somewhere along the extreme boundary. The butterflies in her stomach were rapidly becoming something else as she leaned against the hard musculature of her husband's back and felt the sway of his hips with the movement of the horse. She hadn't forgotten a moment of their night together, and fear mixed with anticipation as they drew closer to his destination. Cade wasn't Jim. He would demand a great deal more from her than a hot meal and a clean house.

They stopped in a small clearing near a babbling brook. The sky was overcast and the pines added to the gloom, but their branches cut off the winter wind, giving the glade an air of tranquillity.

In the glade's center sat a tepee similar to the one Cade had taken Lily to back in the Indian village. As Cade helped her down from the horse, Lily stared at it with nervous interest. The heavy buffalo hides were overlaid enough to keep out any wind. With a small fire, it would be wonderfully warm. And solitary.

Cade had ensured that they would have complete privacy for their wedding night. Or day. Lily threw a look to the sun hiding somewhere directly overhead. It was only noon. Did he mean to take her to bed at noon?

"Go inside, out of the wind. I will have a fire started shortly." Cade gently pushed her in the direction of the tepee.

Lily hesitated, throwing him an uncertain look. "Is it yours?"

Amusement crinkled his eyes briefly as he met the questions in hers. "A tepee is transportable. It is mine. I brought it down from the village some weeks ago."

She wasn't going to question why he had done that. She knew damned well why he had done that. Giving him a sniff of disapproval, Lily turned, threw back the skin covering the doorway, and entered the darkened world that was Cade's only home.

She had reason to remember the soft furs of the buffalo robes covering the dirt floor. Brightly woven blankets sat neatly stacked at the bottom of what she assumed was to be their bed. An assortment of baskets and pottery was gathered to one side as if ready to be used upon the owner's return. Cade could move in here at any time and have all the comforts of home.

He entered, carrying wood for the fire, and the tent was suddenly narrow and confining. He filled the space with his presence, even when he knelt to lay the fire. Standing as far from him as she could, Lily shivered and rubbed her arms as she watched him work. He was the only man she knew who could make her feel small. She wasn't at all certain that she liked the sensation. How did other women accept this feeling of vulnerability?

When the flames began to flicker into life, Cade stood, measuring his height to hers. He met her gaze gravely before reaching out one big hand to remove Lily's shawl. He folded it carefully in half and laid it beside the baskets. Completely unsure of herself in this setting, Lily remained passive, waiting for his guidance. She felt no fear, only a dreadful uncertainty. She was his wife, but she didn't know him.

Dark eyes held hers as Cade reached to release her hair, and Lily shivered slightly at the intimacy of the gesture. The ribbons slid out easily, and he spread his fingers through her braid, separating it into a cascade of gold in the firelight.

His touch sent heated sensations flooding through her. Confronted with Cade's broad chest and towering height and hands that seemed to move like magic, Lily felt lost, as if she had no control over what was happening. Already his fingers were unfastening the tiny shell buttons of her bodice, and her heart was pounding so fast she feared it might leap from her chest as his knuckles brushed against her breasts.

"I have dreamed of how you would look in the daylight, without this burden of cloth." Cade skimmed the gown from Lily's shoulders, tugging the long sleeves loose until they hung from her waist.

There was only the thin muslin and ribbons of her best chemise to hide her from his gaze. Lily raised a hand to cover herself, but Cade caught it and held it to her side. He didn't speak but he didn't have to. His gaze devoured her near-nakedness, and she began to shiver beneath the intensity.

He released the ties at her waist. Her one petticoat fell unfastened to the floor, followed by the blue gingham. Chill bumps rose up and down Lily's arms, but it wasn't from the cold. The fire's heat was already sending smoke up the opening at the crown of the tent.

Cade's large hands closed over her shoulders, then slid

downward over her arms, drawing her closer. Stiffly, Lily obliged. He was her husband. She would obey.

But obedience had nothing to do with the kiss she fell into when Cade's mouth closed over hers. Lily's hands reached to grab his biceps for support as the kiss deepened. When his tongue claimed her mouth, her legs shook and she held on tighter. Desire, hot and heavy, flooded through her, and she returned the kiss with unexpected fever.

Her chemise followed the rest of her garments to the ground. The shock of her bare breasts grinding into the soft cotton of Cade's best shirt as his hands cupped her buttocks stimulated new sensations. Lily ignored the sudden draft across her skin. She was on fire inside.

Cade carried her to the buffalo robe and lay down beside her. Fully dressed, he covered her nakedness with his length. While his hand explored, his mouth implored, filling Lily with his need and extracting hers until all hesitancy had flown, replaced by the same urgency that had overtaken them once before.

As his hand found the moistness between Lily's thighs, Cade groaned and pressed against her, but he was determined to do this properly this time. Pulling away, he jerked his shirt from his pants and began to pull it over his head.

The absence of Cade's warmth left Lily fully exposed to her nakedness, but as Cade's shirt followed her clothing to the floor and his gaze burned across her skin, she no longer felt embarrassment. The broad brown chest hovering over her filled her with excitement, and she raised a hand to stroke the muscular planes thus exposed.

Cade didn't leave her time to explore. Determined to have her completely naked, he bent his attention to her few remaining garments. His hand kept touching her in intimate places, making the task more complicated than necessary, but Lily was nearly wild with desire by the time they finished.

"Beautiful," Cade murmured as he pulled her down to the furs again, his hand skimming over her breasts and coming to rest at the slight swell of her abdomen. His kiss brushed against her lips before moving to suckle at her breast, and Lily felt her hips lift in wild abandon, demanding equal attention.

Cade still wore the new buckskin trousers he had donned for the occasion, but he sat up to peel them off now. Lily gasped at the sight of his full nudity, but she wasn't given time to feel fear. He was over her and between her legs before she could take in the full extent of his size. Bronzed, hair-roughened thighs pushed against her pale soft ones, spreading them as he rubbed against her entrance.

"I don't want to hurt the child. Tell me what I must do to protect it," he demanded.

That simple request opened Lily's heart to him more surely than anything else he could have said. She spread her fingers across the rough squareness of his jaw and met the intensity of his gaze with a newly awakened tenderness.

"The child grows well above where even you can reach. Just be gentle with the child's mother."

His face flushed dark with desire, Cade bent to kiss her. The kiss deepened and enlarged and grew frantic until Lily curled her legs around him and pulled him inside even as he adjusted himself to the entrance of her body.

This time she could see the bronzed breadth of Cade's chest as he held himself over her. She dug her fingers into the thick trunks of his arms as he tried to curb his actions, but the urge was too strong for both of them. With a cry, they wrapped themselves together and thrust and fought until they found the rhythm that multiplied and climbed to a frantic crescendo.

Lily felt as if she were part of a mountain ready to explode as they reached the peak and climbed even higher. The tension carried her to near madness until the explosion came, shaking them both over and over. Even when the trembling stopped, Lily felt as if she had been reduced to little more than hot ashes. It was done, and she was his. There was nothing else left of her.

Somewhere in the mindless darkness that followed, Cade must have rolled his weight off her. Lily gradually grew aware that she was wrapped in his arms with a blanket pulled to cover their nakedness. She felt the heaviness of his arm around her, the soreness between her legs where even now he stirred, and the utter contentment of lovemaking. It was enough. She closed her eyes and slept.

She woke to find herself on her stomach and Cade straddling her legs. His kisses nipped at her ears and throat, and when his hand slid beneath her to press the place he had just taught her to respect, Lily instinctively rose to allow him entrance. His other hand encompassed her breast, and she gasped with the sudden eruption of desire he brought on as he entered her.

It was incredible what he could do to her. Even as she pumped against him in frantic need, he turned her over and slammed into her, driving her to new heights of desire. It couldn't go on, but she continued to cling to him even when there was nothing left but the hot liquids of their lust between them.

Cade pulled her against his chest and whispered soft words in Spanish against her ear. Lily recognized some of them, but not all. Perhaps he spoke in Apache. She just knew the sound of them warmed her heart.

"It's never been like this before," she murmured in wonderment as her hand boldly tracked the broad expanse of Cade's chest. Now that she had time to look, she could see the tattoos of his tribe on the upper part of his arm, and her fingertips moved to trace them.

"I am glad I do not hurt you." Cade's hand traced a path down her spine as his breathing slowed.

He had shown her an ecstasy she had never dared imagine, and all he could say was that he was glad he did not hurt her. Lily smiled against his shoulder and kissed him there. They came from such different worlds that they must look at every subject from different angles. It should be an interesting combination.

"Are we going to stay here like this all day?" Lily could feel the lower part of him stirring against her again.

She didn't think she had the strength to repeat their performances.

Cade turned her back against the rug and hovered over her. "All day and all night for as long as we can. You have made me wait forever."

Lily frowned slightly as she drew her hand along his chest. He was the same color all over. Perhaps his arms were a little darker. And his throat. She touched him there, learning all she could about him with her fingertips, admiring the contrast of white and dark. "I should have made you wait forever. We know nothing of each other but what we see. We cannot spend the rest of our lives together in bed."

"You worry too much. We have a roof over our heads and food in our stomachs. What more can we ask? There will be children and you will teach them as well as you have taught Roy. I will watch over your cattle and see that the herd grows bigger and that we get the best prices for them. Life is very simple."

Lily smacked his arm and tried to sit up. Cade obliged by moving aside and watching her. His hand continued to stray over the fullness of her breasts and occasionally lingered with curiosity over the curve of her abdomen.

"Don't give me your Indian monologue, Cade. That was a Spanish lawbook you were reading. I doubt that there are three men in all of Texas who could read that, much less understand it. You ought to be a lawyer, not a damned cowherder."

"My mother would cringe at your language. You are fortunate that she is dead and I do not have to take you home to meet her."

"That's a stalling tactic if I ever heard one, and I've heard lots of lawyers. How old are you, Cade?"

Perhaps he wasn't distracting her with his attentions, but he was distracting himself. She was even more beautiful than he had imagined. Her legs seemed to go on forever, and Cade wanted to feel them around him again. Her hair fell like desert sunshine down her back, and it was even light where he held his hand now. He felt her breathing grow irregular as he caressed her there, and he watched her lips part and grow moist, though they both ought to have been thoroughly satiated.

"I would say I have seen thirty-two winters. Why?"

Lily had almost lost her train of thought as Cade's fingers played dangerous games, but she focused on his eyes, reading their intensity, knowing it wasn't all lust. Caution lurked there, and he hid behind it.

"Where have you been for thirty-two years? What have you been doing? You didn't learn to read lawbooks riding Colonel Martin's range."

"The priests taught me those few years I consented to stay with them as a child. I'm a drifter, Lily. Don't make more of me than you see. Unless you wish me to make love to you again, you had better pull that blanket around you. I need to find you something to eat or our child will starve."

Lily made no move for the blanket, and in the end, they made love again, slowly this time, drawing the pleasure out until they were weary and exhausted and beyond caring where they were or what they wanted.

It was full dark and the fire had grown cold before they woke again. This time, they woke to their new responsibilities as husband and wife. Lily's stomach was growling with hunger, and though lying beside Cade she didn't feel the cold, it became noticeable when he moved. She imagined the life growing within her complaining of this treatment, and she reluctantly took Cade's hand as he helped her to stand.

"I will bring water and firewood while you dress. The snares I set should have found rabbit by now. I will be back shortly."

Cade pulled on his buckskins and strode out and Lily felt an odd lurch in her middle at the sight of the bronzed breadth of his back. He was her husband. She had married an Indian. Her sisters would have absolute fits when they found out.

She glanced down at her rounding stomach and smiled. He would give her the children she craved. She would have to spend the time between children worrying about how to prevent them from happening too frequently. She didn't think Cade was likely to tire of coming to her bed anytime soon.

And for some reason, Lily found that thought fully satisfying.

Twenty

Standing by their pallet before they retired for the night, Cade pulled a small object from his pocket and, catching Lily's hand, gently twisted it onto her finger. "I meant to give you this when we signed the book. There didn't seem to be an appropriate time."

Lily looked down at the flicker of silver in the firelight. The band was wide and heavy and intricately carved with delicate traceries of dark and light. It looked very Spanish and very old. There was no room for shyness between them anymore, and she looked up to meet Cade's gaze with the warmth of their astonishing intimacy. "Your mother's?"

He nodded, then with reluctance he offered the explanation she deserved. "It belonged to her mother and her grandmother. She gave it to me to sell so we might have food. I kept the ring and stole the food."

Lily felt a queer stirring in her stomach at this first voluntarily offered piece of Cade's past. She touched the wide band, then lifted her fingers to brush back a thick lock of black hair from his forehead. The ability to allow herself this boldness thrilled her, and she stepped closer, until he was forced to put his arms around her and she could lean against his shoulder. She sensed he had been reluctant to do so after his admission, but he wasn't in the least bit reluctant to hug her close once she was in his arms.

"Someday, will you tell me about your mother? I don't know how she could have survived in an Indian camp. She must have been a very strong woman."

"In her way, she was, but in the end, she wasn't strong

enough. Returning to civilization killed her." Cade pressed his lips to Lily's hair and the soft scent of the soap she had used filled his nostrils. The kind of women he had known in his life these last years had never smelled clean and healthy. Perhaps that, along with her hair, was what attracted him.

"You can't stop there. Why must I drag every word out of you? If you go back to grunting instead of talking, I'll pinch you."

Since he wasn't wearing a shirt, she had an ample expanse of skin to choose from. Cade grunted when she picked a small piece of his back just below his armpit. She twisted, and he punished her with his mouth. They were on the bed and laughing before either of them knew it.

"I knew you could laugh if you wanted." Lily wiggled free of Cade's hold and sat up. She wore no more than her chemise and a blanket, and the blanket was losing its grip on her shoulders.

In the firelight Cade could see the shadow of the valley between her breasts. She wasn't large, but well-rounded. He liked to think that his child added to that fullness. It gave him a feeling of belonging, something he hadn't known in a very long time.

"Indians don't laugh," Cade told her solemnly.

She didn't even give him a warning. Diving at him, Lily feathered her fingers beneath his arms and tickled until Cade was rolling with laughter as well as his attempt to hold her off without harming her.

"Cry uncle," she demanded, wiggling one hand loose from his grasp to tickle his ribs.

"Tio," he laughed, turning her over and strapping her spread-eagled against the robes.

"It's a good thing for you that Juanita has taught me some Spanish," Lily informed him with gravity, "or I should have to continue tickling you unmercifully."

Since he held her completely helpless, this was a lie of magnificent proportions, and Cade nearly doubled up with laughter at her audacity. He couldn't remember ever feeling this way, not even as a boy. He caught her in his arms and rolled over and began to lavish her with kisses.

"Stop that, Cade, before you break something," Lily admonished, struggling for a position a little more dignified than sprawling across his chest. As much as she enjoyed what this would lead to, there were other things here to consider, and she wasn't the kind to give up easily.

Cade instantly let her go and stared up at her worriedly. "Am I hurting you?"

With a lift of her eyebrows, Lily allowed her gaze to drift down Cade's rather awesome chest to the place where his buckskins covered his hips. "I was more concerned about you. I don't wish to wear you out too soon."

Cade gave a bark of laughter and grabbed her hair, tugging her down to lie curled against his side. "If I don't nip your boldness at once, you will become impossible. You do understand I don't intend for you to be my boss lady anymore?"

"Not that I ever was," Lily said, unperturbed. "Now tell me about your mother."

"She died."

In exasperation, Lily pinched him again. "Do you want to start this all over? You can talk. I've heard you. Why do you persist in this imitation Indian sign language?"

"Habit. What's the point of talking if no one is listening?"

Lily propped her elbows on his chest and glared down at Cade's strong, angular features. In this light he looked neither Indian nor Spanish. He was just Cade, a man with a chip on his shoulder a mile wide. Impulsively, she leaned over and bit his shoulder. It was solid and hard to grip, but she managed to sink her teeth in enough to register.

He hollered and jerked her back. Glaring, he asked, "What was that for?"

"I thought maybe I could chew my way through that chip," she said sweetly. "Did you think you'd married a fool white woman who would be content to have a man in her bed and a child in her stomach? I'd better give this ring back if that's the case."

Cade grunted and pulled her back to his side again. "I'm not stupid. You play the part of docile wife and daughter very well, but you're more like a wild mustang that stands still until the moment someone puts a saddle on its back. I don't mean to saddle you, but I'll put a bit in your mouth if you bite me again."

Cade could feel the soft heaves of Lily's laughter against his side, and he untensed long enough to allow himself a grin. He hadn't known he was taking on an undisciplined brat, and he rather suspected she hadn't known it either. The years of childhood that had been stolen from her were rapidly emerging. He just didn't know why he had been the one to set them free.

She began to nibble at his side and the sensation shot straight to his groin. With a growl, Cade jerked her head up to rest on his shoulder. "Unless you're ready for me to ride you again, you'd better behave. What did you want to know about my mother?"

Her stomach was resting near his hip, and Lily rather liked that sensation. "What would you like to tell me about her?"

Cade sent her an irascible look, but in the gathering darkness she couldn't see it. Surrendering, he sifted through memories he preferred not to think about. "She was very beautiful. My father had seen her out riding and led a war party just to steal her."

"Your father doesn't strike me as the kind of man to do that. He seemed peaceful enough to me."

"My father is a Lipan Apache, a warrior. Thirty years ago they controlled much of the territory west of here. Young men were expected to show their bravery. At the time he wasn't much interested in killing or stealing baubles; he wanted a wife. Stealing one was a mark of skill and bravery."

"Then Apaches are as foolish as those idiots in town who thought Juanita would be delighted to welcome the attentions of three of them at once. Men are stupid everywhere."

Cade stroked her hair. "Sometimes, yes. But my father did not rape my mother. Even my mother agreed to that. He made her his wife and when she was ready, he took her to his bed. Do you find it so hard to believe that a lady could desire an Apache?"

"Not in the least." Lily kissed his throat. "I find it hard to believe that she could know desire when so completely out of her element. He was a stranger. His people were strangers. They didn't speak the same language. He probably lived in a tent and she was no doubt used to an elegant home and servants. She must have been terrified."

She had automatically assumed that his mother came from wealth. In a country where poverty reigned supreme, that was an odd assumption, even if a correct one. Perhaps the ring had given it away. Cade found the peak of her breast and caressed it, enjoying the knowledge that the same jolt of sensation swept through them both at the touch.

"My father taught her not to be afraid. He knew some words of Spanish. Apaches have been dealing with the Spanish for years. My father is not an ordinary man. He sees the future when so many look to the past. He knew there was no stopping the white man. There were too many whites and too few Indians. That is why, when his tribe died, he took a wife among the people that you call Wacos. White men will not allow Indians to follow the buffalo much longer. They must learn to farm the land as the white man does. The Wacos have the knowledge to do this."

It was more information than she had ever expected to have from Cade, and Lily savored it. There was much to think about in what he had told her, but she didn't want his words to dry up while she pondered them. Storing them away for future perusal, she persisted, "If your father was so special, why did your mother leave him?"

"Because she could not learn Indian ways. I did not hear these things from my father or mother but from the old women of the village. My mother nearly died when I was born. I was too large for her. My father was a mighty warrior, and it was expected of him to look after the women of his wife's family. That is how it is done. If a woman has no husband or father to feed her, she will die, so she goes to her sister's house. The sister is grateful for the help not only in the many chores but also in the burden of bearing the warrior's children. If the wife has no sister, the warrior will look elsewhere."

"Your father brought home a second wife," Lily stated flatly. "It is a wonder your mother didn't kill him."

It wasn't amusing, but Cade chuckled at her tone. "I take it you will not appreciate it if I try to relieve your burdens by bringing home another woman, even when you are heavy with child."

"I am certain your consideration will so overwhelm me that I will take a shotgun to your hide. Anytime you are even tempted to look at another woman, you'd better remember that Travis is right at hand, and what's good for the gander will do for the goose. We're building a marriage out of next to nothing. What we have in bed is our only bond. I won't share it with another."

Cade wasn't laughing anymore. His big hand caught the nape of Lily's neck and held her where he could see her face through the darkness. "I only need one woman. Don't turn me away and I will never have need to look elsewhere."

Lily felt that command in the pit of her stomach. She was tied to this man for the rest of her life. This wasn't a game that would end with the dawn. No matter what he did or how angry he made her she would have to take this man into her bed or destroy everything. It was an intimidating thought, and she began to have some understanding of Cade's mother.

"I don't think it was all your father's fault," she whispered. The change of subject made Cade blink, and when he didn't answer, she continued, "I think your mother must have been afraid after you were born. I think she probably denied your father."

That was a very distinct possibility. Cade settled her back against his shoulder again. "Let us get this story finished so I can make love to you again. It does no good to try to guess what we will never know." At Lily's nod, he hurriedly completed the tale. "I grew up thinking my mother hated my father. He would teach me one thing and she would teach me the opposite. I did not understand their differences then. It was only after she persuaded a trader to take her back to civilization that she began talking to me as if I were old enough to understand. By then, she had learned that white men weren't as honorable as my father. They thought her an Indian whore. When she returned to San Antonio and found that her family had left for Mexico, she was without protection, and she was treated as a whore. I was eight when we left my father. I was twelve when she died."

His tone had grown bitter, and Lily knew better than to question more. To have so many words out of the taciturn foreman she had known was a miracle not to be denied. Gently, she kissed the place where she rested, and when he did not immediately respond, she began exploring his chest with her lips. When she found his nipple and tugged at it, Cade growled deep in his throat, and soon she was lying beneath him while his tongue taught her lessons she would never forget.

Later, much later, Lily lay beside Cade listening to him sleep. One hand went to cover the curve of her stomach while the other rested on the flat hard expanse of her husband's. None of this seemed quite real yet. Perhaps after they had had a few weeks of seeing each other over the breakfast table, arguing over money or the lack of it, listening to each other's complaints—perhaps then it would seem real. Now, she could only believe she was dreaming this man at her side and his child in her womb.

When she woke in the morning it was to a warm fire and a cold bed. Cade was already up and about. Realizing she was completely naked beneath the covers, Lily pulled the blanket around her and gradually forced herself to sit up. She could feel the imprint of Cade's body on every portion of hers, and just the thought made the various sorenesses burn. Lightheaded, she bent her head to her knees and remained motionless. This morning, the heavy silver band on her finger felt like a noose.

Cade came in to find her in this position, and he was

immediately on his knees beside her. "Is something wrong?"

The obvious concern in his voice revived her somewhat. Lily managed to look up and give him a small smile. "Nothing that another few weeks won't cure. I'll be fine. Just give me a few minutes."

"I didn't know the child was making you ill. You should have told me sooner."

Lily pressed her forehead back against her knees, avoiding the accusation in his eyes. "Normally, it doesn't. I suppose I overexerted myself. Or it doesn't like roast rabbit. I'm just a little queasy. I've been fine."

Only partially appeased, Cade threw some coffee grounds into a pot of water boiling over the fire. "I will take you home where you can rest."

So much for their wedding night. Lily wondered if Cade was regretting the things he had told her last night. She wondered if it would ever be possible to bring the laughing, talkative Cade back into the world as they knew it. She didn't think so, but if she dealt with him right, perhaps she could occasionally be the beneficiary of that hidden side of him. Or perhaps their children would learn to know him as he really was.

It would help if there were love between them, but there wasn't. Travis had pretty well taught Lily that love was an ephemeral emotion, more like an affliction of romantic young girls. She and Jim had got along well enough these last years. She could learn to do the same with Cade. It was just that there was only one side to Jim, whereas Cade had a hundred facets to explore.

"What are you going to do about Travis?" Lily asked, apropos of nothing as the queasiness eased and she lifted her head to watch Cade over the fire.

"If he's the man I think he is, he won't be there. If he comes back, he can use the cabin I've been using."

That seemed fair. Lily sighed and accepted the tin cup of coffee he handed her. "I hope I'm doing the right thing by Roy. Should I tell him the truth?"

"If he asks." Cade threw her an impassive look. "I'm

not the only one with secrets. Are you going to tell me about Travis?"

Lily shrugged. "There's nothing to tell. I was sixteen and the household was upside down with excitement over my older sisters' impending weddings. Travis appeared out of nowhere. We talked and laughed together. We were both young and lonely. I didn't know what we were doing when I slipped out to meet him at night. My mother was dead and no one had ever explained the facts of life to me. Travis made me feel beautiful and feminine, and I very much needed to feel that way. I thought that meant we were going to be married. Instead, I woke up one morning to find his wagon gone and no word of him to be had. Three months later, there was still no word and I'd learned what happened to girls who dallied with itinerant peddlers. Jim was looking for a wife and I offered myself. It's not a very original story."

"That's twice you've married because you had to. I won't say I'm sorry. I'd do it again."

"I know that, but I don't know why. If it's not the land, what is it?"

Cade gave her a curious look. "You have to ask?"

Lily became suddenly aware that she was sitting here naked talking to a man who the day before had been only her foreman. She glanced around for her clothing while struggling with his question.

She reached for her chemise as she replied. "I suppose I'm the only single woman over the age of fourteen for fifty miles around, except poor Anna Whitaker, perhaps."

Cade's impassivity gave way to exasperation as he gathered up her clothes and dropped them in her lap. "There are women enough out here for men like me. You're the first lady who has ever looked at me."

Lily looked up at him in surprise as she pulled her chemise on. "I doubt that there's a female over the age of fourteen who doesn't look at you. My word, Cade, we'd have to be blind not to see you."

He grinned and handed her a piece of toasted bread. "It's good to know my size warrants notice, at least. But that's not what I meant, and you know it. You're a lady, but you didn't pull your skirts away in distaste when I looked at you. You didn't talk to me as if I didn't have sense enough to eat. You listened, even when you were talking a blue norther."

Pulling on the gingham, Lily left it unbuttoned as she tried the toast and wrinkled her forehead at this striking new knowledge. "I can't pull away skirts I don't wear, but I suppose it's something to know you married me because I know how to talk and listen. I'm sure that's as good as being married because I know how to cook and clean."

A low rumble came from Cade's chest and Lily was rather uncertain as to its source, but when he came up from his crouched position to push her back down on the robes and kiss her, she thought perhaps he might be laughing at her.

"Anyone can cook and clean. No one can do what you do."

Cade didn't tell her precisely what she did that no one else could do, but Lily rather hoped that what followed was his way of showing what he meant.

She had to get dressed a second time when he was done making himself clear.

Twenty-one

They rode to the ranch a more rumpled version of their prior day selves. The children didn't seem to notice. Serena screamed a welcome and ran to Cade's arms while Roy ambled onto the porch and glanced uncomfortably from one to the other.

When Lily tried to hug him, he announced, "Travis is gone."

Lily merely smoothed his hair and smiled. "Travis is always gone. That's the way he is. He'll be back. Since Cade will be moving in with us, we'll set up a place for Travis in Cade's old cabin and he can stay there anytime he likes. Will that be all right with you?"

"Does that mean I can have my old room back?" Since he'd broken his leg, Roy had been sleeping downstairs in the main cabin and Travis had taken over his loft over the bedroom. He looked almost appeased at the thought of having the loft back.

Cade came up behind them carrying Serena. "The loft is yours. We'll put Serena where you're sleeping now. Now that there's a little time before planting, maybe we can start building an addition to your mother's cabin. There will be a new baby come summer, and I don't think your grandfather would enjoy sharing his room."

Roy looked shyly at his mother at this casual mention of a baby, but she merely took Serena and tickled her as if the news were of no moment. He nodded like a man of the world and went back inside to inform his grandfather of the changes that were coming.

Lily didn't hide her relief as she looked up at Cade. "He's taking this rather well, don't you think?"

"About as well as can be expected. He's a good boy, Lily. Quit worrying."

That was easy for him to say, but not so easy for her to do. While Cade took his horse back to the paddock, Lily followed her son inside. Her father was calmly rocking in her chair, listening to Roy's chatter. He threw Lily a speaking look as she entered.

"So your new husband is going to allow me to stay?" he inquired acerbically. "Does he think I have nothing better to do than watch over a passel of brats?"

"There was never a question about that, Daddy. The choice has always been yours. I just thought you were enjoying it out here. You've worked all your life. Why shouldn't you have a chance to sit back and decide what you want to do next? You must have someone capable running the store if you've been comfortable being away this long."

Ephraim sniffed and gave his daughter a skeptical look. "Your sisters thought I was too old to run the store anymore. Elizabeth's husband hired a man to take over. If you would have married that Travis fellow like I asked, we could have gone home and taken it back."

"Travis doesn't want to leave Texas any more than I do. And it was Ollie you wanted me to marry. I'm sorry, Daddy, but nothing is going to make me go back there again. You're welcome to stay. As cheap as whisky is out here, maybe you could start another store. You certainly know the business."

"Now that's a thought. I'll give it some consideration."

Lily left him there to consider it. She knew perfectly well why Elizabeth's husband had hired someone to take over the Emporium. Her father was already well into his cups and it was scarcely noon. What dowry they had was wrapped up in the Emporium, and a drinking man could destroy it easily. She wouldn't begrudge Elizabeth saving what she could, but her sister could have been a little softer on their father's pride. He'd done his best to hide the hurt these last months, but it was showing today.

Lily didn't understand what made a man turn to drink when he knew what he was doing to himself and to his family. Whenever her father picked up a bottle, it was as if he were rejecting her. The hurt never quite went away, but she was learning to live with it. She had too much else in her life for it to be any other way. Every day put that much more distance between them. After nine years, the distance was fairly complete. She would respect him as her father, but he couldn't influence her life any longer.

Juanita sent her a sidelong look when Lily entered the kitchen, but the contentment in Lily's expression was evident even beneath the frown over her father's behavior, and Juanita gave a covert smile.

"No esta un monstruo?" she asked innocently as Lily checked the pots cooking over the fire.

Lily blushed and blamed the heat from the flames. "Cade is not a monster. He is a good man."

"There is no such thing, just different levels of evil. They are all of the devil."

That was quite a mouthful from Juanita. Lily put down her spoon and confronted the smaller woman. "I have been fortunate in the men I've known. My father drinks too much and makes my family unhappy, but he is not evil, nor is he a devil. He is a good father when he is not drinking. Jim was not a particularly brave man or a wise one, but he did his best to be fair. Did you ever see anything evil about him?"

Juanita shook her head. "But he desired land like other men desire women. He could have been."

"Desire is not evil. You desire children, don't you?"

Juanita looked uncomfortable and returned to kneading her bread rather than answer.

"I know you do. That desire isn't evil. Stealing a child might be evil, but desiring one isn't. Those men back in town desired you. That wouldn't have been evil if they'd come to court you and showed you respect. But they were drunk and wicked and they took what they wanted instead of earning it. That was evil, but it does not make them devils."

"You are wrong. There are devils. You just don't wish

to know of them. Ask your husband sometime. He knows of devils."

Lily gave up. Juanita's beliefs were ingrained, and there was no chance of persuading her out of them. She doubted that Cade had any superstitions, but Indians were known for their strange beliefs. Perhaps he did. She didn't want to hear of them, if so.

But Juanita wouldn't leave the subject alone. That night when they gathered around the table for supper, she daringly spoke directly to Cade—unheard of for a woman who seldom said two words to any man and only then if coerced.

"You will tell her the devil exists." Juanita slammed a plate down in front of Cade as he took his seat.

Cade took the demand in stride. Reaching for a piece of bread, he broke it in half and without even inquiring as to the origin of the subject, answered, "I've seen him walk on two legs, yes."

Lily glared at him. "Shame on you. Don't encourage her nonsense. She will be feeding us ground cactus to prevent hexes if you don't watch out."

Cade raised a questioning eyebrow in her direction, then proceeded to slather his bread with the newly made butter. "No ground cactus for me, Juanita. Good is the best preventive against evil."

Lily threw up her hands in disgust and returned to cutting Serena's food into small pieces. Roy was the one who eagerly grasped the topic.

"Have you seen the devil, Cade? Granddad read me a story about the devil in the Bible."

"There are many sorts of devils, Roy. Your main concern is not to become one. It's very easy to do if you turn your eyes away from what is right."

That wasn't what an eight-year-old wanted to hear. He persisted. "How do you know a devil when you see one?"

"By his actions. He thrives on the pain and suffering he brings to those around him. Now eat your meal."

Roy chewed on his thoughts along with his food and gradually came back to the subject that bothered him. "There was a man in town yesterday after you and Mama left. I heard some of the men call him a Spanish devil. I saw him kick a dog, but the lady he was with seemed to like him real well."

"That's just Ollie's friend from Béxar," Lily objected. "The men don't like him because he's Mexican, but he's been helping Bert Dixon with the boundary lines. There are a lot of Mexicans who are making claims to some of the lands west of here. Just because he's different doesn't make him a devil."

"A man who kicks dogs isn't a saint," Cade said drily. "What is his name?"

Lily frowned as she tried to remember. "He's not around often or for very long. Ralph or Bert mentioned his name once. Ricardo?"

Cade froze, then slowly lowered his knife to the table. "Ricardo? Short, distinguished-looking? Gray at his temples?"

Lily looked surprised. "I suppose. I only caught a glimpse of him once. Like I said, he's not here much."

Cade looked to the small woman hovering near the fire who refused to eat with them. "Juanita, he is the one?"

Hesitantly, Juanita nodded.

Cade picked up his knife again. "Juanita is right. Evil walks on two legs. Stay away from this man."

When he said nothing else, Lily wanted to kick him, but Roy had been distracted by the pie Juanita hurriedly placed on the table, and she wasn't ready to expand upon the subject for his benefit.

Later, Lily was too flustered by her father's ribald comments to Cade as she prepared the children for bed to return to the subject of Ricardo and evil. Her father's suggestive words seemed to roll right off Cade's broad back as he put up a shelf Lily had requested beside the fireplace. But Lily's face felt like it was on fire when it was time for her to retire. She tried not to show it, but pregnancy made her sleepy, and there was never time to sneak a quick nap.

"I'll not keep Cade up too long," Ephraim called to her as Lily tried to slip out the door to the dogtrot. "I figure he'll pound a hole in that wall if he has to wait much longer."

She wished her father wouldn't drink. He was a much nicer, more understanding man when he didn't. But he had so isolated himself from the world by now that the bottle was his only companion. Trying to be understanding, Lily slipped into her room and hastily began to wash.

Cade entered before she was done. It was going to take a while before she grew used to this. Jim had always politely waited until she was nearly asleep. Cade evidently wasn't even going to give her time to wash. He was unfastening his shirt as he came across the room toward her.

He took the soap she dropped in the washbowl and began to scrub himself while he watched her. She had removed her gown and pulled her chemise to her waist, leaving her breasts uncovered to his gaze. Lily thought of hiding herself, but it was a ridiculous thought considering what they had done the night before.

As if she did this every night of the week, Lily pushed her chemise off and bent to pick it up and put it away.

"Don't tempt me, Lily. If you want to get some sleep, put your nightgown on and get in bed where I can't see you. I'm about to bust my pants just looking at you right now."

Lily held the chemise to her breasts as she turned and looked at him. Cade had soap lathered across his chest and under his arms, but her interest lay a little lower. She let her gaze fall to the fastenings of his trousers, and she felt a lump form in her throat. He wasn't being facetious. He had changed into the old denims and she was quite certain they were about to give way beneath the strain of what he kept hidden behind those buttons.

Her gaze traveled back to his. "I'm ready when you are," she murmured complacently.

Cade gave a sigh of relief and grinned as she sashayed back to the bed, giving him a full view of her swaying hips and firm buttocks. He had been told by other women that he asked too much. For a lady like Lily he was fully prepared to grant concessions, particularly when she carried his child. He was thoroughly relieved to discover that she meant to ask for none.

So the question of good and evil and a Spaniard called Ricardo disappeared with the night.

Lily caught a glimpse of Cade entering the barn, and grimly, she threw off her apron and hurried out of the house after him. She was sick and tired of being confined to the house for one reason or another, and this time she had a bone to pick with Mr. Cade de Suela, one she preferred to pick in private.

Cade was taking a harness down from the wall when she entered. He continued what he was doing as she approached. Despite what went on behind their bedroom doors, he wasn't the kind of man to show any emotion outside of them. He nodded warily as Lily placed her hands on her hips and confronted him.

"I heard you've got the men plowing under the cotton field."

Since there wasn't any particular reply he could make to that, Cade waited.

"Did they collect the late crop? If we're not going to get the cattle to market we're going to need the extra seed next year."

"We won't be growing cotton." Finding the weak place in the harness he had been checking while she talked, Cade pulled the rotten piece of leather off and threw the harness in a stack to be repaired. Callused brown hands moved with swift assurance over the rest of the tackle. Lily's words seemed to roll off his broad back.

Lily tried to hold her temper. "Don't you think that's something we ought to discuss? Don't I have some right in this decision?"

"Cotton requires too much labor. I won't hire slaves." As if that was the last word on the subject, Cade began moving toward the door.

Lily ran around in front of him and slammed the barn door closed. "And I won't let you run this place into bankruptcy. Cotton is our only cash crop besides cattle.

How do you propose we stay alive if we don't sell either?"

"Corn." He could easily lift her away from the door and walk out, but Cade kept his hands to himself and waited for her to move aside.

"There's no market for corn!" Lily declared with exasperation.

"There will be if we grind it. We can sell it here and save the shipping. If we were closer to San Antonio, we could sell milk and butter. People in the city can't supply their own."

"You want to make us backwoods farmers! One bad year and we could be wiped out. Grow corn if you want, though Lord knows where you'll get a mill to grind it, but I want cotton in that field. Go plow your own if you want corn."

Cade simply waited.

Lily glared at him with mounting fury. She was virtually helpless in this debate. The men would take orders only from Cade. If she told them to do something, they would consult Cade first. Except for Jack and one or two of the others, the hands they now employed had all been hired by Cade. They had no difficulty accepting his taciturn authority. Her frustration escalated when he refused even to discuss her opinions.

"I mean it, Cade. You told me this is my land. I ought to have at least some say in how it is used."

"I won't have slaves. You cannot have cotton without slaves."

"We can hire Ralph's for one more year, just until we have a little cash ahead."

"No."

"Damn you, I wish I'd fired you when Ollie told me to." Defeated but refusing to admit it, Lily swung on her heel, threw open the door, and marched out toward the paddock.

Before Lily could reach the horses, Cade was behind her, catching her waist and holding her kicking to his side. Always aware of his greater strength, he spread his legs and braced himself so he could pull her up against his chest where neither of them could harm the other.

Lily's head jerked angrily, and her long braid swung from her shoulder and down her back as she glared at him, face to face.

"If you ride, you must take someone with you."

"Says who? You're not my boss. Put me down, Cade. I'm a grown woman. I can go anywhere I want."

"Jim was a grown man and he lost his life out there alone. Promise me you will go nowhere without company."

"And if I don't?" Here was an area where she could defy him, and Lily faced him triumphantly. The fact that Cade held her so close his belt buckle pressed into her stomach did not go unnoticed, but she was too angry to react differently.

"I will have Abraham follow you around all day. If you want to pay one of the men to watch over you, then defy me in this."

And Abraham would do anything Cade told him. Wriggling violently, Lily escaped his grasp and spat, "I hate you," before retreating indignantly to the house.

The honeymoon was over. Cade watched her slam into the cabin, and then he returned to the barn to get the poncho he had left there. The rain could turn to snow before the day was over. February weather was like that.

Twenty-two

The tension between the newlyweds escalated to a noticeable degree when Cade rode out leaving only a message with Juanita that he would be back in the morning. Lily couldn't believe her ears when she received the message, but she refused to make their arguments public. Acting as if Cade had already discussed his departure with her, Lily merely went about her chores as usual.

With Lily's last words still ringing in his ears, Cade maneuvered his gelding through the dense thicket of trees in the direction of his father's camp. Her words had torn through him as no other's could, and he knew the injury inflicted would be slow to heal. He wanted Lily's respect, not her hatred. He was accustomed to hatred. He had learned to live with it. But not from Lily. He wasn't certain what to expect from a wife, but he wanted it to be more than he'd received in the past from the people around him. He knew he was running away from the problem, but he hoped he was running in the direction of a solution.

The horse practically knew the way, so Cade had more than enough time to ponder the argument. He had desired Lily from the instant he had seen her wearing those hip-hugging denims and sitting straight in the saddle staring down a group of men. At the time he had considered her unobtainable, but when he had found just how obtainable she could be, he had not hesitated, even knowing the number of difficulties he would create. Now he was going to have to start resolving them.

He had wanted Lily because she was a lady, but because she was a lady he couldn't treat her as he would a whore like Maria. A whore's pleas could be ignored to a great extent because she was being paid to do as he pleased. In this case, the tables were turned. Lily was giving to him. Granted, Cade knew his knowledge of this land and the men who worked it was as valuable as the land itself, but it was not a tangible possession, and mankind thought in terms of tangible possessions. So in Lily's eyes he ought to be doing as she pleased, not the other way around.

But now that he had a lady wife and a child on the way and lands behind him, he was in a position to do more than just survive. There was a debt owed him that he had given up for lost many years before. Lily had returned hope and the need for a future. It was time to call in that debt. Knowing Ricardo was in the territory gave him a better incentive. The white man's arrow in Jim Brown's back was becoming just a little clearer.

This time, however, Cade was in a position to take the offensive. He wouldn't wait until Ricardo had him cornered and he had no choice but to kill or be killed. The timing was wrong, though. With the damned rebels holed up in the Alamo, begging Santa Anna to come after them, it wasn't a time to be on the roads, particularly in that direction. He was going to have to decide whether to act now or wait to see what spring brought.

His father greeted him without surprise. The older man's fringed buckskin shirt hid most of his scars and tattoos, but he didn't look any less fierce for that. His warlock had turned gray but was still worn knotted long and decorated as became his status. The women and children went off chattering on their own business as father and son sat beside the fire sharing a pipe. Cade accepted the stew he was given and waited for his father to grant permission to speak.

"When will the child come?"

That wasn't the opening he had been hoping for, but Cade answered obediently, "When the corn reaches its height." He shouldn't be surprised by his father's knowledge. El Caballo had taught all his sons well. The youn-

gest two walked boldly through town when they wanted
and hid in the grass when it suited them to do so. They
were only part of his father's eyes and ears.

"It is past time you raised warriors of your own. You
have chosen your woman well. She will bear you many
sons."

"Unlike your mother," the unspoken words said. Right
at the moment Cade wasn't entirely certain that was a
correct assumption, but he wasn't here to argue with his
father. "She is strong," he agreed. "But I would not have
her travel when she is great with child. Have you had
word from Béxar?"

His father drew deeply on the pipe before answering.
"The walls are being rebuilt." He gave his son a long
look. "It is not good to return to that place. Your sons
will grow strong here."

"My mother's lands belong to me," Cade replied simply.

That was a concept his father could understand. His
first wife had brought no dowry in the way of horses or
any other wealth to add to the consequence of her children. Land was not something that could be possessed as
far as El Caballo was concerned, but his son had grown
up learning a white man's ways. If that was the dowry his
mother possessed, then it was up to Cade to claim it. His
father nodded a reluctant understanding.

"Their army approaches," he warned. "The snow
slows them. They are fools to travel when the days are
short."

It was going to be a race against time. Cade stiffened
at that knowledge, allowing his mind to run over all the
possibilities to extract the probable ones. It was a dangerous game he played. He didn't want to involve Lily or the
children in it.

Accepting his father's offer of a bed in his lodge rather
than seeking out the tepee he had shared with Lily only
a week before, Cade retired alone with his thoughts. He
had slept alone most of his life, but this past week had
taught him how much more desirable it was to share a
bed with a warm and willing woman. Even when he

could not be with Lily, he desired her. Surely that need
would disappear with time, but for now just his wish to
know how she and the child fared became a pressing
urge. If it were not the height of foolishness to ride
through the darkness, he would return to Lily and the
cabin tonight.

Cade set out at daybreak, but he hadn't gone far before
he realized he was being followed. Suspecting the iden-
tity of his followers, he hid his grin. He needed to talk
with those two.

He carried a rifle, but he used it only when he needed
game. He reached for it now. The slight rustle of an ev-
ergreen branch ahead could have been a squirrel. A white
man might never have noticed, but a red man would. The
boy had a lot to learn.

When the slight figure leapt for his back, Cade was
ready. Twisting, he caught the boy in one arm while
wheeling his horse from the path and the other mischief
maker's attack. He caught the boy in the stomach with the
stock of his rifle, knocking him from his pony and onto
the pine needles of the path. Leaping from his saddle with
a mighty whoop, carrying the younger one with him,
Cade straddled one half brother while holding the other
one throttled at the neck with his arm.

They glared at him in silence until he grinned.

"Don't try it on any Comanches until you practice
more," Cade admonished in their tongue.

At his lack of animosity, the younger one began to
chatter excitedly while the older grudgingly climbed out
from beneath Cade and sat in the path, listening.

Cade gave the silent one an affectionate cuff on the
head. "We have the same father. We know the same
tricks. You are good. I can use your help."

The boy didn't visibly brighten, but his sullen look dis-
solved into one of wary interest.

"I am going to Béxar. I need someone to watch out for
my woman and household while I am gone, but I don't
wish them to know. If there is trouble, you must judge
whether or not you can deal with it or if it will take many.
Our father can get word to me if I am needed. Do this

well, and I will show you where the buffalo can be found when I return."

This last was the persuasive argument. Watching after women and children was unrewarding, but a buffalo hunt would make warriors of them. Wacos were not warriors. There were no men in the tribe willing or able to search out the herds that lingered too long in Comanche territory. Cade's offer was the best they'd ever heard.

The bargain was struck, and Cade rode off feeling a little better about what he intended to do. His half brothers were young, but they were skilled. They would have no defense against a Comanche attack, but that wasn't the enemy that Cade feared. They could out-fight and out-maneuver any white man in town.

When he returned to the ranch, the men were carrying out the orders he had given them before he left, and Cade was at leisure to return to the house and settle his differences with Lily. When he saw the gaudily painted wagon in front of the cabin, he cursed.

When Cade entered, Travis was leaning against the fireplace sampling a piece of cake and teasing Juanita about his granny's cake being better. He looked up at Cade's entrance and grinned.

"Sure am glad I'm not in your shoes, *hombre*. Lily's not a mean-tempered woman, but I know a storm a'brewin' when I see one. Want me to soften her up some first?"

Cade gave this insolence the respect it deserved. Ignoring Travis, he swung Serena into his arms and asked Juanita, *"Donde está?"*

Juanita replied in the same language, "She rode out to the cotton field."

Unconcerned that his knowledge of Spanish went only as far as the word *"hombre,"* Travis continued nibbling his cake, interpreting the exchange without need of translation. "She took Ephraim with her. She's already polished the old man off this morning. Told him he wasn't going to get another sip of whisky until he got out of the house and got some exercise. I think Roy is riding shotgun."

At least she had obeyed one of his orders, although Ephraim and Roy weren't precisely the company he had meant for her to take.

Cade handed Serena to Juanita. "She needs to go to the privy."

Wordlessly, Juanita took the child and left the two men alone.

"What's the word from San Antonio?" The Americans seldom added the name "de Béxar" to the old town. Cade had learned to blend in with his surroundings a long time ago by using the language of the company he was in.

"Crockett's arrival has raised spirits some. Houston wants the fools to get the hell out. The mercenaries want to take the offensive and march on Matamoros. Far as I can tell, all the settlers went back to their farms. I doubt if you could get any three people to agree on anything right now, and even if you could, they'd change their mind the next day."

"They know Santa Anna is coming?" Cade helped himself to the cake.

Travis watched him shrewdly. "Nobody knows anything. Rumor has it that some of the Mexican citizens on our side have spies down on the border, but it's not likely Bowie's men are going to pay attention to anything a Mexican tells them. Most of them are drunk half the time anyway. The army in Goliad created such havoc that all the citizens have fled, so they have the place to themselves now. Have you heard anything?"

"He's coming, all right. It's just a matter of when he gets here."

Travis stuck his hands in his pockets and regarded Cade warily. "I want to be around to see what happens. If it's war, you're going to need all the hands you can get. Roy is all the family I've got; I mean to look after him."

Cade nodded stoically at this admission. "If you're staying, take my cabin. Roy's moved back to the loft." Licking his fingers clean, he strode out without further explanation.

Finding a fresh horse, Cade rode out for the cotton field. Lily was less apt to say things she didn't mean in public. Of course, there was always the chance that she wouldn't say anything until they were behind closed doors and she could flail his hide. Living with another person was going to take some getting used to.

She'd evidently persuaded the men to stop their plowing until she had time to go through the remnants of the cotton, salvaging what hadn't been ready when the hired pickers went through. Cade cursed as he watched his wife stooping to the labor, her father and Roy working the rows on either side of her.

She hadn't yet surrendered trousers, but she was wearing baggy ones instead of the tight denims. And the way she wore her loose shirt tied over top and covered by his old poncho told Cade she couldn't get all the buttons on these pants fastened either. The damned braid glittered golden in the weak sunshine.

Inspiration struck Cade as he dismounted and crossed the field. Lily was doing her best to ignore him, but that couldn't go on forever. He took the sack from her shoulder and waited for her to straighten. He half expected her to come up swinging, but she merely raised her fists to her hips and glared at him coldly.

"Why did you bother returning? Didn't your squaw stroke your masculine pride?"

He didn't know whether to kiss her or hit her. Judging neither to be appropriate, Cade shouldered the bag and threw a damper on her hostility. "The child will need clothes. I have come to ask if you will go to town with me to buy the appropriate materials. Perhaps you would like some for yourself also. And Roy."

Lily stood there for a minute and stared at him. She supposed other men would have come with a mouthful of apologies and a handful of flowers. Cade simply skipped all the in-between arguments and pleas and went on to the next subject. She might as well try arguing with herself.

"You're not forgiven," she informed him. "And I'm not going anywhere until I gather the rest of this."

"Me and Roy will do it tomorrow," Ephraim intruded, seeing Roy's crestfallen expression. In the end it was easier to surrender than to fight. Lily gave in to the majority and agreed to accompany Cade to town. She knew perfectly well that the trip could wait until Saturday, but now that it had been mentioned, she was as eager to go as Roy was.

Not that they needed to spend a lot of money on infant clothes. Lily had carefully packed all of Roy's away against the time she would need them again. And the chest of drawers Cade had carried into the house for Serena was filled to overflowing with everything a little girl would need. But just the idea of looking at a few soft flannels and maybe an eyelet or two made the child's coming a little more real. She had been afraid to admit its existence earlier. Now she wanted to revel in her accomplishment.

Lily held the sprigged cotton across her work-roughened palms, then brushed the fabric's softness against her face. The child would be born during hot weather and wouldn't need much clothing, but perhaps for the cooler nights of autumn . . . ?

It was an extravagance they could ill afford. Moving to the unbleached muslin, she began to count the yardage. Washed and dyed, it would make any number of sturdy garments for all of them. She could use a new chemise now that her old one was beginning to stretch its seams. And Serena could use a simple shift that was easier to wash than the extravagant laces Cade had bought for her.

The usual idlers weren't around. Most of them had gone to Gonzales and San Antonio to urge the rebels on. Some of the men might have even joined the army to speed the progress of the war. The steady stream of immigrants demanded the opening of more land. With Santa Anna refusing to release land to Americans, there was every reason to expect violence. The idlers expecting to profit from land sales would see to that.

Lily didn't hear Ollie come in until he was beside her.

Surprised, she turned and smiled. "Ollie! Has the council done all its work then? Do we have new laws I need to know about?"

Ollie took her elbow and steered her around the table of yard goods. "I need to talk to you. Come back here and . . ."

For a large man, Cade walked very lightly. He had stayed outside while Lily and the children shopped, but he was at Lily's side now before anyone heard his entrance.

Cade never touched Lily in public, but his position behind her was proprietary as he greeted the storeowner. "Clark," he nodded. "Thought you were in San Felipe."

Ollie's expression was grim as he replied, "I could wish you were elsewhere also."

Lily grabbed a bolt of eyelet and held a length out between the two men. "Wouldn't this be lovely for a christening gown?" She turned ingenuous blue eyes to Ollie. "Do you suppose if we're going to be a republic we could have preachers? I'd dearly love to see a church again. Perhaps by the time the baby comes we could have a preacher for the christening."

Cade's arm came around Lily's waist and he pulled her behind him as Ollie's big hands clenched into fists and his face took on an almost purple hue, but the tall man managed a curt nod and a respectful reply to Lily's question.

"We'll have freedom of religion. That should bring them running. I heard the Methodists are already arriving. Now, if you'll excuse me . . ."

The grip on Lily's waist relaxed as Ollie made his way past the barrels and crates to the back of the store. Lily carefully put the eyelet back in its place.

Cade picked it up and handed it back to her. "You will need it for the christening gown. If the preachers don't arrive, we will go to Béxar. I know a priest there."

"It is too costly, Cade. Elizabeth showed me how to tat. I will try to remember enough to make a bit of lace. It isn't as if the gown will have much use."

Before she could put the bolt back on the table, Cade

took it to the counter and the silent woman who had watched the whole episode without blinking. She blinked now as Cade loomed over her.

"We will have some of this," he said slowly, as if she were deaf or stupid.

The woman blinked again, then looked to Lily for instruction.

Cade picked up a bolt of the cotton with tiny lavender nosegays and added it to the eyelet. "Enough of this for a gown for my wife."

Lily opened her mouth to protest, then shut it again as she saw the fierce intensity of Cade's dark eyes. Grabbing the unbleached muslin before he could discover the silks, she shoved it into his hands. "We will need the whole bolt of that, Cade."

The clerk's stare came unglued then. Hastily reaching for a slip of paper, she began to record the sale. Satisfied, Cade glanced around the shop to see if there was anything else to be added to the order. He found Roy staring wistfully at a display of hats.

Cade walked over and located the smallest one. The stiff felt came down over Roy's ears.

"We will need to make one that fits," Cade said when Roy's face fell with disappointment at the size.

Roy eyed him warily. "Can you make hats?" Since Cade never wore one, the question was reasonable from a boy's point of view.

Cade appeared to measure Roy's head with his hand. "Raccoon looks like the right size. Would raccoon do?"

Roy's eyes lit with delight. "Real raccoon? One of the Tennessee militia had a raccoon hat. Will it have a tail and everything?"

"Ever seen a raccoon without one?" Cade lifted Serena from Juanita's arms and put his hand into the candy barrel. "Lady, put four pieces of hoarhound on that bill," he called to the clerk. Dividing the candy between the children, he freed a hand to reach in his pocket to produce a pouch that clinked with coins. Handing it to Lily, he said, "Get what you need. I'll take these two outside."

Lily's fingers closed around the pouch in astonishment. It crinkled with real cash money as well as coins. She hadn't seen cash since the days of her father's store. Practically everything they had done since coming to Texas had been by barter or credit. Jim had always dealt what coins they acquired sparingly. Before she could question or refuse, Cade had gone out the door.

Juanita and the store clerk stared at Lily until she felt forced to look in the pouch. "Oh, my," she murmured, before drawing it closed and reaching for the brushed cotton she had admired earlier. Cade's child would have a few things of its own.

"Ain't never seen an Indian with cash money before," the clerk spoke for the first time since they entered, curiosity getting the better of her. "It's not wampum now, is it?"

"I recognize real money when I see it." Finding a particularly pleasing blue linen, Lily laid it on the counter with the rest. She would be confined to the house before long. It wouldn't hurt to measure Cade for a new shirt. She would be able to take a break from tiny baby clothes.

"You really married to an Indian?" The woman's curiosity, once released, was unquenchable.

"I am married to a man." Lily slapped the bolt on the counter. "Let me see your threads and buttons."

When Lily finally left with her purchases, Cade was leaning against the storefront, hands in pockets, watching Roy lead Serena around on his pony. At Lily's appearance, he hastily stood up and grabbed the packages. In doing so, he bent near her ear and whispered, "A man, Lily?"

"A stupid one," she responded, sticking her nose up and heading for the wagon.

"Not as stupid as Clark. I didn't let you go." Undaunted, Cade flung the packages in the wagon and helped Lily up.

"Ollie isn't dumb. He's a coward. He lost Miss Bridgewater because he was terrified to court her. She married a lesser man out of desperation. I cannot imagine how he found the gumption to come out and visit me the few times he did."

Cade had a thought or two on that himself, but he had as yet been unable to confirm them. Whistling to himself, he disregarded Lily's insult and allowed the balm of her approval to ease an earlier pain.

Twenty-three

The shots rang out as the oxen wagon rolled out of town.

Fear pierced Cade's heart more surely than any bullet as he kicked his horse into action. He had come out with just women and children, leaving Ephraim and Travis behind. His overconfidence could be the end of the future he had so brashly thought to carve for himself.

"Get down, all of you! Roy, move! Get back to town." Riding his horse between the wagon and the attackers, Cade waited to see his orders obeyed before galloping in the direction of the shots. They could blow him to hell, but he wasn't going to give them another chance at Lily and the children.

Another shot rang out, sending the gray gelding skittering nervously, but Cade had his target located now. Smoke drifted from behind Ollie's barn, and Cade, his jaw set grimly, swung to the side of the horse, Indian style, out of the attacker's range as he spurred it on.

People were pouring out of the buildings in the previously sleepy town. Gunshots on a Saturday night were to be expected, but midday and midweek called for explanations. Several of the men were saddling up, and Cade prayed they had the sense to cover the wagon. He didn't have the time to linger and find out.

By the time he reached the barn, the sniper had disappeared. Ollie came running up from the store, and Cade cast a suspicious glare toward him, dismounting to investigate the spot where he was certain the man had stood just moments before. The air reeked of gunpowder, and close inspection turned up a carelessly lost bullet. Cade tossed it in his hand as he gazed at the trampled grass and mud, then looked at Ollie's feet as the other man came up beside him.

Ollie wore ill-fitting leather shoes, as most men in this country did if they weren't wearing moccasins. Cade looked again at the distinct heel print in the dirt. Boots were nigh onto impossible to find unless one came from Mexico City and had money to throw around. The sniper had worn boots.

"What happened?" Ollie demanded, clutching his shotgun at his side as his gaze drifted nervously to the woods beyond the barn.

Cade glanced back to the wagon where Lily and the children waited. Men were surrounding it, and even Roy was riding back now that the shooting had stopped. Cade gave the other man an angry look. "I could ask you that, but since the fool was too far away to do any damage, I'll let it go this time. But if anything should happen to Lily and the children, I'll be back."

Mounting the gray, Cade left the other man to stand furiously in the mud as he urged his horse back to the road. Ollie hadn't done it, but Cade ventured to guess a certain friend of Ollie's had. Damn. He had thought he was ahead of the game this time.

Lily looked worried as Cade approached, but she had the sense to keep quiet while the men around them asked excited questions. Serena was crying and Juanita rocked her, crooning quietly while the men badgered Cade.

"Probably a kid shooting rabbits," Cade dismissed the episode disinterestedly. "The range was too far for anything else."

There seemed to be some reluctance to accept that, and several of the men rode over to the barn to see for themselves, but the excitement was over and there was little to be done. Several gave Cade suspicious glances and the murmur of "Indian" was heard more than once as they talked among themselves, but with Lily present, nothing else could be said.

Lily took a weeping Serena into her arms, and Cade tied his horse to the back of the wagon, climbing up beside Lily to handle the oxen. He sent Roy on his pony an anxious glance, but the boy was safer if he could ride away from the slow-moving wagon.

"You did right, boy," he told the child. "Think you can do the same if we're further down the road?"

Taking a deep breath to steady himself, Roy nodded nervously. "Yes, sir. Do you think they'll come again?"

So the boy hadn't accepted his explanation either. Sending the wagon rolling away from the spectators, Cade spoke reassuringly. "Nope. We scared them off. But you never know when something else might come up. I want you to be ready."

"Yes, sir!" Roy danced his pony a little farther from the wagon, making a show of watching the surrounding countryside.

Unimpressed, Lily waited until Serena had calmed to ask, "Who was it?"

"I can't say for certain, but stay away from Ollie's friend Ricardo." There was no point in insulting Lily's intelligence with anything less than the truth. She needed to know who their enemies were, although Cade feared she wouldn't like the explanations.

Lily had a dozen questions, but she had learned from Cade's taciturnity. Holding Serena curled in her lap, with Juanita murmuring Spanish imprecations behind them, Lily had the sense to hold her tongue until they were home.

Roy, unfortunately, couldn't be counted on to do the same. At the first sign of the cabin he yelled and sent his pony into a gallop. By the time the wagon arrived in the yard, Travis and Ephraim were stumbling out of the cabin carrying every weapon that had come to hand, and their questions were curt and angry.

"Roy, take your horse back to the barn and tell Abraham to come get the animals." Cade climbed out, took Serena, and helped Lily down. Travis had already rounded the wagon and lifted a still shaken Juanita from the back. He held the small maid briefly, as her legs seemed about to give out from under her, and then released her when she shook herself free.

As Juanita fled to the safety of four walls, Travis confronted Lily and Cade. "Roy said you were attacked." He gave Lily a look of concern, but she was pulling her old woolen pelisse around herself and Serena and heading for the cabin to get out of the cold February wind.

Cade shrugged his shoulders. Muttering, *"De nada,"* he followed Lily. The shopping expedition he had hoped would lighten her heart had become an even greater wall between them.

Lily took coffee from the fire and poured a mug for Cade and another for herself, lingering in the warmth as the men entered. She felt Cade's towering presence behind her as he picked up the mug, but she couldn't turn to him in the company of others. She wasn't certain she should turn to him at all. She knew very little about this man she had taken for her husband. Others had warned her, but she had been entranced by a flute and a dance and a seductive touch. Now she and her family might have to pay for her foolishness.

"Were you attacked or not?" Exasperated, Ephraim stamped into the cabin, setting the shotgun aside as he glared at the two young people by the fire. The golden-haired child sat contentedly between, cooing over her doll, unconcerned by the stiff backs of the tall adults on either side of her.

"Rabbit hunters," Cade offered, sipping at his coffee.

"Hogwash," Travis concluded, not putting his rifle down but coming into the center of the cabin and holding it at his side as he glared at Cade. "Juanita is shaking like a leaf. Roy can't get two words out in one direction, and Lily looks as if she's seen a ghost. You could at least offer her a chair, you know."

"I know where the chairs are," Lily snapped. "I can look after myself."

The challenge was thrown and Cade reluctantly took it up. Pulling a chair to the fire, he pushed Lily into it. She sank into it surprisingly easily, and Cade cursed his inadequacy when it came to gentlewomen. Lily was so strong that he managed to forget that she hadn't been brought up as he had been and that the child drew strength from her.

"If they weren't rabbit hunters, then they only meant to scare us. There isn't a rifle made that could have reached us from that distance."

Ephraim grunted and reached for the jug. "So you do have something to say. I was beginning to wonder."

"I do, when anyone's willing to listen," Cade conceded. Still not looking directly at Lily, he rested his hand at her nape. She stiffened, but then relaxed as he did no more than knead the muscles there. He needed to know she was on his side. It had never been important to have someone with him before, but he wanted it now.

"We're listening." Finally setting the rifle aside, Travis took a chair at the table and, resting his feet on another, sat back and waited expectantly.

Cade hesitated. He had only speculation to go on. It seemed foolish to mention it, but remembering he needed to leave for Béxar shortly, he overcame his reluctance in the name of caution.

"It could be nothing. It could have been rabbit hunters. If so, the hunter wore boots."

That meant nothing to the two men who had just come from back East where boots were readily available. They stared at him expectantly.

"Spanish boots, with heels." Cade emptied his mug and set it aside. Juanita rapidly filled it, and he realized she was listening as closely as the men. "I don't know any men around here who wear anything that expensive or hard to find."

"But you know someone from somewhere else." Lily spoke softly, finally looking up at him. The blue of her eyes was as wintry as the skies outside, but Cade didn't think the cold was for him. The murder he read there was more for the man who had endangered her family. Cade moved his hand to the chair back, not daring to touch her when all he longed to do was take her in his arms. It weakened a man to think that way, and he resisted.

"There is a man who thinks he has reason to hate me. He has never tried to kill me before. I think the shots were just a warning, part of his plan. He stirs up trouble like winds breed storms." He didn't say the man might have shot Jim to make it look like an Indian attack when Cade was the most obvious Indian in the area. The strategy had worked well once before, but the explanation wouldn't make things better.

"Who is the bastard? We'll find him and take care of him." Travis was practically on his feet before Cade shook his head and motioned him back.

"You plan to talk him into behaving?" Cade asked wryly. Cade heard Lily's inelegant response to this insult, but Travis seemed to be taking it in stride. Sometimes he almost liked the slick-talking salesman. "We can't touch him. He's a Mexican who has gained some authority with Austin and the settlers. He is supposed to be working with the council."

"Ricardo," Lily said softly.

"Ricardo de Suela, he calls himself now, but he is not a de Suela. My father's first wife was a widow. He is her son."

"So why does he hate you?" Growing interested now, Travis put his feet up again and smiled widely at Juanita as she refilled his cup and offered him a plate of corn pone.

"He hated my mother. She refused to marry him, even after she returned to Béxar after leaving my father. It is a family matter. I do not wish to drag others into it. I only tell you to warn you. I must go into Béxar, and I would not leave you unprepared."

Lily shoved back her chair and jumped to her feet, knocking the chair over as she glared at Cade. "Leave us? Some friend of yours shoots at my family and you talk about leaving? Do you plan to join those suicidal idiots at the Alamo?"

"Lily . . ." Travis and her father both came to their feet, but Lily only had eyes for Cade. He met her glare with the same stoic facade he had used the day they met.

"There is something I must do there. I know nothing of white men's wars, but for a few hundred men to stand against an army of thousands is the work of either fools or great heroes. I cannot help them either way. My business takes me beyond those walls."

"And I suppose I have no right to ask what that business is? I am only your wife, after all."

"This is business between myself and one other man. I have already told you more than should be said."

"How can you do this?" Lily whispered, so furious she did not dare speak louder.

"I can do this because you do not need me here. You have told me yourself that you can stand on your own. You have a father and friends here. You will be safe with them."

But would he be safe without her? Anguish tore through Lily as she met the implacable look in Cade's eyes. He wasn't going to give an inch. She hated him as much now as she had ever hated anyone.

"You're right, I don't need you. I don't need anybody. The whole lot of you can go to Béxar. I'm going to take a nap."

Lily walked out, leaving the room behind her crackling with unspoken emotions.

Neither Ephraim nor Travis said anything as Cade took the back door toward the barn. The cabin was too small for all of them. Newlyweds ought to be allowed their spats in private. This, however, had the makings of something more than a lovers' quarrel.

Excusing himself Travis belatedly left for the cabin he was renting, wondering if the Indian meant for him to look after Lily and her family. He had never had to look after anyone other than himself before, but he was willing to learn. He had a stake in this family too.

Cade returned in time for supper, but Lily wasn't speaking to him. She had already fed the children and sent them off to bed. She helped set the food on the table, then filled her plate and took it to join Juanita at the fire.

Ephraim and Travis raised a protest, but Cade said nothing. She was telling him he was treating her as a servant and not an equal. He did not know how to tell her that he felt it was the other way around, that he should be the one sitting by the fire. He had done nothing yet to earn his place at the table. But to earn it he had to leave her.

When Ephraim and Travis gave him furious looks, Cade sighed and picked up his plate. Crossing to the fire, he set the plate down on the shelf he had just built and with a nod of his head sent a worried Juanita to his place at the table. Instead of taking Juanita's unstable stool, he sat cross-legged at Lily's feet and began to eat.

Lily tried to ignore him, but it was like trying to ignore a mountain coming to sit at her feet. Cade's black hair gleamed in the firelight, and she knew he was too warm when he rolled back his sleeves and she could see the sheen of perspiration on his bronzed arms. It was his own fault. He had no one to blame but himself. She hadn't asked him to sit there.

When it came down to it, she hadn't asked him to marry her. He could take himself to San Antonio any time he liked and stay, for all she cared. It wasn't as if their marriage meant anything more than a name for the child and maybe an occasional tumble in bed.

Lily knew pregnancy was the reason for the tears in her eyes. She was a practical woman and had done the practical thing by marrying the father of her child. She had no reason to expect more, and she shouldn't be surprised or disappointed when she didn't receive it.

But the nights they had spent together in that bed had given her a different impression. With Cade sitting so close, Lily didn't have to stretch her imagination far to remember how it felt to lie beneath him, to feel the pulse of his body inside hers, to know the tensing of his muscles as he strained against her in the heat of passion. And then there was afterwards, when he held her and murmured against her ear and stroked her breasts and the place where their child grew. She wouldn't think about afterwards. That was what had given her the false notion that she meant something to him.

Lily cleared her plate and quietly went about cleaning up. Juanita joined her, and the two women scraped food onto a plate to take out to the pigs, poured hot water into a bowl to clean the dishes, and silently did their woman's work while the two men at the table finished their coffee and darted furtive looks at the large man still sitting by the fire.

When Lily went off to bed, they waited for Cade to follow. When he finally rose, they breathed mixed sighs of relief and fear. When he walked out the back door, they looked at each other in puzzlement.

Lily heard the window open, but she was already stripped to her drawers and chemise and there wasn't time to grab a robe and flee. She had pulled the door latch in to indicate her displeasure, but she hadn't expected that to deter Cade. Actually, she hadn't thought he would even bother to try. The window had never occurred to her.

He stepped through as silently as the Indian he was. His silhouette filled the window, and the light of the candle flickered across his sharp features, shadowing his cheekbones into copper. Lily couldn't read the dark depth of his eyes as he crossed the room to her. She held her breath and tried to keep her gaze from the broad expanse of chest revealed by his untied shirt.

Twenty-four

Cade reached for Lily and gently began to unbraid her hair, pulling the silken strands through his fingers until they settled in a pale cascade over her shoulders and back.

"I am coming back, Lily." Cade spoke quietly, as he would to a skittish horse. He had grown up with animals as his only friends. He knew no other principles to apply.

"Jim didn't." Lily set her brush down firmly and pulled away from Cade's comforting hands. But there was nowhere she could go without walking out the door or over to the bed.

"I am not Jim. I have been taking care of myself most of my life. What are you afraid of, Lily?"

Her back stiffened. "Nothing. Go where you will."

Cade didn't know what to do. He couldn't leave with this anger between them, but he didn't know how to alleviate it. He could wrestle a steer to the ground, track a man through open prairie, live in the wilderness with ease, but he didn't know how to talk to a woman.

His hand dropped to his side. "There's some things a man has to do, Lily."

She swung around and glared at him. "No, there are some things a man *wants* to do. It's his choice. There's a difference."

She was a slender flame in the darkness. Cade wanted to reach out and touch the beauty of her, to know for certain that she was actually his to have and to hold, but flames burned. He kept his hands to himself.

"I don't want to leave you, Lily. It would be much easier to stay here and hold you in my arms and let the world go by, for the present. But not for the future. It is our future I seek, Lily. I may not succeed. I may come back empty-handed. But I have to try. Lily, can you see that? I have to try."

There was almost a plea in his voice. It seemed impossible to believe. His eyes were as dark and impenetrable as ever. The angular lines of his face revealed nothing. Without thought to what she did, Lily lifted her hand to touch the stony line of his jaw. It was warm and very, very human.

Cade gave up the fight and jerked her into his arms. Just her touch shattered something inside of him, something that had held him immobile for too long. He did not know what it was to need someone. He did not want to know. But right this minute he needed her.

Lily's arms slid around his neck, and Cade held her close, doing nothing more than feeling her breathing against him. "I don't want you to hate me, Lily."

"I don't." She rested her head against his shoulder. "I was angry. And afraid. I'm afraid of you, Cade. I'm afraid of what you do to me. I'm afraid of what you are. I'm afraid of what I don't know."

He could understand those emotions, but he couldn't admit it. He ought to just carry her to bed and end this foolishness, but she had touched something inside of him that he hadn't known existed, and bed wasn't enough any longer. Caressing her back with one large hand, Cade asked, "What do I need to do to show you, Lily? Show me what you want."

"It isn't that easy. There has to be trust. We don't know each other well enough to trust." Lily had lain awake most of the previous night discovering these things. When she had married Jim she had been too young to do anything else but trust an older man as she would her father. She was older now and wiser, and she trusted far less easily. And Cade didn't trust at all.

Cade pressed his cheek against her hair and drank in the fragile scent of her. She was light in his arms, with the suppleness of a willow wand. She had the same kind of inner strength, the kind that might bend but would never break. He knew he had chosen wisely, but he did not know how to make her see him in the same light.

"I would not have given you Serena and my child if I did not trust you, Lily. I do not know how to make you trust me. It will not be easy with men like Ollie whispering words of hate in your ears."

"You would have married Maria if she would have taken Serena off your hands. You'll start sounding like Travis if you're not careful, Cade." Lily jerked free from his arms and strode to the window, staring out at the rainy night and remembering the day she had come across Cade and Maria fighting in the street.

"Where in hell did you get that idea?" Growing angry at this resistance, Cade came up behind her, refusing to let her get away with this.

"I heard the two of you fighting the day before you were to come out to the ranch. You offered her a home and respectability. You knew you couldn't take the job without someone to take care of Serena. She refused you."

"She was keeping Serena in town. I wanted her here at the ranch. I offered Maria a home and a way out of the life she was living. I didn't offer to marry her. Maybe that was what made her mad. I think it was more a matter of her finding life out here with only one man too boring to consider."

Lily took a deep breath and stared at the cabin just visible from this corner of the room. It could have been worse. Maria could have been living out there now. She felt Cade standing behind her, knew his massive solidity and his gentle hands. She couldn't fault him for what he had done in the past. She had known there were other women. She wasn't precisely an innocent herself. They had to go forward from here.

"I'm trying to move ahead, Cade," she whispered to the window. "I didn't want to marry again. I didn't want another man taking away my choices. But it's happening all over again, and I don't like it. Can you understand that, Cade? Can you understand how I feel?"

His hands captured her shoulders and pulled her

around. His face loomed over hers as he spoke. "Give us time, Lily. We can make it work. Living without anyone else is an awful lonely business."

He didn't give her time to argue. Closing his mouth over hers, he drew the sweetness of her response with his tongue, found an answering eagerness in the swell of her breast, and carried her to the bed.

Before they slept, Lily felt Cade's hand slide to her side and test her growing roundness. Sleepily, she murmured, "He is larger than Roy at this stage, I think. I am getting fat already."

"You'll never be fat. You are beautiful. I want to hold both of you." Cade adjusted her so she lay contentedly against his side.

He had called her beautiful. No one had ever called her that before. Smiling, Lily finally drifted off to sleep.

Cade lay awake a long time later, learning what it felt like to have another person in his life, making certain that what he meant to do would not in any way harm what they had between them. It couldn't. What he had to do was too important to him. Lily would have to understand that.

Lily didn't understand it at all when Cade rode out the next day despite an icy downpour, but she held her tongue. He had called her beautiful and told her he trusted her, and like the young fool she once had been, she had believed him. Since there wasn't anything she could say to stop him, she might as well take what consolation she could.

The cotton would be wet and moldy and not worth picking after the downpour. Cade had given the men their orders for the length of time he would be gone. At this time of year there wasn't much they could do beyond mend harness and watch over the cattle. A norther could catch the herd out on the prairie and freeze them if they weren't kept somewhere protected. Newborn calves could die or be carried off by wolves. The men were experienced enough to know what needed to be done. There was nothing Lily could tell them.

Juanita read the misery in Lily's eyes easily enough, but there was little she could say. When Lily sat down, Juanita dumped Serena into her lap and went to fix her some coffee and cake. Food was the only solace that she knew.

While Roy worked at his lessons, Lily read to Serena from one of the old books she had brought with her from Mississippi. But after a page or two, Lily was too restless to sit still any longer. Serena protested at being put down, and Ephraim held out his hand to take the book. Gratefully, Lily gave it to him, and Serena willingly exchanged laps.

With the rain pouring down outside and the fire spreading a cozy warmth inside, she should be feeling safe and comfortable. She had much more than the average woman on these plains did. Perhaps the comforts weren't quite as civilized as those back home, but they were hers, and that's what should matter.

But all Lily could think of was Cade riding out in the storm with nothing more than an old buckskin shirt and poncho to cover him. She had made him wear Jim's old felt hat, but that would be little protection against cold winds.

Lily went to the shelf and got out her sewing basket and the material that she had bought—or rather, that Cade had bought for her. She had never asked where the money came from. Perhaps it was better not to know.

Travis came in and helped Roy with his arithmetic as Lily spread the material across the table. Lily noticed that Juanita was immediately on hand to serve coffee and ask what Travis needed, although she should be preparing dinner for the men. Lily lifted a questioning brow to Juanita, but the other woman didn't heed her.

She really ought to learn to spin and weave and make her own cloth like some of the other women, Lily thought. As she smoothed one of Roy's old baby gowns over the soft material as a pattern, Lily tried to imagine herself doing something so domestic, but the image failed her. Sewing was about the only household task she could manage with any dexterity, and that was because it was challenging and creative. There was nothing creative about spinning.

The rain stopped after dinner and Lily gave a sigh of relief. Cade would dry out before nightfall. She didn't have any illusion that he would shelter for the night in any cabins along the way. He would be taking the Indian paths, staying out of sight of civilization and the dangers of being mistaken for what he wasn't. He would sleep on the prairie tonight.

She didn't know why this should concern her. It was his own damned choice. But she couldn't bear to sit inside and think about it any longer. She pulled on Jim's old cracked leather boots after stuffing socks into the toe and heel, wrapped herself in an old deerskin coat, and went outside to see to the horses.

By this time word had gotten around that she was pregnant, even though she still wore Jim's trousers. The men in the barn raised hell when she tried to take a horse out, and even when she convinced them she was only going to take a look at the river, one of them insisted on going with her.

It was too early in the season to be worrying about flooding, but Lily felt better once she was outside the house. The air was brisk and damp, but it didn't smell of smoke and burned grease and wet clothes like the cabin. She surveyed the rising river and the damp cotton field, noted the plowed river bottom where Cade meant to put the corn, checked on the horses in the near field, and quietly rode back to the house, with Red trailing behind her.

She heard his curse before she noticed anything else. Red was new, but she had already noticed he had a tendency to preface every sentence with an epithet. When he thought she wasn't listening, he quite frequently used a curse word as a descriptive to every noun. Lily found it more amusing than offensive and didn't think twice about his cursing now. She merely looked up to see what he was seeing.

And then she added her curses to his. Digging her heels into the horse's side, Lily sent it galloping across the pasture in the direction of the house, with Red following as fast as he could.

Ollie and his companion hadn't had time to climb from their horses before Lily appeared at a gallop to stop them. They stared at her uncomprehendingly for a moment before realizing that the rider in fringed leather and trousers was a woman. Only when she was close enough for her long yellow braid to be seen did they realize who she was.

"Lily! What in hell are you doing out here in weather like this? If that husband of yours doesn't take better care of you than that . . ."

"Shut up, Ollie. What are you doing all the way out here? Did you find who was shooting at us?" Lily stayed in the saddle. She had a sneaking suspicion that Cade wouldn't approve of the man sitting quietly on the other horse. She had seen him only once, but his was a distinctive face. Pointed features and olive coloring combined with a black mustache and the strand of gray through otherwise polished black hair gave him a certain fascinatingly distinguished look. His lack of height, however, diminished the fascination. Between Ollie and herself, he appeared to be not much larger than a boy.

Ollie's handsome features closed, and he seemed prepared to offer another scold when the front door opened and Travis came out to stand on the porch. Clad in his embroidered black waistcoat and fitted frock coat, Travis was the epitome of everything the rough-clad storekeeper was not. The two antagonists glared at each other.

"Don't mind me, old man," Travis said, as he sauntered toward the red peddler's wagon. "I'm just going after some of my fine medicinal liqueur, guaranteed to take the ache out of the old bones on a day like this. Have you tried some, gentlemen? I started with a recipe from an old voodoo doctor down New Orleans way, then using my scientific training, I experimented until the brew was just right, aged to bring out its medicinal properties and strong enough to kill any incipient diseases before they can strike. Only two bits a bottle will buy you health, gentlemen. Will you be trying some?"

Lily nearly broke into laughter at the expressions crossing the visitors' faces as Travis tried out his patter on them. It had been a long time since she had heard him at work. He hadn't lost his touch, although she realized he was merely using the talk to take stock of the situation. If he had really wanted to sell them something, they would be off their horses by now, begging to buy a bottle at any price.

"I think the gentleman jests," the Spaniard said softly when Travis paused to take a breath and let someone else get a word in.

Scowling, Ollie turned his back on the wagon and Travis and faced Lily. "We need to talk with you, Lily. I think it's best done in private. We've been friends for a long time and out of respect to Jim, I don't want you hurt. Is there a place in the house . . . ?"

Lily wanted to tell him his friend wasn't welcome in the house, but she didn't think it wise to let them know that Cade had warned her. Did they know Cade wasn't here? Even if they didn't, they would think he was out with the cattle. Ollie knew enough to know that Cade worked incessantly.

Travis swung down from the wagon with a bottle in his hand. "You're missing a fine opportunity, gentlemen. I've only a few bottles left, and the winter is far from over. I know Mr. Clark here, but I don't believe we've been introduced, sir. I'm Professor Mangolini, but my friends know me as Travis." Genially, he held up his hand to the small man on the elegant Arabian horse.

"I am Ricardo de Suela." He ignored Travis's hand and focused his attention on Lily. "I come only because my friend asks it of me. He fears you will not believe his concern and wishes someone to confirm what he says."

Lily's gaze dropped briefly to de Suela's feet. They were encased in expensively stitched Spanish leather boots. She raised her eyes and they reflected the color of the cloudy sky. "We are friends here. You may say what you like in front of my friends."

Red eased his horse a little closer to hers. Not understanding all that was happening, he did understand the fact that Lily hadn't invited the stranger inside. His hand dropped to the rifle he kept tied to his saddle.

Travis returned to the porch and leaned against a pole, waving the bottle of "medicine" happily. "We're just one big happy family here, gentlemen. Health and happiness are some of the benefits of my medical training. This liqueur isn't the only example of my trade. Warts? Rashes? Hives? I have a powder that will cure them all. Spread the word and the entire populace will be grateful to you. There is only one thing this beautiful country lacks, and that is the services of a fine physician. I'm here to rectify that error. Gentlemen, what will it be?"

"Lily, can't you shut that joker up? This is important."

"You might do better to try his medicine than talk to me. Why don't you wait until Cade is here?"

"It's about Cade, and you know it. Send all these people away and just let you and me talk. Can't you trust me enough to do that?"

Lily glanced around to see who "all these people" might be. To her surprise, she found her father in the doorway, blocking it with his rifle to keep the children from coming out onto the porch. The men idling away a rainy day in the barn had come around the side of the house, and they, too, seemed to be armed. It was as if a warning had spread across the ranch without a word being said. Cade had done his work well.

She shrugged and met Ollie's gaze again. "I don't hide anything, Ollie. Speak up or go on about your business."

"Damn, Lily, you're the most stubborn . . ." Ollie shut up as Ricardo jostled his horse and brought his attention back to the subject. Grimacing, he proceeded as instructed. "That shooting the other day could be just the beginning. Word's got around town about Cade, and there's a heap of resentment about an Indian and a Mexican taking over some of the best land in the territory. He's the enemy, Lily. If Santa Anna came through here today, Cade could turn us all in as traitors and have us killed. The people in town don't like it."

Lily had to struggle to keep a grin from tugging at her mouth. The ploy was much too obvious. She looked pointedly at de Suela. "I believe a few Mexicans have been known to resent a dictatorship and fight for our cause." She turned back to Ollie. "Do you want to try Indians now? Do you think he's going to tell the Comanches where to find you?"

"This isn't funny!" Ollie shouted. "I'm trying to warn you. I don't want you or your family hurt, but that's what's going to happen if Cade hangs around. Sell the place and move elsewhere if you're determined to have him for a husband, but you'd do far better to tell him to beat it. People will understand."

Lily was beginning to get angry now. The jest was growing old. "Thank you for the warning, Ollie. I'll make certain everyone out here is well armed in case any concerned citizens decide to come to my rescue."

"You do not understand, Mrs. Brown. Ollie is trying to be kind. He does not tell you everything. Listen to him."

Lily pulled the reins of her horse until it danced impatiently. With deceptive softness, she replied, "My name is de Suela, sir. Would you care to say more?"

The man blanched with fury, but Ollie was in front of him and didn't see. "Damn it, Lily, he's lied to you just like Ricardo said he would. Cade's not a de Suela. He's a bastard half-breed and a cold-blooded killer. You haven't heard the story from Galveston, have you? He shot a man in the back with an arrow and stole a small fortune off him. Where do you think Cade got the money he gave you yesterday? And folks are saying it's awful convenient that Jim dropped dead in the middle of the prairie for no known reason at all just in time for Cade to ride in and take over. Do you think there could have been an arrow in his back, too?"

Lily went livid and reached for the rifle on her saddle. Before she could unhook it, Travis's slow drawl interrupted, and she glanced down to see he had a pistol in his hand.

"I believe that's enough for now, gentlemen. We'll be seeing your backs, if you please. Boys, will you be so kind as to escort these two gentlemen from our property? And if you see them come back, I'd recommend shooting first and asking questions later. It's an old policy my granddaddy taught me. Works well with rattlesnakes and any other varmints that cross your path."

Red jerked his head, and the other men slowly moved into a circle cutting Lily off from her visitors. Ollie scowled, but Ricardo was already swinging his horse around, his silver spurs jingling his outrage as he kicked his elegant horse into a run that Red's muscular mustang couldn't match.

Lily could almost hear Ricardo's curses over the trample of hooves. Wearily, she allowed Travis to help her down.

"You'd damned well better hope none of that is true, Lily, or I'll kill the man myself," Travis murmured as he handed her up to the porch.

And the state of her nerves was such that she didn't take objection to the insult. She merely walked away.

Twenty-five

T he adobe walls rising like a fortress from the flat
mesquite grasslands could be seen miles away, so
Cade had no illusion that his arrival would be unexpected.

He had passed this way many times since he was a
child. The place had held him in fascination. It had been
deteriorating when his mother first brought him here. The
adobe had cracked in many places and the outer layers
had fallen away to reveal the old logs and mud within.
The main house had become a home for dust and spiders,
and eventually there was evidence of snakes and coyotes
and any other creature of the prairie that might wander
through. Another time Cade had noticed that the flat roof
had sprung a leak in a spring storm, and the water had
seeped in and frozen during a bad winter, destroying
much of the once-lovely tile floor. It had been little more
than an abandoned ruin for this past year or longer.

But the adobe gleamed intact against the black winter
sky as Cade approached now. El Caballo had been right.
Someone had returned.

He wouldn't get his hopes up. He had waited for this
day for years. His efforts to trace his mother's family had
led to nothing in all that time. Cade suspected that there
was a conspiracy to keep the knowledge from him: there
had been more than enough hints that they were protecting someone. But even if the people who had come to restore the *ranchero* were not related, they must know of
his grandfather. They had to buy the land from him.

Cade rode forward slowly, giving the men standing at
the guard post on the inner wall a chance to see that he

was alone and relatively unarmed. He was glad that he had stopped in Béxar to wash and change into clean clothing. He was still wearing the old felt hat Lily had given him, but he now sported his best white shirt and a red bandanna and fresh buckskins. All he needed was a sash around his waist and a bolero, and his costume would be complete. Even his horse wore the Spanish saddle with the high pommel of a *vaquero* instead of the low-slung American one. His size was the only evidence that he wasn't as he seemed.

The gate swung open to let him enter without his requesting it. Cade had half expected to be met with an army and guns, but as he rode into the outer courtyard there was only the guard and one old man.

Swinging down from his horse, Cade eyed his host warily. The man was tall, taller than most but not as tall as Cade. He was so slender as to be almost frail, and the ebony walking stick in his right hand added to that image as he braced himself on it. He was dressed in little better fashion than Cade, although his trousers were of a wide-bottomed cut and made of an expensive black fabric that gleamed in the right light. He wore no coat in the winter wind, as if he had just come from the house after being warned of a stranger's arrival.

A boy scurried forward to take the horse's reins. Cade released them reluctantly. He was unaccustomed to any form of hospitality. The old man's wariness seemed more natural. Surrendering his only means of escape, Cade faced his host.

Leaning heavily on the stick, the old man stepped slowly forward, his gaze never leaving Cade's face. The ravages of age had left deep lines on his visage. His eyes were nearly shrunken in his head, but they were bright and fierce and black as Cade's own. His mouth worked slowly, as if the joints were unused and in need of grease. He stopped a foot from Cade and measured him with his eyes.

"You are bigger than they said. If your father looks like you, I could understand a few things a little better."

"He is not so tall but more striking. My mother loved him when she did not hate him."

Tears formed in the old man's eyes, and he nodded curtly and strode in the direction of the house. "You had better come in. The wind grows cold and I am an old man."

Standing there for a moment, Cade let the cold Texas wind cut through him as he looked up to the high, scuttling clouds and around to the massive mud walls. He had dreamed of this moment all his life. He needed to remember it now. Dust swirled around his moccasins and he drank deeply of air stronger than whisky. Then he turned his eyes to the sprawling house ahead and the impatient old man silhouetted in the doorway.

He had come home.

"Granddad, hold me!" Serena held up her three-year-old's chubby arms and pouted prettily.

Frying bacon over the tiny iron stove Jim had hauled up the river after selling his first crop of cotton, Ephraim frowned down at the child. "I'm busy, girl. Go pester your mama."

Lily looked up from her sewing to smile at the exchange. It was Juanita's birthday, and she had been ordered to take the day off to go into town with Travis. It had been Lily's intention to do the cooking herself, but she hadn't protested when her father had insisted that she stay off her feet. She was scarcely five months into her pregnancy and already she felt like she was ready to deliver. Roy had never been this large, she was certain.

So she sat comfortably ensconced in the corner of the tiny kitchen, instructing Roy and Ephraim in how to cook. Men ought to have some knowledge of the basic necessities of life. It was a good lesson for both of them.

"Roy, you'll need to crack more eggs than that or someone's going to go away from the table hungry. The cook eats last, you realize."

Roy frowned. "But that's all there are. I didn't find any more."

"Those hens aren't as dumb as you think. They're hiding them from you. Did you check all the stalls?"

Roy flung off his borrowed apron with disgust and went back outside to rummage in the hay, swearing he was going to let the hens into the bunkhouse where they could at least nest on sheets.

Ephraim grinned as Roy slammed out. "You've got a fine boy there, Lily. He's going to grow up right. Always wanted a boy, but I think you've done a better job than I would have. I'm proud I got a chance to know him."

"I'm glad he's got a chance to know his grandfather. I hope you've decided to stay out here. Cade and Travis will push Roy awful hard. He'll need you to spoil him a bit." Lily handed Serena a wooden spoon and bowl, and the child settled contentedly to making dinner for her doll.

Ephraim's drinking had tapered off considerably these past weeks as Lily had found more and more for him to do and Travis hadn't obliged in joining him at the bottle. With Cade gone and Lily increasingly incapacitated, both men were beginning to shoulder more responsibility. It was quite a sight to see sometimes. Lily wondered what Cade would do if she told him he was fired when he returned.

When the child fluttered and turned within her, Lily closed her eyes and leaned back in the rocking chair. If he returned. It had been nearly a month. How long did it take to get to Béxar and back? The rivers were rising. Travel would be difficult. Perhaps Cade was waiting for the weather to improve. There hadn't been anyone through here in weeks. She had no idea what was going on in the rest of the world. Dear Lord, she thought, make it the weather that delays him and not something more disastrous.

Lily didn't know when she had gone from hating Cade for leaving her to waiting anxiously for his return. Perhaps it had been when she had finished sewing the linen shirt and wanted him to try it on. Perhaps it had been the day she had felt the baby move. Anything was possible. It was possible that she still hated him. He had a lot to answer for. But she wanted him here to answer personally.

She didn't let any of the confusion show. If anyone was going to take Cade apart piece by little piece, it was going to be her. She really didn't believe the hateful gossip Ricardo was spreading around with the help of Ollie, but Cade ought to be here to defend himself.

Ephraim's shout of pain brought Lily to her feet without further thought. Roy was coming in the door with a bowl of eggs and dropped them with a splattering crash, dashing to his grandfather's aid.

Flames leapt from the older man's sleeve as he screamed and tried to find water to douse them. Roy grabbed the pail kept by the stove while Lily tried to get her father to hold still so she could beat at the sleeve with a towel to smother it. She gasped in relief when Roy managed to lift the heavy pail and hit the flames with the first throw. The fire died, leaving the acrid stench of burned flesh.

Where was Travis and his cock-and-bull medicine when she needed him? Together with Roy, Lily led Ephraim back to the house, Serena trailing behind them. Ephraim stoically bit back his moans, but Lily could tell he was in great pain, and it tore at her to feel so helpless. She should have warned him about the dangers of that damned stove. The sparks flew all over the place and caused more burns than Indians caused deaths. There ought to be a safer way to make stoves, but now wasn't the time to complain.

Inside the cabin Lily removed her father's destroyed shirt and found enough lard to smear over the burned area. Ephraim groaned as she applied it, but she knew of no other remedy. When she was done, she handed him the jug of whisky. It was the best painkiller in the house.

Roy helped her to make a pallet beside the fire where they could keep an eye on their patient. Ephraim protested mightily and refused to lie down until Lily informed him she could hurt herself if she had to lift him when he passed out.

That seemed to occur quite soon after he lay down.

Worriedly, Lily left Roy to keep an eye on his grandfather while she went to the kitchen to finish throwing together some kind of meal. The men would have to make do with biscuits and eggs and ham. They wouldn't be happy, but it was all she had time for.

After she saw the men fed, she hurried back to the cabin. Her father was still unconscious, and Roy's brow was puckered with worry as he tried to keep Serena quiet and watch over the groaning man at the hearth.

"Go climb into Travis's wagon and see if there's any medical books in there. Maybe we can find something else to do for him." Doing anything was better than nothing, and it seemed to relieve Roy to be useful.

He came back with an armload of books on anatomy and diseases and a book called *Gunn's Domestic Medicine*. Lily jumped on the latter and hastily devoured the contents page, cursing when she couldn't find "Burns" and then flipping quickly to the "Scalds" section. She read the pages hastily. She should have applied more cold water. They didn't have ice. They didn't have sweet oil. Would lard work as well? When she came to the recommendation for "Turner's cerate," she pointed it out to Roy.

"See if you can find some of that in the wagon. It says it will cure any burn."

Lily checked the unbandaged arm as she waited. She didn't see any signs of infection yet, but it was red and swollen. Perhaps if Roy found the medicine, she could start all over, wash off the lard and soak the arm in cold water, then apply the salve. Or would that just serve to wake her father to the pain?

The rain began to fall again, and Lily wanted to cry with frustration. The skies had been like lead for weeks. Couldn't it let up for just a little while? If only Cade would come home . . .

She heard the ox wagon pulling up and almost cried with relief. Travis and Juanita hurried in with Roy a moment later.

"Let me take a look at him, Lily. You go sit down. My

God, you're white as a sheet. Juanita, get her something to drink."

Travis moved briskly through the room, taking command, and Lily let him. She was terrified she had already done all the wrong things. Ephraim shouldn't have passed out so quickly. The burn wasn't that serious, was it? There ought to be something more that could be done.

"Here, drink. Travis will make him well." Juanita poured some of the whisky into a hot cup of coffee and handed it to Lily.

Juanita's saying a good word about any man was cause to wonder, but Lily didn't even notice. She sipped at the coffee and watched anxiously as Travis went to work.

He actually did seem to have some idea of what he was doing. He mixed some potion to clean the wound, causing Ephraim to wake up cursing. When Ephraim sat up, Juanita handed him a cup of the potent coffee and he sipped at it while he watched Travis warily.

The salve Travis dug out from his store of supplies apparently stung, for Ephraim howled and cursed when it was first applied. But when Serena woke and started wailing, he quieted and beckoned the child to crawl in his lap. He told her some wild tale about a rabbit that talked while Travis finished bandaging his arm.

"It's going to hurt like hell for a while, but you'll be as good as new in a few weeks. Give you a taste of what you're in for if you don't repent your sinful ways." Travis stood up and cleaned his hands in the bowl of water Lily kept at the sink.

"You're expecting enough for me to believe a snake-oil salesman knows anything about doctoring. Don't ask me to listen to your preaching, too." Grumpily, Ephraim accepted Travis's hand and stood up, weaving unsteadily until he found a chair.

"I'm about ready to believe anything Travis tells me right now, so you'd better treat him nice." Relieved, Lily scolded as she found a pillow for her father's arm and one for his back and fluttered around him until she was certain he was almost back to normal.

Dinner was a fairly quiet meal. Surprisingly, Juanita

kept up much of the conversation, telling of the silk ribbon Travis had bought for her, the arrival of a new shipment of fabrics, and her conversation with her cousin. Travis encouraged her by drawing her out about the Indians they had seen boldly walking through town in their leather leggings and shirts and hideous tattoos. When Lily asked if there were any news of the war, Travis shrugged and changed the subject.

That did not bode well, but Lily was too tired to argue. Swearing he was well enough to retire to his own bed, Ephraim dragged himself to the dogtrot and up the stairs early, carrying a jug with him. Lily made no objection to the liquor. His pain was too evident.

When everything was cleaned away and the children in their beds, Lily asked to borrow the medicine book and took it to her room with her. The supply of candles was running low, but she would indulge herself for one night. She wasn't sleeping much anyway. The bed seemed empty and almost haunted. She didn't want to think about it tonight.

She read the section on pregnancy and wished Cade were there to discuss it with her. She wasn't certain what to make of the doctor's treatise on the woman who felt compelled to steal when pregnant or the one who stopped stealing only when she was pregnant. Did that mean the child was controlling their behavior? Perhaps the one child had inherited a tendency to steal and was showing his true nature by forcing his mother to do so. She wished the doctor had gone on to observe the children that resulted from this strange behavior.

Maybe she would talk to Travis about it in the morning. It was hard to believe that Travis actually had some skills behind all his talk. Cade might be relieved to know he was worth more than the few coins he paid in rent.

Blowing out the candle, Lily settled down to listen to the sounds of night. She was exhausted, but she couldn't sleep. The child stirred, and she covered her growing stomach. There wasn't anything in the book about how long a pregnant woman could make love before she had to give it up. Jim had not made love to her until quite some time after she had delivered Roy. It was one of those things that had made her worship him. But with Cade it was different. She wanted him to make love to her. She needed the reassurance. But if she grew any bigger, it didn't seem possible, and all that business about the womb pressing downward—she should never have read the book.

A whistle split the night air. There was nothing heart-stopping about a whistle unless it came in the middle of a quiet night when everyone should be in bed. Lily sat straight up, suddenly aware that she had dozed off. Had she dreamed the whistle?

She smelled smoke. It had to be her memory of earlier that day, when the stench had been hideous. Surely not twice in one day.

A shout had Lily leaping from the bed and hunting for slippers and robe. More shouts, and thundering feet on the stairs outside. What was happening?

The stench of smoke nearly rocked Lily back on her heels when she threw open the door. Running outside, she could see the flames leaping from the cabin roof, and she screamed mindlessly.

Her first urge was to run toward the house, but someone jerked her away from it. Lily struggled, and Jack's curt tones woke her further.

"There's others as can carry the children out faster. Don't give us another one to hunt for."

Juanita came running from her kitchen pallet, hair streaming in ebony lengths behind her as she caught Lily's arm and stared in horror with her while men pumped water and handed it up the chain forming to the roof. Abraham came rushing out of the main cabin with Serena in his arms at the same time Travis appeared from the loft over Lily's room and handed a sleepy Roy over the railing to someone waiting below.

That left only one person unaccounted for, and Lily held her breath as figures appeared through the smoke pouring out of the big loft. They weren't figures she recognized immediately. Slight and erect, they carried a heavy burden between them. Her urge was to rush forward and give them aid. But the men on the stairs were already catching the unconscious man, hauling him downward, releasing the two young Indians from their burden.

Indians. Lily expelled a breath and, shaking free of Juanita, ran to them. Some of the men were already glaring at the youngsters with suspicion.

"It was your whistle I heard! Thank you. I owe you more than horses this time. Cade isn't here. I'll tell him . . ." Near hysterics, Lily tried to reassure the two boys Cade had called his half brothers while letting the men know that the boys only meant to be helpful. She didn't even know why they were here. It didn't matter. They could have all burned in their beds if the boys hadn't seen the flames and warned them.

The elder one, the one who looked most like Cade, touched her arm and gestured with his hand. The seriousness of his dark eyes brought Lily to her senses. She wished it hadn't. She would have preferred to go on babbling mindlessly just a little while longer.

Instead, she turned in the direction he indicated and stepped toward the man lying on the muddy ground. Travis was already bent over him, breathing into his mouth, pumping on his chest, and cursing with every word he had ever heard in between. Lily tried not to make a sound, tried to do nothing to distract him, but tears were pouring down her face and she was stumbling to her knees before she could control herself.

"Daddy! Wake up, Daddy! It's me, Lily! You've got to wake up now. You're scaring me, and it's not funny. Please, Daddy. I'll play for you. There's a piano back in town. You haven't heard me play it. I'm sorry I haven't had time to play it for you yet. We'll go tomorrow night. Or maybe Saturday if you're not feeling up to it. Please, Daddy . . ."

Someone pulled her away. Someone else half-carried, half-led her to the barn and out of the rain that was finally starting again. Lily knew Roy was sobbing, heartbroken. She could hear Serena crying and Juanita hushing her. Someone was speaking to her, handing her a cup of something. But she couldn't taste it. She couldn't see them. She had to see that her father was all right.

Lily tried to get up and go to him again, but they held her back. She screamed and tried to fight them, but there were too many. When Travis entered, he shook his head as he looked at her. That's when Lily knew it was over.

Weeping openly, she collapsed on the hay and cried for Cade, and for herself, and for the father she would never know again.

Twenty-six

Cade saw the leaping flames as he rode his exhausted horse out of the woods. His heart nearly stopped in his chest, and he urged the weary gelding to a greater pace.

They had been riding for twelve hours or more. He was soaked to the bone and should have found a camp hours ago. But the thought of spending the rest of the night in bed with Lily had been too compelling for common sense.

Cade tried to focus his gaze on the flames, but they were already fading from sight. Perhaps it had been lightning, but he couldn't remember hearing thunder. The direction was too uncomfortably close to the house. No campfire would reach that high. Something was wrong.

Sensing home and shelter, the gelding responded to Cade's urging with one last surge of energy. They raced across the prairie in the direction of the ranch.

She wasn't even aware he was there until he was gathering her in his arms. Weeping hysterically, Lily threw herself on Cade's shoulder and allowed all her fear and sorrow to pour out.

As he held her, Cade glanced at the other men standing helplessly about.

"Smoke inhalation. He was dead before we carried him out. I tried, but it was too late." Travis shrugged and looked at Lily in bewilderment. He had never seen her like this. Even as a sixteen-year-old girl, she had been headstrong and sure of herself. He didn't like seeing her fall apart.

Cade's gaze had already taken in a white-faced Roy and a sobbing Serena. It drifted now to the long body covered in an old horse blanket. Ephraim. First her husband. Now her father. The gods were exacting their price already.

"It's all my fault. I shouldn't have let him take the bottle to bed. He would have seen the fire, smelled the smoke, if he hadn't been drinking. He's been doing so well ... He was just telling me how proud he was of Roy, how he'd always wanted a son. Why, Cade? Why does this have to happen?"

"Because he'd made his peace with the world, Lily, and it was time for him to go. Don't fault yourself. There was nothing you could do." Cade glanced back at Travis. "Is there anything habitable? She's shivering. We've got to get a fire going."

"The roof is gone on the main cabin and rain is going through the loft floor. I'd be afraid to use the chimney. Lily's and Roy's bedrooms weren't touched." He hesitated, then offered, "I think Ephraim had one of his cigars before he went to sleep. He'd been in pain earlier and he'd told me he slept better after a good cigar. It could have fallen in the blankets and smoldered. He was probably asphyxiated before the flames started."

"No, no." Lily shook her head violently against Cade's shoulder. "Daddy wouldn't have smoked in bed. I told him it smelled too much, and he said he wouldn't smoke them anymore."

Travis and Cade exchanged glances. The old man had smoked a cigar every night before he went to bed. He just waited for Lily to leave the room or took it upstairs with him.

"Let's get you inside where it's warm." Cade helped Lily to her feet, then glanced at a grief-stricken Roy. "Would you rather sleep downstairs with us? There's not much of the night left."

Roy looked uncertainly to his mother, but Lily was too caught up in her grief to comprehend his need right now. Travis dropped a reassuring hand on the boy's shoulder. "Let's you and me go back to my place and fix up something hot to warm our insides. Your mom will feel better in the morning."

When Roy went off with Travis, Cade spoke to his half brothers, who had grown restless and uneasy with the number of strangers staring at them. They replied in their native tongue, and Cade gestured with his head to Jack. "Fetch the boys some blankets. They'd rather sleep out here in the barn with the animals. I don't want them trying to ride out tonight."

Jack looked slowly from Cade to the two young Indians; then, deciding that Cade knew what he was doing, he went off to carry out his orders.

Lily had managed to follow this much of the conversation, however, and she tugged at Cade's poncho anxiously. "It's too cold out here, Cade. There ought to be room in the bunkhouse."

"If I tried to make them sleep in there, they'd bolt. I don't want to have to hunt them down in the morning. Come inside. You can't stay out here any longer."

Wrapping Lily in a blanket someone handed them, Cade led her back into the night. He stared bleakly at the scorched remains of the main cabin. All Lily's prized possessions were in there: her table and chairs hauled all the way from Mississippi, her crates of books, her new sink and pump, all the things that came so dearly out here. The front window would no doubt be shattered too. Caught up in the more devastating loss of her father, she hadn't noticed this lesser loss yet, but it was coming.

And there was worse yet to follow; he could feel it. That was a topic best left for morning.

Juanita carried Serena off to the safety of her cabin. The dresser with all the child's clothes would be in the charred wreckage of the main room. It was only a miracle that Serena had been saved from the same fate. Cade offered his thanks to Whoever watched over them as he helped Lily into their room.

Jim Brown had neglected to build a fireplace for this side of the house. It made sense, for it was dangerous to leave a fire burning all night in these timber-framed chimneys, but Cade cursed the lack now. The house would be uninhabitable for the winter without any means of heat.

Gathering Lily in his arms, he carried her to the bed—blanket, robe, and all. He pulled up the quilts at the bottom of the bed and tucked her in, then discarded his own damp clothes. Leaving them lying on the floor, he climbed beneath the covers and hugged Lily's huddled body into the curve of his own.

He could feel her sobs lessen as exhaustion claimed her, and as she quieted, Cade allowed slumber to cover his senses. There would be time enough in the morning to survey their choices.

Lily woke feeling thoroughly ill. Her head hurt. Her throat was raw. But there was nothing wrong with her nose. The disgusting smells of wet, charred lumber and other undetectable materials seemed to fill her nostrils.

Her stomach stirred in protest, and she squirmed uncomfortably in the cocoon of wrappings around her legs. She needed the chamberpot. A hand pulled at the quilt muffling her head, and Lily leapt fully awake.

She turned and found Cade bent over her, concern evident in the depth of his eyes. The previous night flashed through her mind, and she stared back at him, grief-stricken.

"Are you well enough to get up? I can carry you to the kitchen where it is warm."

She didn't want to get up. She didn't ever want to get up again. Why couldn't her father have been taken when there were a thousand miles of distance between them? Why did it have to happen now, just as they were coming to know each other again? Just as he seemed ready to start a new life?

Lily's eyes hurt too much to cry, and she shook her head. "I need to get dressed." There were certain demands of the body that had to be met. She couldn't linger here feeling sorry for herself.

The child within her stirred in agreement, and she realized she was hungry. Unwrapping herself from the cocoon of covers, Lily pressed a hand to her restless insides. Cade's hand instantly came to cover hers.

"The child moves?"

"Can't you feel him? It is early yet, but already he uses my stomach for a kicking post. I think he's going to be as large as you when he is born." It made Lily feel better to speak of the babe. She had wanted another child for so long, she couldn't lose her joy in this life even in the presence of death.

Cade burrowed his hand beneath her robe and covered the hard pear shape of her abdomen with his palm. He could feel a slight stirring movement, and he stroked her there, feeling the child respond.

"Let me bring you breakfast. There is no need for you to get up now. It is early yet."

He was swinging out of bed before Lily could register surprise. She turned and watched as Cade hastily pulled on one of his old chambray shirts and searched for his denims. Someday she would have to buy him some long johns. He kept his back to her, but she could very well imagine what he tried to hide. It had been a month since they shared a bed, but her needs were buried beneath grief right now. Cade was doing his best to respect that.

She would have to match his thoughtfulness. If she wanted this to be a partnership, she was going to have to shoulder half the burden. She could do it. It was just a matter of setting her mind to priorities and keeping it from wallowing in guilt and grief.

"I want him buried on the rise near the oaks." Lily threw back the covers and stood up. She wouldn't think about the empty, charred room across the dogtrot. There were more important things to consider. "We need to find some way to thank your brothers. They saved our lives."

Safely buttoning his pants, Cade turned and watched her worriedly. She sounded hoarse and there were huge circles under her eyes, but this sudden energy was better than the night's hysterical grief. "I have promised them a buffalo hunt. They do not expect more than that. If you are truly grateful, you might give my father permission to camp where he is now for as long as he likes. I think he is ready to accept the fact that he cannot fight both Comanche and white men."

"How could I object?" Embarrassed by her distorted body, Lily pulled her drawers up beneath her nightgown as she spoke. "Your brothers have saved Roy and now everyone in the household. I do not understand why they were out in such miserable weather, but I am grateful for their quick actions."

Cade didn't think she would appreciate knowing the boys had been watching her since he left. He merely nodded agreement and then impulsively reached for her nightgown and pulled it off before she could hide any more of herself beneath it.

Cade stared in satisfaction at the fullness of her breasts and the slope of her belly. "Don't hide yourself from me. Your beauty is one of the pleasures of my life."

He bent and kissed her, then left her staring after him. Lily looked down at herself, then back at the door Cade had closed behind him. The man was definitely mad.

She tried not to look at the ruin of her lovely house as she scurried through the slashing rain to the privy. She needed to talk to the children and see that her father had a decent burial. Then she would need to notify her sisters. There would be time to take stock of the situation when all that was done.

She kept herself going, one task at a time. The men had to be fed. She ignored the way Travis and Cade talked in low tones between each other, leaving her out. She was getting work done. She would find chores for them to do soon enough.

The men built a coffin out of scrap lumber, and Travis scaled the dangerous upper story to see if any decent clothes could be salvaged from Ephraim's wardrobe for his laying-out. Lily scrubbed the ones he brought her and methodically hung them in front of the kitchen fire. The tiny kitchen was going to be crowded if they all had to stay in here for warmth, but the fireplace was far down on her list of things to do immediately.

The rain let up enough by afternoon for the men to carry the makeshift coffin and its heavy burden out to the grave that had been dug in the mud that morning. Lily concentrated on holding Roy's hand and the words she wanted to say. She couldn't break down again. Too many people depended on her.

Tears began to roll down her cheeks as Travis read a few passages from the Bible and said a few words of his own. Cade accepted the book next and quoted a psalm without opening to it. Roy began to sob, and Lily knelt to hug him. Any words she had wanted to say disappeared with her tears, and she didn't mind when the men kept the Bible and nodded for the first clods of dirt to be thrown in. She couldn't speak now if her life depended on it. Perhaps, just occasionally, she didn't need to do everything herself.

Serena was too young to understand death, and she danced in happiness at having Cade home again as they made their way back to the house. She talked incessantly, saying nothing, filling the silence that surrounded them.

They were almost back at the house when the first rider appeared over the horizon. Lily wouldn't have noticed, but Cade caught her arm and the sudden tightening of his grip warned her. Several of the men began running toward the road. The rider came from the direction of Béxar, and they hadn't had news in weeks.

Cade glanced at Travis, and Lily intercepted the look. This time she wanted explanations. There was so much wrong in her life right now, she didn't want to be surprised by any more burdens.

"What is it? What are you keeping from me?"

"I think you are about to find out." Cade gestured toward the road where already several more riders could be seen, followed by a wagon rolling at a pace guaranteed to destroy every joint in it.

"Santa Anna," Lily breathed, not even needing to question. "He's arrived, hasn't he?"

"He laid siege to the Alamo well over a week ago. I've not seen any Texan reinforcements marching in that direction." Cade guided Lily toward the kitchen and warmth.

"The men out there are running from him, aren't they? Does that mean we've lost already?"

"The Alamo couldn't win without reinforcements. I

know nothing more than that. You will have to make choices, Lily."

Lily could hear the furious shouts of the first arrivals as she came around the kitchen. "There was thousands of them, like ants! They kept on coming, but our boys mowed 'em down. When they tried to run their own men ran them through, so they kept marching. There's dead everywhere, and the Mexicans marched over them. They say Crockett and Bowie were fighting them barehanded towards the end. But Houston never sent reinforcements. They're all dead. Santa Anny murdered them all."

Lily turned wide eyes of horror to Cade and started to hurry toward the speaker, but Cade caught her arm and jerked her toward the kitchen.

"The men will report back soon enough. You don't need to hear the details."

To her own surprise, Lily didn't protest this command. She really didn't need to hear the details. The larger picture was all too clear. The gallant young men holding San Antonio had died a horrible death. That was all anyone needed to know.

"What happens now?" she whispered as the children ran to take the warm milk Juanita was pouring for them.

"Those people out there are running for the border. If they can get across to Louisiana, Santa Anna won't dare follow. I expect his troops won't be too far behind, although he's more likely to head for Goliad first. If he has as many men as they're saying, he may split them up and send them to Gonzales, too. I doubt he'll send any this way, but we don't know for certain." Cade studied Lily's face to see if she comprehended what he was saying. It was difficult to tell. The grief and horror were plain, but they had been there all day.

"What do conquering armies do to innocent citizens?" she asked quietly.

Cade was uncertain how much to tell her, how much would be too much, but he had to make her understand what they were up against. He had known it when he rode in last night. He had hoped to have a little time to make a decision. The speed with which events were proceeding was rapidly eliminating all alternatives.

"I have it from a very good source that Santa Anna is not quite rational. He is taking opium and is beyond the point where anyone can guess what he will do next. I don't think it will be safe to stay anywhere that he might send his armies. He may intend to wipe out all Americans for all I can tell."

That definitely wasn't rational. Lily attempted to digest this information as Travis returned from talking with the runaways. He quickly confirmed what Cade had already told her, and both men looked solemn as they took seats at the table, forcing Lily to sit with them.

"You can't stay here, Lily," Travis said first. "As the news spreads, the whole countryside is going to empty. The nearest army is at Gonzales and they can't possibly protect you. There are rangers at Bastrop, but there's not enough to hold back a thousand Mexican troops if they come up the San Antonio road. We've got to get you out of here." He threw a stony look at Cade. "And I'm going wherever you decide to go."

Letting the men play their games, Lily considered what she had been told. They were hundreds of miles from the border. The river was already overflowing its bed. She finally looked at Travis with incomprehension. "How? How can we run through the mud and the floods and stay ahead of an army riding horses? I've got two children to consider, Travis. There has to be another way."

Since Cade had offered no objection to his company, Travis left it to him to reply. Cade waited until Juanita had poured a hot cup of coffee and shoved it into Lily's hands.

"Two," he spoke abruptly. "We can join my father in the woods and hope the army does not leave the road. They will see the ranch, but they will not come looking for what they cannot see."

Lily looked uncertain, but she did not reject the opportunity out of hand.

"Or we can try to follow the prairie and reach my grandfather's house. The journey is shorter than going to the border, but it is very dangerous. The only reason I suggest it is that my grandfather is a man of influence. If Santa Anna wins, he may be able to save your land. And you will be more comfortable there than living with my father."

"Save the land" was the key phrase, and Lily almost immediately responded to it, but she held her tongue just a while longer in favor of more information. "Your grandfather?"

"Antonio de Suela, my mother's father. He has returned to Béxar." Cade sat patiently at the narrow plank table usually used for cutting and mixing. His big hands surrounded his mug, and there was no nervousness in them as he discussed this question so vital to their future.

Lily looked from those steady hands to Cade's expressionless eyes. He would give her no clue as to his choice, but she knew it without his saying. For some reason, he wished to make the terrible journey to Béxar again, against the onrush of fleeing settlers and a victorious Mexican army. She wasn't certain she understood his reasoning, but she was beginning to trust it.

"How will we get there?" she asked.

And the men immediately began to plan.

Twenty-seven

"The men are going to join Houston at Gonzales."
Lily tried not to look as desperate as she felt as she rummaged through scorched chests for blankets and quilts they could take with them. "Are you and Travis planning to follow them?"

Cade gave her a sharp look as he packed supplies into a canvas bag. "We will decide what to do next after we see you and the children safe. Are you worried which side my loyalties are on?"

"I don't care about men and their damned loyalties. I will fight for my land in any way I have to, but it is men and their damned talk and arrogance that started all this. They knew the Mexicans didn't want slaves, that's just one of their excuses to grab land that isn't theirs. If the men left things alone, someone would have shot Santa Anna in another year or two and they might have someone more reasonable to deal with. And everyone knows the government in Washington was trying to buy Texas. There had to be other solutions besides this."

Anger was better than grief. As she left the lovely, delicate linens that had been her mother's in the chest and closed the lid, knowing they reeked of smoke and damp and she could do nothing, Lily stoked her anger further. They could lose everything.

She stared at the gutted room, at the charred timber that had scarred her carefully polished table, at the soaked baby clothes lying in a pile and covered with soot and ashes, at the three-legged stool Roy and Jim had so proudly worked on. Some of these things could be saved were she given a chance to stay and undo the damage.

But she was being driven out of her home by men and their stupid arguments.

She wanted to kick and throw things, but she quietly bundled up the blankets she had retrieved and crossed the dogtrot to her bedroom, where she had gathered the rest of the necessities they would take with them: blankets and food. They were crossing the prairie in a cold March rain with nothing but blankets and the clothes on their back.

The others fleeing down the road had filled their wagons with possessions, carrying as much with them as they could pile in. But the refugees were following the road, and even then they would lose much of their loads before they reached the border. Cade had said they would have to avoid public roads if they were going in the opposite direction, and a wagon couldn't be pulled across fields of mud.

Lily had to believe Cade knew what he was doing. She didn't want to lose her land. She didn't want to go fleeing back to Mississippi with nothing to show for these last nine years. This was her life. She would defend it in whatever way seemed best. Right now, following Cade seemed the most reasonable solution. And the activity relieved her mind of thinking of the endearing smile she would never see again, of the affectionate hugs she would never feel again, of the man who would never be there again for her to turn to.

When they mounted her on a broad-backed mule the next morning, Lily wasn't so certain that this solution was as reasonable as she had thought. With no sidesaddles available and her condition making it dangerous to ride astride, she had no alternative but to accept this means of transportation if she wanted to follow the others. Glaring at the mule as it turned a beady eye on her, Lily kicked it into motion.

The mule had no intention of responding to her lamentably one-sided kick, but he reluctantly stepped into line when the horses began moving out. Cade had abandoned his high-pommeled saddle for an Indian blanket so he could prop Serena in front of him as he rode. Unable to manage a horse, Juanita had also been given a small mule, and she cursed hers as vividly as Lily did. Behind them two packhorses carried their worldly possessions and pulled the travois carrying Cade's tepee, thanks to his brothers' quiet efficiency. Travis and Roy brought up the rear.

The animals had been driven as far back on the prairie as was possible before they left. Lily glanced over her shoulder when the little caravan rode off, praying they would return in time to keep the entire herd from going wild and drifting away. It was all the livelihood she had now. The chances of spring planting this year looked mighty slim.

The rain poured down steadily as the day wore on. Every so often they came close enough to the road to hear the noise and clatter of others fleeing toward the Sabine, but mostly Cade kept them to the ridges and out of sight. They stopped under some trees for the noon meal, stretching their legs and filling their gourds from a torrential stream. Cade watched Lily with concern as she held her back and tried to walk away the cramp, but she refused his suggestion to cut their day off early. They mounted and rode on while there was still daylight.

It didn't seem likely that they would meet Comanches or thieves in weather like this, but that night they used the old trick that every traveler learned of making a campfire and eating at one place, then packing up and setting up camp several miles away. Cade seemed to have no difficulty reconstructing the tepee even in the dark, and Lily accepted its shelter with relief.

They had no privacy. Travis and Cade took turns keeping watch while Lily and Juanita slept with the children between them. The men lay down wherever there was an inch to spare. All that mattered was that the buffalo hides kept them dry.

When they rose in the morning, Serena was as bubbly and cheerful as if she had just risen from her trundle bed in the warmth of their home. Roy played games with her while Lily and Juanita tried to cook over the sputtering flames of the fire. The rain didn't promise to let up any-time soon.

"Who's that?" Playing an old game, Roy pointed at Juanita.

Serena grinned and raced to plant a kiss on Juanita's cheek. " 'Nita!" she cried triumphantly.

Juanita pointed her toward Lily. *"Quién es?"*

"Mama and baby!" Serena climbed into Lily's lap for a hug.

As Cade bent his large form beneath the flap to join them, Lily pointed in his direction. "What's his name?"

"Papa-*padre*-daddy," she crowed, laughing as Cade lifted her and sat down with her in his lap. She liked hav-ing several names for everything and everyone, and could chatter incessantly in two languages.

Cade pointed at an unshaven Travis who glared blearily at their laughter as he untangled himself from his damp bedroll. *"Qué esta?"*

Unaware of the Spanish niceties as to being addressed as a "what" instead of "who," Travis glared at their cheerfulness until Serena flung herself at him and hugged his neck.

"Snake-oil man!" she cried.

Laughter erupted all around—despite the dreary rain, despite their fear and weariness. Welcome waves of amusement relieved some of the tension, and they gave in to it gladly. Travis growled and tickled Serena until she ran to Roy for help, then grinning slightly, he met Cade's eyes. "Can't you teach her something else to call me?"

"Tío Travis?" Cade suggested.

"Tío, tío!" Serena cried, sticking her tongue out at Travis and hiding behind Roy's back.

"Why do I get the feeling that means 'snake oil' in Spanish?" Travis muttered, reaching for the tin cup of coffee Juanita offered him.

"It means 'uncle.' Whether you know it or not, you've just adopted a niece. That means you get to carry her to-day." Cade took his cup and settled back cross-legged be-side Lily.

"I don't think I'm ready for the responsibilities of a

family man. I'm not even certain how I got into this." Travis threw Lily a wry look. "You're more trouble than you're worth, you know."

"Look who's talking." Undisturbed, Lily called Serena to come eat her breakfast. She had spent eight years raising Travis's son. It was time he took on a little responsibility.

Travis shrugged his shoulders, unabashed. "You could have had a smart, good-looking man like myself and you chose that man-mountain over there. You lost your chance, Lily."

Lily didn't need to reply to that. She merely looked at his rumpled curls and beard-stubbled face and grinned.

Relieved that she could still find humor in the midst of her grief, Cade finished his food and leaned over to kiss her before rising to finish packing the horses. Lily watched him go with astonishment. Cade never made public displays of affection.

Their mood was a little less somber when they set out this time, but the constant drizzle and occasional downpours took some of the light from their day soon enough. The children complained. Lily felt as if she would never stand again. And after some undetected incident at their midday halt, Juanita quit speaking to Travis.

By the time they reached the rain-swollen Guadalupe River, they were all too exhausted even to consider searching for a place to cross it. Not even bothering to go through the game of moving their camp after the fire died, they set up the tepee and collapsed for the night.

Gunfire woke them at midnight. The children woke up crying with terror, and Travis didn't bother searching for his shoes as he grabbed his rifle and ran out. Cade was on watch, and Lily clutched the blankets around her as they waited in fear for some report.

Both men came back a little while later, soaked and cursing but unharmed.

"They were after the horses. It's all right. No one was hurt," Travis assured them.

Cade said nothing, but his eyes sought out Lily, telling

her there was nothing to concern herself about. She didn't
know how he knew she needed this extra reassurance, but
she relaxed and nodded her understanding, obediently
rolling up in her blankets once again.

But when they rose in the morning it was to discover
that Lily's mule had somehow made its escape, with or
without help.

Travis cursed, but Cade merely took it in stride, dis-
tributing the saddlebags on his horse to the two packhorses and holding his hand out to Lily. "You'll ride
with me."

Lily looked at the swirling river they had to cross and
shook her head. "You'll have to carry Roy and Juanita
across first."

Travis rode up with Serena on his lap to find the reason
for the delay in time to hear Lily's reply. "Much as I hate
to admit it, she's right. I can carry the brat here across on
my saddle, but the gelding is larger and safer. Do you
know a crossing or should I test the river?"

"There's a beaver dam and some other obstructions just
down past the bend. We can cross there." Cade caught
Lily by the waist and threw her up on his horse. "You'll
ride with me till the crossing."

The muddy river seemed to swirl closer to their feet
with every passing minute. Lily didn't see how they could
possibly cross without boats. Feeling Cade's arms close
around her as he got up behind her, she tried to tell herself everything was going to be all right, but she glanced
worriedly at Roy. He was trying to look brave, but his
face was pinched with cold and fear. Should anything
happen to him too . . .

They found the jam of old logs and silt and tree roots.
Water grew steadily deeper on one side, seeping through
in slow eddies and giddy currents in several places, but
the dam blocked the flow sufficiently to lower the water
level on the far side.

Lily stood at the river's edge where Cade had lowered
her and watched as Travis eased his horse into the current, holding Serena securely in front of him. She didn't

realize she was holding her breath until she saw him safely emerging on the other side.

Cade lifted a terrified Juanita in front of him and leading her mule, set out down the muddy bank. Lily reached for Roy's hand as he sat on his pony, following every movement with his eyes. His small fingers curled in hers, and she wished she had the power to warm him. His whole world had come apart since Jim died. He was holding up remarkably well, but this journey was not one she would wish on the strongest of men. Perhaps she should have accepted Cade's offer to house them in the Indian camp.

Lily stifled a scream as the gelding lost its footing and slipped into deeper waters, but Cade held on to Juanita and the reins, releasing the mule to make its own way, and managed to steer them to safety. Braying loudly, the mule followed up the slippery bank.

Giving Serena to Juanita, Travis followed Cade back across. He commandeered the packhorses while Cade took Roy and his pony. Lily wished she could close her eyes, but she couldn't. It was as if by watching she somehow helped them make the crossing. If she didn't watch, anything could happen.

The dam began to crack when they were only halfway over. Lily could hear Juanita's scream of fright as the massive construction creaked and a small torrent of water poured over the place they had just crossed. The water level rose rapidly with this new addition, but Travis and Cade kept their frightened mounts under control and brought them out on the opposite bank.

Juanita caught Roy and hugged him as Cade lowered the boy beside her, then turned and hugged Travis when he climbed down to check their packs. He looked thoroughly surprised, but offered no objection, and went about his work grinning widely.

Just as Cade started back across, a major portion of the dam collapsed beneath the rough stream. Lily stepped farther back up the bank as the water poured under the mud cliff, weakening the ground where she was standing and sending it swirling into the already muddy waters. She looked across the misty river to find Cade determinedly returning his horse to the rushing current.

It was sheer madness. The water roared as high as the gelding's withers, and Lily knew for certain Cade was going to be swept away. He hauled on the horse's reins and kept coming.

A log broke loose and swept dangerously near, and a second followed as the dam fell apart beneath the torrential current. Lily screamed as Cade caught one log with his foot and kicked it aside, nearly losing his seat, but he never faltered as he came back for her. It was like watching an irresistible force meet an immovable object. He was out of the water and up the bank a few seconds later.

He leapt down and Lily flung herself into his arms, clinging to his muscular back as he wrapped her in his embrace. Still he said nothing as he lifted her up to the horse. There was nothing to be said. They had to go on.

He sought a safer crossing, however, following the river until a sandy bar indicated a shallower place in the wide riverbed. The water still poured around them, soaking them to the skin, but the logs were fewer and farther between and the danger less.

When they finally rejoined the others, Travis had his hands full with two terrified children and a weeping Juanita, but he managed a shaky smile as they rode up.

"Couldn't have done it better myself, redskin. I guess you win the fair lady."

Cade grunted something incomprehensible and swung his horse back to the trail. The morning had just begun. They had a day's ride ahead of them.

By evening, Lily's raw throat had worsened so much that she could barely swallow, and she knew she had a raging fever. There was nothing that could be done about either, so she said nothing when they dismounted for the night.

The rain had turned to a mild drizzle, and Lily simply clung to the saddle while the men set up the tent and the children scavenged for small tinder that might dry quickly. When she tried to walk, her head seemed to swim, making it exceedingly difficult to reach a secluded spot where she could relieve herself.

The trees had become less frequent as they traveled westward. The land was given to rough mesquite and dwarfed oaks. Lily succeeded in reaching one of these as the men worked, but returning, she nearly slipped and fell in the mud. Roy saw her and hollered, and Cade was there in a few long strides, catching Lily's waist and half-carrying her back to the completed tent.

"She's burning up. What have you got in your medicine bags for that?" Lowering Lily to a hastily spread bedroll, Cade held a hand to her head and sent his cynical question toward Travis.

Travis knelt on her other side, and Lily tried to shake them both off by sitting up, but Cade caught her shoulder and held her down while Travis grabbed her waist and sought her pulse.

"She should never have been out in this damned rain. Her whole system's weak. She needs to be confined to bed for a month or so."

"Don't be ridiculous, Travis," Lily croaked. "See if we can't make some hot tea and let me be. I'll be fine." Lily could see the children gathering behind Cade, and she meant to firmly impress on them that there was nothing wrong with her. There was too much turmoil in their young lives as it was. She sat up again.

"You look like hell, and if you don't take care of yourself, you'll lose that child. Now sit there quiet and don't move a muscle until you're told to." Rising, Travis ordered Juanita to look for the tea while he went outside to rummage in his saddlebags.

Grimly, Cade brushed Lily's hair back from her face and pulled a blanket around her drenched clothes. "Change," he ordered. Then, gesturing to Roy, he led the boy outside, giving Lily the privacy she needed.

" 'Don't move,' " Lily mimicked. " 'Change,' he says." Tugging at the soaked trousers she wore half-fastened under her old dress, she pulled them off. "I'm going to throw the two of them back in the river."

"Babies scare them," Juanita offered pacifically,

handing Lily a tin cup of the brandy she had hidden in the cooking supplies. "The fire isn't hot enough to boil water yet. This will do you good."

The brandy burned all the way down, but it helped. By the time Cade let anyone back in the tent, Lily had changed into only slightly damp long underwear and her flannel nightgown. She hadn't come away with a large wardrobe.

"The books never tell you what to give a pregnant patient," Travis complained as he sat down beside her with a bottle of Professor Mangolini's Cure-All. "But a hot toddy never hurt anybody, and this stuff comes close enough to that. We can warm it up with some hot tea when the fire gets going."

Lily looked over at Juanita, who giggled, making Lily giggle too. She lowered her head and tried to hide the sound against her knees. Travis looked worried and threw a look to Juanita. "Are you ill too?"

That made them giggle more. Hearing the sound, Cade entered the tent to find both women on the verge of laughter and Serena happily toddling between them, urging them on.

"Magic cure you have there, professor. Is it contagious?"

It hurt to laugh, and Lily tried to calm herself, succeeding only in developing a case of the hiccups instead. Holding her head to her knees to keep it from spinning, and hiccuping, she swung her tin cup airily. "More, Juanita. We'll teach this child to be a Texan."

Cade grabbed the cup and sniffed. Holding it out to Juanita, he demanded, "I'll have some of that, too, if you please."

Travis jerked the cup out of his hand and handed it back to Juanita. "That's just what we don't need, a drunken Indian. Tea, and now, Juanita. We'll drink it cold if we have to."

That sobered Lily, and she lifted her head quietly. She could see the fury bubbling up inside Cade, but no one inexperienced in observing his impassive mask would have noticed. She held her breath, waiting for the explosion to come.

Instead, Cade glanced down at her, read the pain in her eyes, and stalked out.

Twenty-eight

Horrified by the long line of uniformed soldiers marching down the road not a day's ride behind the wagonloads of settlers fleeing for their lives, the small party lay low behind a small outcropping of rock and tried to stay quiet. They had stumbled across the road and its dangerous occupants at the wrong time, and it was too late to try to run. Any movement was almost certain to draw the attention of the troops marching across the horizon.

Even the children were sensible enough to know they should be quiet, but the mule wasn't. Its bray brought a quiver of interest from the ranks, and Lily watched in horror as a few of the soldiers peeled away from the line and looked in their direction.

Before she realized what he meant to do, Cade was on his horse, towing the mule while riding at right angles away from the road and the army on the move. The rain had let up slightly and the air was warm, and Cade wore only the white full-sleeved shirt and tight trousers he had worn every day since they had left. The shirt was open halfway down his copper chest and accented by a bright-red sash at his waist that held his knife. Lily thought he looked a pirate or worse, but the soldiers striking out after him weren't reaching for their weapons.

"He looks like a damned Spaniard," Travis whispered at Lily's side. "How does he do that?"

With years of practice and an Indian talent for deception—but Lily didn't say that out loud. She was gradually coming to learn that Cade was like a chameleon, able to blend in with his surroundings for safety.

She didn't like to think of the child he must have been to grow up that way, but it certainly helped to survive in this chaos that was Texas.

Lily restrained a gasp of terror and Travis reached for his rifle as one of the officers lifted his musket and aimed it at Cade with a hoarse shout. Cade turned around, but made no move toward his own weapon. He merely slowed his horse and replied in Spanish that Lily couldn't catch.

Although they could see this little tableau from their position behind the rocks, Lily was aware that Cade had led the officers far enough away from the road that the army marching out of sight over the horizon couldn't see. She was equally aware that Cade's American rifle could reach farther and with more deadly accuracy than the old-fashioned muskets of the soldiers. Between Travis and Cade it would almost be possible to pick off all three soldiers and have no one be the wiser for some time to come. But Cade didn't reach for his weapon, and Travis was forced to lower his to protect their hiding place.

"Doesn't he know what that damned gun is for?" Travis asked irritably as he felt Lily grow tense at his side. If the soldiers chose to take Cade prisoner, they couldn't fight an entire army to rescue him.

Lily relaxed a moment later as the men exchanged words and the soldier lowered his musket again. To her amazement, the one soldier gallantly swept off his hat and offered his hand in friendship and Cade accepted it with an almost regal nod. She had the sudden urge to grab Travis's rifle and shoot the arrogance out of him. Didn't he realize he was fraternizing with the enemy? Who in hell did he think he was?

When the soldiers turned and galloped off after the departing army, Cade kept up his charade of riding in the opposite direction until they were out of sight. Then wheeling his animals around, he galloped back to his hidden family.

"What in hell did you tell them?" Travis asked irritably as he stood and tried to mop some of the mud from his clothing.

Cade reached to help Lily up, but she stood without his aid, ignoring his outstretched hand. He could very well have just saved their lives, but her suspicions were beginning to mount ever higher, and she needed answers first.

When Cade showed no inclination to answer Travis, Lily wiped her hands off on her bedraggled skirt and confronted him. "How did you know you could talk them into leaving? Wouldn't it have been safer to shoot them or tie them up or something? What if they had decided to shoot first? Or take you prisoner?"

Cade heard her anger, but he hoped he also heard her concern. There were things she didn't understand as yet. He didn't feel qualified to explain them. Throwing Roy back into his saddle, he answered without emphasis, "They knew my grandfather. They would not wish to incur the wrath of a de Suela."

That made about as much sense as anything else she had seen or heard this day. As far as Lily could understand, Cade was the barely legitimate son of an Indian and a woman whose family had deserted her. Perhaps invoking the de Suela name was a type of incantation that frightened off the superstitious Mexicans with just its utterance.

She said nothing more as Cade took her up before him. Her fever hadn't lessened to any noticeable degree, but without the constant drenching rain she felt considerably relieved and didn't complain. If she allowed herself to admit it, being held in the security of Cade's arms against the formidable strength of his hard chest was as good as lying in bed and pampering herself. His closeness was a source of comfort in itself, and his calm assurance as he held her and urged the horse into motion had the benefit of pushing all her fears into a box where she didn't have to confront them. It was foolish to put herself and her family into a man's hands without question, but she had been foolish from the first moment she had seen this man with a kitten in his lap. She couldn't fight it now when she was so weak.

"Do you think we'll be home in time to have the

baby?" she murmured as she rested her head against the bulk of his shoulder.

Cade's hold tightened slightly as he set his gaze on the horizon ahead. "We'll be home," he assured her. He didn't say which home he meant.

By the time they rode into the *ranchero,* Lily had no awareness of their arrival. Even curled inside the blanket that Cade had wrapped around her, she shivered, and she remained unconscious as Cade lifted her into the hands of Travis and climbed down.

The old man was already hurriedly coming forward into the growing gloom to greet them. He bowed with Old World grace over Juanita's hand, leaving her flustered and embarrassed. Cade said nothing as he took Lily back from Travis and started for the house, the children trailing after him.

Without asking where to go, he entered the high-ceilinged hallway and turned to his right, carrying Lily to a room with a wide bed with an ornately carved frame. When Serena lifted her arms to be picked up and placed beside Lily, Cade took her in his arms but carried her back to the hall where the others waited.

Depositing the child in Juanita's hands and giving Roy a look that included him, Cade commanded, "Watch after them." Turning to the slightly bewildered old man, he asked, "Is there a physician? My wife is ill."

Antonio de Suela looked down at the petite Mexican beauty cuddling the golden-haired child, then back to the hall where his grandson had taken the ill woman. He had seen enough to know the other woman was tall and blond and obviously not Spanish or Indian. He had assumed . . .

But it was wisest not to assume anything with this dark stranger who was his flesh and blood. He replied with care, "The Americans have gone. We have no physicians. I am sorry. Is there something I can do?"

"Have someone bring hot water for a bath and boil some tea or coffee if it is available. And have you any onions? If there are, they need to be boiled." Travis stepped forward with an air of authority.

At Cade's nod, de Suela ordered a hovering servant in Spanish to find the needed articles.

Following Travis's instructions but refusing him entrance to the room, Cade bathed Lily and wrapped her in a flannel nightgown that had been dried before the kitchen fire. He unwrapped her hair and scrubbed it clean, knowing she would want it that way even though she couldn't be roused enough to answer him if he asked.

Her labored breathing terrified him, but the steaming water seemed to help. Holding her in his lap with a blanket wrapped around her while her hair dried, Cade attempted to get a little of the hot tea into her. She drank when pressed, but mostly she lay inert in his arms, and Cade sat for long moments in the dark bedroom, staring at the walls closing in around him.

He could feel her breathing, feel the beat of her heart against his chest. If he turned her just right, he could feel the slight fluttering kicks of their child. He tried not to experience anything beyond these physical sensations, but he couldn't ignore the immensity of what he had done, what he was doing.

He was responsible for another human life, two lives. He knew how to accept responsibility, but he didn't think he knew how to cope with the results if he should fail. That fact had never occurred to him. Ephraim's death was weighing heavily on his mind. Coupled with Lily's illness . . .

Lily wasn't supposed to get ill. She was as strong and independent as he. Cade tested the long lengths of her silken hair and finding them sufficiently dry, he determinedly lifted her to the bed, fighting the suffocating sensation of helplessness. Life was fleeting. He would learn to cope with whatever happened as he had learned to cope with all that had come before. Emotions were a luxury he couldn't afford to indulge in. He was going to survive, and if Lily would just recover, he would show her how well he could take care of her.

He would show her now, although she wouldn't be aware of it. Wrapping the poultice of boiled onion around her neck as Travis had instructed, Cade patiently began inserting spoonfuls of camomile tea between Lily's lips. She would be better in the morning, and then he could begin to make her understand.

The others wandered in and out of the room throughout the night. Cade comforted Serena and Roy by telling them Lily was tired and was just sleeping. They could see the truth of that with their own eyes and went away to sound sleeps in comfortable beds for the first time in a week. Travis and Juanita weren't so easily fooled, but Cade refused their offers of assistance, allowing them only to bring more tea and poultices and vinegar water.

Cade applied the cool vinegar water to Lily's head when the fever seemed to grow stronger. When she began to sweat and toss restlessly, he peeled her gown from her shoulders and bathed her shoulders and breasts. She seemed to grow quiet with his touch, and he continued the soothing motion until she felt cooler again.

When he was certain that she slept peacefully, Cade stripped off his clothes and joined her beneath the covers. They hadn't been together like this for so long. He pulled her into the curve of his body and rested his hand protectively on her swelling belly. His child grew there, and he protected what was his. He had so very little, he would fight for what he had.

Exhausted, Cade slept. He dreamed of his mother's voice, Lily's tears, Serena's laughter, and Roy's wary confidences. They became intermixed somehow, forming a potion he was meant to sip. It was a heady brew, sweet-tasting and going down warm, fermenting into bubbles when it hit his insides, where it became a part of him as the baby was a part of Lily.

When he woke, Cade could still feel the magic of it burning in his middle, but his more immediate response was to the woman's body so conveniently pressed against his need. His loins hardened almost painfully as he rubbed against the soft curve of Lily's buttocks. When she answered his quest by pushing closer to him, seeking the same solace he required, Cade eased the interfering nightgown up to her waist.

He touched her breasts, and Lily moaned with pleasure.

Kissing, caressing, Cade felt her hips move rhythmically against him until he could no longer bear the pressure. Fearful of causing her harm, he entered her gently from behind, and she sighed her need just as he felt he would burst with his.

Lily woke to the feel of Cade inside her, his fingers gliding between her legs to spread her pleasure until she thought she would jump out of her skin when he moved and made himself deeper. Crying out, she moved with him until they were both gasping with desire. The moment, when it came, burst upon them with unexpected suddenness. They weren't ready, and their bodies continued to press and twist and cling to the closeness their joining should have satisfied.

Filling his hand with her breast, Cade forced himself to stillness. The heat of the night had left her, and he kissed the shoulder he had bared during the fever. "How do you feel this morning?"

"Ravished," Lily croaked, surprised at the sound of her voice. At Cade's chuckle and the gentle brush of his hand over her nakedness, she realized how thoroughly she had succumbed to him—again—and she stiffened.

"You are not to move from this bed," he warned softly as he moved away, pushing her down into the pillows and pressing a kiss to her forehead. "I will be back shortly with your breakfast."

Lily ached in too many places to argue. She still felt him between her legs, and irrationally, she wanted him there again. At the same time, she wanted to throw things at him and demand explanations. Cade was too good at slipping through the cracks, avoiding the questions that just his presence raised. But she hadn't the strength to lift her head from the pillow.

She watched as Cade went to the wardrobe and pulled out a white shirt of the finest linen weave, even finer than the one she had made for him. She had seen him wear only three shirts in the entire time she had known him, and suddenly he was wearing his best dress shirt through mud and donning rich clothes that made him seem a stranger.

He pulled on a pair of skintight trousers that appeared to be satin, and Lily's breath caught in her chest at the sight he presented. She couldn't keep her gaze from straying to his narrow hips and the crotch of his trousers. He was her husband and she knew him intimately, but his new clothing made her interest seem almost obscene.

He covered himself with a short jacket embellished with silver braid and added a cravat that hung in loose folds over his elegant shirt. His thick, straight hair brushed the cravat, but in all other respects he looked like a Spanish gentleman. The sharp Roman nose and high cheekbones now resembled aristocracy more than it revealed his Indian heritage.

There was no expression in his dark eyes as he came to stand by the bed and adjusted her pillows before leaving. Lily fingered the expensive quality of his coat with curiosity, but he didn't answer the questions in her eyes.

"Rest. I will be right back," Cade assured her before plumping the pillows one last time and walking out.

Yes, but who would he be when he returned?

Serena came in and threw herself upon the bed before Juanita, following behind, could stop her. Even Juanita looked different this morning. Her hair was braided in shining loops at her ears and she wore a new blouse that was scooped in the neck and full in the sleeves and totally inappropriate for cooking. She had silver bangles in her ears and on her arms and jangled them surreptitiously, with a child's wonder, when she thought Lily wasn't looking.

It was as if everyone had set out to make her understand that this was a Mexican household, that she was in someone else's territory and not her own. It was a strange feeling. Even when she had moved to Texas, Lily had been confident that the cabin they built was home and not a strange new way of living. In the Indian camp, she had felt awkward, but she hadn't known those people. Here, she was surrounded by people she knew, but she didn't know them.

Cade came in with a tray and, seeing Juanita, left her to deal with the complexities of feeding an invalid. Lily wanted to shout at him to stay, that she needed a few answers, but he seemed impatient to be off and her voice wouldn't do more than croak a few protests. She threw a pillow after him when he closed the door.

Serena laughed at this new game and threw a pillow at Roy when he came in a short while later. Sullenly, Roy threw it back at her, and she went laughing into the covers, completely oblivious to Roy's displeasure.

At Lily's frown, he reddened slightly and put his hands behind his back. "Are we going to live here forever?" he demanded.

"No," Lily managed to croak. She reached to brush a straying hair from his face.

"Good. Everybody speaks Spanish, and I don't understand a word they're saying." He helped himself to one of Lily's tortillas and settled into a corner of the room to munch.

Lily sipped her coffee and glanced around at her new living quarters. Wherever she was, it was more elegant than anything she'd ever had at home, even in Mississippi. Besides the ornately carved bed with its rich covers, the room contained matching wardrobe, washstand, and a chest of drawers. The wood was heavy and dark and artistically embellished and accented by glittering brass candleholders and crystal containers and silver hardware. A tapestry in silver-blue and gold depicting a bullfight hung on one wall, and similar colors were repeated on pillows and covers and tablecloths. The linen she slept on was almost like silk. Lily knew she would never own such niceties if she lived to be a hundred.

She found it hard to believe that a man who owned all this would accept a half-breed into his home. Surely Cade's grandfather knew of Cade's heritage?

Worried, Lily stared out the window to a plain devoid of the green she called home. Why had Cade brought her here?

Twenty-nine

"**I** wish to speak with my grandson's wife." The old man stood in the doorway, his sharp eyes ordering the servant blocking his path to move away.

When Juanita stepped aside, he entered the bedroom without further ceremony. His gaze immediately swept to the woman sitting up in the bed. She was pregnant and ill; he took that into consideration. Her face was weathered by sun and cold, and dark shadows circled her eyes. Her baby-fine hair was pulled back in a braid that fell over the simple white gown she wore. Even taking all the circumstances into consideration, he could not call her beautiful, as both of his wives and his daughter had been. But she met his stare with a strong blue gaze that reminded him sharply of the differences between himself and his grandson. For now, he would give her the benefit of the doubt.

Barely glancing at Juanita, Antonio nodded toward the door. "You will leave us," he commanded with all the authority of one accustomed to being obeyed.

Lily hid her dismay as Juanita unhesitatingly did as she was told. Her throat was still raw and hoarse, and she made no attempt to contradict the old man's orders. Instead, she shifted her focus to examine this new obstacle in her life.

She could only assume that this was Antonio de Suela, since no one had bothered to introduce her. He was nearly as tall as Cade, but only half his breadth. Had she been well and feeling like herself, she could almost believe that she would be stronger than this frail old man gazing at her with such intensity. He leaned on a gold-handled walking stick, but his black eyes were alert and observant as he turned more fully toward her.

"You are carrying Luis Philippe's child," he stated without preamble.

The name did not sound strange on this man's tongue, but it took Lily a moment to respond to it. She merely nodded her head in reply. She had a feeling she would need to save her voice for what would follow.

"I had hoped my grandson would find a wife among his own people." Antonio lowered himself to a bedroom chair but continued to hold himself stiffly.

Lily lifted an inquiring brow. His own people? Had the man forgotten that Cade was equally Indian?

Antonio scowled at her response. "Among my people. It would be easier to show that he is a de Suela if he had married appropriately."

This man had come here with an axe to grind, and nothing she could say was going to stop him. Why waste her voice in trying?

She reached for the shawl on her bedside stand and wrapped it around her without speaking. After all, there was nothing she could say to the man's pronouncement.

Her silence forced de Suela to realize this, and he nodded. "He tells me you are a wealthy lady in your own right. I should not complain. I apologize. I am an old man and have come to realize that many of my dreams will never come true. For many years I have wished for a child to carry on my name, but I thought it was not to be. Now that I have found my grandson, I wish him to be everything that I would have made of him. I forget that he is already a man of his own."

"Very much so," Lily whispered, finally hearing something with which she could agree.

Antonio nodded sagely. "I think you are a good woman. We will make the family see that you are one of us, as they must come to see that Luis is mine. It is good that he takes my name. The child you carry will be a de Suela. Luis has done the right thing by bringing you here. I am not so old that there is not time to see my destiny passed on to my grandson and his child."

Lily felt a flicker of alarm, but the old man was already rising, and the shakiness of his hand on the stick kept her from protesting aloud. She was in no state to argue, and in any case, this was not the man with whom she wished to argue. "Luis" had a few questions waiting for him whenever he deigned to put in an appearance.

Antonio made a gentlemanly bow over Lily's hand. At the sight of the silver ring on her finger, he hesitated, and an expression of such deep sadness passed over his face that Lily wished she could reach out and comfort him. He seemed about to speak, but then he merely kissed the ring, wished her well, and departed.

Determined to show the old man that she was not his daughter and he could not arrange everything to suit himself, Lily prepared herself for the fight. When Juanita returned, she was struggling to get out of bed. "Where's Cade?" she whispered hoarsely before the maid could even say a word.

"He and Travis have gone into Béxar. You are supposed to stay in bed. We have none of us slept for worrying about you. If you make yourself ill again, we will never forgive you. Back!" Juanita ordered, bustling about, pulling at the covers and plumping the pillows.

"I want to get dressed. I will sit right here and rest, but I want to be dressed when they come back." Lily slid from the high bed to her feet, swaying slightly as she did so. The fever had left her weaker than she had thought, but she clung to the bed and maintained her balance.

"Your clothes are being washed and pressed. There is nothing for you to wear. Now is not the time to be modest. They have seen you in your nightgown before."

Lily didn't know whether Juanita was referring to their nights in the tent or if she was hinting at Lily's past relationship with Travis. There was a slightly sharp edge to Juanita's tone that made her think the latter. Reluctantly, she returned to the massive bed with its suffocating feather mattress. Crossing her arms over her chest, Lily scowled at thus being thwarted.

"I am not an invalid. What am I supposed to do here all day?"

"Sleep. Travis says you are to get much rest." Juanita jerked the light curtains across the windows to conceal the winter sun.

"And since when have you paid any attention to what Travis says? He is a man like any other." As long as she was going to be bored, she might as well draw Juanita out on a few subjects that had been intriguing her. Unfortunately, her throat still hurt enough to keep her from saying as much as she would like.

"He is not evil." Juanita gave a haughty sniff, but there was a color to her cheeks that had not been there before.

"No, he's too damned charming for his own good. Unless you have decided to raise a child on your own, you'd better stay away from him." Lily couldn't make her warning any plainer. Travis may have matured over the last few years, but she couldn't see him settling down to a Mexican maid and the role of country physician.

Juanita blushed more deeply and stalked out without a reply. Lily stared at the window on the far wall and wondered if her life would ever be the same again. Less than a year ago she had thought herself safe and secure. Suddenly she was married to a man she didn't know, living in a house that wasn't hers, and wondering who the hell she was and what she was doing here.

She wanted to go home, but the chances were good that she no longer had a home to go to. She wouldn't even be able to return to Mississippi once she wrote to tell her sisters of their father's death. They would probably sell the house faster than she could travel.

The past was gone, and she had only an uncertain future to look forward to. Leaning back against the pillows and placing her hand over the child resting trustingly in her abdomen, Lily vowed to right that situation as soon as possible. She would have a home again. Her home. Not some stranger's.

When Cade returned, Lily was asleep. He laid the present he had brought for her over a chair back and hesitated near the bed. Asleep, she looked little more than an innocent child, but the evidence was there to prove that he had stolen any claim to innocence. He touched the bulge of her stomach beneath the bedclothes with his brown hand, and she instantly awoke.

"Cade." The word was a sigh of relief and a warning all in one. Lily struggled to rise, and Cade placed pillows behind her back. She rested against them gratefully. The child was already kicking up a storm.

"Have you heard news?" First things first. Lily studied Cade's dark face for the truth. There was nothing of the triumphant in his expression as he spoke.

"The news is not good. Tell me how you are feeling. Can I get you anything?"

"You can get me out of here, and you can tell me the truth. How bad is 'not good'?"

There was a stiffness between them that should not be there, but Cade did not know how to erase it. He fully intended to make this house his home, just as he had made Lily his wife, but he had lived thirty-two years without either and it was taking some time to adjust. He knew she was uncomfortable with the situation, but Lily was as strong as he. She would learn.

"It will not be good for the child to hear the details. Houston's army is retreating. Do not ask me more. Shall I call Juanita to bring your supper?"

Cade had promised that his grandfather would help keep her land if Santa Anna won. She would have to trust in that. Not comfortable with the notion, Lily turned away from Cade's expressionless face to stare out the window. "I can't stay in bed forever. Are my clothes dry yet?"

She hadn't even noticed the gift he had left across the chair. Not certain how to react to that, Cade spread the gown across the covers. "Will this do?"

Lily glanced down in surprise. She had seen the dark cloth thrown across the chair, but since she didn't recognize it, she had thought nothing of it. Now she picked at the rich velvet bands of mourning against the heavy silk of the skirt and turned uncertainly to Cade. "It is lovely. Whose is it?"

Cade rubbed his hand over the back of his neck, suddenly uncomfortable with these civilized clothes and gestures. He knew what to do with a woman in bed. He wasn't at all certain what to do with one who was ill, in mourning, and carrying his child. He groped desperately for the right words.

"Yours, I thought . . . because of your father . . ." Her face lightened with comprehension, and Cade made no attempt to explain further.

"You've bought me a mourning gown! Cade, that wasn't necessary. It's so expensive . . ." Lily smoothed the rich silk lovingly. She didn't think she had ever owned something of such value. Sixteen-year-olds weren't given silk, and there had never been the money for anything but the house and land since. "I could have dyed one of my other gowns. You shouldn't have . . ."

"You are my wife." He said this with firm conviction, as if it answered all that was between them, but in reality Cade was uncertain of anything that had to do with Lily. He had thought this matter of taking a wife a simple thing, but he was finding that it led to all manner of complications with which his experience wasn't equipped to deal. Her illness had terrified him, shattering more defensive barriers than he was willing to admit. Her pallor now made his stomach tremble with fear. Cade wanted to keep her in that bed and not let anything happen to her, but he had enough understanding of the woman he had married to know that was impossible. He stood helpless before her, but he hid that fact behind his implacability.

"If it fits, may I come to dinner? I am tired of sitting here by myself." Inexplicably uneasy in Cade's presence, Lily countered with as much boldness as she could command. Standing there in a rich black brocade vest she had never seen before, his linen shirt open at the throat as usual, Cade was a commanding presence and a stranger. And this was his home, not hers.

"I would like that. I wish to introduce you to my grandfather."

"He has introduced himself," Lily replied wryly, finding a topic on which she was on firmer ground. "I'm not at all certain that I meet his approval."

"He is living in the past. Come, I will help you dress."
Cade held out his hand.

Lily glanced down at the swelling of her stomach beneath the covers and back to the handsome stranger beside the bed. She couldn't reconcile the Cade who had
given her this child with the Luis Philippe who expected
her to sleep in elegant Spanish beds and wear mourning.
She shook her head, and his offered hand dropped to his
side as he regarded her a trifle impatiently.

"I will send Juanita."

Cade turned to leave. Lily hesitated, then called after
him, "Cade why does your father think we mean to stay
here?"

Cade swung around. "Because this is my home."

Lily felt a flutter of fear at the hardness in his dark
eyes. "But he will help us to return to my land when all
this is over?"

"I will not let you lose your land." Cade reached for
the door.

Setting her jaw, Lily forced herself to inquire, "I asked
if we would be returning to my land?"

Cade kept his hand on the door latch and looked down
at it rather than turning. "I have waited twenty years to
claim this place. I am in no hurry to leave."

With that, he walked out.

Shattered, Lily continued to stare at the doorway long
after he had passed through it. What had she thought she
was doing when she married this man? Hiring a permanent foreman? Why hadn't it occurred to her that he
would have a life of his own—one that didn't necessarily
require her? And why did she find that possibility so
frightening?

Refusing to give in to fear, Lily struggled out of bed
and, leaning against the washstand, began to bathe as best
as she could. She would show Cade Luis Philippe de
Suela that she wasn't a straw doll to be placed where he
would. She might not know where she stood in his life,
but she had a life of her own. She was a landowner. He
would learn to understand that.

Juanita clucked and scolded when she came in to find

Lily balancing precariously on the edge of the bed and struggling with her new gown, but something in Lily's expression kept her from saying anything more. Between them, they settled the elegant folds over Lily's shoulders and pulled it down to encompass her new waistline. Cade had obviously mentioned to the dressmaker that his wife was *encinta,* because the seams had been adjusted accordingly. Either that, or the original owner of the gown had been pleasingly plump.

Not caring to delve into the origins of the gown, Lily stood and pulled the full skirt down over her legs. The silk had been layered in ruffles from the waist down, easily disguising her fullness in the fullness of the gown, although her waist was much larger than was pleasing. The gown had a faintly exotic look to it and wasn't at all what Lily was accustomed to, but she felt rich and not herself wearing it, even to the point of allowing Juanita to play with her hair.

By the time Cade returned, wearing a long frock coat over the brocade waistcoat he had worn earlier, Lily was ready. She eyed the ruffled tie at his throat dubiously while he inspected the golden-brown ringlets of her hair with interest. They had been man and wife for over five months under Indian law, but their knowledge of each other would fit into a thimble.

Taking Lily's arm, Cade escorted her from the room without a word. If she had been expecting a comment on her appearance, she was destined to be disappointed. To Lily's surprise, Travis waited in the corridor, but it was Juanita's arm he took when she came out. Lily sent her friend a questioning look, but Juanita merely made a shrug, taking the offered arm without a smile.

"I like your hair like that, Lily," Travis offered genially as they traversed the clay tiles of the corridor into the courtyard that opened onto the public rooms.

"I don't." Cade's tone was ominous. "I like it down around her shoulders." The look he gave Lily left nothing to translation, and even the couple behind them grew silent.

Lily felt his meaning to the bottom of her toes. The

only time she wore her hair loose was when Cade had unraveled it and pulled it down around her shoulders before
bed. Nervously, she looked straight ahead, admiring the
shrubbery that struggled to survive in the neglected courtyard. The Cade who spoke and the Cade she saw were
two different people. It would take time to reconcile the
differences.

The doors to the dining room were opened to the courtyard to allow the circulation of air. As they entered, the
old gentleman waiting inside rose from his chair and
made an elegant bow.

"Good evening, ladies. I have ordered my best wine
brought in to celebrate the occasion. I would welcome all
of you to your new home, and most particularly, *señora,*"
he bent over Lily's hand, "I would welcome you and
hope you will have many long years as lady of this
house."

As the servants poured the wine into delicate crystal
glasses, Lily gave Cade a smoldering look that should
have scorched him to his soul.

He took the glass as if he had handled such daily, instead of the crude gourd that had been his water supply
for the better part of his life. With a slightly lifted eyebrow, Cade raised the glass in salute to Lily and her new
position in his household.

Thirty

Lily's silence set the mood for the remainder of the evening. As the others sipped politely at their wine, Lily held hers, setting it by her plate untouched when the time came to take a seat. She noticed that Cade readily accepted a second glass and he gave her a look of warning over the rim as he sipped it, but she had no intention of nagging or complaining in public. She had been raised a lady, and she maintained some modicum of respect for the conventions of reticence.

Accustomed to doing as he pleased but not accustomed to a woman who did not throw tantrums when thwarted, Cade matched his grandfather glass for glass as the evening progressed. It had taken twenty years of searching and waiting for this day. He didn't mean for his triumph to go unmarked.

He knew the moment was a precarious one. Ricardo, raised as Antonio's son, had every reason to expect this land to go to him. Antonio de Suela was an arrogant, opinionated man who expected his wishes to be followed, and Cade wasn't at all certain that he would follow them. But for right now, he was being accepted as a legitimate part of the family, and that was more then he had known in a lifetime. He would settle for that. Lily would have to learn to adjust.

"What do you think of the land?" Antonio inquired casually, although the look in his eyes was far from casual.

"The irrigation ditches will have to be re-dug. The river is flooding and taking your soil. Few of the cattle are left. We will need to drive some up from Mexico. The vineyards are gone. Some of the orchard is left, but it is

too old to produce. Much work needs to be done." Cade
catalogued his discoveries without inflection. He knew
his grandfather was testing him. He knew the old man
had returned from Mexico to test him. He didn't mind.

"I will hire men to begin work on the ditches." Antonio
broke a piece of his bread and chewed it thoughtfully before continuing. "You will have to go to Mexico for the
cattle. I cannot make that journey again. I will give you
letters of introduction."

"Not yet, *mi abuelo*," Cade answered gently. "There is
another matter I must see to now that Lily and the children are safe."

Cade was aware that all eyes at the table focused on
him. Travis already knew what Cade planned. They had
discussed it long since and were agreed. His grandfather
was watching intently, and the look on Juanita's face was
one of concern, undoubtedly concern for Lily. Cade felt
the daunting blue of Lily's eyes the most. Everything he
said or did could affect her and her family. Cade realized
this, but he had done the best for them that he was able.
It was time now to do what was necessary.

"The future lies in the hands of the man who wins this
war," Cade said, giving his explanation for Lily's benefit
as he never would have done for anyone else. "I do not
relish working for a dictator. I will be joining Houston, if
he will have me."

Even though he was looking at his grandfather as he
said this, Cade knew when Lily's hands quietly dropped
her silverware to the table. He turned to see her lay her
napkin beside the plate. Because the alcohol slowed his
reflexes, he could not rise in time to catch her before she
fled the room. He stood there stupidly staring at the place
where she had been while Juanita rushed after her.

Shaking his head to clear it, Cade fell back to his seat.
He would not fool himself into thinking Lily's flight
meant she feared for his safety. She hated him. She was
angry that he had not sought her approval first.

She would learn that he was his own man, that he did
not take orders from anyone. She had the child to con-

sider now. She could do or say nothing to deter him. When he came back, perhaps they could start over again.

His grandfather was looking at him with more interest than displeasure. Cade lifted his wineglass in salute. "To women," he murmured.

It was late when Cade finally found his way to Lily's room. He did not mean to spend the night in the chair beside the bed again. They had been separated for too much of their marriage. There could be many months of separation ahead. Tonight, he would lie with his wife, he decided with drunken arrogance.

She was asleep when he entered the room, curled up in a ball in the center of the bed. Her hair was pulled back in those accursed braids, but Cade had a vision of her golden loveliness in the candlelight at the table that night. He should have said something polite as Travis had done. But he had said what he meant. He wanted her hair loose and flowing, wanton as her passions.

Unsteadily, Cade stripped off his new clothes, dropping them on the floor without a care for their cost. His grandfather was a generous man when he was getting what he wanted. It didn't hurt him to wear the clothes that made his grandfather happy. He had learned that lesson a long time ago. Tonight, however—with Lily—he would be himself.

Stretched out naked beside her cotton-clad form, Cade eased Lily into his arms. He had never played the part of chameleon in bed, simply because there had been no need to deceive women he had paid to share it. Now he did not know how to be anybody other than himself when he came to her.

He had been terrified that he would frighten her off. If there had been any way to disguise what he was in those moments of intimacy, he might have tried. But he knew of no way of hiding his desire, changing his size, or denying his heritage once they were naked and alone.

And it hadn't mattered—not to Lily. Her desire had been as overwhelming as his own, without any need for disguise. Her body had conformed perfectly to his. And she had not looked at him with disgust in the dawn's early light. And that's when Cade had known that he had done the right thing.

He still had his doubts now and then, but not when they were in bed together. If they shared nothing else, they shared this. Cade's hand smoothed the fabric of Lily's nightgown over her breast and felt her murmur in her sleep as he stroked the nipple rising to his touch. He was already roused and ready for her, and he pressed against her buttocks, hoping to stir her from sleep to better appreciate his needs as she had that morning.

She snuggled closer and sighed, but he received no more response than that. Cautiously, Cade slid her nightgown upward and spread his hand over her abdomen, stroking downward until he touched the soft nest between her legs. She sighed again and grew moist beneath his ministrations, but she did not wake.

It wasn't until he pulled himself up to wake her that Cade saw moonlight winking off the bottle beside the bed. Even in his drunken state he recognized that bottle, and he reached to grab it off the table.

In the flickering light he stared at the label of Professor Mangolini's Sleep Nostrum. Laudanum. Frustrated, Cade flung himself back against the pillow and stared at the ceiling. His loins burned with a need that only Lily could satisfy. And he had driven her to taking sleeping drafts.

No one had told him that marriage was such a damned complicated business.

When Lily woke in the morning, Cade was gone. She knew he had been there. The scent of him lingered on the covers. The nightgown tied in knots around her waist spoke for itself. And her careful braids had come uncoiled to spread in tangled waves across the pillow. Touching herself where he would have touched her, she felt the familiar ache and wished he would return.

It was then that Lily turned and saw the flute lying across the imprint of Cade's head upon the pillow. He was gone.

She tried not to feel the desperation that brought. Carefully lifting the flute, Lily examined it in the morning light. It wasn't the same one he carried in his pocket. That one was faded and worn to Cade's fingers. This one was polished and untouched, carved to fit her smaller hand and embellished with an intricate vine along its side. She knew nothing of reeds or woods and didn't know how he had come to make it, but Lily knew Cade had made this one for her.

Tentatively, she placed the mouth of the instrument to her lips and blew across it. The sound was sweet and pure and full of promise.

In a fury of self-pity, Lily flung it across the room.

Unable to wear the carefully washed and folded trousers placed by her bedside, Lily donned the mourning gown she had worn the day before and set out in search of Juanita. It didn't take long to discover that both Cade and Travis had ridden off at dawn. Juanita's tight-lipped expression mimicked Lily's own.

They should have known this was coming. Men loved war. They would do anything rather than stay home and be domesticated. It really was no surprise.

But as Lily went through the days feeling Cade's child kick more strongly inside her, listening to Roy and Serena prattle Cade's words back at her, watching Antonio for those similarities of feature and expression that so resembled Cade's, Lily knew it was more than anger that she felt.

She didn't want to feel more than anger. Anger could be dealt with. She could slam doors, scream at the children, scrub down her room, uproot a garden and start over. But none of these activities could relieve the gnawing emptiness and fear that began to fill her nights and spill over into her days with Cade's continued absence.

Lily couldn't believe she was afraid for the hulking savage who had walked into her life and turned it upside down. He was a monster, just as Juanita had warned. She ought to be glad he was gone. Except that she mourned his absence as much as or more so than she did her father's.

She blamed her melancholy on her father's death and the loss of her home. She blamed it on her lack of anything constructive to do in this household where women knew their places and didn't venture out to the barns and stable unescorted. She blamed it on loneliness for familiar neighbors in this sea of strangers. But when she went to bed, it wasn't Jim's quiescent presence that she missed. It was Cade's passionate caresses.

Lily shoved the flute into a drawer with her few articles of clothing and ignored it. She was entering her sixth month of pregnancy and certainly didn't need thoughts of lust. She simply needed something to occupy her mind and hands while she awaited the child's arrival.

Cade had been gone well over a week and the sun had begun to dot the prairie with the first April wildflowers when the horrifying news of Goliad arrived.

Lily had learned the hard way that her Spanish host and his hired help believed women should be seen and not heard and that the delicacy of female ears could not withstand their male conversation. So she had learned to work in the courtyard garden while Antonio entertained visitors in the salon, often leaving the doors and windows open to spring breezes. Her Spanish was increasing daily with her concentration on these male conversations, and she was learning much more than the men ever suspected.

She had heard of the capture of Fannin's army in Goliad days after Cade had left. She didn't know how old the news was or if it had been the reason for Cade's departure. She only knew that Cade had said he meant to join Houston, and therefore he couldn't have been in on the disaster that befell Goliad.

Still, Lily cringed as she heard the whispered words of horror describing how Santa Anna had ordered his hundreds of Texan prisoners released only to deliberately have them marched to their slaughter while they thought they were on the way home. The man was mad, as Cade had said. Even Antonio's visitors agreed with him. Santa Anna meant to destroy all that the settlers had done in these last ten years. With the American settlers gone, the Indians would return. What hope was there for the Tejanos in that?

Lily suspected it was no coincidence that Antonio de

Suela had returned from Mexico to his lands in Texas after a twenty-five-year absence at a time when his presence here could lend a steadying influence to a country at war. He made no secret of his distaste for Santa Anna, and the men who came and went from the newly repaired fortresslike walls of the hacienda often spoke of their desire for democracy. Even Lily could translate that word.

She gave Cade's grandfather the respect he deserved, but she couldn't deny her frustration at being treated like a china doll to be wrapped in cotton and protected from the outside world. She could almost sympathize with Cade's mother for staying with the Apache warrior who had stolen her. Knowing what she did of Cade's Indian family, Lily suspected his mother found herself considerably more useful and more challenged mentally as well as physically by the Indian way of life than by this suffocating world of the hacienda.

But with the world outside these walls collapsing in blood and chaos, and the child inside her womb making its demands increasingly known, Lily could do nothing but wait for freedom. She taught Roy and Serena their lessons. She worked in the courtyard garden. She sewed new baby clothes to replace the ones lost in the fire and during their escape. And she waited for word from Cade.

None came.

It was the day that Ricardo arrived that Lily realized she could wait no longer.

She heard the noise of a stranger's arrival, the tramping of dozens of horses as the gates opened, the shouts and yells of men as they brought their beasts under control and greeted each other. She knew at once that the new arrivals weren't the furtive men from Béxar with their news of the war. With hope in her heart, Lily made her way through the house to a darkened salon overlooking the front entrance.

She could make out nothing from the scene other than that they were a mixture of Tejanos and Americans. She saw no one resembling Cade or Travis, recognized none of the horses. Her hopes plummeting, she made her way to her room to freshen herself before the guests entered.

She was even beginning to think like a cosseted female with no other concerns but her appearance.

Scowling at that thought, Lily tucked a straying hair into her chignon and adjusted the black mantilla Cade's grandfather had given her. The flowing lace had a multitude of uses, the best of which was to hide her recalcitrant hair. Checking her image in the cheval mirror, Lily smoothed the wide row of ruffles over her abdomen and examined the extent of the bulge. There was no disguising Cade's child any longer. She looked more like she was in her ninth month than her sixth.

Somehow finding that thought comforting, Lily went to greet their guests. So far, Antonio had not been able to persuade Lily to keep to her room until she was summoned. If their guests had news of the war, she would hear of it, one way or another, and she wasn't waiting for a summons to find out which way it would be.

When she walked into the salon and found Ricardo insolently smoking a large cigar and sitting in Antonio's favorite chair, Lily regretted her impulsiveness. When she noted the other booted and spurred strangers sprawling across the heavy old furniture, she considered turning around and fleeing.

Only Antonio's painfully gaunt figure held her as he gestured with his hand in welcome and introduced her.

"Señora, my stepson, Ricardo. Ricardo, this is my grandson's bride, Lily."

Looking up, Ricardo gave a malevolent grin. "*Buenos días,* Mrs. Brown." His eyes dropped to her protruding stomach. "Another Apache bastard. How interesting."

Even without the epithet, she could see the danger in his eyes and knew the threat this man represented to Cade, to her child, to them all. He would see them all dead, if he could.

Lily knew in that moment what Cade and Juanita meant when they said evil walked on two legs.

With a shiver of fear, she turned her back on Ricardo and walked out, but her mouth tasted of ashes as she sought the safety of her room.

A man who could hate an unborn child was more than evil; he was without a soul.

Cade wanted her to reside with his grandfather, and Lily struggled to reconcile her instincts with his wishes, but the two were irreconcilable. The threat of Ricardo's presence hung over the hacienda like a thick pall. Lily watched as Juanita retreated to her locked room and refused to come out. She held her tongue when the children clung to her skirts whenever Ricardo appeared. But when Antonio de Suela no longer left his chamber or entertained his friends, Lily let her instincts be her guide.

Placed between the devil and the deep blue sea, she chose the vagaries of the sea.

Thirty-one

"How can we do this? It is mad," Juanita whispered frantically as they slipped into the paddock where only the rustling, nickering noises of the animals could be heard.

"What choice do we have?" Resolutely, Lily searched for the placid animals that had brought them here among the restless, half-wild beasts that Ricardo had brought with him.

Juanita had no answer to that. Joining in the search, she helped locate the mules and ponies they needed, leading them out of the paddock with grave misgiving. Roy waited there, holding hastily packed saddlebags and stolen harness. Wrapped in a blanket near his feet, Serena slept quietly.

At least the weather had improved. The night was clear and mild as they loaded the animals. Lily had feared the horses would be guarded, but Ricardo was too sure of himself to waste manpower inside the hacienda walls. The guarded gate would be their difficulty.

Juanita resolved the problem easily. Slipping into the shadows along the wall, she located the man responsible for manning the gate, and holding out one of the silver bracelets Travis had bought for her, she bribed him into complacency. The gates opened, and they rode out without hindrance.

It was too easy. They had surprise on their side, Lily knew. The men never expected a handful of women and children to boldly ride away from the hacienda's protection. Lily was quite certain that Ricardo considered them prisoners as surely as he did his grandfather. The guards posted on the walls could mean no less, and he would not have made his contempt and hatred so plain elsewhere. That he was so confident of his power that he did not immediately imprison them was the only reason Lily could find for the ease of their escape.

As they rode into the dangers of the night, two women and two children, with no guide but the moon and stars, Lily couldn't help but wonder if they had not fallen into Ricardo's trap after all.

April 21, 1836

The noon sun heated the thick magnolia leaves overhead, and the fetid odors of decaying foliage from the rain-swollen bayous stifled the senses as the army buzzed angrily in its hiding place among the trees.

"Santa Anna's whole damned army is moving in, and Houston lies there sleeping! What are we waiting for?"

"We should've gone at dawn and caught them all napping. I'm tired of runnin'. It's time to fight!"

Cade sat silently on his horse and listened to the ceaseless complaints murmuring around him. His gaze, like everyone else's, was fixed on the enemy encampment waiting across the grassy plain, less than a mile away. At dawn the Mexican army had been waiting for them behind hastily erected barricades. By mid-morning, reinforcements had begun to arrive. Now, at noon, the Mexican camp was settling down in the lazy afternoon sun. A few figures were still stirring, but the men who had marched all night would be sound asleep.

Cade was tired of running, too. He wanted this battle over with. He had never lifted a gun to harm another man before. He wasn't at all certain that he could do it now. Something in his nature found it repellent to take life needlessly. Ricardo had that reticence to thank for his life now. But Cade knew that, for the future of Lily and his child, he had to make a stand. The line had been drawn and sometime, somehow, someone had to cross it. He wasn't a coward. He knew how to fight. He just didn't know if he could kill.

Cade's thoughts drifted back to that day with Ricardo and the rattlesnake. It would have been better for everyone if he had ended Ricardo's life that day. But even then, even before the priests had taken him in and taught him the wisdom of turning the other cheek, Cade had been reluctant to make what was in reality God's decision. Had Ricardo kicked the box with the snake, it would have been of his own volition. He would have been responsible for his own death.

Standing here now, waiting for the command to kill, Cade couldn't find the desire for death in his soul. Those men in the other camp were there for the same reason he was here: because the men in power couldn't agree. He couldn't find the rage to kill that the men around him possessed. What had happened at the Alamo and Goliad had been horrendous and inhuman, and Santa Anna deserved to die for that. Houston's army would be slaughtered in the same manner if they did not fight to win. Cade understood that. But he wished he was home with Lily.

He had spent thirty-two years surviving. He wanted to live for a change. He wanted to plan for a future, not contemplate death. Lily was the first person to offer him that opportunity, and instead of building a life with her, he was here, prepared to destroy the lives of others. It didn't make sense, but Cade knew he had to do it.

He glanced at Travis, who was nervously smoking a crudely rolled cigarillo. Travis barely knew how to shoot a gun. This wasn't even his war. He didn't have land here. But he was prepared to fight for a cause he thought just. They were all mad.

And getting madder. The arguments behind them were growing more vociferous. Houston hadn't slept in weeks. Why he had chosen this morning to sleep was beyond anyone's comprehension. Travis had whispered "opium" at one point, but exhaustion was as good an explanation as any. How anyone could sleep with the enemy on his doorstep was beyond Cade's comprehension.

A wave of relief passed through the ragged troops in the woods when Houston woke, but the angry murmurs grew louder when he did nothing. Guns were cleaned and polished. The twin cannon were readied. The men practically had their targets picked out, but no call to arms came.

When the enemy camp had finally settled down completely to a lazy afternoon siesta, the flat plain glistened in the spring sun, with only the call of birds to intrude upon the silence. Cade felt it coming. He had wondered if Houston wasn't waiting for reinforcements from the American army across the river, but his men weren't prepared to wait much longer. A rustle of elation passed under the magnolia leaves and through the pine forest as Houston's decision reached the front lines. The word came to march.

Cade rode out in the first vanguard, pulling one of the cannon through the open field, an enviable target for anyone watching. No one watched. Amazed at the incredible stupidity of an army without pickets or scouts, Cade released the cannon when ordered within two hundred yards of the breastworks and prepared to ride. The main part of the army was more than halfway across the wide, open plain before the first shots were fired.

Later, after he heard of the atrocities committed by Houston's army in the name of revenge, Cade was glad that he had been one of the first to fall. Even an enemy scared out of its pants and with weapons too crude to aim straight couldn't miss a target as large as himself. But as he was falling, Cade didn't feel grateful. He felt only sorrow that he would never know the cries of his newborn child or the warmth of Lily's arms again. He hoped Lily would find the kind of man she deserved. He didn't want her to suffer any more than she already had.

The initial blossoming of pain exploded to wrack Cade's body as the army poured around him. Screams split the air, but they weren't his. Cade had learned silence at an early age, and he practiced it now, while the world erupted in violence around him. Blood poured from the wound in his shoulder and he knew he would soon lose consciousness. He tried to pull himself up, but the fall had done something to his leg. He fell down again,

and the bright day faded to an odd twilight, as if the sun
had gone behind a cloud.

Curses filled his ears, closer than the screams and
shouts and gunfire. Pain had too much control of his body
for Cade to concentrate on anything else. Someone was
there, but it was almost too late. A body could hold only
so much blood, and there could be little more to pour out.
If he could fully believe in the pearly gates of the priests
or the spirits of his father, he might welcome the knowledge of death, but all Cade could think of was Lily.

It was odd that he had spent twenty years of his life
simply surviving, only to spend his dying minutes dreaming of a woman who hated him for giving her all he
owned. Closing his eyes, Cade felt the warmth of Lily's
body close to his. She didn't hate him completely. Her
body was too warm and alive to his touch to hate him entirely. Had there been time . . .

"Damn you, you Indian bastard! You're not leaving me
to tell Lily of your death. You're going to get up and
walk out of here if it's the last thing I do."

But it wasn't likely to be. The battle had surged onward, into the Mexican camp and beyond, driving the enemy backward into the swamps and rivers amid screams
of desperation. The grassy field was empty except for the
fallen. Travis reached for his saddlebag and his spare
shirt. He knew how to stop the bleeding. He didn't know
how to bring back the dead.

Weeks later, Cade sat in a dark, one-room cabin, his
mending shoulder aching like hell as he glared at his sav-
ior with ferocity. "What do you mean, she isn't there?
Why wouldn't she be there? The damfool messenger just
got lost and is too stupid to admit it." But in the back of
his mind, Cade knew why Lily wouldn't be at the hacienda: because it was his home and not hers.

Undaunted, Travis took a sip of water from the dipper
he had carried in for his patient. If Cade wasn't going to
drink it, he wasn't too proud to drink it himself. Feeling
the liquid slide down his parched throat, he gave a gasp
of pleasure before answering Cade's cross accusations.

The implacable Indian had turned out to be one hell of a catankerous patient.

Besides, the moment gave him time to organize his words. Travis knew that as soon as he gave Cade the whole truth, the obstinate Indian would be out of bed and heading for his horse. Travis couldn't think of any way of preventing it short of lying, and he couldn't lie about something as serious as this. His own inclination was to run for his horse, but he knew next to nothing about this country, and his chances would be better with a little planning and an experienced guide.

If the guide was too ill to move, he would have to wait. "The fool messenger found the hacienda, no mistake." Travis laid down the dipper and waited for Cade to shut up and pay attention.

Cade glared at him and waited.

"Ricardo is there."

Cade began shoving off the quilt covering his legs. He wore nothing under it, but that didn't deter him.

Travis watched idly as Cade tried to stand and stumbled against the wall. The fall from the horse had damaged something in his knee. The swelling was going down, but he hadn't walked on it in weeks. It wasn't going to support him easily.

"The 'damfool messenger' didn't trust Ricardo, so he hung around and asked questions."

Disregarding Travis's sarcasm, Cade straightened and reached for the saddlebags on the table. He had to lean on the table to open them, but he succeeded in tugging out his denims. When Travis didn't continue, Cade threw him a killing look.

Travis shrugged. "There's no women or children there. No one knows where they went. Your grandfather is supposedly ill and confined to his room."

Cade finally spoke. "Supposedly?"

"Ricardo has had a lawyer camped at his door, not a priest or a doctor." Travis turned around and walked back outside to the well. He didn't want to hear Cade's fury. He wasn't ready yet for whatever Cade would decide. Travis had been on his own since he was fifteen. Lily and their son and Juanita were as close as he had ever come to family since then. Even the little brat, Serena, had carved a place in his heart. He wasn't made like Cade. He longed for the warmth of human emotion. He even missed that old rascal Ephraim. He didn't care about the damned land or the cattle or whatever else it was that drove men to fight. Travis required Juanita's shy adoration, Roy's admiring phrases, Lily's rare laughter. Ricardo could have the damned hacienda. Travis wanted the women and children.

He was afraid Cade wouldn't think the same. These past weeks had made it obvious that Cade had a single-minded fascination with the Spanish family and the hacienda he had been denied all these years. When he was coherent, he had spoken of the changes he would make, the plans he had for that mesquite-studded acreage. When he was fevered, he had cursed Ricardo, cursed every obstacle that had ever stood in his way, and sworn oaths that made Travis shiver. Behind that stoic facade lay a lifetime of hate and longing. He didn't want to think about the decision that Cade had to make now. Lily and her small farm had only been an afterthought in that lifetime.

When he returned to the cabin, Cade was dressed and checking his rifle. He looked up and asked, "Are you ready to go?"

The man could barely walk. He had recovered from fever scarcely a week ago. His shoulder wouldn't hold together under the tug of a rein. And he was prepared to ride out without a moment's notice.

Travis grinned. "Whenever you are."

They had never formally entered the army and didn't formally discharge themselves now. The wounded Texans Travis had been treating were almost all on their way home. The slaughter that had left over six hundred Mexicans dying in the fields and bayous had killed only nine of the Texans. Most of Travis's patients were Mexican prisoners, and there was little else he could do for them.

Cade was the one he worried about. His shoulder shattered from the first explosion of the Mexican cannon, Cade had lost enormous amounts of blood before Travis

had found him. He had a long way to go before he regained his strength. Travis watched warily as the big man
rode uncomfortably in his saddle, driving himself as he
always did. How in hell was he going to keep Cade alive
long enough to find Lily?

And the others. Travis tried not to think about the others. Lily was strong. If anyone could survive, it would be
she. But the others . . . He wouldn't apply names to his
concerns, but wounded dark eyes watched him from behind every tree, screaming their hurt and need. He knew
all about hurt and need. He knew nothing at all about
solving them.

So he followed Cade, forcing the other man to rest
when the May sun got too hot for comfort, feeding him
meat as often as they could find it, bandaging and
rebandaging his wound when it began to bleed. Cade was
Travis's only hope of finding the family he had come to
think of as his own. He would do whatever it took to
keep the damned Indian alive.

It wasn't an easy task. Cade pushed himself like a man
possessed. They rode through the darkness until he was
nearly falling off his horse. Too exhausted to hunt when
they stopped for the night, he had to be forced to eat what
little Travis could put together. After a night crossing of
a spring-cold river, Cade crawled to his horse when
Travis refused to help him get up. Cursing, Travis hauled
him into the saddle and tied him there so they could ride
on.

It was with great relief that Travis recognized the road
they followed. True, the road ultimately ended in San
Antonio, but it had to pass by the little homestead where
they had all come together. If Lily had gone anywhere of
her own accord, it would have been to her own home.

Cade seemed to have the same thought. His pace
quickened as they approached the town. He rode through
without stopping. He was slumped over the gelding's
neck and holding on with his last strength as he galloped
toward the sunset and the little farm snuggled between
the pines and the prairies.

He even refused to give up when the charred ruins of

the house came in sight and no flicker of light showed from its remaining windows. Travis leapt down and stood ready as Cade nearly fell from the saddle in his desperation to get to the cabin. The house was silent and dark. No childish laughter winged through the windows. No scents of baking bread drifted from the kitchen. A steer stood munching at weeds in the garden Lily had so carefully cultivated the year before. No one came out to greet them.

They should have known what to expect after seeing the broken wreckage of the red peddler's wagon, but they entered the dogtrot and began throwing open doors anyway. The charred main cabin, like the wagon, had been ransacked of what few viable goods had remained. Even the sodden baby clothes had disappeared, and every lamp, candlestick, and mug had been removed from the shelves. The heavy, damaged dining table remained, its polished wood warped with the rains and cold.

Cade stood still in the doorway to the bedroom that had been the source of the only happiness he could remember. The mattress had been gutted by someone looking for hidden wealth. The bed frame and washstand had been used for firewood. The porcelain washbowl and pitcher with their colorful roses and greenery lay shattered on the floor. And Lily's elegant windows had been blasted by a shotgun.

Cade was a proud man, and a strong one. Nothing in all his life had ever brought him to his knees, but he was on the verge now. Clinging to the door frame, Cade held himself upright by sheer force of will. Lily's cries of passion still haunted these walls. He could almost hear the sound of a flute as he clung to the wood. He had wanted to give her music and happiness. He had wanted to lay the world at her feet. He had wanted . . .

He had wanted.

And this was the result. Everything she had, destroyed. It was a poor return for everything she had given him in those few short months. Cade closed the door and walked away.

Lily carried his life with her. He knew it as the soul

knows the stars are out of reach. If Lily lived, he would survive. If she did not, he was a walking ghost. He could not return to being the man he had once been. He could not live alone again.

He turned and started for his horse, ignoring Travis's vehement protests.

Thirty-two

Travis cursed again as the damned Indian set out across the fields like a man possessed. Nothing he had said or done could convince Cade to remain here for the night and start out in the morning. Travis had half a mind to let the madman go ahead without him and follow the trail of blood come dawn to pick up the remains. If he did, it would be just his luck that Cade would somehow manage to leave him behind, just when they had come to the part of the search where Travis could not begin to look for himself. A handful of women and children could disappear into these vast open spaces and never be seen again.

So Travis rode as close to Cade's gelding as he could, waiting to catch Cade when he fell. The man was barely hanging on now, clinging to the horse's mane and letting the animal follow some unseen track on its own. Travis prayed silently that the horse knew where it was going, because he sure as hell didn't.

They seemed to spend an eternity walking the horses through the pine woods, but the moon was still high in the sky when a clearing opened ahead. Travis could hear the river. At the same time he caught a whiff of wood smoke, and hope surged through his veins.

Lily kept Serena's chubby body curled tightly against her own and prayed as she had prayed every night since Cade's departure. She had been furious with him at first. Then she had felt rejected, as if she were of no account in his life. The feeling was aided by the fact that Cade had never said or done anything to contradict it. But then she had begun to remember things—the kitten in his lap, the flute on her pillow, his pain in setting Roy's leg, the fierce passion of his lovemaking—and she had to wonder if these weren't Cade's way of showing how he felt. A sliver of hope had begun to fill Lily's heart then, and she had nourished it in the days since, hoping to block out the growing fear when there was no sign of Cade even after the battle was won.

Lily had come to accept the fact that Cade would return to the hacienda first. There would be some kind of collision with Ricardo, if so. So she had two things to worry about: had Cade survived San Jacinto and would he conquer Ricardo and come out whole?

Lily couldn't allow herself to think of Cade as anything but whole. He was the solid oak in her life. She might never receive affection or tenderness from him, but he was the support she had come to rely on, however wrongly. Perhaps she could take care of herself, but she didn't want to anymore. She had quit telling herself she didn't need Cade. She needed him more with every passing day, as the child grew larger and more active and became more real. She needed the comfort of Cade's arms, the solidity of his presence, the assurance of his actions, the music of his flute.

And she needed his love, but she knew better than to ask that. She had known her father's selfish love. She knew she wasn't particularly lovable. She had lived all those years with Jim without love. She could survive—if she just knew that Cade would return. Without him, the future had the blank face of hopelessness.

She didn't know what had happened to her independence. Cade had shot it all to hell somehow. Holding her adopted daughter to her, Lily tried to pretend that Cade would be home soon and everything would return to normal. They should be planting the fields now that the rain had stopped. It was late, but they could still get out a crop. She counted steers in her head, hoping to discover sleep in the process.

Listening to the night, Lily knew the instant the Indian camp changed. In the months since they had arrived here, she had come to appreciate the infinitesimal changes of daily life: the day the first pigeons returned, the planting done under the new moon, the celebration of the first green shoots in the field. It was a peaceful life, and it had healed many of the wounds of these last few months. She was ready to accept whatever changes Cade wished to make.

But the unexpected call of a nightbird at this hour was more warning than the changes Lily had in mind. She listened, hearing the sounds of running feet where there had been none before. Someone in the lodge began to stir. A shadow passed through the doorway, and she was afraid.

These people were still strangers to her. They had taken her in, given her a bed, allowed her to help in their activities, but she still could barely speak their language and found their customs strange and foreign despite Juanita's reassuring presence. She worried about Roy sleeping with the other young boys on the other side of the lodge. She kept her ears open, terrified of the danger the night could bring.

A murmur of voices and the sound of horses approached. More shadows rose and walked the floor. This was the lodge of Cade's father. His sons were young enough to still sleep here, but mostly the building contained women and children. Lily was uncertain of all the relationships, but she seemed to be just one more dependent among many. The shadows were definitely male.

When someone stirred the fire in the lodge's center, Lily gave up any pretense at sleep and unraveled herself from Serena. The child had taken to Indian life with the same joyful innocence as she did everything else. She continued sleeping soundly now as Lily reached for her clothing.

Lily almost screamed at the appearance of a large silhouette in the lodge's open doorway, but recognition came swiftly and surely, with a surge of joy. She was afraid to run to him, afraid he would be angry with her, afraid still that he would reject her newfound and tender feelings.

Cade stepped inside, and the figure at the fire rose to

greet him. It was only then that Lily realized something was wrong, terribly wrong, and her heart leapt to her throat as she left her pallet, unconsciously holding her hand out in her husband's direction.

Lily's movement caused Cade to turn. In the small flickering light of the fire he caught a glimpse of gold, saw the white shadow of her welcoming palm, knew the graceful height of her silhouette, and knew he was complete.

He toppled slowly, like a mighty oak collapsing into the forest. Lily screamed. Travis leapt out of the darkness to catch him. And other lithe figures inserted themselves between the big man and the ground, lifting him carefully and carrying him to the pallet Lily had just deserted.

A torch was lit beside the bed. One of the young Indian women came and carried the still-sleeping Serena away. Bowls of water were carried in, and Lily carefully bathed Cade's face as Travis ripped at his shirt to examine the newly opened wound.

Outside, a drum began to pound, and Lily could hear the stirring of the village to the call. She could feel the concern of the people behind her. One of their own had fallen, and they would intercede with the spirits to protect him.

"He is fevered," Lily murmured as she bathed Cade's forehead and felt, more than heard, his moan.

"He was wounded at San Jacinto. He was just recovering when he heard that you had disappeared. He has been obsessed with finding you ever since." Travis swore at the extent of the damage to the injury he had so carefully tended. "How do I tell them to bring me my saddlebag?"

Lily turned to the tall man hovering in the background. With a few words of Spanish and a gesture of her hands, she made the request clear. The man spoke curtly, and one of the young boys raced to do his bidding.

"I'm going to get Juanita to teach me how to do that." Travis looked up suddenly, his eyes dark with pain. "She is here?"

Lily nodded. "We're all fine. Roy has the makings of an excellent guide. I'll let him tell you how he got us here." She smiled to share her appreciation of this jest at a small boy's pride, but the relief on Travis's face indicated that his thoughts were elsewhere.

The bags were brought and Travis re-cleaned the wound, but its festering edges were obvious even to Lily. They exchanged glances in the shadowed light, both aware of the threatening presence of Cade's father nearby. The drums beat steadily now, and the air was beginning to fill with smoke. From somewhere in the distance, a man chanted. Cade's life lingered somewhere between heaven and hell, and their own could very well depend on it.

Lily stroked the strong, angular jut of Cade's cheekbone, bringing her hand down to caress his chin. Cade's eyes opened briefly. She thought she saw recognition in them, but they closed again and she could only draw her own conclusions. Whatever had gone before or would go afterward, he needed her now.

With a bravery she didn't feel, Lily looked to the waistband of Cade's trousers. He was wearing a stained and stiff pair of buckskins that she would have buried, given a chance, but her hand went unerringly to the place where she knew Cade kept his knife. She slid it out of its leather thong and handed it to Travis.

He stared at it in horror before accepting the bone handle and examining the width of the blade. Neither of them had to speak to know what had to be done. They had both seen it done before. Neither of them had ever had to do it.

Lily held her breath as Travis shoved the shining blade into the center of the torch's flame. Lily felt Cade's father come closer, and the tension around them rose to a new level. She was half afraid of the man and didn't dare turn and seek his comfort, but she wished desperately for some kind of outer strength to prop up her rapidly dwindling resources.

In the torchlight, Cade's magnificent copper body danced with shadows that accented its muscular planes and ridges. Lily wanted to stroke them, to reassure herself that he lived and breathed, but she contented herself with clinging to his hand. With a word, she ordered one of his brothers to hold the other hand. As if understanding what would happen next, someone else held his feet.

As Travis laid the flaming knife against the wound, Cade jerked and howled. The stench of burning flesh filled the air, but Travis grimly held the blade in place despite Cade's concerted efforts to fling him off. Only when he was certain that the wound had been sealed against infection did he remove the instrument of torture. The room seemed deathly quiet in the aftermath of Cade's screams.

"If you have any sense, you'll keep laudanum poured down him until he's healed." Travis slapped the knife down beside the bed and rose. "Where's Juanita?"

By this time, everyone in the lodge was awake, including the children. A wide-eyed and terrified Roy staggered into Travis's path, and Travis bent and scooped him up as if he were as small as Serena. Lily didn't watch the reunion. Her attention was focused wholly on the unconscious man in the bed.

Hugging Roy, Travis glanced back at Lily with sadness in his heart and let the last piece of his dream go. She had been a bright part of his adolescence, of his growing up. He was grown now, and as a child surrenders the comforters of his past, Travis surrendered any notions he might still have harbored about the mother of his child. He didn't want to let his son go, but the woman was already lost to him.

Reassuring Roy and sending him back to his bed, grinning at a sleepy Serena who tumbled to his toes and sat there staring up at him, Travis knew he had found his home. He just needed to set his sights on a different woman, one who thought he was a man to be admired and not the scared young boy he had been. Perhaps in time he could learn to be what she thought he was.

Travis's determined questioning finally took him out of one lodge and on to another. He didn't know why Juanita wasn't with Lily. He wasn't in any position to question Indian customs. He only knew that when he got there Juanita was waiting for him, standing outside the doorway, watching him with a wrenching mixture of trepidation, pain, and hope. Travis held out his hand and Juanita took it, and then she was in his arms, and he was shaking with the strain of emotions suddenly unleashed.

It took a moment before he realized that they were surrounded by women, many of them giggling young girls. Lifting his head up, Travis finally understood: Juanita was staying in a lodge that housed all the unmarried females of the tribe. He groaned, and sought Juanita's eyes.

Shyness lingered in her gaze as she replied to his unspoken question. "There is nowhere else."

Travis thought of his destroyed wagon, of the charred cabin and the torn mattress. He hadn't inspected the outbuildings, but it could be expected that they were in the same disarray. Everything he had ever possessed was gone. He looked down at Juanita. She wasn't his, but she could be.

It was a major step for him to take. He could seduce her with words; he was very good with that. But Travis knew Juanita's background. Lily had explained it succinctly, so even he could understand her fear of men. It didn't bother him that she wasn't innocent. Neither was he. At least she was innocent of wrongdoing—which was more than he could say. So if it wasn't going to be seduction, it was going to have to be something more permanent, and he didn't know if he had anything to offer her.

Reluctantly, Travis released her. "I've been sleeping on the ground this long. Another night won't hurt."

Too terrified to do anything else, Juanita let him walk away.

Legs curled on the ground and head resting on her arm on the pallet where Cade lay, Lily finally drifted into sleep holding his hand. She was vaguely aware of figures coming and going during the night, of the erratic beat of the drums, and sometime in the dawn, the lilting notes of the flute. She smiled in her sleep and drifted deeper into unconsciousness.

Cade woke with a clearer head than he had known in days. He knew instantly where he was, and he lay silently accepting the familiar sounds of dogs barking and women chattering. The aromatic smells of roasting venison and boiling porridge drifted through a doorway on a spring breeze. There were the less pleasant smells of untreated sewage and animal offal, but they were the smells of home, and he didn't disparage them.

Cautiously, Cade let his senses focus on the presence beside him. He remembered his dream of Lily. He had seen her face, seen the golden flash of her braid, but it was a strange Lily, one wearing the deerskin of an Indian. He wanted to cling to the image because it hadn't been hatred he had seen in her face, but he had to separate dreams from reality. If she wasn't here, he had to find her.

Opening his eyes, Cade looked up to the tightly bound grasses of his father's roof. The sun was shining through the chinks. His hand felt trapped, and he tried to move it. When there was no response, he struggled to sit. Pain ripped at his shoulder, and he groaned.

She was there instantly, her hand brushing his forehead, her worried face hovering just above his own. Cade let out a breath and scanned the pale outline of Lily's features, then let his gaze drop to the fullness of her breasts hidden beneath the thickness of deerskin. It was beautifully tanned deerskin, the hide weathered and beaten to a luminous black and decorated with tiny beads and quills as only these people could do it, but it was on a woman he had last seen in silks.

His gaze fell farther, to the swelling where his child grew, and he relaxed. She was safe, and so was the child. "Lily," he said with some satisfaction. It was good just to be able to say her name. There had been a time when he had thought he would never be allowed.

"Don't ever do that to me again, Cade," she whispered somewhere near his ear. "If this child is born terrified of its shadow, it's all your fault."

That made some sort of illogical sense. Pain consumed him, but Cade concentrated on the softness of her touch, the tenderness and fear in her voice. She bathed his face, and then his chest, and he was certain he had died and gone to heaven. He couldn't remember anyone ever caring for him before. He could remember countless times lying in misery in whatever lonesome shack he had occupied at the moment, but no one had ever come to bathe his face and body. It was almost worth the injury to know this sense of belonging.

"Papa." A soft, pudgy little body plopped down beside him and spoke with cheerful satisfaction. "Papa, *padre,* daddy." And then with what could only be described as a guttural giggle, she added her Waco version of the word "father."

Cade grinned, although he was almost certain that it came out a grimace. He couldn't lift himself to see Serena, but he reached to stroke her hair. Satisfied that she had waked him sufficiently, the little imp scrambled off the pallet and ran to join the others.

"She's like a ray of sunshine. I don't know what I'd do without her."

Unable to keep his fears from his eyes, Cade looked up to the woman who hadn't stopped touching him since his return. He knew nothing of the emotion he saw in Lily's face, but it was far from the contempt he had inspired most of his life. Content with that knowledge, he squeezed her hand and slipped back into sleep.

Lily glanced worriedly to the feverish streaks around his wound and continued to hold tightly to Cade's fingers. She was just coming to know this man. She couldn't lose him before they had time to explore what could be between them. She hadn't dared hope since that day Travis had disappeared from her life. Please, Lord, don't destroy that hope again.

Thirty-three

"He sleeps?" Cade's father asked in his heavily accented Spanish.

The grass lodge was nearly empty except for some of the smaller children. Lily looked up in surprise at the Indian's entrance, then answered hesitantly, "*Si.*" She certainly hoped Cade slept. Travis had said that Cade had ridden here like a man obsessed. She didn't know how to interpret that action, but his sleeping seemed natural. "His body must gain strength."

Her Spanish was awkward and equally accented, but Cade's father seemed to understand. She could not pronounce his Indian name, but his Spanish one was El Caballo, The Horse. At one time, the description was most probably apt, particularly if one could see the father through the son. El Caballo was older now, and some of the muscle had turned to flab with the sedentary life of his wife's tribe, but he was still a large man.

"I talk with him. You go." El Caballo sat down crosslegged beside the pallet where Cade rested.

Lily hesitated. "He needs sleep," she warned uncertainly. She didn't wish to anger this man. She felt fairly certain the other women would not argue with him, but Cade's health was more important than this man's pride.

El Caballo scowled and gestured for her to leave, but Lily thought there might be something of amusement in his eyes as he replied, "I wait. You go. You sleep."

His broken Spanish was quite clear, even to Lily. Rising, she glanced uncertainly back to Cade's sleeping form. She wanted to be there when he woke again, but she supposed that was being selfish. El Caballo had as much right to be there as she did, and she had the child to think of. She needed sleep.

She found a pallet on the opposite wall and lay down to take a nap. She would rather be sleeping beside Cade, but there was no privacy to be had in this place. She supposed it was better this way, but separate beds held little appeal.

Despite the fact that his father waited, Cade slept longer than Lily did. She was up and about when Travis returned for a second time that day, and when he shook his head with concern, Lily was beside him instantly.

"What is wrong? What can I do?"

Rested now, with the light of day to see her in, Travis grinned and gave her an admiring look. "I wish I'd been there to see you grow that big with Roy. A woman never looks better than when she's carrying a man's child."

That was Travis talking, but for some reason, Lily felt the words deep inside her. Her sisters had always made her feel less than feminine, and the shame and humiliation of her first pregnancy had erased any womanly notions she might have had at the time. But Travis had touched on an emotion she had only recently begun to recognize. Lily truly felt like a complete woman for the first time in her life, and her hand proudly touched the bulge of life growing within her.

Ignoring Travis's smile, she demanded, "Is Cade going to be all right? Is there something I should be doing?"

Travis grew serious as he threw a glance toward the large man lying still on his pallet and the old man sitting patiently beside him. "I would say that his body needs rest, but it also needs nourishment. Has he eaten at all?"

"No." Lily frowned and stared at Cade. "Should I wake him?"

"Damned if I'd try. Even with that shoulder he's likely to come up out of that bed with murder in mind if we startle him. There were times when he was fevered that I thought he'd throttle me. For a man who likes children and animals, he's got a lot of violence in him."

"I daresay he has his reasons." Lily had never spent much time questioning Cade about his past, but what she knew of it was enough to give her some understanding. Thoughtfully, she considered the problem. Food was plentiful. She had helped often enough over the cookfires when needed, but her pregnancy apparently gave her special dispensation to stay with the children most of the day. The other women in the lodge did most of the cooking. Since the day was warm, they were outside, but Lily could smell the broth now. It was just a matter of getting it into Cade.

She didn't know what would work, but she could experiment. Leaving Travis to find his own way out, Lily went to the small satchel with her few possessions and removed the flute that Cade had given her. It was a little more worn now, the polish developing a patina from use, and Lily regarded it with satisfaction. It had taken hours of practice, but she was beginning to learn its use.

Sitting on the opposite side of Cade from his father, she began to play. El Caballo frowned slightly. Music was not woman's work or something to be taken lightly, but Lily played very well. Even the man in the bed thought so; he began to stir.

Cade's eyes opened and came to rest on Lily. The opaque depths that had once kept everyone out softened as he watched her with the flute. Then sensing they were not alone, his gaze turned unreadable again as he turned to his father.

Lily didn't need El Caballo's warning look to know when she wasn't wanted. Putting the flute down, she awkwardly found her feet and went in search of food. Cade's father had better learn to speak quickly.

"I owe you my life," Cade said simply, expecting this man to understand that his life was Lily. He didn't know how Lily had come to be here. He knew nothing of what had transpired these last months, but he knew she was safe and his father was the one who had offered safety.

"There are no debts between family." El Caballo sat stoically beside his eldest son. "I have lost three sons to war. I would see my last ones live in peace. I do not teach them to be warriors. You, I would have taught. That is why your mother took you from me."

Cade contemplated this latest piece of the puzzle that was his past. Although he had no memory of it now, he knew his father had taught him much of the Apache way. At the time, it had been boy's play and meant little to him. Still, he knew he had none of the bloodlust that was necessary for a good warrior. Whether his mother or the priests were responsible, he could not say. All his life he had known that his greater size intimidated, and that had been all the protection he had ever required.

"I am a poor warrior," Cade admitted. "But I know the white man's ways and can take care of my own."

El Caballo made a gesture that indicated the whole camp, then another that encompassed just the lodge. "These are your own. Their future is yours."

That was a huge responsibility to lay on a man who wasn't even certain he was capable of taking care of his immediate family at the moment. Cade knew what his father meant, but it seemed a hopeless task. He had lived in the white men's world, knew their hatred for Indians and their reasons for it. He also knew the other side of the argument. Two diverse cultures living in the same land were bound to clash. How could he possibly stand in between?

Cade knew the instant Lily entered the lodge, and he grunted with relief. Here was the reason his father had hopes of living in peace, although he was quite certain Lily didn't realize the expectations she had raised. Were there more people like Lily, perhaps the impossible could be done. Unfortunately, he had met only one Lily in this world.

Carefully, Cade shifted himself onto his one good arm and took in the aroma from the bowl she was carrying. His stomach rumbled in appreciation. Lily's answering smile made his insides tumble. She wasn't mad at him. He would pin his hopes on that.

"Travis did a very poor job of keeping his patient in bed. I will have your promise that you will stay put until I tell you or I will drug your food so you can't get up."

Since she was managing the awkward business of settling her unwieldy body on the floor while holding the steaming bowl, Cade could assume she wasn't planning on drugging anything just yet. Forcing his injured arm into motion, he took the bowl so she could sit.

"Do you expect me to watch that performance regularly and still lie here?" Cade asked calmly, returning the bowl to her when she was settled. "We will have to go back to the cabin just so you can have a chair to sit in."

Lily looked at Cade's father. She didn't want to argue in front of him. The older man managed an inscrutable expression even better than Cade, but his words as he rose indicated his appreciation of her problem.

"My son is like the oak, but sometimes it is better to be a willow." In his own language, he turned to Cade and said, "You will lie here or I will have you strapped to a travois and carried home."

The idea of being strapped humiliatingly to a travois like an old man or an invalid made Cade scowl as his father walked away. He turned the expression to Lily, but she calmly held out a spoon of stew for him to eat.

"I hope he said he was going to hold you here at knifepoint. You are of absolutely no use to anyone dead, and that's where you'll be if you strain yourself any more. I don't think the cabin is going to be any more comfortable than this is."

Remembering the disaster of that once comfortable home, Cade had to agree, but he wasn't ready to give in. "I will have Travis find someone to start rebuilding. I wish our child to be born in our bed."

"Our child was conceived in an Indian bed. There is no reason he cannot be born in one. Besides, here there are women who can help me when the time comes. There are none at home."

"I will bring Dove Woman to you when your time comes. A lady should lie in her own bed." Cade swallowed the food she shoved into his mouth.

His words were very attractive, if Lily were truthful with herself. She longed for a bed off the floor, with clean linens instead of the innumerable fleas that resided in furs, but Cade's health wouldn't permit any exertion. She set her jaw stubbornly. "You may tell Travis to do as he wishes, but you cannot go anywhere until you are well. What if Ricardo should return?"

That was a touchy subject, one Cade did not dare broach entirely. If his grandfather was in danger, he needed to go to him. But he had no desire to frighten Lily any further now that it was so close to her time.

"Ricardo is a bully who picks on the helpless. He will cause us no harm. What did he say to drive you from my home?"

"He threatened the child. And Juanita is terrified of him. We could not stay where he was welcome." Perhaps they should have. Perhaps they should have driven Ricardo from the hacienda that Cade claimed as his, but Lily had thought first of the children. They had to be removed before she could fight, and the child within her needed that same protection.

"And my grandfather did nothing?"

"What could he do? He is one old man against half a dozen bullies. He does not see Ricardo the same way a woman does."

It had been coming for a long time. Cade ate silently as he contemplated the man who had smashed his foot into Cade's face at every opportunity. Over the years Cade had come to understand that Ricardo was probably personally responsible for not having reported the return of Cade's mother to Béxar or Cade's existence to his grandfather. There had to have been communication between Antonio and Ricardo during that time, if for no other reason than that Ricardo made regular trips to Mexico City for some reason besides his health. Cade couldn't know at what point Antonio had become aware of his existence, but it certainly hadn't been through Ricardo's good intentions.

Every misfortune of his life had been prefaced by Ricardo's arrival. It was like being haunted by an evil genie. Cade didn't believe in genies or coincidences. Ricardo wanted him dead, but he didn't mean to sully his own hands in the process.

And now it wouldn't be sufficient for Ricardo to rid himself of Cade; there was the child to consider. If Antonio was determined to leave his lands to someone besides Ricardo, Cade's child would be next in line. Cade had been prepared to turn the other cheek for himself, but for the child, he would fight.

He couldn't tell Lily that, though. Tired, his stomach satisfied, Cade leaned back against the pallet and closed his eyes. He felt Lily's gentle fingers caressing his brow, and he reached up to hold them. For Lily, he would wait, but it wouldn't be a passive waiting. He would plan, and when the time came, he would win.

Cade felt the brush of Lily's lips against his own and felt a desire so bright it illuminated the future. He had never thought to have a future, but it was all he thought about now. He craved it with all his heart and soul, with the hunger of a lifetime of denial. He clung to Lily's hand as he clung to his dream. He would make it happen, one way or another.

Travis appeared again later, checked Cade's wound, and drew Lily aside after he changed the bandages.

"If you can keep him resting, he is on the road to recovery. You won't need me. I want to go back to the cabin and start setting things to rights."

Lily looked dubious. "We have no hired hands. What can you do by yourself?"

"The men who joined Houston think they'll be paid with land, but there isn't any way all that land can be surveyed and titled anytime soon. They'll need to eat. They'll be back. There just needs to be someone there when they come. Let me go, Lily."

He was almost pleading with her. Astonished, Lily gazed at the man who had given her a son and wandered off to follow his own dreams. She knew Travis as a smooth-talking salesman, and in many ways, he still was. She couldn't see him as a farmer, not for long, but for some reason, he needed to be one for just a little while. She had nothing to lose by agreeing, except his company.

"It's Roy's home. I would see it repaired and the land made to prosper again. I have no money, and I'm not certain that Cade is willing to invest in it any longer. What can you do?"

"I don't know, but I want to try." Travis slipped his hat back on his head and regarded Lily slightly uneasily. "Lily, about Juanita . . . Do you think she'd rather . . . Hell, I know she has reason to hate men, but I'd be happy with just her company. Do you think she'd come? Do you think I should ask her?"

Lily didn't think she would ever see the day when Travis Bolton, the womanizer, would look nervous over a female. Amusement curled her lips at the thought of shy Juanita causing his despair. He had a whole heck of a lot to learn if he thought Juanita was going to fall docilely into his arms. She very much suspected that when Juanita was ready to commit herself, she was going to lead him a merry chase. It would serve him right.

"I think you'd better be looking for a preacher if you want her for anything but a cook, but go ahead and ask. She'll not take your head off. Or any other part of your anatomy."

Travis stared at this boldness on Lily's part, then grinned at the laughter in her eyes. "I reckon it's a damn good thing I didn't show up when you were carrying Roy. I don't think you would be so reticent."

"You could very well be right. I've butchered many a chicken with you in mind."

Travis laughed outright, causing heads to turn as they stood there in the day's dying light. Their height alone made them stand out, but there was something in the assurance of their carriage, in the way they reacted to each other, that made them seem invincible. Anyone could see that they had the blessing of the gods.

"I'm glad Cade's the one who got you. You'll have a hard time putting a harness on him, and I can't imagine you respecting anyone you could harness. Can we stay friends, Lily, even if I turn back into a snake-oil salesman?"

"You'll always be a snake-oil salesman, Travis, and I'll love you for it. You're what I can never be. I've got to give you credit for that."

With this recognition of what Travis was and was not, Lily put the past behind her where it belonged. No longer would she curse Travis or condemn herself for what was done. They had created something beautiful between them and gone their separate ways. She held out her hand in friendship and he took it.

Travis grinned appreciatively. "Maybe you could explain to Juanita about the benefits of salesmen and play down what a fool I am. I'll need all the help I can get."

Lily watched him walk away without a qualm. He would always be Roy's father, but he would never be anything else to her. She glanced back to the lodge where Cade lay sleeping. That was where her future waited, and hope danced in her heart again.

Thirty-four

"Lily, I do not like to leave you. I should not go with him. But he says he needs me . . ." Juanita looked helplessly from the woman who had taken her in five long years ago to the man who waited patiently now by the horses, ready to take her away.

The sun of late May beat down upon their heads, warming their hair, making them regret the heavy Indian clothing. Lily thought longingly of the cottons in her cool cabin, but she could not return there yet, not until Cade was ready to travel.

Lily looked at Travis, his curly dark hair grown long with neglect, his laughing eyes solemn now as he waited in the distance for the two women to confer and make this decision. Then she looked at Juanita. "I do not want to make you do anything you do not wish to do. You are more sister to me than my own. We have grown up together. Travis will do nothing you do not wish, if it is him that you fear."

Juanita glanced down nervously at her moccasin-clad feet. "I do not think I could ever be to him what he wishes me to be," she said softly. "I would go with him to make the ranch ready for your return, but that is not all he wants, I think."

"He will not force you, Juanita, this I can promise."

Juanita didn't look up. "It was Ricardo, you know. He was the one who did this to me."

Shocked, feeling the shock in her very center, Lily could only stare at her friend's bent head. Ricardo? The dapper Mexican had lowered himself to force a child of no certain background? It did not seem likely, but there was no reason for Juanita to lie.

Misunderstanding Lily's silence, Juanita hurried to explain. "He is evil. You must understand that. He did not lay a hand to me, but he told the others what to do. They ... they used ... things." She could not describe the instruments of horror that had been used on her in addition to the normal male equipment that had torn away her innocence. "When they could not perform anymore he told them what to use and how to use it. And all because I would not give him freely what they stripped away."

Lily choked and closed her eyes, swaying slightly with the horror of it, grabbing her stomach as if to protect the child within from such words. "Why did you never tell me this?"

"Because I was afraid. Because he said he would do worse should I ever mention what happened. I did not know his name then. I know it now, and I spit on it." Juanita did as she said, her eyes blazing fiercely as she finally looked up. Suddenly seeing Lily's expression, she grabbed Lily's arm. "I did not mean to make you ill! Come, we will sit down. He does not need me. I will stay here with you."

Lily grasped her spinning senses and shook her head. It was quite obvious what she needed to do now, for Juanita's own good. Juanita needed a man like Travis, a man who could say the sweet words and lies that made a woman feel like a woman without even touching her. Even if Travis should eventually leave her, Juanita would discover that lovemaking was not what one perverted monster had made of it. To do otherwise would leave her a victim forever.

"Dove Woman will look after me. You must go with Travis. He needs you more than I do. I would not tell you to go with him unless I trusted him. Help him," Lily whispered, but her prayers said "Help her" as she looked up to Travis's forlorn figure in the distance.

Reluctantly, Juanita left, and Lily watched them go until she could see them no longer. Then she turned her feet back to the lodge and the man waiting restlessly inside. Cade regained his strength too rapidly to be a good patient.

"They have gone?" he demanded as soon as she entered. He sat propped against the wall with a bundled buffalo hide as a cushion.

"You knew it was Ricardo who ordered her raped, didn't you?" Lily accused the minute her eyes adjusted from the brilliant sun to the dim interior.

Cade watched her warily as she lowered herself to the ground beside him. "She is lucky there was no brothel she could be sold to. He has done that also."

Lily could not comprehend a wickedness so immense. "Why? What does he gain from such acts?"

"Power. Ricardo craves power. It is the way of some men. Women are easy victims. He chews them up and spits them out as a man would practice shooting at targets to keep his sight skilled."

"What is it he wants with my ranch?"

Cade took his time answering, formulating the words slowly. "I think mostly he wants land because land is power in Texas. There is little money here, but land can be traded for anything, including positions of power. I think he is among the speculators grabbing every acre they can find. Your ranch may not be so important to him now that so many have left Texas and he can buy cheap, except now he knows you are my wife. Now, it is not your land he wants, but me."

"He does not want the land to grow things, but to trade things? And he wants you because your grandfather means you to have his land?"

"The name de Suela carries much distinction in Mexico. Ricardo covets that distinction for himself, but my grandfather has always denied it. He wished Ricardo to prove himself; instead, Ricardo denied him the knowledge of my mother and myself. He left Ricardo to look after the ranch, but Ricardo sold parcels and left to ingratiate himself with Austin and the others who would someday take Texas from Mexico. I do not think my grandfather even yet knows the whole truth of Ricardo's despicable character, but he knows enough not to believe his lies."

Cade restrained himself from saying that he must return to see that his grandfather was safe. Lily was too close to term for him to leave her for that length of time. The last few months had taught him a few things about their relationship, but he did not know how to tell her that.

Lily leaned back beside him and allowed Cade to wrap his good arm around her while she rested her head against his shoulder. It was good to have him back. She couldn't think about letting him go again. "I wish we could have brought your grandfather with us, but I did not think he would come."

She was quite right there. Antonio de Suela would not be caught dead in an Indian camp. Cade grinned and allowed his hand to roam. Pregnancy had slowed his wife down and made her a good deal more complacent about allowing such liberties in the broad light of day. He had no aversion to taking advantage of the opportunity offered by his forced idleness.

"Why did you come here and not to the ranch?" he demanded.

Lily knew what he was doing but offered no objection. The heavy layer of deerskin offered protection enough, and she was too unwieldy to do more than enjoy his caresses. She contemplated Cade's question before replying. "You said the ranch would not be safe and that your father's camp would be. I did not think I had the right to endanger your child by going against your wishes."

"You did not like it at the hacienda," he stated, sliding his hand beneath the fringed edges of her smock. "But you will stay in an Indian camp?"

Lily gave an involuntary gasp as Cade's warm hand inserted itself between her breasts and began to stroke and squeeze. Liquid warmth flowed between her thighs, and she had to adjust herself uneasily as the sensation grew more demanding. She did not reply readily as her breathing grew more uneven.

"Neither place is my home, but I will stay where it is safe."

That gave Cade something to think about besides the reaction of his recovering body to Lily's lush proximity. He should not be feeling this way about a woman who was heavy with his child, but his loins seemed to have a mind of their own.

"Travis will tell us when the cabin is ready for our return. I will take you home then."

Lily listened to this pronouncement in astonishment, but her mind was clouded with the sensations Cade was driving her to. She knew he wished to go to his grandfather. She knew he considered the hacienda his rightful home. She knew neither of them was in particularly good condition for going anywhere. But all she could wonder was how long it would be until dark and whether there was any way they could satisfy these urges with her belly in between them.

Cade didn't satisfy her curiosity that night or in the other nights they spent in his father's house. El Caballo had a new wife, one scarcely older than his adolescent sons, and their coupling could be heard in the darkness when all else was quiet. Cade and Lily lay stiff and silent in each other's arms, their desire driven below the surface by the communal living. It was becoming obvious that they could not stay here much longer. Lily regretted leaving Cade's tepee in their escape. That would at least have allowed them some privacy.

At the end of the week, Cade signaled his brothers and conferred with them on the progress being made at the ranch. Their response evidently did not please him, for he scowled and increased the exercise of his injured arm despite Lily's protests.

By the time Travis returned, Cade was still limping, but he was also pulling himself off and onto his gelding without any seeming effort. Travis glared at his patient in the corral and then went to a worried Lily, leaving Cade to discover his presence whenever he tired of his heroics.

"Should you be standing out here in the hot sun? You ought to be lying down, resting."

"If he doesn't, I don't." Lily glared at her recalcitrant husband, who was now performing tricks for the amusement of his youngest brother. She switched her gaze back to Travis. "How is Juanita?" There was a world of questions in that one, but she did not dare ask them any plainer.

Some of the laughter in Travis's eyes died, and his reply was a little stilted. "She is well. She is a whirlwind of energy. If she could only build cabins, everything would be done. As it is, she keeps all of us fed, has somehow managed to restore mattresses to the beds, and is busily mending anything that falls into her path."

The courtship was obviously not doing well. Lily let the matter slide in favor of more pertinent questions. "Us? Have some of the men returned? Will they be able to help rebuild? Was any of the livestock saved?"

Travis grinned and took Lily's arm as he saw Cade come stalking in their direction. "We will find someplace comfortable to discuss this. The only way your obstinate husband will be able to hear the answers is if he sits down and joins us."

Cade growled and appropriated Lily's arm before they entered the lodge, but he made no objection to taking a place on the mat and letting one of the women fetch them something to drink while he listened to Travis's recounting of the repairs in progress.

"There are chickens all over the damned place, enough to make a dozen mattresses and have stew every night. The hogs have gone wild, but we've been rounding them up and fencing them in. Jack says the cattle are still out there somewhere, but there's not been time to count them or brand them or anything. We're lucky the Comanches didn't burn us out like they did Bastrop. I guess one scorched building was sufficient to convince whoever robbed the place that there was no point in burning more."

"Then it was Indians?" Somehow, that relieved Lily to some extent. She hadn't seen the destruction Cade had described, but she hated to think it was caused by people who knew them.

Cade and Travis exchanged looks. Cade answered for him. "It was everyone who came through, I suspect. People about to lose everything tend to do desperate things. They were probably hoping to take any kind of portable wealth they could find. Comanches are more likely to fire the place after taking what they want. They would want to drive us out never to return. There could have been some of the Mexican army involved, although I would have thought they'd have stayed farther south of here. They cleaned out everyone they crossed. Some of them had never seen clocks and mirrors or tasted white sugar or owned candle wax. It was an open market to them."

"Thank God we weren't there." Lily shuddered. She resented the loss of the personal possessions she had worked so hard to own, but her family and friends were still alive and relatively unscathed.

Cade dismissed the unpleasant subject sharply and turned to Travis. "Are you going to stay and help us out?"

Caught by surprise, Travis hesitated. His gaze drifted not to Lily but to the curly-haired boy playing in the dust with his new friends. When his attention returned to Cade, his mouth was set in a firm line. "I have in mind to start a family of my own. I'll be looking for land, but I want it nearby. Roy is still my son."

Cade remained expressionless. "We will have need of all the help we can get. You are welcome to use the cabin until you find what you want. I would not keep you from your son any more than I would keep Lily from him."

They had been through too much by now for either man to speak of debts or gratitude. Travis nodded his acceptance, and Cade returned to the subject uppermost in his mind. "If there is a place where Lily can lie down, we will return with you now. There is much work to be done."

Travis gave him a glare of exasperation. "Lily is in her eighth month. How do you propose to move her back to the ranch? And if I take a look at your shoulder now, is it going to be raw and bleeding again after that asinine performance you just put on?"

Cade peeled back his shirt to reveal an ugly brown mass untouched by bandage but also untouched by the red streaks of infection or the flow of blood. The wound was starting to heal. "I will carry Lily in front of me, as before. The horse has a gentle gait. We will manage."

It was obvious there would be no arguing with him. Imperious as ever, Cade ordered his horse haltered and their belongings packed. Lily could only stand by in amazement as he gave Dove Woman instructions for following them when the time came, bade his father a calm farewell, and told his brothers the buffalo hunt might have to wait until fall. Buffalo hunt? Perhaps she had misunderstood that part of the conversation. In any event, he managed to stir the whole tribe until it hummed like a hive. No wonder he had never made a good employee. He was too accustomed to being the royal prince.

That wasn't a fair accusation, Lily knew, but it helped her to accept Cade's tyrannical habits a little easier. Whatever his background, he was certainly a man more inclined to giving orders than taking them. Without consulting her wishes on the matter, Cade took her onto his saddleless horse when all was ready, and Lily kept her doubts to herself. She wanted to go home as badly as he did. With Serena propped in front of Travis and Roy on his own pony, they set out from the Indian camp.

The gelding's walk was every bit as gentle as Cade had promised, and Lily leaned back against his chest and relaxed with the swaying movement, drinking in the fresh, cool scent of pines as they crossed under them, relishing this freedom. She had felt almost as stifled in the Indian camp as she had at the hacienda, but now she was going home, to familiar territory. Tonight, she would be in her own bed, and Cade would be by her side.

At that thought, she turned her head upward to catch Cade's dark glance looking down. Lily burned with the intensity she found there, and colored as she noted the direction of his gaze. Juanita had sent a gathered blouse as a gift. The low-cut neckline would have been barely acceptable before her pregnancy; now it was barely decent. It was insane to think Cade could be looking at her with lust, but Lily felt his look as if it were his hand caressing her breast.

She grew restless after that and squirmed impatiently until they were in sight of the ranch. She heard Cade's muttering curses at her wriggles, but this had all been his idea. Let him pay for it. With the ranch in sight, she settled, her gaze sweeping over the familiar buildings, and she breathed her relief at the sight of men on the roof nailing down shingles on the main cabin already.

Serena was scrambling out of Travis's arms before he could come to a stop, and Roy rushed his pony on ahead, galloping into the yard and yelling his joy until men came running to discover the source of the ruckus.

Cade read the satisfaction in Lily's eyes as she gazed around her, felt the relaxation in her body as she discovered home almost as good as she remembered it, and recognized the bitterness of defeat along with his relief at her happiness. This would never be his land as his grandfather's would, but Lily had given him something he had sought all his life and craved more than he craved land—acceptance. He had thought to mold her to his way of thinking, but he had come too close to losing her to ignore her wishes any longer. If she could be happy nowhere but here, then here they would stay.

Cade didn't admit his defeat as he helped Lily down from the horse and into the newly refurbished cabin. It wasn't precisely defeat. Lily would give him the handling of her ranch now that she had the child to keep her occupied. Cade knew that. So it was a compromise of sorts. A compromise with definite advantages.

He circled his arms beneath Lily's breasts as she leaned into him to admire all the work completed in their absence. The damage to the mahogany table couldn't be completely repaired, but it could be concealed beneath a gaily embroidered tablecloth. The warped veneer of the chairs had been lovingly tacked down until the damage was scarcely noticeable. Serena's little cubicle sported a new mattress with a ruffled coverlet, and odds and ends of every kind of pottery and tinware that could be found were stacked neatly on the shelves, ready for their next meal.

"You've been spending money again," Lily murmured quietly as she felt Cade's arms tighten around her.

"I spent a lifetime saving that money until I had someone to spend it on. I think I've found what I was looking for."

Lily glanced up swiftly, but she could discern nothing unusual in Cade's expression. He had meant nothing more than that he had found a home. She could be happy with that. She would be certain to make this the kind of home he would never wish to leave.

Straightening, Lily turned and looked him in the eye. "Shall we inspect the rest of the house?"

Since the rest of the house meant their bedroom, Cade willingly agreed, a gleam coming to his eye as he followed her out. Even carrying the heavy weight of their child, Lily managed her slender height gracefully, and Cade watched the swing of her hips with interest. He had made an inquiry or two while he was occupying himself in his father's camp. Dove Woman had been particularly knowledgeable. The barren desert of the remaining months of pregnancy and recovery had an oasis or two to be discovered, if he could persuade his wife to the journey.

And judging by the look in Lily's eye, she was willing. Whatever their differences might be elsewhere, they had one thing in common—and the bed they now inspected held equal interest for both of them.

Thirty-five

"Cade, what are you doing?" Lily whispered a trifle breathlessly as he came to bed and immediately began tugging her nightgown off.

"Taking advantage of one of the privileges of married life. Besides, it is too warm to be wearing this thing."

Since he was boldly, blatantly naked without showing any evidence of shivering, she could accept his word for that. As Cade knelt beside her on the bed, pulling her gown off, however, Lily felt as if she were about to be scalped by a savage. When he next reached to unplait her hair, a shiver went down her spine.

"Cade, this is foolish. I look like a beached whale. Allow me some decency."

Instead, Cade flung the covers to the floor and straddled her legs, leaning over to rest his ear against her stomach. "I think he speaks Apache, but I can't understand a word he says."

Lily laughed softly and tried to push him away. She was too aware of the muscular hardness of the trunklike thighs on either side of hers, and she couldn't ignore the extent of his arousal. She tried to concentrate on his damaged shoulder, lifting her hand to touch the broken skin. "What language is it that you and your father speak?"

"Apache," Cade replied calmly, leaning farther to place a kiss on her breast. "Any child of mine will know it through his mother's womb."

Lily gasped and arched upward to encourage his lips as they tugged at her nipple and sent spiraling sensations through her center. "Stop it, Cade! Oh, don't . . . It's not fair." She silenced as his lips found hers and drank deeply of a kiss they had denied each other for too long.

"Nothing is fair. It is up to us to take what we can get," Cade murmured against her mouth as he turned to his side and pulled her with him.

"This is insane. You can't rape a fat woman."

The unholy gleam in Cade's eye was pure Indian as he slid his hand downward and between her thighs. "We'll save rape for a more appropriate time. For now, I mean a simple ravishment. Hold still, wife, and let me become better acquainted with my child. I would learn if you carry a boy or girl."

"Both, assuredly," Lily gasped as he increased the pressure of his fingers, bringing her to a responsiveness that was scarcely necessary given her state of complete starvation.

Cade eyed her stomach with interest. "Ugh. Two. Do you think it's possible?" Without waiting for an answer, he slid downward and assaulted her senses with his tongue.

Lily gave a breathless scream at this unexpected attack. Surely it was immoral. Jim had never done anything like it. But those protests were worthless as her body exploded in convulsive waves with every swirl of Cade's tongue. He lifted her close and delved deeper until there was nothing left of her but a damp rag that he laid gently back to the mattress as he carried his kisses upward, extracting every last bit of pleasure from her skin.

And then he turned her away from him, placed a pillow under her for support, and entered her from behind, catching the last of Lily's shivering contractions and propelling them a little while longer until he reached his own.

That was the way they fell asleep, complete and more at rest than they had been in more months than they cared to remember. They had earned this peace, and Cade closed his eyes and relaxed thoroughly for what might have been the first time in his life. His home was here, where Lily was. It didn't matter whose name was on the deed.

The sun was fully up and the heat had risen sufficiently

to leave a sheen of sweat across their bodies before they woke. They woke together, the stirring of one causing an equal reaction in the other. Lily thought maybe this was what it meant to be man and wife in every sense. Cade's dark hand lay splayed across her pale abdomen as if safeguarding their child, and his large body curled protectively around hers. She felt more secure than she ever had in her life. Perhaps this was what love was all about. She had certainly never expected to find a man who would hold her and love her as Cade had last night even when she was at her ugliest. Any man who did that had to care for her to some degree. That was all she needed to feed her hopes.

If he could truly care for her above and beyond what they had in bed, she would do everything within her power to make him happy. Sighing contentedly, Lily covered Cade's brown hand with her own and wriggled herself more comfortably against the length of his body.

He responded by kissing her shoulder and pushing her back against the bed so he could see her face. "Don't tempt me any more than I already am, *querida*. There is much work to be done, and we will both need our strength to do it."

Lily smiled and stroked the aquiline jut of his arrogant nose. "I have married a monster. I suppose hard work is one way of preventing all the children we are likely to have if left to idleness."

"Or of supporting them when they inevitably arrive. We will have to beware of planting seeds under the new moon in the future, or we will have a lively crop spilling out the walls." Cade swung from the bed and splashed in the pan that had replaced the porcelain washbowl.

Amused, Lily levered herself up from the bed. "Is that how you succeeded in getting me pregnant with just one try? You planted me under a new moon?"

Cade dried his face in a linen towel and came up grinning. He watched admiringly as the golden sun played across his wife's proud figure and danced through the silken strands of hair tumbling down her back. "Plowed and seeded, *querida*." He stopped smiling and reached to pull a stray strand of her hair over her shoulder. "Do you still regret it?"

Lily tilted her head and studied his face. "I don't think I ever regretted it. I want this child, Cade. Does that seem strange?"

"No." Because he wanted it too, but it was a concept Cade couldn't explain. He didn't want just any child, but he wanted this one—carried by a woman alien to anything he had ever known in his past but similar to him in so many ways.

He kissed her then, not the usual kiss of lust that they shared, but a gentle kiss of understanding—and something else, but neither of them was ready to recognize it.

Lily only knew that she felt warm all the way to her middle for the rest of the day. She smiled contentedly as Travis and Juanita skirmished whenever they came in contact, which seemed to be altogether too frequently. She laughed and rescued Serena when the child climbed to the top shelf in search of cookies and couldn't find her way back down. And she even managed to hold her tongue when Cade agreed that Roy could help in rounding up the cattle. Such serenity couldn't last forever, but it was good to discover that it existed somewhere inside of her.

It was also good to discover that she didn't have to fight all day, every day, to make herself heard. When she suggested over dinner that Travis might want to restock his medicinal supplies, the topic was discussed among them all and the ways and means were decided upon without the idea being dismissed as a woman's foolishness. When she went outside to see if she could salvage her kitchen garden, Cade sent a hired man to begin the hoeing without her even having to ask. She had learned how to nag and manipulate Jim to her way of thinking, but Cade seemed to be always one step ahead of her.

Paradise couldn't reign all the time, of course. As the heat increased in the June sun, tempers flared. The corn had been planted before any work had been done on the house, and Cade complained about the crookedness of the rows and the depth of the seed, with Travis defending his ignorance of

farming and his reliance on the hired help. Neighbors returning to their own ruined farms came asking for help and lured
away the few available workers with promises of higher
wages that no one could actually afford. Reports of Comanche raids to the north and west had everyone's nerves on
edge, and any sudden movement could result in gunfire.

Sewing baby bonnets and gowns and tending her garden, Lily managed to ignore most of the strife. When
Travis and Juanita started arguing in the middle of the
yard, she calmly dumped jugs of water over both their
heads and left them to laugh or curse as they chose. She
noticed Cade struggling to hide a smile as he came in a
little later and decided the method had been effective.

"Are the lovebirds kissing and making up yet?" Lily
asked with a trace of cynicism as she fed Serena a lunch
she'd had to fetch for herself from the kitchen since
Juanita seemed otherwise occupied.

"They were rolling in the mud when I came across the
yard." Cade helped himself to a pitcher of water and
gulped it thirstily, ignoring the cup Lily held out for him.
Setting the pitcher down again, he shrugged. "Juanita was
pulling his hair and cursing him for a fool, among other
less polite things, and Travis seemed to be admonishing
her to remove her clothing before she caught cold. He appeared to be well on the way to accomplishing it. Do you
think I ought to carry another basin of water out there?"

Lily pushed aside the mosquito netting that now
adorned her window and peered outside. There didn't
seem to be any hair pulling going on now. About all she
could see of Juanita was her arms around Travis's neck.
Lily let the netting fall back in place.

"I would recommend just keeping everybody out of the
yard for a while. If you dump water on them now, we'll
only have to suffer through this all over again."

Cade muffled a laugh in the piece of bread he had stolen from the table. Black eyes dancing, he watched as
Lily calmly returned to setting the table. "You're going to
lose a cook if Travis takes to the road again."

Lily favored him with a derisive glance. "The road is
going to lose a peddler if Juanita decides to keep him."

"Do women always win these wars?" Cade buttered a piece of bread for Serena.

"Women seldom ever win these wars, but Travis is smart enough to realize that Juanita needs the safety of familiar faces around her. He might decide she's not worth staying here for, but he won't take her away."

Cade thought about that as he chewed his own bread. Lily had been strong enough to follow her husband to a new land and start a new life when she was only sixteen and carrying a child. She was strong enough to start a new life at the hacienda if he asked it of her. But he rather thought she was strong enough now to tell him to go to hell, that she had no intention of leaving her home again. Lily had given him everything he had ever wanted except this one thing. It was a small price to pay.

Before Cade could make any reply, a muddy and decidedly disheveled Travis stumbled into the cabin. "There's a rider coming. He's alone. Should I call the men just in case?"

Lily looked up in surprise at this indication that they were expecting someone and meant to greet whoever it was with an armed force. Nothing Travis said revealed these plans, but she had some experience in reading between the lines. They didn't usually call the men out to greet a rider coming down the road.

Cade strode to the front and pulled back the netting. "Looks like Clark. Call them in and keep them out of sight. Station someone in that stand of pines along the road. Keep everyone away from the cabin."

Travis grabbed a rifle, buttoned his muddy shirt, and departed, leaving Cade and Lily to stare at each other.

"You've been expecting this," she accused quietly, trying not to disturb the child happily chasing her peas across the table.

"Around here, you'd have to be a fool not to expect trouble. I didn't expect Clark. Why don't you take Serena and go out to the kitchen with Juanita? There isn't much Ollie can do by himself, and I might get more out of him if you're not in the room."

Lily might have resented being treated like a helpless

female, but Cade's explanation made his commands go down easier. There had been a time when he wouldn't have offered explanations. Perhaps life with her had had some civilizing influence. Smiling at the thought, she reached over and kissed his cheek as he checked his rifle's breech. She was already picking up Serena before Cade could do more than look up and watch her with surprise.

He didn't have time to ponder her action for very long. Setting the rifle close to hand when the loud rap came on the door, Cade moved to answer it.

Ollie looked nervously at Cade's forbidding features and glanced into the room. "I thought maybe Lily or Travis would be here."

At one time, that would have been right, but Cade had taken to staying close to the house now that Lily was so close to her time. Dove Woman had warned Lily might not carry the baby to term since it was so large. Cade didn't explain any of that; instead he met Clark's gaze coldly. "They're around. What do you want with them?"

"That's not precisely hospitable," Ollie answered uncomfortably. He relaxed as he noted Travis coming through the other door. "I've brought some of that new whisky I ordered for the medicine. It's out in my bags. Just a minute."

As Travis came into the room, he and Cade exchanged glances but no words while Ollie went to bring in the supplies. Personal delivery service didn't usually come with the order.

"Have you got some cups?" Ollie asked as he returned bearing arms full of liquor. "We might as well give it a try and see if it's what the doctor ordered." He laughed at his own joke.

Travis obediently grinned and helped set the heavy load on the table, but Cade merely frowned and waited. Travis was the one to produce the cups, and Ollie poured, extolling the whisky's qualities as he did so.

They switched to discussing Travis's pharmaceutical business as they lifted their cups to taste the liquor. Absently keeping an eye on the window, Cade lifted his cup from habit, but the strong odor of spirits he hadn't tasted since the fiasco with wine at his grandfather's house jarred him back to what he was doing. He still started to sip at the whisky until his glance came to rest on the table decorated in gaily colored cloth and set for a family dinner—a table that had once gleamed with polish and Lily's pride. A stubborn old man and whisky were responsible for that cloth being there. It could just as easily have been Serena that timber had fallen on.

Without drinking, Cade set the cup aside and moved toward the window. Ollie was up to something. He didn't need to be drunk while he discovered what. He didn't need to be drunk at all. Things had changed, and he had no objection to changing with them.

"Come on, Cade, you can do better than that. I've seen you put away a jug of that before. Can't you stomach the good stuff after all that rotgut you've drunk?"

If the scorn was meant to rankle, it didn't succeed. If it was meant to challenge him into drinking, it failed dismally. Cade merely turned and gave Ollie a look that should have made his scalp tingle.

"Cade's a family man now. He doesn't drink," Travis explained genially. "It's good whisky, Clark. I daresay it will do just fine, but I need the rest of the supplies before I can get started. When do you think they'll come in? I'd not have you riding all the way out here again just because we haven't got time to get to town too often these days."

Ollie made himself comfortable at the table without invitation. "Everybody's up to their ears with planting and repairing, and no one gets to town much anymore. That's why I'm out delivering. You don't think Lily'd mind if I stay to dinner? I've got a couple more stops to make before I get back. Here, give me your cup and let me top it off. Takes the heat off the day."

Cade watched this performance cynically, but he moved to call the anxious women. Travis was going to need the food in him if he meant to sample any more of that whisky.

Juanita reverted to her usual uncommunicative self as

she carried the dishes to the table, but Lily directed the conversation with the expertise of her Southern upbringing as she set another place and arranged the table seating to her satisfaction.

"We haven't heard any news in forever, Ollie. Tell us what is happening. Are we really going to be a republic now, or are we going to petition to join the states?"

"I imagine it's going to come to a vote. President Jackson's eager for us to join the union, but I can't say for certain what will happen." Ollie held out the whisky bottle sitting in the center of the table. "Sure you don't want some, Cade? It's mild as water. I won't charge for this bottle in exchange for your hospitality."

Since Cade had noticed Travis surreptitiously watering his own cup, he could imagine how mild the liquor was. There had been a time when Cade would have suffered agonies over having to refuse the offer, and there had been a time when he would have accepted it out of reckless defiance, knowing what it would do to him. And there had been a time when he would have sought it without prompting to erase the pain of existence. Even now, he could almost taste the alcohol and imagine the stirring in his blood that it would cause, but he merely took another bite of his chicken and shook his head. There had been a time when he had needed oblivion. That time was gone.

Besides, he was obviously foiling Ollie's plans, and it was tickling Cade immensely to see the man squirm in his seat as his scheme collapsed. Lily had watched the interchange with suspicion, and when Ollie refilled Travis's cup, she discreetly stood up and began clearing some of the empty bowls from the table. The whisky bottle went with them.

"I have heard tell that there's some trouble with the legal titles over toward Béxar and the Tejanos are up in arms," Ollie mentioned conversationally. "Seems a lot of these Spanish land grants have been awarded several times over, and no one's precisely sure who owns what. They've been looking into some of the property round hereabouts, too. But I'm sure Jim must have gotten a clear title before he built all this."

Cade calmly continued eating, but Lily could tell he was as tense as a panther about to spring. The muscles stretching his old shirt across his back were knotted and rounding to striking power. She didn't dare touch him for fear he would leap out of his seat. But he kept his fury under control, and no one else at the table seemed to notice.

Besides worrying about Cade, Lily didn't like this talk of titles. Jim hadn't been a man who had much concern for bits of paper. He was a man who knew the sun and the soil and how best to apply them. He would trust other men to be as honest as he was. If there had been any problem with the title to their land, he would never have known it, but she kept that fact to herself.

"I'm willing to take Mr. Austin's word that this land was ours for the taking, but tell me more about the land in Béxar. Haven't those people lived there for decades or longer?" she asked.

"They're lazy, shiftless Mexicans, Lily," Ollie replied with scorn, ignoring the fact that his host was half that maligned breed. "They can't do anything right. There's no surveys, no written records that anyone can find, nothing to show what belongs to whom. I hear Houston is ready to see them cleared out if he gets the presidency. There's those that are ready to clear them out now. A new republic doesn't need that kind around."

Travis hurriedly shoved an overlarge piece of bread into Juanita's mouth when she opened it. Lily had insisted that Juanita take her rightful place at the table when they returned here, but this was one of those times when she would regret it. When Juanita chose to speak, she had a vocabulary that could singe the hairs off a mule skinner.

Oblivious to the rage boiling up around him, Ollie looked around for his bottle and, not finding it, scratched his head in puzzlement and rambled on. "Well, anyway, it's been a fine meal, Lily. I do appreciate your invitation. I wouldn't worry too much about these land-jumping claims, especially if, like Cade said when you got married, the land is in your name and not his. If they're going after Tejanos, just imagine what they'd do with an Indian. Well, let me leave you folks to your work . . ."

He seemed to look around in bewilderment one more time for the nearly full bottle, which would have made an excellent end to the meal, but he retained enough manners not to mention its absence. Lily smugly stood in front of the child's bed with its ruffled covers pulled over a whisky bottle and waved farewell as Ollie departed.

She then turned hurriedly to the two men standing solemnly behind her. "Where's the damned deed? If it burned with everything else . . ."

No one wanted to consider that notion.

Thirty-six

Cade overruled the confusion that ensued by the simple expedient of talking louder.

"Lily, where did Jim keep the deed?"

"He kept all his important papers in a metal box under one of the floor planks. I think it was that one over by the fireplace."

Since the area she pointed toward was an area that had suffered the most damage during the fire, Cade turned to Travis. "Was there anything down there when you had those planks replaced?"

Travis scratched his head, trying to remember even as Juanita went to that portion of the floor and began searching for loose boards.

"I wasn't always here while they were working. Nobody told me about any box."

"Lily, I'll send Roy in to pull up the planks. Travis and I are going to ride out and take a look around. I don't like the way Ollie was plying that whisky bottle. Something's going to happen, and they don't want us ready for it."

Cade was gathering up his rifle and ammunition as he spoke, and Lily felt the first real heartbeat of fear. "Maybe it would be safer if you stayed here instead of looking for trouble?" she suggested tentatively, knowing in advance that she would be refused.

Cade gave her an impatient look. "I'm going to send someone over to Langton's. He ought to at least be warned if there's trouble brewing. You can go over there if you get worried."

Like hell she would. Lily kept her sentiments to herself as she watched the men get together instruments of war and head out. She would be damned if they were going to push her out of events this time. This was her home, and she would defend it as fiercely as they.

Roy had been eating in the bunkhouse with the men, but he came in now with a crowbar and began prying at the planks under Lily's direction. It didn't seem possible that the men would have nailed new planks over a metal box and left it undisturbed, but they would have to see. If it wasn't there, then someone had removed it without informing Travis. That did not bode well at all.

While Lily worried over the deed, Cade calmly directed the men to their positions with the authority of a general before a battle. Some of the hands had been hired since the rebellion and didn't understand the need to jump when Cade said jump. They tended to argue, but they shut up rapidly when Cade swung his rifle up and unrolled his whip. No one had ever seen Cade use the rifle or whip, but just looking at the big man wielding them was sufficient to convince them he would. The new men rode out with the same haste as the old.

Cade turned to Travis, who waited on his horse for his orders. "I'm going to have to stay here near the women and meet any unexpected visitors. You'll have to be the one to go to my father. If there are strangers anywhere around, he'll know. Do you think that smooth tongue of yours can get the message across?"

"I know about as much Spanish or Apache as you know Latin, but if those brothers of yours are around, I'll make myself understood. The fiendish little devils know about as much English as I do, I'd wager."

Cade hadn't really thought about it, but it wasn't a wager he'd take. His brothers were clever enough to keep their mouths shut and let the white men around them make fools of themselves. He nodded and let Travis ride off across the prairie toward the woods and river.

Cade was essentially alone now. He'd never really learned to rely on the help of others when there was trouble. If everyone followed orders, that was well and good, but Cade didn't intend to count on them. Ollie was a bumbling ass, but someone had put him up to this, and he didn't have much trouble imagining who or why. Whoever it was had made a mistake in sending Ollie, though. If someone had come here and said the de Suela claim was being stripped, Cade would have ridden out today and left the ranch practically undefended. Instead, they had sent a man whose interests were here and not in Béxar, and he had concentrated on Lily and not Cade. That was a major tactical error.

Humming to himself, Cade rode out to the pasture where part of the cattle herd had been gathered. There were several young and restless bulls in the herd. They ought to be cut out and separated sometime. Now was as good a time as any.

The summer sun was beginning to sink slowly behind the line of trees on the distant horizon when a piercing whistle split the air. The men waiting listlessly in the dry pine needles and old leaves of the forest along the low-lying ridge looked around in puzzlement for the source of the sound. Several mounted up, and others checked their rifles as they watched the road below them.

To their incredulity, the big Indian on his gray gelding suddenly came riding down the road, calmly cracking his whip over a herd of young bulls. Red lifted his hat to scratch his head and whistled softly to himself.

"Hell, ain't never seen one damned man ride herd on the sons of bitches like that. Think he's plumb gone out of his friggin' haid?"

The rest of the men gathered around to watch Cade keep cool control over some of the meanest, most rambunctious animals on the range. Their bellows of rage echoed clearly even up here as Cade forced them in the direction he had chosen and not one to their liking. The man had to be loco.

"Look. Over there," Jack whispered to Abraham, nodding in the opposite direction.

Down the road from town came a cavalcade of riders and a single wagon. The riders were heavily armed. The wagon carried surveying equipment. They rode hell-bent for a collision with the animals stampeding just around the bend.

For stampeding they now were. Whereas Cade had maintained full control over the bulls up to this point, he seemed to have suddenly misplaced his magic spell. The animals were screaming their fury and galloping flat out along the path of least resistance—the open road.

Abraham chuckled and swung up on his horse. "That man ain't gonna need us. He done got full charge of the sit-che-a-shun."

And so it certainly seemed. The rampaging bulls charged straight ahead, tossing their horns and scattering the trespassing horses and their riders off the road and across the prairie as each bull broke from the pack after a different target. The wagon horses screamed and raised their forelegs and broke into a wild gallop that sent the wagon careening through baked-mud ruts. Tools flew everywhere. The driver leapt for his life. And the wagon itself finally smashed into splinters as the horses attempted to escape on either side of a live oak.

The small group of men in the trees rode down to help when they saw Cade casually stop and make inquiries of the driver. They arrived in time to hear Cade say, "Poor timing on both our parts. My men were just gathering some rogue cattle. Are you hurt? My wife can see to that bump, if you like."

The driver was still staggering to his feet and cursing raggedly as he looked up to see the motley collection of cow herders ride down on him. He spit to check a loosened tooth, then glared at the massive Indian in denims and blue work shirt.

"You don't run bulls on the road, you fool." He looked around to locate his scattered surveying equipment. "Have your men gather up my tools. They're too valuable to lose."

Helpfully, Jack leapt down beside a shiny piece of metal on a wooden stick. An ominous crack followed his landing, and the surveyor spun around in fury just as Jack bent to pick up the now-mangled tool. "This yor'n?" he inquired innocently, handing it back.

The rest of the equipment was swiftly gathered in much the same manner. By the time a few of the horsemen escaped their rampaging attackers, the surveyor was in near-hysterical tears, ranting and raving and stamping his feet in the road as the bent and mutilated equipment was gathered in the remains of the wagon bed.

Cade still sat majestically upon his gelding, surveying the destruction with calm authority. He lifted a questioning look to the furious horsemen jerking their mounts to a halt before him.

"You're going to pay for this, Injun," one burly scout snarled.

"I'm going to pay?" Cade glanced out over the prairie, where the dust rising over the grass was the only indication that his cattle had ever been present. "You just drove my herd halfway to Galveston and you think I'm going to pay? I'd suggest you check your maps. This is a private road. You're trespassing. I think it's time I had a few explanations."

The click of several rifles being placed in firing position caused the intruders to glance around nervously. The previously inept lot of cow herders now sat menacingly in their saddles, backs straight, rifles cocked, ready, and held deceptively loosely in their hands as they surrounded their quarry.

"There ain't no such thing as a private road," the surveyor blustered.

"Is it on your maps?" Cade leaned over his horse's neck to inquire. "Check your maps, and if you're any kind of land agent at all, you'll see that this piece of land is square in the middle of property deeded to Jim and Lily Brown in the fall of 1824. Jim cut this road to get his cattle down to the San Antonio highway. That makes it a private road, gentlemen, and I can't think of one good reason why you should be on it."

The burly rider recovered fastest. Unfastening his rifle from his saddle, he held it in hand but raised it no farther as half a dozen guns rose in response. Still, he sat confidently as he replied, "That's the reason we're here. That deed ain't worth the paper it's written on. This land wasn't Austin's to sell. It belongs to another land grant, and Mrs. Brown is the one who's trespassing. The true owner wants the place surveyed and prepared for sale."

Cade still didn't bother lifting his weapon, but the tension in his muscles was evident as he straightened and gave the interloper a steely look. "I can guess who that imaginary owner is. Tell Ricardo to give up and I won't add his scalp to my collection. Otherwise I won't bother wasting my time with the law and the courts again. I'll have his scrawny neck instead. I'll make him sorry he ever messed in my wife's business."

The other man bristled at the threats. "I don't know any Ricardo, mister. I'm just doing my job. If you don't keep out of our way, we'll have the law after you."

Cade smiled, and the men around him stared in astonishment. Cade never smiled, and they hoped he never smiled again. The look was pure malevolence, and they glanced at the intruder to see if he shivered as they did when Cade spoke.

"Try it, gentlemen," was all he said. Turning his horse, he rode away, leaving his men to get across the message that trespassers had better turn back.

By the time Ralph Langton caught up with him, Cade looked more like a tired farmer than a menace. The other rancher kicked his horse to ride beside Cade.

"Heard there's trouble."

Cade swept him a sour look. "Isn't there always?" Without waiting for a reply, he finished, "It's Ricardo. You'd better beware. If he's decided to rewrite the records to declare this side of the river part of his land grant, you're in danger too. He won't let a small thing like revenge stand in the way of a profit."

"He can't rewrite the records. We've all got deeds."

Cade watched a hawk floating toward the sunset. "Deeds are worthless if he declares Austin had no right to issue them."

The other man remained silent for a minute. "We've got friends we can call on," he finally answered.

Cade sent him a smoldering look. "Even if I had any

friends, I wouldn't put them in Ricardo's path and still call myself friend. Stay out of this, Langton. It's time I took care of Ricardo. I don't think turning the other cheek works against devils from hell."

"You can't go taking this into your own hands, Cade. Think about Lily."

"I am thinking about Lily. If I weren't thinking about Lily I'd be out of here now, chasing Satan back where he came from." Cade paused and gazed at some spot in the distance, then turned his head to Langton and asked, "Do you think the courts would accept Indians as witnesses?"

"Nope. What are you getting at?"

"Hell, I don't know." Tiredly, Cade admitted, "I think I've got a witness to Jim Brown's murder. I've spent the better part of my life studying Mexican law to keep myself and Ricardo's victims out of trouble, and now there's no damned law at all. I don't have any choice left, Langton. I'm going to have to go after him."

Langton stared at him but didn't question further. He knew as well as Cade that an Indian witness would be worthless even if there were a court to bring him to. "There will be a law," he said slowly. "You've just got to be patient. Law or no law, you can't kill a man without getting hung. There's too many willing to witness a good hanging."

"Then I guess I'll just have to hang him." Stating that with quiet finality, Cade spurred his horse into a gallop in the direction of Lily and home.

She was waiting for him anxiously. Seeing the worried look on her face, Cade attributed at least part of her concern to himself. He needed to feel wanted for just a little while. He swept her into his arms and held her close and allowed the warmth of her embrace to ease his hurts just a little.

"You've been gone for hours. I was afraid you weren't coming back," Lily murmured against his open collar.

Those words were balm to his angry heart, and Cade pressed a kiss to the golden spill of her hair. "I came as soon as I could. You'll have the child all stirred up and complaining if you go working yourself into this state just because I'm out for a little while."

"Out for a little while!" Lily tore herself out of his arms and, hands on her hips, glared at him. "You go riding out of here with your troops and stay the better part of the day and come back and pretend you were out stargazing? What the hell happened, Cade de Suela?"

Her worry might be balm to his heart, but her fury was balm to his spirit. Cade grinned and, lifting her up, deposited her in the newly repaired rocking chair. "Sit. I don't want that child leaping out to get me with a hatchet in his hand." He turned to a worried Juanita. "Bring me something to drink. Rounding up cattle has me parched."

"Rounding up cattle!"

Cade had Lily in a state halfway to fury by the time Travis ambled in. As a tin cup came flying across the room, Cade ducked and Travis jumped out of the way, letting it slam against a far wall with a satisfying crunch.

Travis lifted an inquiring eyebrow at the woman with the wild throwing arm as she stood with her golden-brown hair halfway down about her shoulders and her eyes flashing with an ire that had never been turned on him. He supposed Lily must look like some Valkyrie, but he wasn't much on other people's legends. He caught the next cup that came flying at him and set it on the table.

"I don't suppose the two of you ever thought of sitting down at the table and discussing things rationally, did you?"

"Look who's talking!" Shoving her straying hair back from her face, Lily looked scathingly at the mud stains on Travis's shirt. "Just tell me what happened out there and don't give me a cock-and-bull story about rounding up cattle. Something's happened or El Monstruo over there wouldn't be grinning all over himself."

Travis shrugged and took the mug Juanita handed him as he sat down at the table. "Can't rightly tell you more than that. I've been up visiting with the Indians myself."

Juanita retrieved his mug and dumped the contents over his head. Travis howled, and Roy—sitting quietly on the hearth—finally gave way to mirth at the sound. Serena, not to be left out, giggled happily and pulled herself into Travis's lap, patting her small hands against his wet shirt and making smacking sounds.

Looking around at the bedlam that was his home, Cade pulled Lily against his side and kissed her soundly before she could offer any protest.

"I'll wager they're married before the baby comes."

"I'll wager she kills him before then." Lily poked a fingernail into Cade's side to indicate the threat worked for both of them.

"You'll not do it," Cade declared boldly. "If you did, who would you have to . . ." he whispered the rest of the sentence so little ears couldn't hear.

As it was, the whispered words singed Lily to her toes and made her cheeks redden. It was obvious she wasn't going to get anything sensible out of him any time soon, but he would regret making her wait. In the meantime, she turned her mouth up for a kiss, bit Cade's lip, stepped on his toe, and sidestepped his grab as she sashayed out the door in search of their belated supper.

Thirty-seven

"The box was there, but the deed is gone. What are we going to do, Cade?"

Lily whispered the words as they lay in each other's arms that night. The day's emotions had taken their toll, and exhaustion weighed heavily on her eyelids, but she was too frightened to sleep.

"There will be a copy of the deed in the *alcalde*'s office, and Austin will have the plat marked in his records. A piece of paper is meaningless if Ricardo means to change the rules. There's such chaos right now that they had to close the land office. Nothing legal can be done until they reopen. It's terrorism that Ricardo wields best."

Lily held her hand quietly against Cade's broad chest, hearing the frustrated fury through her fingertips as well as with her ears. He had made it more than evident that Ricardo had been the bane of his life since he was a child. He had made every effort to stay out of Ricardo's way, to disappear into the vast open spaces of this land, but Ricardo had always found him. And now he was threatening more than Cade. Lily had been surprised when Cade hadn't run to save his grandfather from Ricardo's clutches. She wondered what held him back now.

"What are we going to do?" she asked quietly.

Cade shrugged, doing his best to keep his anxiety from her. "We'll wait. There's nothing else that can be done." Trying to ease the mood, he stroked the place where his child grew. "We'll watch our child grow and wait for the corn to rise."

That was what she wanted to hear, but Lily had a feeling that wasn't what Cade wanted to say. She could almost feel him erupting inside, feel the frustration and the fury tearing at him. She knew that despite his size, Cade wasn't a violent man, but there was a limit to how much any man could take. Lily very much suspected Cade had been pushed to his limit, but still he lay here calmly telling her he was content to wait for events to happen. She didn't think she was a fool, but she couldn't interpret his actions, either.

"I think, perhaps, it is time for you to go to your grandfather," she suggested tentatively, testing the waters.

Cade stiffened, but he forced himself to relax again. "Béxar is several days' journey. I would not leave you now. My grandfather has friends who will watch over him."

Lily pushed up on her elbow and stared down at him incredulously. "You are staying because of me?"

For him, she had worn her hair unplaited, and it spilled across her shoulders and breasts now. Cade took a deep breath and admired the sight. Running his fingers through the silken strands to her breast, he answered, "You and the child are more important to me than all the land in the world."

Lily couldn't believe she was hearing this. She searched his face for lies, but whatever Cade might be, he wasn't a liar. The wall that he had built around him was finally opening, and she could see the shadows of his doubts and fears in the look he returned to her. Lily found herself caught in the wicked trap of her emotions.

If she loved him, she would have to let him go. It wasn't a pleasant notion. Returning to Cade's side, Lily curled there, fear and desperation and a terrifying wave of love sweeping over her and drowning her senses. She meant more to him than the land. It wasn't a gallant, romantic declaration of love, but it spoke the truth as Cade knew it. And it sent her hopes swirling, spiraling upward to new and previously unexplored heights. She hadn't thought love was real, but whatever this was had the force of a hurricane. She couldn't control it, couldn't rationalize it, couldn't even speak of it, it was so new—and terrifying.

Lily found herself saying what came to her heart, responding to the emotions in Cade, reaching out to ease his ache despite her own. "I am in no danger here, Cade. Your grandfather might be. It could be weeks yet before the baby comes. I think we will both feel better if you find out what is happening."

She chose the words as carefully as possible. She didn't tell him to seek out Ricardo and kill him. She didn't tell him that the idea of having this child alone scared her to death, but Ricardo scared her more. She didn't tell him to do this for himself, but for both of them. She knew how to use words to say the right things, and she did it because she loved Cade, not for her own sake. She would probably never understand this if she lived to be a hundred, but it was done.

Still absorbing the impact of this unexpected freedom, Cade lay quietly holding Lily until he could find the words to speak. "I spent the months with Houston regretting leaving you. When I heard you were no longer with my grandfather, I thought I had lost you. I don't ever wish to live through that time again."

Perhaps Cade would never say the words Lily wanted to hear, but she had never thought to hear them anyway. He had spent a lifetime trapped inside himself. She couldn't expect him to come out too often. What he had just told her was sufficient proof of the tie binding them, a tie she had never believed could exist between the taciturn Indian and herself. She could learn to accept what little Cade could give. It was amazing what she could do once she knew it was more than lust binding them.

"I do not want you to go, but I know you must, just as I knew you had to go with Houston. I'm not going to leave you, Cade. We're bound together for the rest of our lives, no matter what is thrown our way. I know the words were never said, but in marrying you, I agreed to be your wife until 'death do us part.' Just don't go getting killed on me. This brat of yours is going to need a man's handling."

Cade smiled at the roof over their head and allowed a sliver of contentment to take root inside him. He had never owned more than a horse and a saddle in all his life, and he knew he didn't own Lily, but she was his, just the same, by her own admission and not his demands. He rather liked the notion of having a companion for life, one who wouldn't walk out when she got bored or irritated. He sure as hell was tired of talking to four walls. And it wasn't just an end to loneliness, it was the beginning of something else. Remembering Lily's heated arguments and equally heated lovemaking, Cade's smile grew broader.

"I think I'll bring a priest back with me. I want to hear those words said before a man of the cloth. I think I will feel much better if I can produce a witness when you start throwing things at me again."

Lily laughed against his shoulder. He was hiding his feelings, but she was being equally secretive with hers. There was too much ahead of them for words to bridge. One step at a time was the most practical policy.

"I'll hold you to that promise. I don't want you disclaiming this child when he starts screaming all night. If you think Ricardo is a formidable foe, you've never tended an infant."

Cade chuckled, and they talked softly for a while longer before sleep overtook them, but both knew their problems weren't solved by a few words whispered in bed. A mountain still loomed ahead, but words couldn't cross it. Only time would tell if it was even traversable.

The garden gate was barred, as Cade had known it would be. Sliding his knife between the gate and the frame, he pried at the dried-up board until it fell to the ground with a soft "thunk." In moments, he was inside the hacienda gardens.

Getting inside the walls had been the easy part. The unexpected that lay ahead would be the danger. Perhaps his Indian training hadn't been thorough, but experience had taught Cade many things. How to walk silently and keep to the shadows was just part of his knowledge.

The lamp in his grandfather's room was still lit. No guard waited in this supposedly inaccessible part of the house. Reassured that Ricardo's arrogance ran true to form, Cade slipped to the hacienda walls and climbed on the timbers jutting through the adobe to look in.

His grandfather looked haggard but well as he sat at his desk, painstakingly writing in his journal. The window was too small for Cade to fit through, but there was no glass to interfere with speech. Whistling lightly, he made Antonio turn.

The old man's face lit eagerly as he recognized the shadow in the window above him. Coming forward, he whispered, "One of the men walks through the gardens at intervals. Beware."

"I will hear him coming. I have heard that you are held against your will. Do you wish to leave here?"

Antonio shrugged. "I have nowhere else to go, so I stay."

The old man's pride needed to be pacified to get an honest answer from him. Cade offered, "I will take you to see my wife if you wish. She worries about you."

The old man's look was wary, but a smile tugged at his lips. "She is well? Has the baby come?"

"The child will arrive any day. She went to stay with my father for a while after she left here. I think it is safe to say that she is well," Cade answered dryly.

Antonio's chuckle held a hint of admiration. "You have an extraordinary wife." He hesitated thoughtfully, then continued, "But I suppose she must be if you have chosen her. Your mother was strong like that. There is much of her in you."

"Will you come?"

"I think I should like to see my great-grandchild into this world. There is a guard outside my door. What do you suggest?"

"Wrap anything you would take with you in a sheet and keep it hidden until I come. Be quick."

He was gone from the window before Antonio could offer any objection.

Trying to keep from whistling to himself, Cade slipped

into the shadows of the lemon tree until the guard walked past on his rounds. Then sliding through the dark, he reached the railed paddock and smiled. Ricardo wouldn't have liked that smile if he had seen it.

Lifting the bars from their racks, Cade opened the paddock fence. A soft whistle to catch the stallion's attention, the crack of a whip to wake the mares, and a shout to send them running was all that it took. Cade stepped out of the way as the stallion ran directly for the path to freedom, his harem not far behind.

As the horses broke into the yard and screamed and galloped in panic through the gardens, men came running from the house and outbuildings and down from the walls. The air filled with curses as whips cracked and horses whinnied and reared and all hell broke loose.

Cade sauntered through the darkness to the rear of the hacienda, entering the back door without interference. Another sharp whistle and the snap of his fingers brought his grandfather's greyhounds racing around the corner of the house. Finding the open doorway, they eagerly entered, running across tile floors and sliding on cotton rugs as they sought someone to play with.

Cade listened with satisfaction as a woman screamed and a man cursed and the dogs yelped down the corridors. A lantern crashed to the ground somewhere, darkening one of the rooms. He put out other lights as he strolled through familiar halls to his grandfather's chamber.

The guard outside was gone, and Cade swung back the door silently. He held his hand out for the pack his grandfather pulled from under the bed, and they slipped down the darkened corridors to the kitchen garden. Outside the walls, Cade's horse and another waited for them.

"Well, this is a surprise, Mr. Dixon. Won't you please come in?" Lily swung open the door and gestured for the *alcalde* to enter.

Bert Dixon twisted his hat nervously and remained where he was. He gave a start when a man stood up in the room behind Lily, but he recited his piece relatively smoothly.

"I've come here on official business, Mrs. Brown."

"De Suela," Lily said pleasantly. "Go on."

"Well, I hate to be the one to tell you this, but questions have been raised about your title to the land. I've done some research, and well, you see, this ain't legally your place. I'm going to have to ask you to leave."

Lily stood out of the way and made a gesture of welcome. "Do come in and have a drink to wet your throat, Mr. Dixon. I'm sure it was a long ride out here, and that sun is downright hot."

Uncertainly, Dixon stepped into the cool dimness of the cabin. Ralph Langton was still standing by the table, but Dixon turned to Lily. "You did understand what I said, didn't you?"

"Of course, Mr. Dixon. Have a seat right over there. Ralph, pour the gentleman some of that whisky Travis keeps on the mantel, if you would, please."

The puzzled lawyer took a seat where Lily indicated and accepted the glass the older man handed to him. "You all are being mighty kind about this. I was afraid you wouldn't understand. The new owner will be arriving any day now. When can I tell him you will be moving on?"

"We won't, Mr. Dixon. Can I get you something to eat? Juanita just made a fresh batch of peach pie, first of the season. Would you like a taste?" Lily settled in her rocker and picked up her sewing.

"No, ma'am, I don't need nothin' else, thank you. Ralph, maybe you ought to explain to her . . ."

Iron-gray hair falling over a brow tanned and weathered by years of sun, Ralph Langton merely crossed his arms over his chest and regarded the lawyer grimly. "She understands. We all understand. When were you planning on coming out to my place, Dixon?"

Dixon took a quick drink of the whisky before answering. "Soon, I'm afraid. All those deeds are worthless. Everything along the river here belongs to another land grant."

"Hogwash, Mr. Dixon," Lily said from her seat in the rocker. "You know perfectly well if there were anything wrong with those deeds that Mr. Austin himself would be out here explaining it to us and offering reparations. Now go back and tell Mr. Ricardo that we're quite happy where we are and we have no intentions of moving."

Dixon stood up. "I'm afraid I'll have to bring the law out here if you refuse to move peaceably, ma'am. I'm sorry it's come to this, but I'm sworn to uphold the law."

Lily smiled gently. "What law, Mr. Dixon? I'm sure the new constitution makes some provision for elected officials, but we haven't had an election yet. The title of *alcalde* came from the Mexican law, and we're not part of Mexico any longer. There is no law, Mr. Dixon, and until there is, you're not moving us."

"You can't do that!" Dixon blustered. "They're liable to come riding in here with hired guns to throw you out if you don't move on. He's got the deed and the title and you've got nothing!"

Langton took Dixon's elbow and began steering him toward the door. "We've got men and guns, Dixon. Anyone stepping one foot off that public road is going to be shot on sight. If I were you, I'd lay low for a while. I ought to whip your hide for coming out here to scare an expectant lady when her husband's not at home. You're only getting this one warning. Now get out."

Dixon tripped over the door frame and stumbled out. Langton slammed the door behind him.

Turning to Lily, he said, "You and Cade are a pair if I ever saw one, Lily. What in hell were you planning to do if I hadn't been here?"

"Did you think I was all alone, Ralph?" Lily looked up with the best imitation of sweetness that she could arrange. At his sardonic look, she pointed toward the window. "I think right about now you'll see Travis riding in from the field. That bell you heard clamoring earlier wasn't for dinner. If I'm not mistaken, you'll soon see men coming over the prairie, and they're not expecting dinner, either. And you'll have to belive me on the rest because you'll not ever see them, but up in that stand of trees are at least two Indians who would have been down here in seconds if I'd hung that red rag there out the window."

Lily smiled at Ralph's astonished look. "Cade just doesn't believe I can take care of myself. What do you think, Ralph?"

Langton picked up his rifle and started for the door. "I think I'll be going home and making similar arrangements. Maybe we better figure out some smoke signals so we can warn each other."

"Two puffs of black smoke every minute, and my men will be there, Ralph," Lily replied calmly.

Slamming his hat on his head, Langton gave her a long look and stalked out.

Thirty-eight

The dapper Spaniard sitting on a cotton bale drew deeply on his cigar while his host kept a fearful eye on the ashes. The man in the sweat-stained checked shirt who had entered just minutes before wiped at his dust-coated brow and eyed the brandy bottle on the table with more than thirst.

"Why are you just bringing me this news now? The old fart has been up at that cabin for two days already. It's a little late to tell me he's not at the hacienda anymore."

"We've been looking for him!" the messenger protested. "We didn't think the old man could get far. Nobody went through that gate. Nobody! We made certain of that even when the damned mustangs were stampeding through the bunkhouse."

The man with the cigar looked weary and lifted the glass of brandy to his lips before replying. "I don't suppose it occurred to any of you that every good fort has more than one exit, did it?" At the look on the man's face, Ricardo spit out his brandy and made a vulgar noise before answering for him. "Of course not! You have to be told everything. Am I the only one who can think around here?"

Bert Dixon reached over and poured a glass and handed it to the checked-shirt messenger, but his words were for Ricardo. "I say we give the game up. Do what you want in Béxar, that's your territory, but I'll never get elected if I try to throw those people out. I know of a couple of plats that no one's come back to claim after the Runaway Scrape. We can sell those off with no one the wiser and look around for a few others. Land's going to be cheap for a while yet, what with the war and the Indians and all. But I hear there's boatloads of settlers looking to find prime land already. We can scrape up enough to make a fortune."

"Prime land means river land. You give up too easy, *idiota*. We have Indians around here, do we not? I heard the Comanches are not too happy that white men are returning. It is just a matter of time before the Indians come this way, and those outlying farms are perfect targets. We'll have the bastards out on their ears before we sell the first lots."

A man in the corner twisted nervously on his barrel seat. "Cade's an Indian. Don't Indians stick together? Why would they burn him out?"

"He's not a Comanche, you fool." Ricardo threw his cigar on the floor and ground it out with the heel of his Spanish boot. "And we're not waiting around for the real things to come down and do our work for us. A little nut juice on the skin, a few arrows, and we burn them out. It will all be over in a few hours. With any luck, everyone out there will suddenly be interested in moving back to town and we won't have to do anything else."

Ollie stared at him. "There's women and children out there!"

Ricardo sighed with a great show of patience. "We're not planning on scalping them. There will be time enough for them to get out." His black eyes glittered with a sudden thought. "But I think I'll offer a bonus to the man who brings down that damned Indian. Comanches have rifles, don't they?"

Back aching, unable to sleep, Lily heard the "thump" of the first arrow in the cabin wall. Thinking it was a wolf after the salted ham in the dogtrot, she dragged herself from the bed and reached for her wrapper.

The shriek of an Indian war cry and the first whiff of smoke sent panic down her spine. Before she could lean over to wake Cade, he was on his feet and reaching for his trousers.

"Get the children and *mi abuelo* into the big cabin. I'll call the others."

It wasn't necessary to call anyone. The sound of racing hooves and war cries and the stench of flaming arrows had men stumbling out of the bunkhouse. Seeing Roy hurrying from one loft and Antonio from the other, Lily checked the kitchen where Juanita slept. Its roof was already in flames, but before she could scream, she saw Travis racing from his cabin with a nearly-naked Juanita in his arms.

Breathing a sigh of relief for more reasons than one, Lily hurried in to comfort a crying Serena and yell orders at the boy and old man who entered behind her.

"Grab the rifles. One of you aim out the front window, the other take the back." As Travis burst into the room, she ordered, "Throw the bar on that front door. Juanita, if anyone gets near it, chop his damned toes off."

From the front window Roy exclaimed, "There's men riding from Langton's! I think the Indians are running!"

There was an exchange of gunfire from the rear, and Lily heard Antonio swear in Spanish as he aimed the rifle. A man's scream followed the rifle's report, and she hurried to hand him another loaded one.

A deathly silence followed, and then there were shouts and running footsteps, and Antonio was limping hurriedly toward the door. Lily couldn't believe it was over so quickly, but the smell of burning wood warned that it wasn't over entirely. Racing to the window, she watched as the kitchen roof went up in sheets of flame.

Her gaze instantly swung over the yard, searching for the one figure she knew best. He was there, bending over a fallen man on the ground, and she breathed a sigh of relief even as she started for the door.

"Lily, don't go out there yet," Travis warned. "Stay here with the children and let me see what's going on."

Ignoring him, Lily walked out. Her back hurt like the devil, and she was quite certain the baby weighed as much as she did. Anybody's back would ache with that kind of weight to carry around.

She watched with surprise as men who were not from

the ranch began a chain from the water pump to the roof, handing pots and pails of water hand over hand to splash on the tinder-dry wood. She recognized Ralph Langton and, to her double surprise, Ollie Clark.

Not taking the time to wonder about this oddity, Lily hurried to Cade. To her dismay, she noted that his shirtsleeve was torn and bloody, but Cade didn't seem to be aware of it as he crouched beside the fallen man, questioning him angrily.

Curious, Lily crept closer. She had to conceal her gasp when she realized the man on the ground was not a savage Comanche but a half-naked white man. She didn't recognize him, but Cade obviously did.

As the fire was brought under control, Langton and Clark hurried to join Cade and the others gathered around the fallen "Indian." Cade's gaze instantly focused on Ollie, but Ollie turned defensively to Langton.

"Clark tried to warn us, Cade," Ralph said reassuringly. "He reached my place first. We came as soon as we could, but your enemies work quickly. Do you know that one?"

"I know that one. He tried to take a shot at me, but my grandfather brought him down." Cade turned to Travis. "See if you can fix him up. I think I've got a witness who can tie him to another incident. He has a fondness for playing Indian." Cade looked up to Lily, but she didn't seem to have any understanding of what he was talking about. That was the way he wanted it.

"Let Travis see to your arm first," Lily said quietly.

Cade glared stonily at Ollie as he rose from his kneeling position. "It's just a flesh wound. I'm fine. I think there's a little meeting I need to attend right now. Right, Clark?"

"There won't be time. Word will already be on the way back."

"I don't think so." Grimly, Cade nodded to the distance where mounted figures were emerging from the darkness, some leading riderless ponies. "If the bastards knew what they were doing, they gave themselves up the instant they were spotted. We'll find the bodies of the ones who didn't when we come back in the morning."

"How many men have you got out here?" Clark whispered with incredulity.

"They're not all mine. I had a little help from some friends." He glanced once more to the distance, making certain two of the riders were the slim young figures of his brothers. Then, catching Lily briefly by the waist, Cade kissed her hair. "Are the children all right?"

"Everyone's fine. Cade, where are you going?"

"To town." Releasing her, he nodded toward the barn and the horses. Taking his cue, the men around them began gathering up their mounts and checking their rifles.

Alarmed, Lily caught Cade's arm. "Cade, you're hurt. You can't go out now. Why can't this wait until morning?"

"Because the time has come now." Looking to his grandfather, Cade gave a curt nod of recognition of the older man's fears. "Stay here and look after my family, *por favor*. It is better that you not see this."

"It is better that you not do this, my son," Antonio said sadly. "Let the law see justice done."

Not deeming that worthy of a reply, Cade swung on his heel and went for his horse.

As Lily watched the procession of men ride out, she cursed at the obstinacy of men and wished she were in a position to follow. Instead, the pain in her back struck sharply, moving around to her middle, and she gasped and held her side until it passed. Then with a look of determination, she turned back to the house and its frightened occupants, clinging to the arm of the tired old man just for the knowledge of his support.

When she entered, she murmured quietly to Roy, "Fetch Dove Woman for me, will you? I don't know that anyone is watching us any longer after this."

Roy looked alarmed, but with a reassuring look from Juanita, he raced for the door.

The dozen men who started for town quickly became two dozen as they rode into town and the word spread.

The general store, with the light still burning in the back room was quickly surrounded, but Cade took little note of the preparation. He was a man who abhorred violence, but Ricardo had gone too far this time. Unfastening his rifle from the saddle, he swung down and strode determinedly toward the back door.

Kicking it open, Cade stood back and waited for whoever was inside to fire. When the sound of only one shot came through, he waited for the lone rifleman to come to the door. Then with a quick motion that the men behind him couldn't see, Cade kneed the rifleman in the groin, brought his rifle stock down over his nape when he doubled up in pain, and flung the guard out of the way.

When he stepped into the narrow back room, Cade was greeted by a trio of loaded rifles aimed in his direction and a familiar figure sprawled across some cotton bales.

"Shoot anytime you're ready, gentleman. It's only a stinking Indian after all."

Cade held his rifle loosely at his side, but his focus was entirely on Ricardo. "Order them to shoot, if you like, but I'll take you with me before I go."

"Don't be ridiculous. Remember, I saw you vomit your guts out when you had to shoot that horse back in Gonzales. You couldn't shoot a jackrabbit if you wanted to." Ricardo drew a cigar from his jacket pocket and calmly cut the tip.

"I had to shoot that horse because your renegades let it loose to stampede over that child. If you'll remember correctly, I was drunk at the time. I'm not drunk now, Ricardo. But if you don't believe I'll shoot, let me warn you that half the town is watching. You'll not get away with one of your back door assassinations this time."

Three guns were suddenly lowered as their owners searched the darkness behind Cade for the truth. Cade obligingly stepped aside, and the room began to fill.

Alarm flared briefly in Ricardo's dark eyes before they shuttered closed again. "Welcome, gentlemen. To what do I owe this honor? I must warn you that I try to stay out of local politics. My only position here is that of land agent for the government."

"I have a man back at the house with a bullet through his middle who is prepared to testify that you ordered the raid on my place tonight. He also mentioned an additional bonus for my death, Ricardo. That's conspiracy to murder, and it's a hanging offense under any law that I know."

"A man with a bullet in his gut will say anything. Your *alcalde* and I have merely been working late tonight to finish up these records so I can move on. I suggest you come up with a better story than that if you wish to strike fear into my heart."

Ricardo rose and riffled through a stack of papers on the table, producing the one that he wanted and handing it to Ralph Langton, the oldest and most responsible man present. "There's the real reason that my friend here is out to cut my throat. It's a will deeding my father's ranch to me instead of to him."

Cade shook his head in disbelief. If Ricardo weren't so much smaller than he, he would strike him now and save his breath. "I'm beginning to think that you believe those stories yourself. These men have only to go back and consult with my grandfather to learn that I drew up his will last spring. You inherit your mother's dowry, as he told you. The ranch is mine, and in the event of my demise, it goes to my heirs. And as a precaution against your taking out your vengeance on Lily and her children, he leaves the ranch to the town of Béxar should anything prevent their inheriting. A copy of that will has been filed in Béxar so they know to make their claim. Try again, Ricardo."

Langton carefully shredded the piece of paper in his hands, and a nervous twitch worked at Ricardo's jaw.

"I am sure these men will be able to ascertain your lies soon enough," Ricardo answered scornfully, "but in the meantime, there is no excuse for this conduct. I have done nothing for which I can be held. I think that it is time that you leave."

"But I'm not done with you yet." Cade lifted his rifle slightly as a reminder. "I want you to tell all these good folks how Jim Brown came to die by a white man's arrow in his back, just like that poor sodbuster back in Galveston."

"You've taken leave of your senses now." Ricardo scowled at Cade. "You murdered that farmer. Everyone in Galveston knows that. His money was never recovered. You never did explain where you got yours."

There was an angry murmur around Cade, but it settled as Cade spoke. He didn't raise his voice, but the deadly menace it contained carried through the room. "I was born half-Indian, Ricardo, but I was raised white. I can't hit the broad side of a barn with an arrow. I've always preferred rifles as more efficient. You might have noticed that if you'd paid more attention to details. That farmer was shot by the same renegade who shot Jim Brown, the same man who tried to take my scalp tonight and got a bullet through his gut for his efforts. The man swore to it in front of witnesses, and I've got another witness who says he saw him shoot Brown. Your imitation Indian also swears you paid him to commit both murders."

"What would I have to gain from murdering farmers?" Ricardo asked over the growing anger forming around them.

"Their land and your money back. I earned my money honestly, but you're carrying a pocket of Tennessee coins that that farmer was going to use to increase his acreage until he discovered you sold him nothing but swamp. And now his land belongs to you, just as you thought Brown's land would become yours with a little persuasion. I'm tired of arguing with you, Ricardo. We'll let someone else judge whether you ought to hang."

"I'm damned well not going to hang for you or anyone else. Ollie Clark is the one who wanted Brown's land, along with the widow. You're not going to nail any of this on me."

Ollie elbowed his way to the front with a roar of rage. "You bastard! I wanted land all right, but I didn't go shooting poor Jim to get it. For what it's worth, Dixon and I will testify against you, but if you had Jim killed, I'm all for hanging you now."

That seemed to be the consensus, and the crowd began to surge forward.

Finally realizing that logic wasn't going to win over rage, Ricardo turned to run for the passage leading into the store.

A shot rang out, and he jerked, then fell sprawling to the floor.

Langton turned in suspicion to Cade, but Cade was leaning on his weapon, staring at the fallen man with disbelief. The only smoking gun in the room was Ollie's.

Thirty-nine

Long streaks of baby blue and gold colored the eastern horizon behind the collection of weary riders trailing down the San Antonio road. Of the two dozen who had set out from town, several had dropped along the wayside to spread the news, and others had ridden in to take their place.

It didn't look like there was going to be a hanging, but a town meeting of some sort needed to be called. But the man who had the most right to call for a trial and jury had no intention of lingering in town any longer than necessary. That being the case, the others followed him home. The extent of the night's destruction needed to be investigated and repaired and the whole story brought out and discussed until some decision could be reached.

Not caring if the whole damned town followed him, Cade set his eyes hungrily on the cabin he called home. Smoke rose in a gray column from the chimney, although the day already promised to be another Texas boiler. His glance went to the ruined kitchen and he judged the cooking had been moved to the cabin, but he urged his mount a little faster. He needed to know that the night had had no other disastrous consequences.

A small figure came flying out the front door at his approach, and Cade's heart nearly stopped in his chest. Flinging himself from his horse, he grabbed Roy as the boy threw himself into his arms.

"Papa, Mama's calling for you! Hurry!"

Terror all but froze Cade in place. Over Roy's head, Cade saw Travis leap from his horse and rush over. Giving Roy a hug, Cade tried to calm the boy's fears along with his own. "I will go to her." Looking at the man who had stood beside him as friend these long months, seeing Travis's expression as another man was addressed by the title he craved, Cade asked, "Roy, you know I am not your true father?"

The boy looked over Cade's shoulder to the man who looked so like himself and nodded.

"Then go to him while I see to your mother." Cade didn't stop to see the light in Travis's eyes as Roy made his first tentative steps in acknowledging his real father. Holding on to his rampaging fears, Cade tried to make a dignified retreat toward the cabin.

But the sight of two young Indians guarding the dog-trot sent him into a distinctly undignified run.

The men behind him were already raising their rifles, but Travis waved them down. At the same time, a gaunt old Spaniard limped into the morning sun from the main cabin, and the men from town were treated to yet another curiosity. Silver buckles and spurs gleamed in the sunlight as the old man called to someone behind him, and Juanita stepped out in her best finery, bracelets ringing on her wrists and silver sparkling at her throat. Sedately following this vision came an old Indian in full tribal dress, tattoos scarring his torso and shoulders, loincloth fringed and beaded, hair looped and feathered and hanging to one shoulder. He remained aloof on the porch, arms crossed over his mighty chest, while Juanita and Antonio joined the men in the yard.

Ignoring their astonished audience, Antonio spoke directly to Travis. "Lily sent your woman out. She says Juanita would never wish to have a child if she watched now."

Juanita glared at Travis, although she swished her skirts and boldly walked up to confront him. "I shall never have children," she declared firmly. "Why go through such pain just to bring another man into the world?"

Wiping his dusty brow with the back of his arm, Travis looked away from the old Indian on the porch and down at Juanita, grinning widely as he looked her up and down.

Her brown skin glinted with golden highlights in the dawn, and the loose neck of her lacy blouse revealed more than was necessary of the narrow valley between her breasts. He had finally been treated to more than just a glimpse of that delight last night, before the raid, and even in his weariness he couldn't control the surge of lust that followed that thought.

"Where would women be if they did not have men to cook for and to warm their beds and to fill their bellies with bonnie babes? And look what fun you'd miss." With one quick grab, Travis hauled Juanita into his arms before she could escape, and he assuaged some of his hunger with the feel of her ripe body pressed into his and her lips opening beneath his kiss.

Several of the younger men whooped. Ralph Langton merely removed his hat and climbed down from his horse, holding out his hand to Antonio. "I don't believe we've met, señor. I'm Ralph Langton. I take it Lily's having the babe?"

Antonio accepted the offered hand and threw a proud look over his shoulder to the cabin Cade had entered. "I am about to become a great-grandfather. I have promised the young ones a fiesta. Come inside and we will begin the celebrations."

Leading Langton to the porch and the impassive Indian, Antonio made introductions in Spanish. "Cade's father, El Caballo—Cade's friend, Ralph Langton."

White man and red stared at each other. El Caballo gave a stern nod. Langton held out his hand. Serena darted between them and held up a cornhusk doll in beaded leather, waving it happily at the tall Indian who was the only grandfather she would ever know. The Indian obediently crouched to pick her up and, holding this bundle of sunshine, solemnly offered his hand to Langton. Juanita hurried past them to fill plates for the starving men who were spilling from their saddles and pouring in and around the main cabin.

Ignoring the entire chaotic spectacle, Cade entered the bedroom just in time to watch Lily struggle with the pain of a long contraction.

"She is not yet ready," Dove Woman informed him calmly in her language.

Cade scarcely heard her. He was afraid to touch Lily as she pulled at the headboard spindles, her beautiful face twisting with pain as the child moved within her. Even now, when the pain ceased and she rested, Cade feared to come between her and her fierce concentration on the child. But his panic was great as Dove Woman wiped the perspiration from Lily's brow and spoke soothing words that Lily could not possibly comprehend.

"Ricardo?" Lily gasped when she finally found the breath.

"He was killed trying to escape." The words sounded flat and stale instead of resounding with the triumph he should have felt. Ricardo's death had no importance in the face of the birth of new life happening here. Cade struggled helplessly for something to say to convey his feelings, but Lily was already straining again against the pain.

"Why does it not come?" he demanded sharply of Dove Woman, who was merely sitting cross-legged on the floor, humming to herself.

"Because it is not time," she repeated calmly.

"But it is killing her! Look how she suffers. We must do something." Cade paced, throwing anxious looks at Lily as she took a deep breath and released the bed once more.

"You had better go out with the others, Cade. There is nothing you can do to speed the child's coming." Not understanding the actual words between Cade and Dove Woman, Lily understood their content.

"I will fetch Travis. He will give you something for the pain."

Before Cade could start for the door, Lily gave a groan of pure agony, and Dove Woman unhurriedly rose from the floor.

"She is in pain! Santa Maria, do something!" Cade dropped to his knees beside the bed and tried to lift Lily into his arms, but she reached for the bed rails as pain twisted through her insides.

"Send him out," Dove Woman enunciated in clear Spanish when Lily rested once more. "It will save pain for both."

Lily looked up at Cade's anguished expression, startled by the immense emotion displayed for the first time on his usually implacable features, and her heart took two leaps and a jump before settling more calmly in her chest.

"Leave, Cade. There is nothing more you can do here," she said softly.

"How can I leave?" he cried in anguish. "I have done this to you. I would take the pain away." As Lily's eyes closed with the onset of the next contraction, Cade panicked. "Lily, I can't lose you! Lily, please . . ."

Dove Woman went to the door and murmured to the two boys waiting outside. The eldest looked rebellious at her words, but he soon disappeared into the opposite cabin. Moments later, he returned with Travis.

Travis pounded on the closed bedroom door and shouted, "Cade, get your royal ass out here before I have to come in and get you!"

Lily's eyes blinked open and she half smiled at this command. "Go, Cade. You can't bring the child any faster."

"I can't leave you here to suffer alone." Cade touched her brow, unwilling to form even in his mind the words for the fear he felt. Her pain was ripping him apart, tearing down the walls of his heart and soul. He didn't want to lose her, and he couldn't leave for fear she would be gone before he could come back.

"I wish there was music," Lily whispered as she surrendered to the pain once again.

Cade caught the wish even as Travis slammed into the room, gun in hand to order him out.

"Cade, damn you, the women want you out!" Travis shouted as the big man swung slowly in his direction.

Seeing only an obstruction between himself and the means to satisfy Lily's wish, Cade calmly knocked Travis's gun aside, floored him with a single punch, and stepping over his friend's fallen body, walked out the door.

In the yard, men ran to find the source of the commotion, but Cade was already half running toward the paddock and the oxen grazing there.

Hearing Travis's shouts and seeing Cade running, two men stepped into his path to halt his progress. Cade plowed his fist into the belly of one, the jaw of another, and broke into a full run.

Cade had the oxen out of the paddock and heading for the wagon before the rest of the crowd came barreling around the corner of the house. As Travis stumbled out of the cabin shouting, Ollie dived full length at Cade's legs, causing him to stagger but not to fall.

Langton ordered two of his men to help hold Cade while El Caballo sent his young sons to their brother's rescue.

Cade roared and flung aside his attackers like so much chaff in the wind. Snatching up harness, he began wrestling the animals into position.

"Hell and tarnation, man, you can't leave your wife while she's havin' your babe!" Red shouted as the two Indian boys jumped on the back of the oxen and began helping Cade fasten the harness.

Jerking a rifle from the man nearest, Cade leapt to the wagon seat and glared defiantly at the gathering crowd. "My wife wants music," was the only explanation he gave as he grabbed the reins and swatted the animals into motion.

Men rubbing sore jaws and aching bellies grumbled at this idiocy, but a light leapt to Travis's eyes. Turning to a sullen Ollie, he demanded, "You still got that piano of yours?"

Having felt like a prisoner on trial since the shooting, Ollie regarded the question suspiciously. "It's there. Ain't anybody gonna steal it real easily."

Leaping to the back of the wagon before it could gather speed, Travis grabbed Cade by the back of the shirt. "You go build a kitchen. We'll find Lily some music."

Before Cade could swing wildly at Travis, someone

else jumped in to grab his arm and jerk it down while others hurried to hold the oxen. A holiday mood had taken over as the men washed the night away with a bottle of Travis's medicinal whisky. Anticipating a brawl, they joined Travis in dragging a struggling Cade from the wagon seat. Landing in the dust, pinned by half a dozen men, Cade roared and fought like a wild man while the wagon rolled off with a party of jubilant piano-seekers.

When they finally allowed him to his feet, Cade could only stare after the departing wagon. His clothes were coated with dust and sweat poured from his brow as he ran his hand through his hair.

In a state of shock, Cade stared frantically at the dust of the wagon and back to the cabin. One of his brothers came up and shoved a flute into his hand, and he looked at it blankly. As the muffled screams from the bedroom fell into a momentary silence in the yard, Cade shuddered, closed his fist around the instrument, and walked determinedly back to the dogtrot.

Sitting cross-legged in the shadow of the breezeway, Cade began to play. The air filled with a wildly haunting melody for which there was no written music, a sound that caused gooseflesh to rise on the arms of his listeners. Serena crawled into his lap and began to bounce her head against his chest in time to the tune, and the music took on a new note, a sweetness that pierced the heart. Cade's father and grandfather and half brothers came to keep vigil with him, and the music swept around them, encompassing them in its wild dissonance. Juanita supplied them with lemonade and spicy tortillas, and in the yard Travis took charge of the pounding and sawing.

Lily heard the flute through a haze of pain and smiled. She continued smiling as the morning advanced and the child still did not come. The erratic, haunting tunes Cade began with gradually became slightly wilder and less stable. Dove Woman looked out the window sometime during the morning, shook her head, and commented "Much people," before going back to tending her patient.

Cade's playing grew increasingly frantic as Lily's muffled screams grew more frequent. Finally, reduced to dance tunes, he switched from one to another and back again without noticing. Lily tried to keep up with them as she bit a rag to hide her pain. Just as she felt the baby move into position, she heard a wild cheer in the yard, and her screams suddenly miraculously became mixed with the tinkling notes of a piano.

Cade heard only her screams. The flute in his hand almost cracked under the pressure of his grip, and he leapt to storm the door keeping him from Lily. Before he could breach it, the wails of an infant drifted through the open window.

More cheers erupted in the yard and the piano began a raucous tune that had the entire company singing in accompaniment, raising an unholy roar to the heavens.

Cade staggered against the door, leaned his head against the wood, then stiffened his shoulders and swung the panel open.

Dove Woman was serenely cleansing a screaming babe in a bowl of water.

Numbly, Cade stared at the fat, healthy infant already raising a fight. Then, with terror in his heart, he turned his gaze to Lily.

Exhausted, she leaned back against the pillows, her hair streaming in a golden-brown cascade over the thin linen covering her shoulders. But a look of unadulterated happiness beamed from her face as she looked up to him and held out her hand, and something inside Cade crumbled to sand as he recognized the significance of her gesture.

Cade fell to his knees beside Lily, and she brushed away the streaks of tears he hadn't realized were there. He wrapped his arms around her and buried his face against her breasts and felt her arms wrap gently around his neck.

"*Gracias, querida, muchas gracias* . . . I love you so much. How can I say it? How can I thank you? I did not know . . . I thought a child would hold you, I wanted you to bear my child, but I did not mean to cause you such pain."

The piano crashed into a resounding "Yankee Doodle Dandy" to celebrate this victorious Fourth, and Lily smiled and stroked Cade's thick black hair, feeling the glory of this day seep into her bones where she could remember and cherish it forever. "It's because I love you that I wanted your child. The pain is just the price we pay to have what we want. Can I see him now? Will you bring him to me?"

Cade jerked his head up to meet the blazing happiness of blue eyes and knew Lily spoke what was in her heart. It was difficult for him to absorb. He had been a man alone for too long, an outcast wanted by nobody, yet this woman knocked down doors none had dared approach to declare her love for him. He stroked her cheek, his dark hand contrasting with her light skin, and she kissed the web of flesh beneath his thumb. Cade accepted that as confirmation of her words and allowed a smile to form.

"I think he is big enough to walk over here." Despite his mocking words, Cade rose to take the child from Dove Woman. He opened the blanket to inspect all the working parts, a feeling of awe encompassing him as tiny fists clenched and unclenched and long legs kicked and shoved at the hot blanket, and he knew this was a part of himself and Lily.

Cade presented the child to Lily, ignoring the clamor of voices outside the door. She held the infant tenderly, laughing at his belligerent cries, and showed no astonishment when the door flew open and El Caballo stood there in all his glory.

"Un niño." Lily held the child out for her father-in-law to admire.

El Caballo looked from his son's exhausted but laughing face to Lily's and grunted something Lily couldn't translate as Cade proudly lifted the child for his perusal. The Indian stepped into the room to observe the babe, poked a finger at his wiry chest, and was rewarded with a fist wrapping around it.

The piano playing stopped, and silence seemed to reign

outside. Travis appeared in the window, but taking in the scene, he chose only to hiss to catch Cade's attention. Caught up in the emotion of the moment, Cade didn't notice.

"Cade!" Travis whispered a little louder. "There's a priest out here looking for you."

As Cade looked up, puzzled, the bedroom door opened once again, this time revealing Antonio.

"Father Juárez is here. Shall I bring him in?" He spoke to Cade, but his gaze focused on the child in his grandson's arms.

Lily looked alarmed, shoving her hair back from her face and straightening her nightgown, looking frantically for a shawl with which to cover herself. Cade merely nodded.

Antonio moved aside and the old priest in his long black robes entered, coming to a halt at the sight of the tall, nearly naked Indian, then letting his gaze drift to the child and the man holding him. He lifted his eyebrows but continued into the room.

"I thought it was a wedding I was to perform, not a baptism." There was a tone of admonishment in his voice.

Held securely against Cade's chest, the child had quieted and slept now as his father looked to the priest. "You have come in time for both, *padre.*" Returning the child to Lily's arms, Cade indicated his wife. "We are married in my father's world and in the legal sense, but we wish to be blessed by the church."

The priest looked with mild surprise from the fair woman crooning over the infant in the bed to the large man he had once known as a bright but rebellious orphan. He did not find it at all surprising that the couple was surrounded by Indians, a sophisticated Spaniard, and a yard full of "Texians," including Tejanos and Negroes. Cade had always been an enigma. Father Juárez rather preferred it that way.

"Then I suggest we get started while the wedding guests are still standing. There seems to be a large quantity of hard liquor being distributed out there." The padre nodded toward the window through which the strains of a dance tune could be heard.

"Ask Mrs. Whitaker if she knows any Beethoven," Lily whispered to Cade.

Cade passed the message to Travis outside the window, who carried it to the woman pounding the piano in the back of an oxen wagon. A few minutes later the first strains of a piano concerto filtered through the air.

"Now I'm ready," Lily announced.

And so the ceremony was performed, with the groom sitting on the bed beside his bride with their child in her arms. When it came time to repeat their vows, Cade held Lily's head cradled against his shoulder as she looked into his eyes and promised "to love and to cherish, until death do us part." He pressed a kiss against her brow when he repeated the same after her.

With a signal from Travis that the ceremony had ended, the piano broke into a slightly bawdy tune and the crowd that had been growing in numbers all morning cheered and shouted and rang bells and shot guns into the air.

The babe woke and began crying, but the newly married couple scarcely noticed.

Father Juárez coughed lightly and inquired, "If you will give me his name, I'll see him baptized."

Lily frowned. This was not a discussion they had held as yet. She looked at the squalling child who would be as big as Cade some day. "Not Mighty Quiver," she announced emphatically.

"Not Luis Philippe," Cade countered.

"How about Travis?" called the aforesaid from the window.

"Not Travis," both agreed in unison.

Chuckling, Antonio led the priest toward the door. "I do not know of any subject that they agree upon, *padre*. It may be a while before you have an answer to your question. Perhaps we can find you a sip of wine to take away the thirst?"

Dove Woman quietly removed the crying babe to the corner prepared for him. El Caballo watched over her and stooped to leave the room when she was ready. Travis wandered off in search of Juanita.

"Not Ephraim! That's an awful name for a boy."

"No child of mine will be called Cadenza."

And the piano played on.

Forty

Beneath the blue bowl of the sky, Lily picked her way over the rough ground to the shadows of the pines overlooking the river. The crystalline notes of a flute drifted on the slight breeze as she lifted her gingham skirt to avoid a horned toad leaping across her path. Smiling, she rested a minute, allowing the breeze to cool her brow while the music stole around her.

She knew where he was. The corn harvest was moving rapidly. They had hired someone to drive the cattle to New Orleans. The kitchen had been rebuilt bigger and better than ever. The roundup would start shortly, but not just yet. And Cade was taking a break from his hectic workday.

He still didn't tell her everything. He stayed busy, he laughed with the children when he came in in the evenings, he held her firmly all through the nights, but he did not say where his thoughts roamed at times like these when he disappeared into the forest and played his flute.

But Lily knew, and today she was going to confront him with them.

Cade looked up in surprise as Lily approached, then leapt to his feet to help her find a seat on a pillow of grass. He had learned one or two things from Travis about how to treat a lady.

"How did you manage to get away?" he asked, knowing the constant demands an infant, two children, and a household of men created on her time.

"Davy is sleeping; Serena is helping Juanita make biscuits; Roy and your grandfather are reading something in

Spanish that sounds vaguely naughty; and I walked out as if I had something important to do."

Cade chuckled and pulled her into his arms, leaning back against the grass so they could watch the wind whisper through the pine branches. "Tending to your husband is important. We must do this more often."

A mockingbird burst into a wild cascade of song to say farewell to summer, and they listened silently until a jay intruded and drove him off.

"I heard Ollie's wife is stocking china and millinery in the general store now." Lily pressed a kiss to her husband's shoulder.

Cade chuckled and began to stroke the bare skin of her arm. "I think letting her know where he was is sufficient punishment for any man. She'll keep him in line better than any prison bars. She terrifies even me."

"Still, it's a pity that Ollie gets punished so cruelly while Bert Dixon was just run out of town. There never was any real evidence that they had anything to do with Jim's death. They were just guilty of greed, and heaven only knows, there's enough of that going around."

Cade shifted Lily more comfortably against his shoulder and feathered his fingers against the silk of her face. "Ollie was the one who shot Ricardo. If we're going to have any sort of law at all, we've got to keep people from shooting when they feel like it. Maybe Ricardo deserved to die, and maybe Ollie was just trying to keep him from escaping, as he said, but no man should be judge and jury for another."

They grew silent, both thinking of the tragedies that had led to that night, both concluding that justice had been served despite the way it had been meted out.

"I think Juanita is pregnant," Lily said unexpectedly into the silence.

"I'll make certain the rogue marries her." Complacently, Cade stroked a straying strand of Lily's hair over her ear.

"I think it is Juanita who must be persuaded. She wants permanence, and she fears Travis has wandering eyes."

"He hasn't wandered very far in these last months," Cade said dryly. "He can barely manage to finish his supper before he drags Juanita off to bed."

Lily giggled softly against his shoulder. Cade had not bothered to fasten his shirt when he came up here to cool off, and her fingers daringly sought the glint of copper skin revealed. "I think perhaps it is time we went to Béxar and left them to themselves," she murmured seductively.

The stroking motion on Lily's arm stopped. Cade lay still a moment longer, then propped himself up on his elbow to gaze down into her lightly freckled face. Her eyes reflected the blue of the sky, and there was nothing of the playful in them as she returned his stare.

"If my grandfather is ready to return, I will take him. You should not risk that travel yet."

"I have been healed this past month or more, Cade. I am not fragile porcelain, you must know. And Davy is certainly strong and healthy enough to travel. There is nothing more for you to do here. It is time to go."

Wariness returned to his eyes as Cade gazed down at her. "You did not like it in Béxar. There is no reason for you to make the journey now. It is safe here."

Lily guessed she was going to have to hit him over the head with a stick to get her meaning across. She reached up and stroked his obstinate jaw, tangling her fingers in his hair. "Then Travis and Juanita cannot come to too much harm if they stay behind. The journey is not that long that we cannot come back to see them, and it might be necessary to allow Roy to stay here part of the year, since this will be his one day and Travis would not like to be separated from him forever. But it is time you started making the changes on your grandfather's *ranchero* that you said needed to be done."

Disbelief rising in his eyes, Cade stroked the hair back from her face with both hands and held her head caught between them. "You wish us to live at the hacienda?"

"Of course," she replied impatiently. "That will be your land someday. It cannot be left neglected much longer."

"But this is your home," Cade insisted. "You did not like it at the hacienda. I cannot separate you from your friends, and I will not go without you."

"Oh, Cade," Lily whispered, running her hands through his hair and down his shoulders, massaging the tight muscles of his arms as he leaned over her. "You still do not understand, do you? I love you, and I want you to be happy, and you cannot be happy while your mother's land goes to ruin. I can help you, if you will let me, and I will be happy just to be with you. It is not the land that is so important to me, it is you. I know this place will be safe with Travis here and you to guide him when necessary. I can learn to make friends anywhere. I cannot find another husband I would want more than you."

Hope finally began to dawn on Cade's face. "You would go to Béxar with me, live in the hacienda, make that your home?"

"Well, it's only fair that Davy be given the same inheritance as Roy," Lily shrugged, trying to hide her delight at Cade's reaction.

But when he bent to kiss her, there was no disguising her joy. Wrapping her arms around the broad muscles of her husband's back, Lily surrendered to the kiss that they had denied themselves much too long. Her body was healed and eager and ready for his. She would not let him back away in fear of hurting her this time.

When Cade touched her breast, Lily lifted herself to press eagerly into his palm. When he tried to retreat, she ran her fingers across his bare skin until she found his nipple, and he gasped and pushed her more firmly against the ground as his mouth came down and made ecstatic demands of hers.

Lily jerked his shirt from his breeches and rubbed her hands over his chest and abdomen until Cade was groaning and pressing himself needfully against the juncture of her thighs. Half against his will, he began unfastening her bodice. When he didn't move fast enough, Lily helped him, sliding her arms from the gingham and pulling the ribbons of her chemise until her breasts were bared for Cade's touch.

When he kissed her there, Lily nearly cried with joy and relief and a desire so deep that she could not control it. Cade's teeth nibbled lightly at the crest, and she gave a cry so primitive that he was yanking her skirts up before either of them was aware of what he was doing.

But when his fingers started on the buttons of his trousers, Cade came to a crashing halt. Looking down at Lily's beautifully flushed nakedness, he grew so hard that it was painful, but he had to stop now, while he still could.

Lily wasn't so easily persuaded. Determinedly, she reached to finish what he had not.

Cade caught her hands and pulled them above her head. "Don't, Lily. I will not be able to stop myself. I forced the burden of bearing a child on you once before. I will never do so again. There must be time for you to grow strong. We do not need to have more children. I would not see you suffer through that pain again."

Lily glared at him defiantly. "I am strong, Cade. I am strong and I am not afraid of bearing your children. And I need you in the same way that you need me and you will drive us both mad if you deny it."

She raised her hips to rub against his and the friction exploded into a conflagration that threatened to consume them entirely. In moments, the front of Lily's skirt was up about her waist and Cade was taking full advantage of her lack of drawers.

The mockingbird began to sing from the top of a pine as a cry of ecstasy pierced the otherwise silent forest. Sometime later, when a triumphantly male bellow split the air, the bird lifted its wings and flew off.

A lone feather floated to the ground and settled in disheveled golden tresses.

An owl's call rang through the distance, an unnatural owl at this hour of the day.

Cade lifted himself to admire his wife's abandoned position beneath him. "I promised them a buffalo hunt," he whispered wryly.

A ring of gold surrounded Lily's head as she smiled

languidly up at him. "I've always wanted to see a buffalo hunt."

He frowned. "You're not going on a buffalo hunt."

A woodpecker began to scold above their heads, and laughter peeled through the answering echoes.

TOPAZ (0451)

EXPERIENCE A NEW WORLD OF ROMANCE

☐ **SWEET EVERLASTING by Patricia Gaffney.** Chance brings sophisticated Tyler Wilkes, M.D. and fawnlike mountain girl Carrie Wiggins together. But something as strong as fate breaks through the barriers of birth and breeding, pride and fear, which has kept them apart . . . as each seeks to heal the other's wounds with a passion neither can deny and all the odds against them cannot defeat. (403754—$4.99)

☐ **BY LOVE UNVEILED by Deborah Martin.** Lady Marianne trusted no one—especially not Garett, the Earl of Falkham, the man who seemed to be her most dangerous enemy. Somehow, in a world of treachery and passion each woud have to learn to trust one another, as a desire that could not be disguised turned into a passionate love that all the powers of the world could not defeat. (403622—$4.99)

☐ **THUNDER AND ROSES by Mary Jo Putney.** Paying a price for his aid, Clare Morgan agrees to live with the Demon Earl for three months, letting the world think the worst. As allies, they fight to save her community. As adversaries, they explore the terrains of power and sensuality. And as lovers, they surrender to a passion that threatens the very foundation of their lives. (403673—$4.99)

☐ **WILD EMBRACE by Cassie Edwards.** Exquisite Elizabeth Easton discovers the real wilderness when the noble Indian brave, Strong Heart, forces her to go with him in a flight back to his Suquamish people. Here both of them are free of all the pride and prejudice that kept them apart in the white world . . . as this superbly handsome, strong and sensitive man becomes her guide on passion' path to unfettered joy and love. (403614—$4.99)

☐ **WHITE LILY by Linda Ladd.** Ravishing Lily Courtland has the extraordinary gift of second sight. Harte Delaney has never met a woman as magically mysterious as this beauty for whom he risks all to rescue and possess. Amid the flames of war and the heat of passion, these two people find themselves lost in a heart-stopping adventure with their own destiny and the fate of a nation hanging in a breathless balance. (403630—$4.99)

☐ **NO SWEETER HEAVEN by Katherine Kingsley.** Pascal LaMartine and Elizabeth Bowes had nothing in common until the day she accidentally landed at his feet, and looked up into the face of a fallen angel. Drawn in to a dangerous battle of intrigue and wits, each discovered how strong passion was . . . and how perilous it can be. (403665—$4.99)

Prices slightly higher in Canada

Buy them at your local bookstore or use this convenient coupon for ordering.

PENGUIN USA
P.O. Box 999 – Dept. #17109
Bergenfield, New Jersey 07621

Please send me the books I have checked above.
I am enclosing $_____ (please add $2.00 to cover postage and handling).
Send check or money order (no cash or C.O.D.'s) or charge by Mastercard or VISA (with a $15.00 minimum). Prices and numbers are subject to change without notice.

Card #_____ Exp. Date _____
Signature_____
Name_____
Address_____
City_____ State _____ Zip Code _____

For faster service when ordering by credit card call **1-800-253-6476**

Allow a minimum of 4-6 weeks for delivery. This offer is subject to change without notice.

T TOPAZ

WHEN THE HEART IS DARING

☐ **STARDUST DREAMS by Marilyn Campbell.** Cherry Cochran, a beautiful actress from earth who witnesses a murder is suddenly swept toward the remotest stars in the spaceship of her mysterious abductor, the handsome Gallant Voyager.... Interstellar intrigue, deadly danger, and a burning desire for love.

(404130—$4.99)

☐ **TARNISHED HEARTS by Raine Cantrell.** To Trevor Shelby, Leah Reese was a beauty forbidden to him by class barriers: he was a Southern aristocrat and she was an overseer's daughter. Trev's tormented past taught him nothing of tenderness, and he wasn't prepared for Leah's warmth and trust. His kisses taught her about passion, but she taught him about love. (404424—$4.99)

☐ **RAWHIDE AND LACE by Margaret Brownley.** Libby Summerhill couldn't wait to get out of Deadman's Gulch—a lawless mining town filled with gunfights, brawls, and uncivilized mountain men—men like Logan St. John. He knew his town was no place for a woman and the sooner Libby and her precious baby left for Boston, the better. But how could he bare to lose this spirited woman who melted his heart of stone forever? (404610—$4.99)

☐ **TOUCH OF NIGHT by Carin Rafferty.** Ariel Dantes was alone in the world and desperate to find her lost brother. Lucien Morgret was the only one who could help her, but he was a man of danger. As Ariel falls deeper and deeper into Lucien's spell, she is drawn toward desires she cannot resist, even if it means losing her heart and soul by surrendering to Lucien's touch ...(404432—$4.99)

*Prices slightly higher in Canada

Buy them at your local bookstore or use this convenient coupon for ordering.

PENGUIN USA
P.O. Box 999 — Dept. #17109
Bergenfield, New Jersey 07621

Please send me the books I have checked above.
I am enclosing $_____ (please add $2.00 to cover postage and handling). Send check or money order (no cash or C.O.D.'s) or charge by Mastercard or VISA (with a $15.00 minimum). Prices and numbers are subject to change without notice.

Card #_____ Exp. Date _____
Signature_____
Name_____
Address_____
City _____ State _____ Zip Code _____

For faster service when ordering by credit card call **1-800-253-6476**

Allow a minimum of 4-6 weeks for delivery. This offer is subject to change without notice.

ANNOUNCING THE

TOPAZ FREQUENT READERS CLUB
COMMEMORATING TOPAZ'S 1 YEAR ANNIVERSARY!

THE MORE YOU BUY, THE MORE YOU GET

Redeem coupons found here and in the back of all new Topaz titles for FREE Topaz gifts:

Send in:

2 coupons for a free TOPAZ novel (choose from the list below);

- ☐ THE KISSING BANDIT, Margaret Brownley
- ☐ BY LOVE UNVEILED, Deborah Martin
- ☐ TOUCH THE DAWN, Chelley Kitzmiller
- ☐ WILD EMBRACE, Cassie Edwards

4 coupons for an "I Love the Topaz Man" on-board sign

6 coupons for a TOPAZ compact mirror

8 coupons for a Topaz Man T-shirt

Just fill out this certificate and send with original sales receipts to:

TOPAZ FREQUENT READERS CLUB-1ST ANNIVERSARY
Penguin USA • Mass Market Promotion; Dept. H.U.G.
375 Hudson St., NY, NY 10014

Name_____

Address_____

City_____State_____Zip_____

Offer expires 1/31 1995

This certificate must accompany your request. No duplicates accepted. Void where prohibited, taxed or restricted. Allow 4-6 weeks for receipt of merchandise. Offer good only in U.S., its territories, and Canada.